A Lady Compromised

Darcie Wilde is the author of:

A Lady Compromised

And Dangerous to Know

A Purely Private Matter

A Useful Woman

A Lady Compromised

DARCIE WILDE

KENSINGTON BOOKS
www.kensingtonbooks.com

KENSINGTON BOOKS are published by

Kensington Publishing Corp.
119 West 40th Street
New York, NY 10018

All Kensington titles, imprints, and distributed lines are available at special quantity discounts for bulk purchases for sales promotion, premiums, fund-raising, educational, or institutional use. Special book excerpts or customized printings can also be created to fit specific needs. For details, write or phone the office of the Kensington Special Sales Manager: Attn. Special Sales Department. Kensington Publishing Corp, 119 West 40th Street, New York, NY 10018. Phone: 1-800-221-2647.

Library of Congress Card Catalogue Number: 2020939497

ISBN-13: 978-1-4967-2087-0
ISBN-10: 1-4967-2087-3
First Kensington Hardcover Edition: December 2020

ISBN-13: 978-1-4967-2093-1 (e-book)
ISBN-10: 1-4967-2093-8 (e-book)

10 9 8 7 6 5 4 3 2 1

Printed in the United States of America

Acknowledgments

A book is not actually written by one person alone. All authors receive support and inspiration from many different sources and directions. I particularly want to acknowledge and thank the many friends who provided encouragement while writing this book, especially the members of the Untitled Writers' Group and my Workantile coworkers. And, of course, my fabulous agent, Lucienne, and Wendy, my editor, who believed in Rosalind from the beginning. And always and forever my husband, Tim, and my son, Alexander.

PROLOGUE

An Urgent Cry for Intervention

They were, I believe, a happy, although not a contented family.

Theodore Edward Hook, *Sayings and Doings*

Let me be in time.

Helen Corbyn leaned low across her horse's neck, the frantic prayer keeping time with the mare's hoofbeats. *Please, please, please, let me be in time.*

It was a horrid morning for a gallop. The lazy spring sun hadn't even peeked over the hills. Fenland mists still clung to the tree branches and swirled across the road. Thankfully, Atalanta was always ready for a run, whatever the weather. Helen held tight to her mount's reins and prayed the mare did not stumble and that the sidesaddle did not slip.

Please, please.

She heard the men approaching before she saw them—a whole gang of jeering, laughing voices. In an eyeblink, a dense crowd of silhouettes emerged from the fog to fill the road to overflowing. They were workers on their way to the new drainage canals, and they saw her in the same instant she saw them. Thankfully, they scattered. Laughter and bawdy song became an uneven chorus of curses and cheers as Helen raced between them.

Another morning she would have laughed and waved in answer. Another morning, she would have enjoyed the feeling of her hair tumbling loose from the few pins she'd jammed into it when she threw on her clothes.

But another morning she would not have been woken by her brother's valet with a sealed letter and the whispered explanation that he'd found it on William's desk, and that he was worried, because William was gone.

Another morning, the contents of that letter would not have driven Helen out into the freezing March morning after her *idiotic* brother.

Atalanta snorted. Her gait slowed. She was getting blown. Helen touched her side with the riding crop, urging her to a fresh burst of speed. William had who-knew-what kind of a head start. She had to catch him.

They had skirted the worst of the fenland, leaving the thickest of mist and shadow behind. There was enough light now for Helen to make out a dark mass on the road ahead. She blinked, and the blur resolved into a landau with two passengers, with a driver muffled in a caped great coat on the box.

In another frantic heartbeat, Helen was close enough to see who it was.

"Peter!"

Peter Mirabeau—the landau's driver—jerked his head around.

"Helen!" He pulled back on the reins, bringing his matched grays to a stop. "What in God's name are you doing out?"

Helen brought Atalanta up beside the carriage and patted the mare's neck. She was sweating badly and would take a chill if kept standing. Helen had run her too fast this morning. She'd had no choice, but perhaps now she would have help.

"William's got himself into a duel, Peter! I have to find him! I have to . . ."

Her words dissolved. Helen squinted hard at Peter. Now, she saw how white he had turned and how still he'd gone. It struck her that it was very strange he should be driving friends about this part of the district, which wasn't on the way to anywhere in particular, especially when the sun was scarcely up.

It was even stranger that a doctor's bag rested on one of those friend's knees.

"Oh no, Peter! Not you!" *We're to be married! You* cannot *be in some stupid quarrel with my brother!*

"It's not what I wanted, Helen." Peter held up his right hand as if taking an oath. "'Pon my soul, I swear it is not. I tried to make an apology, but Corbyn—William—would not accept. He absolutely refused to let the matter drop, so in the end . . . I had no choice."

Shock and fury threatened to bubble over inside Helen. She wanted to scream. If she'd been on foot rather than on horseback, she might have actually used her crop on him, fiancé or no fiancé. As it was, she could not risk spooking Atalanta, and had to settle for shouting.

"What on earth could induce you to exchange shots with my brother! My brother the *cavalry colonel!*"

Peter just shook his head. "I can't tell you that, Helen. Please don't ask me."

The two passengers in the carriage shifted uneasily. Now she recognized the one without the bag. That was Earnest Worthing. He opened his mouth to say something. Helen glowered at him and tapped her crop against her skirt. Earnest closed his mouth.

"All men are blasted idiots!" Helen declared through gritted teeth. "Where is it to be?"

But Peter wouldn't budge. "Helen, this isn't your place. You have to trust that I have already taken measures to keep things from going forward."

"If that's true, what are you even doing out here now?"

Worthing cleared his throat. This time, it was Peter who glared at him.

Helen drew herself up. She threw every ounce of pride and breeding she possessed into her words, and her glare. "Mr. Mirabeau, if you think I'm going to leave my brother to this . . . this travesty, you are very much mistaken. I do not care if the affair is of his own making, I will put an end to it. Now tell me where he is!"

Peter shook his head. "No, Helen—Miss Corbyn. I can't."

"Mirabeau . . ." Worthing shifted uneasily in his seat. This time it was Peter who glowered at him. Worthing sagged backward. He looked pleadingly at the doctor for help. That estimable gentleman just shrugged his shoulders and drummed his gloved fingers against the bag.

Helen swallowed pride, swallowed anger, swallowed everything she had and was. She nudged Atalanta closer to the landau so she could reach out and grasp her fiancé's arm.

"Help me, Peter," she begged. "You know how William is since he got back from the war. He cannot possibly want to quarrel with you! Not really. If . . . if I can get to him first. If I can be there . . . it will all have to come to nothing. No one's going to shoot if I'm standing between you! Then you can both blame me for it not going off. No one can call either of you a coward, or repeat—whatever it is that's got you so upset. Please, Peter!" Tears stung Helen's eyes. "Don't risk yourself, or my brother!"

Peter's fist tightened around the reins, but he twisted around to face his friend.

"Worthing, I can rely on you to keep quiet about all this?"

"As the grave." Worthing touched his hat brim. "Word of honor. Said the whole thing was a mistake from the beginning, didn't I?"

Peter nodded. "We're to meet at the foot of Bale's hill," he said to Helen. "Now, before you stopped us, I was thinking there's something wrong with my landau's axle. I'd better check it while I have the chance, or we'll never get there at all."

Helen didn't bother to reply. She pressed her heels against Atalanta's ribs, sending the mare leaping forward.

Peter Mirabeau watched her vanish around the bend in the road.

Is another such horsewoman in the county? he wondered with a heady mix of pride and not a little bit of fear. As Helen disappeared into the trees, he found himself wondering as well if he had made the right choice to let her go on ahead.

Later, however, he and Helen would understand that this was the choice that saved both their lives.

CHAPTER 1

The Parting of Friends

*Or are you following the fashion and
turning novelist?*

Theodore Edward Hook, *Sayings and Doings*

"Are you certain you're not nervous?" asked Alice Little-field as Rosalind entered the dim front parlor carrying the tea service. "Because if I was about to be shut up for weeks on end with my former fiancé's mother, *I* would be dreadfully nervous."

"I will be visiting a grand manor house on an estate of thousands of acres," Rosalind corrected Alice mildly as she set the silver tray down. The elegant service dwarfed her small tea table. Very little of the Thorne family plate had survived their abrupt shifts of fortune. Thanks to several domestic miracles, however, the tea service remained intact. "And it isn't as if I'll be just sitting in the parlor. I will be helping get Louisa to the altar in as much style as the local church can offer. It shall be a positive whirlwind of activity that's hardly going to leave me 'shut up' with anybody." Rosalind paused. "Besides, Lord Casselmaine cannot be called my former fiancé. We were never formally engaged."

"Formally, you weren't, but practically you were. You cannot deny that."

"I could, but would it get me anywhere?"

"Probably not." Alice helped herself to a somewhat lopsided bread-and-butter sandwich.

Rosalind had fixed their tea herself. Her housekeeper, Mrs. Kendricks, was fully occupied with the work of closing up their small London house for the three weeks of Rosalind's stay in the country. In this room, all but one of the lamps had been emptied of oil and wicks, and all the most valuable movables were already locked away in the back cupboard. As soon as Alice left, Rosalind would spend the remainder of the day with her correspondence. She had to be sure all her accounts were as settled as they could be, and then answer a last few notes from friends and acquaintances. There was the pair of unusually important letters that she must forward to Mr. Sanderson Faulks. These would need to be delivered by hand. Mr. Faulks was an old friend of Rosalind's, and her family's, and he had recently begun holding some particularly sensitive correspondence in a sort of trust for her.

"Then there's the fact that your former fiancé is now a duke," Alice went on. "And is possibly planning on offering for you . . ."

"All right, Alice!" cried Rosalind. "Yes, I am nervous. Does that satisfy you?"

Alice put down her cup. "No, I'm worried about you."

Rosalind felt her brows arch. "Why should you be?"

Alice took her time in answering, which was surprising. Normally, Alice Littlefield spoke and moved and thought with a speed that was difficult to keep pace with. Rosalind, on the other hand, had always been far more deliberate, with a habit of looking steadily at whoever was speaking that some found disconcertingly direct.

The friends contrasted in their looks as much as in their temperaments. Alice was petite and dark haired, with a warm complexion and lively brown eyes. Rosalind Thorne, on the other hand, was tall and golden haired, with a figure more suited to sweeping skirts and cinched bodices of the grand dames of the previous era than the high-waisted Josephine gowns and pelisses that were currently in fashion.

"Rosalind, I know you better than anyone, even my brother," said Alice finally. "You won't deny that Lord Casselmaine represents a dreadful temptation. He's rich, landed, and titled, and it's not just any title, but an old one that puts him in the very first circles. If you married him, you would be returned to society in grandest possible style. It's a dazzling prospect, and it could easily keep you from appreciating the alternatives."

"And what is it you see as my alternatives?"

"Remaining as you are. Acknowledging for once and for all that the *haut ton* is no longer where you live, it's just someplace you visit. And keeping on with your business. I know"—Alice held up her hand before Rosalind could interject—"it is contrary to all accepted etiquette that I should accuse a gently bred woman of engaging in business. But women come to you with their problems, and when you help them, you are materially compensated for your time and effort. That's a business, and you are very good at it. It's new and it's different and you like it and it makes you happy, and you won't be able to do any of it if you're swaddled up as the Duchess of Casselmaine.

"There." Alice folded her hands. "I've said my piece. You may now reprove me at your leisure."

But all Rosalind did was smile and take up a sandwich for herself.

"Alice, everything you just said—those are all the reasons I have to go. If I hold back, I will always wonder if I was afraid, and what might have been. And," she added with a bracing breath, "I shall not just be idling about on picnics or helping Louisa write her thank-you notes. I've had a letter."

Rosalind went to her desk, pulled the letter from off her

stack, and unfolded it for her friend. While she returned to her tea and sandwich, Alice read:

Dear Miss Thorne:
I am writing to you on the recommendation of my confidential friend Louisa Winterbourne. Louisa tells me that you have a proven ability and willingness to help women who find themselves with difficulties that may be very much out of the ordinary. She tells me you have intervened successfully in cases of blackmail and theft, and even helped uncover the blaggard behind that terrible incident at Almack's.

Louisa further informs me you are to come down for her wedding. Miss Thorne, I beg that once you do, you will agree to meet with me privately. I am in the midst of such a quandary and I know not where to turn. I am told by everyone that the matter is dealt with and that I must forget it. But I cannot, and I fear if I do not find answers soon, I shall run mad. This may sound like a girl's hysteria, but I assure you it is not.

Please write as soon as may be with your answer, Miss Thorne. Louisa will know how to get any letter to me.

Yours, Most Sincerely,
Helen Corbyn

"Well." Alice refolded the letter. "I'm afraid she undoes her claim of not being a hysteric by her connection to Louisa. That girl's always had more than a touch of the dramatic about her. Why, she went into full mourning when that actor died. What was his name . . . ?"

"Yes," agreed Rosalind. "But at bottom, Louisa's a sensible young woman. I do not think I can turn down a friend of hers without a hearing . . . Now what is that for?"

Alice was frowning at her.

"I'd say it's nothing at all," replied Alice. "But I know

you'd be cross with me. So, I will say I am making a quiet wager with myself."

"On what point?"

"You'll find out once you have completed your restful stay in the idyllic English countryside," Alice told her. "You know, I wish I could go with you, but we lady novelists must stick to our work. And, of course, you're not the only one with a wedding to plan."

"Have George and Hannah set a date?" George Littlefield was Alice's older brother.

"It's to be in October. Hannah wants time to make her dress, and there are other arrangements . . ." She let the sentence trail off.

Alice currently kept house with George, and while both her brother and his fiancée had insisted Alice was welcome to stay, she had no intention of wearing out that particular welcome. She wanted new rooms for herself, but with her limited means, respectable places were proving difficult to find.

"It will all come together in time, I'm sure," said Rosalind. "Now, tell me how A.E. Littlefield's novel is progressing."

The friends finished their tea, all the while chatting about Alice's work, mutual acquaintances, and the end of the season flourishes Alice had attended as a society writer.

At last, Alice gathered up her things and Rosalind showed her to the door.

"You will write to me, won't you?" said Alice.

"Of course I will. Daily if you like."

"Probably we needn't go that far but . . . I don't know, Rosalind, I still worry."

Rosalind smiled and pressed Alice's hand. "I'd tell you to stop, but I know that never works. Therefore, I will promise to take good care of myself and not to let the Dowager Lady Casselmaine intimidate me in any way."

Instead of answering, Alice gave Rosalind a quick peck on the cheek and took herself out the door.

The parlor seemed quieter than ever without Alice to help

fill it. Rosalind found herself returning to the sofa and swirling at the dregs of her tea distractedly.

When she was a girl, an invitation to stay was a cause for excitement. It meant seeing old friends, buying new clothes, and of course, the possibility of flirting with young men. But it had been a long time since she had been invited anywhere simply as a guest.

Her family's assorted failures meant Rosalind had spent the past seven anxious years making her own way in the world. Now when she received invitations, they were all to house parties she had helped a hostess organize. During her stays, she had chores to complete and tasks to be accounted for, not to mention an endless array of plans to set in motion on behalf of her hostess.

But this time was different. This time, Rosalind Thorne, daughter of Sir Reginald Thorne, baronet (and forger, drunkard, liar, and suspected panderer), was invited to spend a month at Cassell House by Devon Winterbourne, Duke of Casselmaine. Ostensibly, it was to help his young cousin Louisa prepare for her wedding. In reality, it was to give him and Rosalind a chance to recommence a courtship cut off by her father's downfall and his brother's death.

And now, it seemed, she would also be helping a young woman she'd never met out of her difficulties.

Alice had been right from the beginning. Rosalind was very nervous.

CHAPTER 2

A Quiet, Country Retreat

*It is true, that a residence in the country is
favourable to the virtues of moderation, order,
and benevolence; but it is equally true, that they
are not necessarily connected with it.*

Althea Lewis, *Things by Their Right Names*

Rosalind was not entirely unacquainted with the country. House parties had been part of her girlhood, at least during those times when her father had been in funds and in friends. Despite this, each time she ventured outside of London, she still felt like she was entering into a foreign country.

She had, however, read enough novels to know that an author typically described the first sight of the hero's ancestral seat with a sweeping groundswell of prose. As the carriage pulled past the tree line of the Cassell House park, however, Rosalind found herself limited to just three syllables.

"Oh. My. Word."

"Yes," murmured her companion, Mrs. Showell. "I quite agree."

Cassell House was a manor on the grand scale. From what Rosalind could see, the house formed a U around a gravel yard, complete with (open) wrought iron gates. Dozens of windows sparkled in the midday sun, each one ornamented with all manner of coronets, crenellations, yet more crests. There were even cupolas sprouting from the rooftops, one for each wing, and a grand central dome that was probably truly impressive when seen from inside.

The overall effect was of a woman in a ballgown made for someone else. Nothing seemed to quite fit.

"It was the late duke's design, I'm afraid, and Hugh's." Mrs. Showell sighed. "The original house dated from Queen Elizabeth's day. It was not grand in the modern style, but it was graceful. I'm afraid I find this new edifice a trifle . . . inconvenient at times."

Mrs. Showell was Louisa Winterbourne's aunt and the sister of the Dowager Lady Casselmaine. A brisk, practical, experienced woman, Mrs. Showell had shepherded her vivacious niece through two London Seasons, to the successful conclusion that was Louisa's betrothal to one Mr. Firth Rollins. She had also kindly agreed to accompany Rosalind on the journey out to the country.

The driver steered them into the yard and turned the carriage expertly so the door aligned with the hall's grand entrance. A liveried footman was there to place the step, open the door, and help Rosalind and Mrs. Showell out.

Rosalind's foot had barely touched the gravel before Louisa herself came running down the hall's front steps.

"Rosalind! Finally!"

"Louisa!" cried Aunt Showell in affectionate exasperation. "You'll be a married woman in two weeks!"

"And I swear at that exact moment, all running out of doors will cease." Louisa ducked around the edge of her aunt's bonnet to give her a quick, affectionate kiss. "Thank you so much, dear Aunt Showell, for going to fetch her!"

Mrs. Showell waved off her enthusiastic niece and Rosalind laughed. "Well, there's no need to ask how you are, Louisa. I can see for myself. You look wonderful."

Louisa Winterbourne might not be heir to title or fortune, but she had inherited the Winterbourne looks, complete with shining black hair and bright gray eyes. If her ruddy complexion was short of the roses-and-cream ideal of English girlhood, it had the advantage of turning a pleasing golden color in summer. She possessed all the usual young lady's frivolities, plus a few extras, but Louisa was intelligent, kindhearted, and trustworthy, and Rosalind was glad to call her a friend.

Just now, though, Louisa rolled her eyes. "Wonderful?" she cried. "I look distracted, is what I look. I'm absolutely buried under a drift of letters, and cards, and what-have-you, and there are more arriving hourly. I don't know where they're all coming from! I've never met half these women!"

"It's no surprise, Louisa," Rosalind said. "You're getting married from Cassell House. The consequence was bound to rub off."

"Well, that consequence won't do any good if I'm smothered to death under an avalanche of paper." Louisa grabbed both of Rosalind's hands. "Swear you're here to help with the replies."

"I'm here to help with whatever you need. We'll get you to church on time and unsmothered, I promise."

"Oh, I'm not worried, exactly. It's more—" But Louisa caught Aunt Showell's deepening frown and cut herself off. "But I'm keeping you standing out in the yard when you're probably exhausted. Come inside." She hooked her arm through Rosalind's and drew her up the steps.

The interior of Cassell House was even more astonishing than Rosalind could have imagined. The light-filled foyer soared upward for a full three stories. The walls and sweeping curved stair were all made of white marble veined with gray and pink. The great Doric columns were polished pink granite. The carpets and hangings reproduced the colors of the Casselmaine livery: pale blue, silver, and nut brown. The tables and chairs were all gilded and marbled, carved and curved in the French imperial style.

It is like walking into an ice cavern.

Porters and pages in blue and silver livery closed the doors behind the women. Young maids in gray and white came forward to help remove traveling cloaks and bonnets, which were handed to yet another group of footmen to be borne back to the appropriate rooms.

"Here is Emerson." Louisa beckoned to a round-faced woman in the severe black dress of an upper servant who stood out like a shadow in all this white and pink. "She's to be your maid and help Mrs. Kendricks when she gets here."

"Miss." Emerson curtsied.

"I'll let you get settled, and then you and I can talk." Louisa hugged Rosalind. "I have a thousand things to tell you! And then there's . . ."

"Goodness, Louisa." Aunt Showell shook her head. "You'll be burying Miss Thorne under your own drift!"

"Not I." Louisa drew herself up into a stance of perfect drawing room deportment. "I'm soon to be a staid old married lady, and a banker's wife at that. I shall have to practice being perfectly dull on someone, and Rosalind knows all about it . . . oh dear . . ." Louisa blushed, but Rosalind just laughed.

"Believe me, Louisa, I have had occasion to observe many of the finer points of dullness across the length and breadth of London. If you want to learn all the current fashions for tedium, I'll be happy to advise. But right now, I do need to change and get myself together. Is . . . is his grace in the house?"

"Casselmaine?" cried Louisa. "Mercy, no! I don't think he's spent more than an hour in the house since he came down from London. He's down at the drainage works. They're surveying for the next canal channel, or something. He'll tell you all about it at dinner tonight, I'm sure. Oh!

Which reminds me, there will be a dinner tonight, a small one, just a few of the neighbors, and Rollins, of course." Mr. Firth Rollins was Louisa's betrothed. "He's staying with the Ablehavens, but he drives over here almost every day. I can't wait for you to meet him!" Louisa caught sight of a fresh frown from her aunt and rolled her eyes toward the distant white ceiling. "All right, all right. I'm quite finished. You rest and change, Rosalind. We'll talk shortly."

"If you'll follow me, miss," said Emerson.

Rosalind did.

Rosalind soon saw the justice in Mrs. Showell's remarks about the hall being "inconvenient." Once they had climbed to the second story, they left the marble foyer for corridors of polished sandstone, painted paneling, and blue carpets. Art-work lined the walls. Statuary and enameled ornaments and urns decorated nooks and tables. But the house evidently extended much farther back from the yard than Rosalind had been able to make out, and the farther they went into its depths, the darker, narrower, and more confusing the corridors became. Formerly straight lines dissolved into a bewildering series of twists and turns, not to mention rises and falls of little stairs. There were also far fewer windows, so one had the feeling of descending into the depths. The ornaments on the table were now augmented with oil lamps and candlesticks.

Emerson looked back to make sure Rosalind was keeping up.

"One soon learns the ways of the place," she remarked.

"I keep expecting to encounter some ancestral ghost."

"Oh, it's all far too new for ghosts, miss. But we did misplace one of the parlor maids a week ago. We may find her yet."

Rosalind quirked a brow. Emerson sailed ahead as if the words had never been spoken.

The door Emerson finally opened was at the far end of the

corridor. Rosalind stepped into a sunny and well-aired suite of rooms all done in shades of pale green and trimmed in cream. The furnishings, in contrast to what she had seen so far, were in the simpler, modern style. A bow window complete with velvet seat graced the boudoir and overlooked an expanse of formal garden in full summer flower.

"Would you care for refreshment, miss?" Emerson asked. "I can send for tea."

"That would be wonderful. And you'll please let her grace, the dowager, know I've arrived?"

"Certainly, miss."

Emerson gave instructions to the chambermaid and then helped Rosalind change her traveling clothes for a light, plain dress of sprigged green muslin with dark green trim.

The tea arrived and Rosalind accepted a cup. She drank while sitting on the curved window seat, simply taking a moment to enjoy the view. Unlike the awkward grandeur of the house, the gardens were truly beautiful.

A fresh knock sounded at the sitting room door. Emerson opened it to reveal Mrs. Showell standing in the corridor.

"I'm sorry to disturb you, Rosalind, but I just wanted to make sure you have everything you need."

"You're not disturbing me in the least." Rosalind came out of the boudoir into the sitting room. "Won't you join me? The tea's just arrived."

"Thank you." Emerson immediately drew another chair up to the table by the hearth while Rosalind fixed Mrs. Showell a cup of tea with lemon. But she barely had time to sip before Emerson went to the door again. This time, she returned with a folded paper.

"A note for you, miss," she said. "With her grace's compliments."

Mrs. Showell knitted her brows. *What's worrying her?* Rosalind opened the paper given and read:

Miss Thorne:
I must ask you to excuse me from receiving you today. If you would be so good as to wait upon me in my rooms at eleven o'clock tomorrow morning, I should be most grateful.
Catherine Winterbourne, Lady Casselmaine

Mrs. Showell was watching her over the rim of her cup. "I suspect that is to inform you my sister will not be receiving you today."

"Yes," agreed Rosalind. "She asks me to come to her tomorrow."

Mrs. Showell nodded and set her cup back down on the tray, clearly trying to arrange her thoughts, and her words. "Lady Casselmaine is not . . . very well just now."

"I am sorry to hear it. Had I known she was ill, I would have of course delayed my visit."

"I'm afraid my sister is quite often ill. Since Hugh died, she has become almost a complete recluse, and that is not a healthy life even for those of a most robust constitution."

Rosalind nodded. Hugh Winterbourne had died six years before. Six years of seclusion must have an effect on the body and the spirit.

"She has her own suite of rooms and attendants, and so on, so that the household is not required to rearrange itself when one of her . . . bouts comes upon her," Mrs. Showell went on. "And, of course, I have been performing the duties of hostess since my arrival. It does mean, however, that you will probably not be seeing much of her during your visit."

"That would be a shame. I had been looking forward to meeting her." Rosalind took another sip of tea and decided to risk a question. "Is it known what caused her . . . bout?"

For a moment, she thought Mrs. Showell might reply with a polite nothing. But whatever her silent thoughts were, she shook her head to clear them away. "There was a distressing event in the neighborhood some months ago now. A man of good family—one of the heroes of the Peninsular campaign in fact—was found dead. A most unfortunate accident. But when Lady Casselmaine heard . . . to her it brought back too many reminders of Hugh's death, and she went into a state of collapse."

"How very sad. May I know the man's name?"

"Colonel William Corbyn. Was it possible you knew him? He was often in London."

"No," replied Rosalind evenly. "He was no one of my acquaintance."

"He was a good man," said Mrs. Showell. "A sound and a decent man. There are those who would say otherwise, but they do not get a hearing with me. He suffered much during the wars, and it left its mark, but a man should not be judged less kindly for that."

"No, indeed," murmured Rosalind. "Was Colonel Corbyn any relation to Helen Corbyn?"

"Her oldest brother. Is it Helen you know?"

"I don't know her personally, but I believe Louisa has mentioned her name."

Mrs. Showell nodded. "Probably as one of her bridesmaids. Thick as thieves the two of them are. And Helen is engaged to be married as well. At least, she was . . ." Mrs. Showell frowned at her tea.

"Did something happen?"

"Oh no. Well, probably not. But the poor girl was devastated when her brother died, and of course everything had to be put off. There was some talk it was all to be put off permanently, I believe, but time seems to have healed that wound sufficiently."

Rosalind thought of the letter she carried in her case and privately doubted this assessment.

"I've met some of Louisa's friends," Rosalind said. "I'm surprised I have not yet met Miss Corbyn, since they are so close."

"Well, the Corbyns were not often up to town. William himself was frequently there, but the rest of the family always kept close to home. The parents also died rather recently, which left no one to chaperone Helen through a Season. Marius, the younger brother, does not care for London social life, for all his grand ambitions."

"What ambitions might those be?"

"He wishes to be an engineer. He talks endlessly of the great, modern world that men may build, the possibilities of gaslight and steam and I don't know what all. I have my doubts, personally, but he is as good as a sermon when the mood is on him. Still, he's not entirely without scope for his ambition here, thanks to Casselmaine."

"Is Lord Casselmaine building a bridge?"

"Oh, he hasn't told you? He's finally talked the councils and the Lord Lieutenant round to his scheme. He's draining the fens."

"Oh! Yes, Louisa mentioned that." Cassell House and the family estate were in one of the southern counties, where rolling, fertile country was bordered by long sprawls of marsh and fen. On the drive, there were moments when their driver had to occasionally navigate around the waters overflowing the ditches. In other places, the smell was so fetid, it would have done credit to some of the narrower London alleyways.

"Casselmaine's certain getting rid of the bad airs will improve the health of the district, and of course it will open up new arable land for the farmers at a good price to compensate for recent enclosures, create room for new roads, and oh, all manner of things." Mrs. Showell waved her hand vaguely. "He's very dedicated about his responsibilities, you know."

"Yes, I do know."

Mrs. Showell grew suddenly serious. "I think it would be good for you and I to talk frankly, my dear. How do you want to manage this?"

Rosalind allowed herself a moment for a long swallow of tea and then set about refreshing her cup so she could speak without quite having to look Mrs. Showell in the eye. "I think I'm supposed to say I'm not sure what you mean, but I also think that would be condescending to us both." She sighed. "The answer is, I don't know."

"Then may I offer my observations?"

"Please do."

"Casselmaine brought you here to see if you two are still suited well enough to marry. That is obvious. It may not come off. That is the nature of these things. But, it also might. Therefore, beginning tonight, it is safest to adopt a strategy of 'hope for the best, prepare for the worst.'"

Despite the riot of her feelings, Rosalind felt herself smile. "Which is which?"

"That is for you to decide. Until then, my advice would be that we introduce you to the neighborhood in your character as a young woman of gentle birth and possibly the new mistress of Cassell House, rather than simply as Louisa's friend and assistant. As you know, it's far, far easier to settle down than it is to move up."

"And I thought the country was different from London."

"It's all the same people, my dear, with all the same hopes and fears. It's just that when there's trouble, it takes longer for those things to reach a boiling point here."

"Since we are speaking frankly, Mrs. Showell, may I know what you think of my . . . situation?"

"I wish I could say my sister will get better and be able to resume her duties as lady of the manor so there is no need to rush into anything, especially since Casselmaine is still a young and ambitious man. But I do not think my sister will recover." Mrs. Showell's words turned bitter. "She has locked her own door and thrown away the key. Casselmaine needs the stability and support that come with a good marriage and heirs. Without them, he, the family, and the district will all suffer. From what I know of you, I think you could credibly turn your hand to the trade of duchess, and Casselmaine very much cares for you. Therefore, if you want my help to secure this marriage, I am willing to give it."

Rosalind set her cup down again, but found she could not stop staring at it. Mrs. Showell said nothing she did not know, but her matter-of-fact presentation sank deeply into Rosalind's skin.

"Thank you, Mrs. Showell," she said, and to her shame the words came out as a hoarse whisper. "You have to forgive my . . . hesitation. I've spent years learning to live with the fact that I am . . . in reduced circumstances, and to treat that situation as immutable. With that came the knowledge that any sort of marriage—let alone a grand one—was impossible for me. This . . . change . . . takes some getting used to."

"I understand perfectly," Mrs. Showell told her. "The world is hard on those of us with . . . indifferent families. Therefore, it is far better that we stand together." She lifted her chin. "May I take it we are decided? We shall conduct your campaign as if all were settled between you and Casselmaine, and if you'll allow, I'll take your usual role as the useful woman and draw up the order of our calls and social activities."

"I would be grateful to have you conduct my entrée to country society."

"Do London ladies clap hands on such things? I know the men would."

"Let us start the fashion." Rosalind held out her free hand. Mrs. Showell clapped her palm against Rosalind's so the two could shake firmly.

"Well, that's settled. I'll leave you now and let you really rest. We're keeping country hours here, so dinner will be sharp at seven." She stood, and then in an impulsive moment, very much like Louisa, she gave Rosalind a kiss on the cheek. "I know you'll be everything Casselmaine could want."

She left Rosalind alone with the tea and the maids, and thoughts of the letter from Helen Corbyn, and the whole great long swirl of the past and the present.

Everything Casselmaine could want? Will I be all that? she wondered. *And do I truly want to be?*

CHAPTER 3

What May Be Said in Private

*The gleams of affection, the flashes of generosity
which had, from time to time, illuminated his
earlier years, had now ceased.*

Althea Lewis, *Things by Their Right Names*

"Marius! Good heavens!"

Helen Corbyn drew her hems back as her brother slouched into the back parlor. Marius was—to be frank—a wreck. He was so coated in mud that it would have been difficult for a stranger to determine the true color of his boots, breeches, coat, or anything else about him, including his skin and hair.

"Where have you been?" she cried.

"Up to my hips in mud, peasants, and Irishmen. Where else should I be?" Marius threw himself into the chair by the hearth. Helen tried not to stare at the footprints her brother left on the carpet. Mrs. Beale would be beside herself. "Those fens aren't going to drain themselves, and if there's no one on hand to crack the whip, those damned grubbing creatures aren't going to drain them, either." He reached for the brandy decanter on the table and poured himself a healthy measure. "As was proven today when a whole damn wall collapsed practically on top of us."

Helen tried not to wince at the sight of her brother tossing back the whole drink. *He's not William.* But the smell of the stuff still curdled her stomach.

"Well, you need to wash, and change," she said, trying to keep her tone light and brisk. "We'll be late for dinner at the new hall."

The elaborate ducal edifice might be formally known as Cassell House, but everyone in the district simply called it "new hall."

"Damn dinner. I'm exhausted." Marius poured another measure of brandy. Little showers of dried dirt cascaded from his sleeves and shoulders.

No. No. You can't mean for us to stay home. Not tonight.

"But you've been counting on this for weeks. It's a chance to meet some of the duke's bankers. You said . . ."

"I'm in no mood to be spending more time with his sainted grace of Casselmaine." Marius drank, sighed, and scratched his neck hard. "Go yourself. It's a friend's house. It's a dinner without any hint of dancing. There'll be a thousand females about, including the old biddy who's taken over running the place from that nun of a dowager, and you'll be out of mourning in another month. Not even the queen could find anything to object to in your going."

Relief flooded her, but Helen did not dare let it show.

"You'll upset the balance of the table, and I'll be the one who has to excuse you." Not that Marius had ever cared a fig for table etiquette, or indeed, a hostess's feelings. But he would expect her to put up some protest, and that was all she could muster.

Helen hated the fact that she had become a "managing" woman, but Marius needed to be humored almost as much as William had. He'd always been close to their late mother, and had decided to adopt some of her methods of dealing with Helen. If Helen failed to negotiate his bad humor, she might find herself denied access to her horses, or the carriage, or anything beyond the garden gate.

At one time, she would have shouted that she could go where she pleased. She would have saddled her own horse and ridden off. But that Helen had dissolved ages ago.

Marius dropped onto the sofa and let his head fall back. "Explain I've caught a disease from an itinerant Scotsman and am at death's door." He stopped and raised his head. "I'm sorry, Helen. That wasn't fair." He took another drink. "But I am exhausted, and you should go. Mirabeau will be there, won't he?"

"Yes, I think so." She tried to sound indifferent, but it just came out missish.

"You should see him. Let him know you're sorry."

"About what?"

"Oh, stop. You all but accused him of murdering William."

"I've already apologized."

Marius set his glass down and came to take her hand. "But have you made him believe you? Don't make that face, Helen. It's you I'm thinking of, you and our family."

"What's left of it." Helen met her brother's eyes. It was harder than it should have been. He didn't know what it had been like, not really. She had been the one trying to take care of mother first, then father. William had been either absent or drunk the entire time. And now, William was dead, too.

"Yes, what's left of it." Marius spoke the words more gently than anything he'd said yet. *He's trying.* "But that's exactly why you need to be married. You need children. *We* need your children, to keep on. To keep house, land, and our lineage together."

"You could get married," she reminded him. "You're a catch . . . now." They'd feared for a while that William had died without making a will, but it had eventually been found among the grand mess of the papers in his three strong boxes. The document contained no surprises. The house, land, and money—apart from Helen's dowry and some legacies for the servants—had all gone to Marius. The result was that Marius was now one of the wealthiest squires in the county.

"Yes, I've been thinking about my marriage, but . . . look, I still hope to . . . work for a while." He swirled the dregs of his brandy. "What is the problem? You want to marry Peter Mirabeau. He's a good man. It's a decent match, and I've got a plan for you both."

"A plan?" Helen frowned.

"Yes, as soon as the engagement goes through, I'll settle some of the land and money on you directly, and hire Mirabeau as my property manager for the rest. You two will have the run of the place, and as soon as the first son comes along, we can draw up a trust for him immediately."

"While you go build your bridges?"

"Yes," he said simply. "It's what we both want, and what we both need. Helen, you're sensible. We have to look past our personal grief. There's only the two of us left now. If anything else happens, our line is *gone*. Then what happens to our land and everything our family's built here? It'll all be parceled out to whoever can raise the purchase price, regardless of what they are. It'll be some half-caste Spaniard or beady-eyed moneylender. Is that the type you want to bring here?"

Helen turned her face away. There was no arguing with Marius when he started talking like this. Fortunately, he took her lack of argument as agreement. "So, we'll hear no more about it. You'll go and secure Mirabeau. I'll stay and recover my humors so I can face superintending his grace's project tomorrow."

"Yes, of course." Helen stood. "I'll say good night then. I expect I'll be returning rather late."

Marius nodded and took up the brandy decanter again. Helen left before she had to see him drink any more. She closed the door behind her, walked several paces through the blue gallery. Only when she was certain she was out of all possible earshot did she let out a long, slow breath, steadying herself with one hand against the nearest table.

"Are you all right, Helen?"

Helen whirled around.

"Fortuna! Don't tell me you've started listening at doors."

"From this distance?" Fortuna gestured around her. "I was just coming to remind you you need to get dressed. Is Marius joining us?"

Fortuna Graves's name was much grander than her person. She was a slight, almost elfin woman. Her hair was pale gold and her eyes a washed-out blue. To Helen, it looked as if the young widow been left out in the sun too long and simply faded. Her dark plum evening gown only emphasized her natural pallor. Despite this, Fortuna radiated solidity. This was a woman who had stood against any number of tests. She had not triumphed, but she still stood.

In the face of that endurance, Helen felt suddenly and heartily childish. "No, he's tired. And coated in mud. He's asked me to make his excuses." *And I should not be so very obviously relieved.*

But Helen had her own plans for this dinner, and she knew Marius would not approve of any of them.

Fortuna took her hand, just as Marius had. *She thinks I'm worried about his temper, or his politics.* "Helen, Marius misses William, too, and all that gossip around the inquest was a blow to him, as much as to you."

"And you," added Helen. "Oh, Fortuna, are you ever going to get tired of managing all us troublesome Corbyns?"

Fortuna smiled, but the expression did not reach her pale eyes.

"I shouldn't have said that," Helen told her quickly. "I'm sorry. We owe you . . . *I* owe you. . . ."

Fortuna waved her hand, but the chill remained in her gaze. "No more dawdling, now. You get yourself ready, and I'll see what's keeping John Coachman. Mable's all ready to go with you."

"But you're coming." Helen spread her hands to indicate Fortuna's dress and her carefully curled hair.

"No, I'll solve Mrs. Showell's table problem by staying home."

"You don't need to do that, Fortuna. Have a night in company. There will be cards and . . ."

"And Mrs. Vaughn's sniping and Henrietta's swanning and Mrs. Ablehaven's meaningful glances. No, thank you." Fortuna sighed. "It's a relief, actually. I'd much prefer a quiet night with a good book and my letters."

Helen glanced toward Marius's door. He still had not come out. Hopefully, he was not finishing off the rest of the brandy.

But he might well be, and she could not leave Fortuna here to face that. "No, I insist. It will look strange if I show up entirely on my own. Mrs. Vaughn and Lady Humphreys and all the rest will spend all her Thursday calls talking about it." *And you.* "And I'll spend months explaining myself. Please, Fortuna. I need you."

Fortuna sighed again. "Well, all right. I suppose I cannot leave you to the mercy of Mrs. Vaughn."

Helen let herself be led away.

The truth was, Helen would have gone anyway, but how she went, and how she looked doing it remained important. Their mother had raised all the Corbyn children to hold appearances as sacred. Nothing that happened inside the house could be allowed to break the surface, no matter how serious it might be or how long it went on. Marius held to that catechism with an iron fist. What was really happening did not matter. The world could only see what the Corbyns wanted seen.

I must pray that Louisa's Miss Thorne can show me the way out of this. And if not . . .

Helen did not let herself finish the thought.

CHAPTER 4

A Small Gathering of Friends and Neighbors

But glances may be read quickly, and construed off hand.

Theodore Edward Hook, *Sayings and Doings*

"Can I come in?"

Rosalind turned away from her boudoir's bow window to see Louisa peeking around the door.

"Of course. I was just taking a moment to admire the gardens."

Like Rosalind, Louisa was already dressed for dinner. She wore a modestly cut gown of vivid pink and gold. Roses and pearls decorated her black curls, and more pearls circled her throat. To Rosalind, Louisa already looked less like the eager girl she'd been in London and more like the young matron she'd be in a fortnight's time.

Do not feel old, Rosalind commanded herself. *You do not have even a full five years on this girl in front of you.*

Louisa came to stand beside her at the window. "The grounds are glorious, aren't they? They're what's left of the old hall. I'm sure Aunt Showell will be happy to take you on the grand tour. She knows everything about them. I can barely tell a rose from a rhododendron." She frowned. "Do you think that's going to be a problem? When I'm married, I mean?"

"I don't think so. And if it is, we can find you some good books on the subject."

"I just . . . I suddenly feel like there's all these things I should know, and be able to do. I've been sitting with Devon's lawyers and trying to understand what's going to happen, with the money and the property. I'm going to have property!" Louisa added suddenly, and her cheeks flushed. "I didn't even know my father had any to leave me, but it turns out there's been this pile of deeds in trust that nobody bothered to tell me about . . . and I'm going to be in charge of my own house, and my own calls, and dinners, and . . . well, I'm going to be *Mrs.* Firth Rollins, so I'm in charge of him, too, and responsible for how people look at him, and me, and everybody's going to be watching and I just . . . don't feel like I'm *ready.*" She twisted her fingers together. "And you're going to tell me it's just nerves."

"Of course it's nerves, but that doesn't mean it isn't real." Rosalind clasped Louisa's hands. "Your life is about to undergo a complete change."

"That's not a help, Rosalind," muttered Louisa.

Rosalind just smiled and gave her hands a gentle shake. "Just remember, you're not alone. Your Aunt Showell will be right there, and your mother"—then she remembered what she knew of Louisa's mother and moved on hastily—"and there will be all your friends, and I'm here, too."

"Thank you, Rosalind, and I'm sorry. I didn't mean to just burst out with all that. But I had to *tell* somebody."

"I understand, believe me. Still, think of this. One of the advantages of being married in the country, in summer, is that you'll have months of relative quiet before the Season starts. You can make your come-out as a married woman gradually, rather than having to do it all at once."

Louisa's expression brightened at this. "You always turn things around so they're easier to see." She paused. "You got Helen's letter?"

"I did."

"She's just arrived downstairs now. Will you come meet her?"

"Of course. Let me get my gloves."

Emerson, of course, was at her elbow, and within moments had Rosalind buttoned into the white satin gloves. Then, Rosalind followed Louisa through the darker corridors into the region of light and polished stone at the front of the house, where they were quickly forced to double back down a broader gallery toward the manor's center, and its rotunda.

If Rosalind had thought the entrance hall monumental in its scope, it was nothing compared to the grand rotunda. Here everything from floor to ceiling was also pristine marble and smooth sandstone, but the decorations were meant to inspire rather than simply awe. Medieval tapestries—or at least some good reproductions—hung on the walls. Greek and Roman statuary—too battered to be anything but genuine—looked down on the scattering of guests from polished plinths.

The whole was capped off by the dome Rosalind had seen from the parkway, and as she'd predicted it was magnificent. In fact, it was painted and gilded and frescoed beyond anything she'd seen outside of a royal residence.

Louisa caught her staring. "Yes, it does tend to take one's breath away. It'll also be cold as a tomb in another hour or so. Blasted Hugh and all his nonsense, and of course I never said that, especially not the blasted."

"Said what, Louisa? I'm afraid I was gazing in wonder at the frescoes and did not hear."

Louisa grinned and gave her arm a squeeze. "Come on, I see Helen down by that half a vestal virgin."

Like the entrance hall, the rotunda was graced with grand, curving stairways carpeted in shades of cornflower and delphinium blue. Here, the steps were so broad, it was impossible to easily step from one to the other. Despite the profusion of lamps and candles, Rosalind thought the space looked dim. The front of the manor might be lined with windows, but no one had thought to find a way to bring any natural light in here.

Inconvenient indeed, thought Rosalind. And then she stopped thinking at all. Because when Rosalind and Louisa finally reached the foot of the stairs, it was not Louisa's friend who came forward to greet them.

Devon.

Devon Winterbourne, Duke of Casselmaine, cut a dramatic figure against the backdrop of the echoing marble rotunda. He was tall and broad and tanned. His smile had never failed to make Rosalind's heart leap, and now was no exception. His wavy black hair had been scraped back from his forehead and pasted down hard against his scalp. He'd been fastened as carefully into his satin breeches, gold damask waistcoat, white collar, and black coat as she was into her cream and blue evening gown.

"Miss Thorne." Devon bowed over her hand. "I am very glad to see you here."

"Thank you for inviting me, your grace."

"You should be thanking Louisa and Aunt Showell." He nodded to Mrs. Showell, who had come up beside him, in her role as hostess and chaperone. "If I'd neglected you, they would have had my head."

That was not true and Rosalind and Devon both knew it, just as they both knew they could not breathe one word of what really brought them standing face-to-face in this showplace of a house. What they said and did now was solely for the benefit of those around them. All Devon's acquaintances and neighbors must see that everything between Lord Cassel-maine and this stranger from London was open, correct, and thoroughly proper.

There were days when Rosalind wished she could throttle propriety and toss it into the nearest duck pond.

Of course, one would have to be careful not to soil one's gloves.

She felt herself smile, and saw the answering flash of humor in Devon's gray eyes. He might not know exactly what she was thinking (which might be for the best), but he intuitively understood her feelings.

He also held out his arm. "Let me introduce you to some—"

"Oh no, Casselmaine!" Louisa cut him off. "She's mine until dinner. You shall have her afterwards."

Devon opened his mouth as if he wanted to protest. Rosalind raised her brows at him.

"You did say it was Louisa I owed for inviting me here," she reminded him. "I can't refuse to repay the favor now."

"I did say that, didn't I? That will teach me. Go, go." He waved his hand. "She's a bride and we have to indulge her, although if she keeps this up, I'm sending her to bed without supper."

Louisa apparently decided the best display of maturity she could offer at that moment was to stick her tongue out.

"Louisa . . ." began Mrs. Showell under her breath, but Louisa ignored her entirely. Instead, she sailed off, with Rosalind in tow, toward the fragment of Roman statuary and her friend Helen.

Rosalind's first impression of Helen Corbyn was of a young woman who had already learned to shoulder her burdens, but not necessarily with resignation. She looked to be a year or two older than Louisa, but that might just have been her serious demeanor. She was slim built but had the rounded frame and healthy, freckled complexion of someone who was used to exercise and the out of doors. Her curled hair was a rich brown that probably brightened to auburn in the sunlight. She wore her modish, dove-gray mourning gown with tolerance, rather than true comfort.

"I'm delighted to finally meet you, Miss Thorne," said Miss Corbyn when Louisa finished the introductions. "Louisa's told me so very much about you. I do hope we'll have a chance to talk tonight."

There was no mistaking the import of those words. Helen Corbyn did not want to wait for some more appropriate, and private, moment to lay out her business for Rosalind.

But then, if it had to do with her brother's death, and whatever put those dark shadows under her bright brown eyes, Rosalind could not blame her.

"I look forward to it."

Helen looked like she wanted to say something more, but they were interrupted by the approach of a pale blond woman wearing a gown of deep plum velvet. Rosalind was struck by the dress, and the woman in it. There was no lace or ribbon to lighten the layers of rich fabric. It should have made the pale woman look delicate. Instead, she looked distant and regal, especially surrounded by all the white marble and younger girls in their creams and pastels.

"Oh, Fortuna," said Helen. "There you are. Miss Thorne, please let me introduce Mrs. Fortuna Graves. Fortuna, this is Louisa's friend, Rosalind Thorne. I was telling you about her at breakfast."

"Miss Thorne." Mrs. Graves made her curtsy. Her voice was low and deep. It was at odds with her slight and pale appearance, and Rosalind wondered if she cultivated the tone. She was, Rosalind felt certain, a woman who knew to a nicety how others saw her.

"We've met," said Mrs. Graves. "Although I doubt you would remember it. It was years ago now, at a card party given by Lady Aimesworth. You were there with your mother and sister, as I recall."

"You'll have to forgive me," Rosalind answered. "But I am very glad to renew our acquaintance now."

"And if I may ask, how are your mother and sister?"

"My sister is quite well, thank you," said Rosalind. "Unfortunately, my mother has left us."

"Oh, I had not heard. I am so sorry. That is very difficult."

"Thank you," said Rosalind, and smoothly changed the subject. "And you, Mrs. Graves, you have family in this area?"

"The Corbyns are my family," she replied promptly. "I'm afraid I'm that dreaded distant relative who comes to stay."

"Don't talk about yourself that way, Fortuna," said Helen. "We wouldn't know how to get along without you."

Helen spoke these words with a deep sincerity, but at the same time there was a tension in her voice and in Fortuna's modest smile.

Louisa felt it, too. "Where is Marius, Helen?" she asked, a little too quickly. "I was sure he'd be at Devon's right hand all evening discussing how many new feet of earth have to be dug before the county worthies decide to threaten his funds again."

"There was some kind of accident at the dig today—no one was hurt," Helen added hastily. "But it left Marius very tired, and he asked to be excused."

There was something unsaid passing between the three women, but before Rosalind could try to find out what it was, Aunt Showell bustled up to them.

"I'm afraid I must steal Rosalind away from you, Louisa. I'll return her shortly, I promise."

She did not allow Louisa any time to make a reply as she led Rosalind way.

"I just wanted to draw your attention to that little grouping by our headless senator," murmured Mrs. Showell, allowing her gaze to rove casually around the gathering. She herself did not look at that gathering. She waved her hand toward the tapestry on the wall.

Rosalind had a great deal of practice at the art of not looking at people. She followed Mrs. Showell's gesture, her gaze passing over the knot of women, who all surrounded a very petite woman in a very large gold turban crowned by a positive forest of ostrich feathers.

"The creature beneath that luxurious plumage is Lady Pennyworth," murmured Mrs. Showell as they contemplated the tapestries, and the lamps, and the relics, anything and everything except the women they were discussing. "The ladies are her court, in case you couldn't tell. They are our neighborhood's board of directors. If you wish to make a good impression here, you must make it with them."

Rosalind lifted her chin and pasted on her most polished look of polite indifference. She also snapped open her fan. "And who is that?" she murmured, flicking her gaze toward a woman who stood a little behind the others.

She was a tall, stout lady. Her claret gown was relatively plain, but she made up for it with her display of jewelry. She wore a diamond and pearl chain about her neck, and garnets and more pearls on her hands and wrists. Diamonds glittered in her ears and on the gold combs in her hair. Yet despite this show of wealth, her position relative to the other ladies marked her as one outside their intimate circle.

"That's Mrs. Vaughn," murmured Lady Showell. "Her husband moved the family here from London eight or so years ago. He was a solicitor in London and made a great deal of money."

"Perhaps he is now focused on his standing in society?"

Mrs. Showell nodded. "And to the family's social misfortune, everybody's noticed."

Which explained that lady's exclusion, her evident awareness of it, and her equally evident determination not to show it.

"You'll hear more about it all from Louisa, I shouldn't wonder," breathed Mrs. Showell. "You see Mrs. Vaughn's eldest daughter, Cecilia"—she gestured idly toward the group of unmarried girls standing with Louisa and Helen Corbyn—"was engaged to William Corbyn when he died."

CHAPTER 5

At Table, and the Aftermath

The dinner hour was come; the guests arrived:
every countenance was to be smoothed, and
gayety and good humour were to prevail.

Althea Lewis, *Things by Their Right Names*

There were few social events where the rules were quite as confusing, or arbitrary, as the dinner party. Beyond the endless niceties regarding appropriate dress, there was the elaborate and messy ritual of "being seated." This required that the hostess thread through the gathering and assign each female guest a male partner with whom to enter the dining room. Custom declared that wives and husbands did not accompany one another, and neither did courting or betrothed couples. Assignment must be made according to an unspoken order of precedence that weighed not only the guests' ranks, but the level of their welcome in the household and, occasionally, the level of affection (or lack of) that the hostess held for a guest. Rosalind had seen women wield this ritual to help cement matches, shore up political connections, and even gain revenge by pairing eligible daughters with deaf bores or second sons with merry widows.

Once the couples paraded through the doors of the dining

room, a particular sort of mob scene occurred. While partners might be (quietly) arranged ahead of time, the seating was not. The couples were left to sort themselves out as best they could. In general, one wished to secure a place near either the head or the foot of the table. There, one might form a closer connection with the host or hostess. No one wished to be exiled to the dreaded middle ground, because unless the host or hostess addressed the table generally, conversation was permitted only with those closest to you, and some hostesses even frowned on anyone—especially unmarried young ladies—talking with the person across the table.

At a large or prestigious party, the competition for good places could include a discreet foot-treading or sharp elbow. Rosalind had recently been to some suppers where hostesses made firm suggestions for seating, as well as for pairings, in an attempt to keep the peace. Rosalind suspected this would eventually become a regular practice, if only to save people's slippers.

Because it fell to Mrs. Showell to perform the hostess duties and create the pairings, Rosalind was not at all surprised to find herself partnered with Louisa's fiancé, Mr. Firth Rollins. Mr. Rollins steered her briskly and faultlessly to the head of the table, only one chair away from Devon. To whom she could of course not speak, until he spoke to her, as his rank exceeded her own.

One day I will write a book and lay all this out, thought Rosalind. *But it will probably all be out of date by the time it comes to print, and I'll have to write another.* . . . Then she thought, *Alice has infected me.*

Then she thought: *Why am I having such a hard time looking at Devon?* Devon had come to stand at the head of the table. At the foot, Mrs. Showell sat, and then Devon sat, and now the rest of them could sit as well.

"Miss Thorne, I trust your journey here was not too uncomfortable?" Devon's gray eyes laughed even while his face remained perfectly serious. He understood how ridiculous it all was, and yet, they both would play their parts.

"It was perfectly comfortable, thank you. The roads were in very good order."

"How unusual," he said with bland indifference. "Tell me, how does our friend Miss Littlefield? Did I hear her brother is getting married?"

"He is, sir. And Alice is very well, thank you. She sends her best wishes to you and your mother."

"Thank you, and please return my congratulations to the family."

Rosalind smiled and Devon smiled. Then he began talking with Mr. Rollins about the current state of the financial world, and thus the opening figure of the dance was completed. They might speak again, a few words, but nothing meaningful. Not here. Not yet.

The dinner moved along at its stately pace. Cassell House was clearly a well-ordered place, and the servants knew their business. There was fish, game, pastry, beef, sauce, and dressed greens in all their late-summer profusion and variation. Rosalind spoke with Mr. Rollins about art, and the roads from London, and the weather. She discovered Lady Humphreys, who sat across from her, had three daughters, and talked with her about fashions, and the weather, and the roads. When the subtle rhythms of the gathering brought their turn round again, she talked with Devon about his drainage projects and the weather, as they had already touched on the state of the roads.

Through it all, the women watched her. Every time Rosalind turned her head, she found some gaze fixed firmly on her.

Rosalind stifled a sigh. What else could she have possibly expected? She had known when she arrived this was not a dinner. This was a staged performance, and she could not miss her lines.

Louisa watched helplessly from her end of the table. Rosalind gave her a small shrug and an encouraging smile, and got an eye roll in return.

Like the matrons, Helen Corbyn kept stealing glances toward Rosalind. Hers, however, were more on the order of a prisoner looking at the guard's iron key. To Rosalind's eye, it appeared the young woman was putting up a polite front, but even from her place four chairs down, Rosalind could tell Helen was straining to keep her attention fixed on the portly man in a clerical collar and bishop's stole who was busy regaling his table companions about . . . something.

At long last, the cheese and fruit were served and duly consumed. Mrs. Showell rose to her feet, the universal signal that the dinner was over. Rosalind stiffened her spine and gathered up the edges of her fraying nerves. Her skin felt as if it had been rubbed raw by the constant, inquisitive glances, and she was still hours away from being able to retreat to her room. The end of formal dining was only the beginning of the evening's third act. Now, the ladies must withdraw from the dining room to the sitting rooms, out of range of those mysterious male discourses that might perturb the delicate balance of the female mind.

The sitting rooms in Cassell House were, unsurprisingly, lush and lavishly decorated. All the doors had been drawn back to reveal the interconnecting chambers, already laid out for music, or cards, or conversation. Once the gentlemen finished their port and argument, the general party would be able to circulate easily among the various entertainments. There was also a variety of approved (non-spiritous) beverages set out for the guests, along with yet more food, in case anyone had not had enough at the table.

Once the ladies entered the first sitting room, Louisa was immediately at Rosalind's elbow.

"You're with me, Rosalind! I want you to meet everybody!"

By everybody, of course, Louisa meant her friends. Rosalind was never so grateful to anybody in her life. She knew she could not put off being quizzed by the matrons forever, but even a half-hour's respite would be welcome.

The young women of Louisa's circle did not care about Rosalind's parentage. They did not care about her manners— or at least, they cared rather less. Instead, they quizzed her with vigor about the latest fashions from London. She was able to delight them all by dropping the name of A.E. Little-field as a family friend, and drew gasps and applause when she announced—quite in confidence, of course—that Little-field was writing a novel. The girls all promised to subscribe the instant the book became available.

The conversation also, of course, gave Rosalind a chance to more closely observe Helen Corbyn, who had joined the rest of the girls in their circle. Given her behavior at the table, Rosalind felt certain Helen would remain distant from the conversation, isolated by her worries as much as by her mourning gown. But Helen seemed determined to be gregar-ious—talking and laughing as much as any of the other girls, if not more.

Like she's starving for this, thought Rosalind. *Or wants to store it all away for later.*

It was a feeling for which Rosalind had a great deal of sympathy. Protected by this group of young, unmarried women, Rosalind could relax. She could laugh and trade friendly ban-ter. She could talk about whether *A Modern Prometheus* had really been written by Percy Shelley, or whisper about whether this new novel—*The Vampyre*—could possibly be as scandal-ous as reported, or whether one should stick to reading *Northanger Abbey* and its cousins. Then there were plays and actors and local intrigues to all be reviewed in detail.

Despite all the temptations, however, Rosalind never lost awareness of the quieter circle near the hearth, where the matrons gathered. Indeed, it felt strange not to be with them already. As a woman in reduced circumstances—a useful, helpful woman—her place would be at her hostess's elbow. From there, she would fill gaps in the conversation, pass cups of tea, and be ready in case small errands needed to be run, or slight problems needed to be solved by dint of some timely suggestion.

That humble and necessary position, Rosalind noted, was currently filled by Mrs. Graves. She sat beside Lady Pennyworth, but was not fully included in the conversation. Rather, Mrs. Graves managed the teapot under Lady Pennyworth's direction, and handed around the plates of cakes and bonbons.

When Mrs. Vaughn dropped her fan, Mrs. Graves looked to Lady Pennyworth for her approval before she retrieved it. Rosalind could see the sourness in that lady's expression even from across the room.

Unfortunately, she let her gaze linger a little too long in that direction. Lady Pennyworth turned, and she caught Rosalind's stare before Rosalind could turn away. She felt her cheeks begin to burn with unaccustomed embarrassment.

Out of the corner of her eye, she saw Lady Pennyworth say something to Mrs. Graves.

And here it begins, she thought.

She was right. Mrs. Graves rose and came over to the girl's circle.

"Miss Thorne," she said. "I must steal you away, I'm afraid. Lady Pennyworth is asking for you."

"Better you than me," murmured one of the girls. The answering giggles were scattered, but audible. Rosalind made herself frown, but she stood. She had to ignore the butterflies in her stomach, as well as the nervous and disappointed glance from Helen Corbyn. Instead, she schooled her features into her best expression of polite disinterest and followed Mrs. Graves to the other side of the room, trying not to feel like a prisoner advancing to the bar.

Trying and failing.

CHAPTER 6

When Being Presented at Court

*Everybody has observed that whenever particular
pains and trouble are expended to make up an
agreeable party, the scheme universally fails . . .*

Theodore Edward Hook, *Sayings and Doings*

"How are you holding up?" breathed Fortuna as they
crossed the room.

"Well enough," Rosalind murmured in reply. "And you?"

"I'm used to them." She looked patient. She looked quiet.
To Rosalind's eye, she also looked like she was expending a
great deal of energy conserving her dignity. Rosalind knew
that particular range of looks intimately.

Mrs. Showell sat with the matrons. She watched Rosalind's approach as closely as the rest of them. Rosalind tried
not to see the worry in her eyes.

"Lady Pennyworth," said Mrs. Graves as she and Rosalind reached the gathering. "Lady Humphreys, Mrs. Ablehaven, Mrs. Vaughn, do allow me to introduce Miss
Rosalind Thorne."

Rosalind made her curtsy.

"Lady Pennyworth," she said. "Lady Humphreys, Mrs.
Ablehaven, Mrs. Vaughn. How very good to meet you."

Everyone—including Mrs. Showell—looked to Lady Penny-worth. So, of course, did Rosalind.

"Charming," Lady Pennyworth murmured. "Do sit with us, Miss Thorne." Her tone managed to mix languor, conde-scension, and authority.

You've spent a great deal of time in London society, Rosa-lind thought as she took the chair indicated. There was nowhere else she could have cultivated that particular verbal effect.

"Mrs. Graves, perhaps Miss Thorne would care for a cup of tea?" Lady Pennyworth suggested.

"That would be most kind, thank you," replied Rosalind. Mrs. Showell nodded minutely at this and lifted her own cup, but did not in any way relax.

Rosalind accepted the tea with a paper-thin slice of lemon. She also accepted a bonbon, which she put on a plate beside her and did not so much as glance at again. To be seen eating during conversation might be regarded as gauche. It also in-vited the possibility of smears, or dropped crumbs.

Lady Pennyworth bent a smile toward Mrs. Ablehaven with the air of one drawing a perfectly sharpened knife. "I was saying to my husband the bishop this morning that it would be so very enjoyable to have some fresh company at the dinner this evening."

"Fresh and genteel," sighed Mrs. Vaughn. "I shall in no way criticize his grace, of course, but Lord Casselmaine does tend to fill his tables with tedious bankers."

"Well, at least it is not lawyers." Lady Pennyworth smiled. So did all the women around her. Mrs. Vaughn drew herself up sharply, letting Rosalind, and anyone else with eyes, know the hit had been scored.

She watched Mrs. Vaughn's eyes as she filed that insult away for later. Rosalind strongly suspected she had many others to go with it.

"A man so attentive to his estate business has many calls

on him, I believe," murmured Rosalind. "They must necessarily extend to calls on his table."

"Yes, perhaps," Lady Pennyworth acknowledged. "And of
course, when consideration to bankers extends to inviting
them into the family, well, what is one to do?" She gave a
minute shrug with one shoulder. "We all must live, mustn't
we? And the Rollinses have done so very much to advance
his grace's grand public works."

Rosalind set her cup down, ignoring the rising look of
panic in Mrs. Showell's eyes. Drawing room wars were petty
things, conducted in glances, meaningful phrases, and elo-
quent sighs. The bleeding inflicted on the unwary came in the
form of a thousand tiny verbal cuts.

And two could very much play the game.

"I am very glad Mr. Rollins could be here tonight," said
Rosalind. "He's been in such demand even with London adjourned for the season, I thought he might not be down for
another se'en night. Have you heard, Mrs. Showell, how his
consultation on behalf the Countess Lieven progresses?"

Mrs. Showell took the hint, and the baton.

"It goes well, I believe. His father, I understand, has stayed
in London to finalize the details. But, of course, it is not
something he can properly speak of to me."

"Oh, of course not," agreed Rosalind. "I did think Louisa
looked particularly lovely when she accompanied him to the
countess's levee. That shade of pale pink is always so becoming on a young woman of her complexion. Even the countess
remarked on it."

All the matrons were now glancing toward Louisa. *She*,
and her fiancé, were received socially by the Countess
Lieven? One of the most glamorous, and powerful, hostesses
in London? And she hadn't *told* anyone? Which meant she
scored a triumph and was above boasting to her neighbors.
Rosalind watched every last one of them mentally rearrang-
ing their estimations.

It was not a change that sat well with Lady Pennyworth. But her pause did give Mrs. Vaughn an opening.

"I believe, Miss Thorne, your father is Sir Reginald Thorne?" Mrs. Vaughn leaned forward. The movement caused her array of diamonds to flash in the candlelight. "Does he remain in London?"

"He's gone to the country, ma'am, with my sister."

"*The* country, but not *our* country, clearly?" Lady Pennyworth smiled archly at her little coterie, who all returned answering smiles at her little joke.

"No, ma'am," answered Rosalind obediently. "My father is recuperating from a long illness. My sister has taken him to the coast for the sea air." This was a lie on several levels, but Rosalind had told it so often, its rough edges had worn away.

"And how do you find us, Miss Thorne?" inquired Mrs. Vaughn. "Are we very dull after your London Season?" Her attention was fastened on Rosalind's dress. Rosalind suspected she was calculating the probable cost of its materials.

Rosalind found her gaze slipping to Fortuna Graves. That lady read the look and nodded in agreement, conspiracy, and sympathy.

"I found this Season a most pleasant distraction," Rosalind said. "But I am always glad to return to the country when I can." This was at least partly true. "Are you often in London yourself, ma'am?"

"Oh, I find London far too fatiguing for my tastes." Mrs. Vaughn waved her much-beringed hand languidly. "I was so delighted when Vaughn moved us here. I positively *dread* having to return for my daughters' Seasons."

At this point, Lady Pennyworth decided she had ceded enough of the attention. "I understand, Miss Thorne, that you are acquainted with Lady Jersey? How does her ladyship?"

Do you mean to let me know you're also her acquaintance? Yes, you do.

"She was in excellent health when I last saw her. Of course, the demands of the Season are always very heavy for her." Lady Jersey was head of the board of Almack's, the most prestigious assembly rooms in London. This made her one of the metropolis's most consequential and busiest hostesses.

"Naturally, naturally." Lady Pennyworth's smile grew even sharper. *She must keep a special whetstone for that expression.* "And, of course, you just told us that you are also on visiting terms with the Countess Lieven?" The reproof was tiny, but genuine. Rosalind had dropped a name, thus opening herself to the accusation of putting on airs.

A thousand tiny cuts.

"Her grace has been kind enough to permit me to call," replied Rosalind, not neglecting the modest lowering of her gaze.

"You must forgive our friend if she seems overly inquisitive," said Mrs. Vaughn, earning herself another glower from Lady Pennyworth. "It's just that ours is such a quiet county, very few persons come to visit us from London—save for the shooting and the races, of course. And then, oh, such riffraff among them!" This elicited a polite murmur of agreement from the ladies, except from Mrs. Graves. "It's nearly as bad as when one travels. There's no telling who one is *really* talking to, actually."

"It is a hazard of London life," Rosalind agreed. She did not look away. She could not help her color, but she would not lose her poise. "Surely, one of the great advantages of country living is that one always knows precisely who people are."

"If only that were true," murmured Mrs. Vaughn, and she quite deliberately let her gaze roam from Lady Pennyworth toward Fortuna Graves.

What have I gotten in the middle of? thought Rosalind.

At that moment, the footmen opened the doors and the black-and-white tide of gentlemen guests streamed in.

Rosalind turned, anticipating rescue, but a single glance sent her heart plummeting.

Devon wasn't with them.

CHAPTER 7

A Well-Tended Garden of Sorrow

In the want of other objects for her affections,
had found one in the indulgence of her affliction.

Althea Lewis, *Things by Their Right Names*

Devon stood in front of his mother's door and felt nothing but tired.

Dinner had been both physically and mentally excruciating. He'd had to spend the entire meal hiding the exhaustion he still felt from helping dig out the collapse of the canal wall. Added to this, for a full three hours and six courses, he'd had to sit beside Rosalind without being able to say one word he actually meant. All of which was compounded by the awareness that everyone at the table—from the Pennyworths, to the Vaughns, to Aunt Showell at the foot of the table—was watching how he behaved toward her, and she toward him.

Rosalind, of course, navigated the table etiquette and small talk with equal facility. Devon had tried to meet her standards. He wished he could be sure he succeeded.

Devon's heart had quite literally skipped a beat when Rosalind descended the rotunda's grand and ridiculous stairway before dinner. Hers had been the plainest dress in the hall—

cream silk and blue-and-silver netting with the barest trimming of beads. Her hair was likewise simply dressed in coiled braids. Nonetheless, Rosalind shone.

Devon didn't cherish any schoolboy illusions about rescuing Rosalind from her (relatively) impoverished life. He knew she worried about that, but he also knew himself to be the farthest thing from a knight errant. If anything, the lost, selfish, lonely boy he still nurtured inside himself hoped she might be able to save him.

But the promise of Rosalind had always been more than rescue. It was the promise of trust, and of friendship. It was the promise that she would help him find the home his heart and soul needed, and that he, somehow, would help her find the same.

Of course, Devon could say nothing of this when they met in front of the other guests. His heart might be filled to the brim, but he must enact his role as the dignified, proper Duke of Casselmaine.

Just wait, he'd told himself a dozen times during dinner. *Be patient. You'll see her in the drawing rooms. You'll be able to find a way to talk to her then.*

If dinner was excruciating, the conversation afterward with the men over the port and brandy was even worse. Devon had struggled to keep his mind on the business at hand. After all, the point of this dinner was to keep the good will of these men for continuing his drainage project. Draining the fens was the right thing to do—for the estate, the district, and for the people who had to live on this land. It seemed, however, that for every problem the project would solve in the future, it created fifty more in the present.

Pennyworth, as usual, didn't see the need for change. Ablehaven feared violence and disorder from the Scottish and Irish laborers. And Vaughn—all Vaughn wanted to talk about was the plague of poaching that had descended upon the realm. It was driven, Vaughn was quick to assure Ablehaven, by those same laborers. They supplemented their wages by selling other people's hares and pheasants to the local tavern keepers. Vaughn was also able to assure Pennyworth that successful poaching by the "foreign element" would actively encourage discontent and bad behavior, and—heaven forbid—popery, among the local population.

None of which was true, and all of which Devon had heard a hundred times before, and all of which he needed to counter, yet again, to keep the project going.

Despite this, or perhaps because of it, his attention would not stay in the room. All he wanted to do was talk with Rosalind, and see her smile. He wanted to continue the slow coming together they'd begun in London, until she remembered how much they'd once cared for each other, and understood how much he still . . .

He didn't even know which word to use. Loved her. Wanted her. *Hoped* for her.

Patience, he told himself. *You'll be with her soon. You'll be able to stand beside her and talk, at least a little. . . .*

Of course, what had happened instead was that Forest had handed Devon this note from his mother.

> *I am retiring shortly. I hope you will be able to find a moment to speak with me before then.*

He supposed he could have ignored it. On another night, he might simply have sent one of the footmen with his compliments and to ask if she required anything specific of him.

This, however, was not a usual night, at least not from Devon's point of view. As aching and tired and nervous—yes, nervous—as he was, his mother's missive worried him. Lady Casselmaine knew, of course, that Rosalind had arrived, and that Devon had specifically invited her. Devon needed to understand her state of mind, so he could be ready to counter its effects. The dowager held tight to her displeasure, and she had developed myriad ways of making it felt.

So, Devon swallowed his impatience, told himself he and

Rosalind had weeks yet to spend together, and knocked on the door.

His mother's maid opened the door, releasing the scent of fire and candles in a throat-catching cloud.

"Good evening, Quinn. How are we tonight?"

"Well, thank you, your grace," she replied in her usual bland monotone. Devon sometimes wondered if his mother had chosen the woman specifically for her complete absence of human emotion.

The apartment's drapes had already been closed for the night. The windows were seldom opened. These were the only plain rooms in the whole of the hall. Others might be unfurnished, or uncarpeted, but these were stark, unpapered, and barely painted. The furnishings had been stripped down to absolute necessities. Much like the woman herself, seated in front of her meager fire.

"Good evening, Mother," said Devon clearly.

The dowager did not look up.

Mother's grief had worn away her flesh, leaving her skin to sag against her bones. She wore widow's black with a plain white mobcap over her hair. Except for her worn Bible, there were no books near her. Likewise, there were no decorations on the walls, except for the portraits of her dead husband and eldest son over the fireplace.

Devon bent and kissed her slack cheek. "How are you this evening?"

"A little better, thanks be to the Lord," she said to her folded hands.

"I was hoping we would see you at dinner."

"No." She said the single word to her small fire.

Patience, patience, Devon reminded himself. His mother had endured great loss after a lifetime of great disappointment. If she wanted to retreat from the world, could he really blame her?

If only retreat were all that she did.

Devon pulled up the slat-backed chair that served what

few guests are admitted to the dowager's presence, and sat. Slowly, as if it were a great effort, she lifted her gaze toward him. Her gray eyes had gone cloudy with tears and cataracts. Devon had urged her to let him bring in the doctor. He pointed out that if she permitted the operation, she would be better able to walk out and to read her Bible.

She replied that she would be cured if and when the Lord saw fit.

"I understand Bishop Pennyworth is downstairs," she said. "I would be glad if he would come up to pray with me a little before I retire. Perhaps you would be so good as to take a note to him?"

Devon sighed. "Yes, of course, if you like."

She levered herself out of her chair. Lack of use had stiffened her joints, and it hurt to see the way she hobbled across the room to her writing desk. Quinn moved forward to help her, but Mother waved her back. She took a folded paper that waited there and handed it to Devon.

"Was there something else that you needed, Mother?" Devon tucked the note into his coat pocket. "Quinn could have delivered this to the bishop."

Again, that heavy struggle to raise her gaze. Again, all that cold, sad regard. "I understand there was an accident at your work site today."

"Not a major one. A rotted support board gave way and part of the canal wall collapsed."

"Was anyone killed?"

"No." *Where are you taking this, Mother? How did you even find out?* Probably it had been through Quinn, who knew everything that happened within a twenty-mile radius, and reported it all to her reclusive mistress. "We were able to get all the men to safety."

Mother was back to contemplating her folded hands. "And you do not understand this as a warning from the Almighty?"

"No, Mother," Devon replied evenly. "I do not."

"No." She turned her eyes back toward the portraits. "It was too much to be hoped for."

"Mother . . ." Devon began, and then lost the words.

"What is it?"

He shook his head. "Nothing, I suppose. I will wish you good night and I will take this note to the bishop, and . . ."

She waited.

"You know that Miss Thorne has arrived."

She sighed, her martyrdom leavened with just the slightest hint of impatience. "Yes, and knowing you would wish it, I have said I will receive her tomorrow."

"Thank you. Mother . . ." *What can I say? What do I even want to say?* "Is there anything I can do to make this easier for you?"

The corner of her mouth twitched, as if he'd spoken some bitter jest. "How could there be?" She did not wait for his reply. "Good night, Devon. I pray for you."

She said this at the end of their every meeting, and he still had no idea how to reply.

Devon turned on his heel and closed the door softly behind him. The corridor was dark, as always, but two of the lamps on the side tables had been lit. Devon gripped the table and stared at the lamp's flame, willing all his burning grief and rage to subside.

She has lost too much. She has a right to her grief. Patience. Patience. Patience.

But every day the required patience became that much harder to muster.

Sudden glittering of movement caught his eye and Devon straightened. It was Aunt Showell in her jet-trimmed gown, now struggling to pretend she hadn't seen him staring at the lamps like he was thinking of throwing them across the room.

She gave it up as a lost cause. "I came to see if I could help." She waved her closed fan toward the dowager's door. "No better tonight?"

"No, I am afraid not," he answered.

Aunt Showell's lips pressed together in that thin line that was her gravest expression of annoyance. "She was always like this, even when we were girls. She considers that each heartbreak is precious, and that they must all be carefully tended lest they fade. I tried to tell our parents that marrying your father was probably the worst possible match."

All Devon could do was nod in regret and agreement. His father's true passion had always been for display: grand houses, great dinners, a wine cellar that passed description, and a string of mistresses that was dictated as much by fashion as it was by attraction. His mother quickly came to understand that her function was to keep the house ready and available for her husband and whatever guests he might choose to bring home, and to keep herself beautiful so she could act as a personal adornment to her husband as the need arose.

Given the truth of her life, it was perhaps natural that once her first child was born, she fell headfirst into love with him. It was also true Hugh had always radiated immense charm, and like the rest of the family, Devon fell into the habit of protecting the endearing, reckless heir to the title.

For Devon, though, that habit eventually became less about saving Hugh for Hugh's own sake and more to try to spare his fragile mother yet one more heartbreak.

In the end, though, all the times he had lied and paid and pulled Hugh out of this house or that before he could be seen, or nicked, or killed had come to nothing. Their father died drunk in the library, and Hugh . . . Hugh died alone in the dark, where he had to be covered up for one last time.

The touch of Aunt Showell's hand on his broke Devon's bitter reverie.

"I am grateful you've given me the chance to help Louisa to something better than my sister found," she said.

Devon smiled at his aunt. *There's more to do than brood,* he reminded himself. *And much more to this world than the past.*

"Shall we go down, ma'am?" He held out his arm. "Our guests will be wondering what is keeping us."

"And perhaps one guest in particular." She gave his shoulder a teasing tap with her fan.

Yes, please. Let it be so. Devon tried not to let his thoughts quicken his steps.

But when at last they reached the drawing rooms and the bright lights and the crowd of well-dressed, gregarious guests, Devon had to struggle to keep his face from falling into blank and obvious disappointment. The rest of the men had, of course, already joined the company. Music was being played in one of the interconnected rooms. In another, couples and quartets were sitting down to cards.

But Rosalind was not there.

Neither was Louisa.

CHAPTER 8

The Perils of Private Conversation

*I was doomed, if not the advising friend of
the family, at least to become the confidant of
the lady.*

Theodore Edward Hook, *Cousin William* or
The Fatal Attachment

It was Louisa and her fiancé, Firth Rollins, who came to
Rosalind's rescue.

As Rosalind sat displaying her too-visible surprise that
Devon did not walk into the drawing rooms with the other
gentlemen, Mr. Rollins threaded his way through the gathering. Louisa came into step beside him, threading her arm
through his.

"Miss Thorne." Mr. Rollins bowed with cheerful formality. "I carry a message from his grace. Lord Casselmaine's
compliments, and he wishes you to know he's gone up to his
mother, but he hopes to join the rest of the party here
shortly."

"And now, you absolutely must forgive me, Lady Pennyworth," said Louisa before Rosalind could make any reply.
"I'm afraid I have to take Miss Thorne back now. You can't
have her to yourself all evening." Louisa beamed. "I know

you don't care for cards, Miss Thorne, but when I mentioned what a great reader you are, Mr. Rollins at once suggested I should show you the library. I know you haven't yet had a chance to see much of the house. . . ."

Rosalind let herself be pulled to her feet. She smiled her regrets to the frustrated Lady Pennyworth and the calculating Mrs. Vaughn.

She also noticed that Helen Corbyn was nowhere in sight.

In terms of its architecture and décor, Cassell House's library equaled the other rooms. Its arched windows were rich with painted glass. The open draperies allowed a view of the grounds illuminated by the house lights and the full moon. It had been plentifully supplied with reading tables and a carved wooden hearth and more tapestries and rich carpets.

The bookshelves were contained in a series of deep alcoves, but those shelves were not filled, or at least, they were not organized. The older volumes looked broken and badly stored. Newer books seemed to be shoved randomly between them. This left all the surrounding grandeur feeling hollow and sad.

"Casselmaine keeps saying he wants to hire a librarian to set the place in order," Louisa told her. "But men who can repair and oversee a collection in such a state are . . . rare."

"I may know some people who can help," said Rosalind. She also tried not to shiver. There was, of course, no fire lit here, and the night's chill had settled in.

"Oh, that would be marvelous. The sight of so many books in such a state . . . It's like finding out a friend has fallen ill, don't you agree?" Louisa dropped onto the sofa in front of the cold hearth. "Now, where is Helen? She was supposed—"

"Here I am." Helen Corbyn slipped through the doors and hurried to the sofa. "I'm sorry. I had to develop a headache to get away. Have you told her . . . ?"

"I've said nothing yet." Louisa seized Helen's hand and drew her down to sit beside her.

Rosalind settled into the nearest wingback chair and tried to will herself to be patient. She tried not to think about the gathering in the other rooms, and what Devon might or might not be doing at this moment.

Or what Lady Pennyworth is saying to him, or Mrs. Vaughn, or . . .

Rosalind shook herself. Helen Corbyn was asking for her help, and she was anxious enough that she could not wait for a moment of genuine privacy. It would be unkind not to give the girl her full attention.

"Don't worry, Helen," Louisa was saying. "Just tell Rosalind the whole story. I'd trust her with my life."

Despite Louisa's assurances, Helen hesitated. Rosalind noted how Helen sat at the edge of the chair, her back as straight as if she had a board strapped to it. Everything about her posture was composed with the absolute correctness that came only from years of rigorous training. Helen Corbyn had been raised in a strict household, and no amount of personal distress could shake her deportment.

At last, Helen said, "You will have heard by now, Miss Thorne, that my eldest brother has died."

"My sincere condolences for your loss."

Louisa made a shooing motion, urging her friend to get on with it. Rosalind lowered her brows. Louisa blushed, then clasped her hands in her lap.

"What you will probably not have heard"—Helen glanced at Louisa, who shook her head—"is how . . . it . . . happened."

Helen stopped again, this time to look around and make sure that no one but themselves could hear.

"It was a duel, Miss Thorne. Or at least, it was supposed to be, except it never happened, except . . ." She shook her head angrily. "I am making such a mess of this."

"It's all right," said Rosalind. "Telling a story can be as difficult as keeping a secret."

Helen nodded and swallowed to clear her throat. Rosalind looked around reflexively for tea or other relief, but there was nothing.

"When did you first know something was wrong?" she asked Helen.

"When Summers, he's William's valet, woke me up. He'd found a letter addressed to me on William's desk and William was not in his bed. The letter said William was going out to a duel with my fiancé, Peter Mirabeau."

Rosalind imagined Helen scrambling from her bed in the dark, calling for her maid, trying to set aside her fear and her anger so she could act with speed and sense. Her heart contracted in painful sympathy. Louisa had surely heard this story before, but her eyes shone with fresh tears.

"I rode out as quickly as I could," said Helen. "I hoped I could be in time to try to prevent them. I had some hope," she added. "First, because I was sure I had not been meant to find the letter for several hours yet, and then because I caught up with Peter while he was still on the road."

You must have ridden like the wind. What had it been like for this young woman? Alone in the cold and the dark with only her anger and her desperate hope to warm her.

"I confronted Peter—Mirabeau—about . . . where he was going. He told me he didn't really want to fight. His friend—his second—Mr. Worthing, he swore it had all been some ridiculous misunderstanding."

The three women looked at one another in sad and frustrated acknowledgment. Dueling was one of the least penetrable of the male mysteries. Rosalind understood pride and, of course, the utter necessity of keeping up appearances. But how those things could drive otherwise sensible men to a kind of ritual murder in front of witnesses—that remained beyond her.

"My brother was not well, Miss Thorne," Helen said abruptly. "When he came home from the wars he was in pain and . . . much changed. The doctors said his nerves had suffered. They said we must take care and not disagree with him too much and do everything possible to keep him calm and comfortable. Mirabeau knew all that. It's why he didn't want to fight, and why he agreed to let me go on ahead."

"You continued alone?" said Rosalind, surprised.

Helen nodded. "I thought—we all thought—that on my own, I might be able to calm William down, or, if that failed, as long as I was *there* nobody could shoot, and nobody could call anybody a coward, because it would be all my fault the thing didn't come off.

"But when I got to the spot . . . William was already dead. Shot through the back."

Louisa clasped her friend's hand again, but Helen pulled away.

Rosalind's heart went out to the young woman. Helen had seen the corpse, and that shock would never leave her. To accidentally find the body of the loved one she was rushing to save—that would be the worst possible nightmare.

Helen stripped off her evening glove and pressed her fingertips against her eyes, gulping air in an attempt to swallow her desire to sob.

"I'm sorry," Helen murmured. "I didn't used to be like this."

"It's all right," said Louisa. "It's horrible, what you've been through."

"It's horrible, it's unfair, it's outrageous, it's . . ." Helen's cheeks flushed, but now it was with anger. "At the inquest, they said there had been an increase of poaching in the area. They said someone had *obviously*"—Helen spoke the word as a long, contemptuous sneer—"set up a spring gun to try to catch the poachers out, and William had tripped the wire. But that's ridiculous! That section of ground isn't part of anyone's preserve. There's no reason to set a trap up there! And if there had been a trip wire, I would have seen it in the mud!"

Perhaps, perhaps not. But Rosalind kept this thought to herself.

"They're wrong," Helen insisted. "Or they're hiding something, all of them—the coroner, Lord Casselmaine . . ." Louisa's eyes went wide. "It's true, Louisa!" she snapped. "You know it's true! They all think I'm a silly girl who is having hysterics, but I know what I saw!"

Rosalind was silent for a moment, watching Helen, and how her rigidly held propriety was at such odds with the vehemence of her declarations. But even when she shouted, her spine did not bend a single inch. This was hardly a hysterical girl. This was a young woman of iron control.

That only made what Rosalind had to ask next worse.

"Have you told Mr. Mirabeau you were going to speak with me?"

Helen stared at her. For a moment, Rosalind thought she was going to try to lie.

"No," she said finally. "Matters between us have been strained. If he heard what I was doing, I'm sure he'd break things off straightaway."

"Why? Does he mistrust your conclusions?"

"No, it's not that. It . . . he . . ." But Helen, it seemed, had finally reached a point where she could not continue.

"Tell her, Helen," said Louisa. "It will be all right."

Helen gulped and nodded. "I swear I do not believe this, but it's stuck in my head and it won't go away. Mirabeau won't tell me what the quarrel was about, you see. He says it's between him and William, and anyway it can't possibly matter now. I asked Mr. Worthing what started it, but Worthing said it was just some old rumor about something that happened during the wars. I assumed William got it in his head that Peter thought him a coward, but then Mr. Worthing said something strange."

Rosalind waited, very aware that her hands had grown cold.

"Worthing said he'd been up early, writing letters and trying to think of something he could say to restore peace between my brother and Mirabeau, and that he saw Mirabeau's landau drive straight past his window without stopping. He supposed Mirabeau was distracted and just missed the drive in the dark.

"But he didn't come back again for a full half an hour."

And from the way you say it, that was probably time enough to get to the dueling ground and to return. "Did you ask Mr. Mirabeau what happened?"

"Yes, and Mirabeau's story was a lot like Mr. Worthing's. He couldn't sleep, either, but instead of writing letters, he'd decided to drive out. He hoped it would clear his head, and perhaps then he'd see some way out of this mess. Those are his exact words," she added, "and I'm quite sure it's true."

"Of course it's true," said Louisa firmly. "It's perfectly natural. Second thoughts and so on probably happen far more often than anyone admits, not that they can go around admitting to duels in the first place, but you take my meaning."

Rosalind said nothing.

"This is why I need your help, Miss Thorne," said Helen. "I remain engaged to Mr. Mirabeau. Both our families want the match. *I* want the match. I love him. But I have to know . . . I have to know . . ."

"You have to know, but you will not ask him directly?"

"I did! But he—" Helen stabbed a finger toward the window, as if Peter Mirabeau was standing in the moonlit gardens. "He won't talk to me! How can I marry him when he's keeping secrets . . . !"

Helen stared at her own outflung hand as if she didn't know whom it belonged to. She drew it back instantly, retreating behind the façade of rigid poise and calm. She lifted her chin, ready to face Rosalind's censure, not for her words, but for her lack of physical discipline.

Rosalind's heart went out to the girl. Whatever she had been through so far in her life, it had not been easy for her.

And this will not make it any easier.

"I'm sorry, Miss Corbyn, I cannot help you."

CHAPTER 9

A Most Unsatisfactory Conclusion

*You put questions to me which I cannot fairly
answer without offending your vanity, or
wounding your feelings.*

Theodore Edward Hook, *Sayings and Doings*

"Rosalind!" Louisa cried. "You promised!"

She had not, but Rosalind made no answer. She and
Louisa would deal with that later, when they were alone. For
now, Rosalind kept her gaze focused on Helen.

Helen was staring at her, her eyes wide and panicked.

"I will help where I can," said Rosalind. "But I cannot fos-
ter secrets between two persons, especially two persons planning to be married."

"You wouldn't be *fostering* secrets!" cried Louisa. "You
would be uncovering the truth! William was murdered!"

Louisa, please stop.

Louisa did not stop. "Everybody knows it's true! They all
said it for weeks after he was found, and after the inquest,
everybody said something was funny about the whole thing!"

Rosalind wanted to point out that Everybody knowing or
doing a thing was exactly as reliable as Nobody knowing it.
"Everybody" did not have a name. Everybody could not be
asked any questions or be required to offer proofs.

"Suppose that I am able to discover that Mr. Mirabeau had nothing to do with William's death," said Rosalind to Helen. "What then?"

Helen swallowed. Her words, when she spoke, were thick, heavy, and graceless. "Then it will be over and done. He and I will marry."

"And when he hears you needed to go to a stranger to find reason to trust him?"

"Who will tell him?"

"No one knows anything outside this room," said Louisa.

"Unless someone has already overheard us," said Rosalind. "We've hardly been quiet." Louisa shut her mouth at once, and her cheeks flushed more brightly.

"It's also possible that the fact that you and I and Miss Corbyn have all gone off at the same time has already revived old rumors."

"Louisa says you would be able to prevent any rumors from circulating," whispered Helen.

"I'm glad to know Louisa has so much faith in me," Rosalind said, more tartly than she intended. "But I am not a magician. No matter what we do or do not do, everyone out there"—she nodded toward the gallery—"already knows we have had a private conversation. Speculation will arise. Conclusions will be drawn."

Helen tried to rally some of her previous spirit. "None of that would matter to me as long as I can be sure of Mirabeau—"

Rosalind cut her off. "Miss Corbyn, however carefully I inquire about your brother's death, people will become suspicious." In her mind's eye, Rosalind saw Lady Pennyworth and her sharp, little smile. "Once they do, how long will it be before Mr. Mirabeau hears? As soon as he does, he will know you do not trust him. He will understand that you, his *fiancée*, are bringing his honor and his word into question. If you've done that as his fiancée, what will he think of you as his wife?"

"I just want to know the truth, Miss Thorne," whispered
Helen. "Please. I have nowhere else to turn."

Rosalind hated what she was doing to this girl, and to
Louisa. She could feel her young friend's anger against her
skin, like a cloud of steam.

I will find a way to explain. She will understand.

What she said aloud was, "There is one more thing you
have to consider. You are afraid your fiancé killed your
brother. But have you considered that he might be afraid that
you committed that act?"

Rosalind would not have thought it possible, but Helen
drew herself up even straighter. Louisa just stared, shocked
beyond words, but not for long. Before Rosalind had a chance
to draw breath, that shock dissolved into anger.

Rosalind did not give Louisa a chance to speak.

"Helen, you knew about the duel and where it was to be.
You rode out, alone and early. You have already told me your
brother was damaged and difficult and that you were angry
and frightened. . . ."

"I never said I was frightened!" cried Helen.

Rosalind did not bother to dispute that. "Do you hunt,
Miss Corbyn?"

"Of course I—". She stopped. "Mirabeau would never
think such a vile thing."

"And yet you thought it of him." Rosalind bowed her
head. "I am sorry," she said. "I will not be your latest secret,
Miss Corbyn. I cannot."

Helen rose to her feet. She was tall, far taller than Louisa,
and she knew how to use her posture to radiate all the dignity of anger.

"You promised me, Louisa."

Helen strode from the library, flinging open the door and
not bothering to close it behind her.

Louisa stared at Rosalind, betrayal shining in her eyes.
Rosalind met her gaze. She could not allow herself the guilty
luxury of looking away. She wanted to plead, to explain,

even to cry, but not because she doubted her decision. Louisa needed to see that.

Whatever Louisa did see, she leapt from her chair and ran from the library as quickly as the skirts of her evening gown would allow. Rose petals flickered from the flowers adorning her curls and fell onto the carpet in her wake.

Rosalind sat where she was for three breaths. Then, she rose. She smoothed her skirt. Once she was certain she presented at least the appearance of calm, she walked, alone, back to the noise and light of the drawing rooms and all the assembled guests.

Devon had arrived before her. He stood by the hearth with Mr. Rollins and a group of other men. Upon seeing Rosalind alone, Mr. Rollins put his glass down, touched Devon's shoulder in apology, and hurried out the door, presumably to try to find Louisa.

Devon didn't even glance back at the other man as he left. He was watching Rosalind, just like every other person among the gathering. Through one of the open doors, Rosalind could see Mrs. Vaughn at her card table. Mrs. Vaughn's brows arched, her fan of cards held in front of her like a shield.

Rosalind met Devon's gaze. Exhaustion and apprehension flooded through her, and to her shame, she lifted her hems, turned her back, and fled.

CHAPTER 10

A Few Light Words over Breakfast

You see . . . the peril in which you are placed,
and behold the dark and dreadful abyss on whose
slippery edge you stand . . .

Theodore Edward Hook, *Sayings and Doings*

"I'm sorry," said Mrs. Showell as Rosalind entered the breakfast room. Compared to much of the hall, this room felt cozy. It occupied an odd little bump-out from the rest of the wing, to make the most of the light, as well as the view of the gardens. The day, Rosalind noted, promised sunshine and fine weather, for a change.

None of which seemed to cheer Mrs. Showell.

"Nothing that happened last night was your fault." Rosalind joined Mrs. Showell at a table filled with plates of sweet cakes and hot rolls. Jam and fresh butter waited alongside the toast and tea. "I have known from the beginning that nothing between Lord Casselmaine and myself can remain entirely private. I should have asked you more questions and prepared myself more thoroughly to meet the neighborhood."

After her undignified retreat, Rosalind spent a restless night staring at the airy canopy above her bed and constructing a thousand different scenarios where she managed to soothe Helen Corbyn and reassure Louisa, quietly.

Where I avoided a scene.

Because that's what had happened. During her first evening in Devon's home, in front of his neighbors—she had caused a scene.

"Well, I know it was not your fault, Rosalind, and you may believe I have had words with Louisa." Mrs. Showell took another slice of toast from the rack and spread it with a healthy dollop of butter. "It was inexcusable of her to put you in such a position! Importuning you about Corbyn's death! Oh no, don't bother." Mrs. Showell waved her words away with the butter knife before Rosalind could even speak. "The cause of the upset was obvious to anyone with half an eye. Even those who don't know the particulars of how you've helped the Aimesworths and the Melbournes—" She paused when she saw Rosalind's look of surprise. "Oh yes, word of that is circulating, I'm afraid. But the real point is that all the world knows Helen Corbyn never got over her brother's death, and that she doesn't want to believe the results of the inquest, and that she is still trying to get people to take her side."

Which, of course, was only what Rosalind had pointed out last night. Being proved correct was very cold comfort.

"With Louisa at least, Helen's clearly succeeded," Mrs. Showell went on. "You know how loyal she is to her friends. She has become convinced that where there's smoke, there's necessarily fire . . ."

"And is there?" asked Rosalind.

"Is there what?" interrupted a man's voice.

Devon walked into the breakfast room. He was dressed in tweeds and corduroys and worn top boots. A loose neckcloth holding his collar closed. He looked ready for a long day out of doors. Rosalind could not help thinking it suited him better than his severe evening dress from last night.

Devon bowed. Rosalind nodded and tried very hard not to blush.

Really. Rosalind busied herself with a roll, and jam and butter, and tea, and milk, and on further consideration, a Chelsea bun. *There is no reason to keep noticing his clothing, or his complexion, or his eyes . . . especially when what you should be doing is devising an apology for running away from him last night.*

"I think I'm supposed to ask what it is I interrupted," said Devon as he pulled a chair up to the table. "But I suspect I already know."

"It's very rude of you, sir, to deny me a chance to rapidly and seamlessly change the subject," said Mrs. Showell loftily.

"My apologies, Aunt." The footmen served Devon coffee and more rolls, which he split open to spread with butter and jam. He also managed to look at Rosalind meaningfully from under his thick brows. "I notice Louisa is not here."

"We will not be seeing Louisa this morning," said Mrs. Showell. "She has a headache and will take a tray in her room."

Devon glanced between the two of them. "Are you going to try to tell me this has nothing to do with whatever happened between Rosalind, Louisa, and Helen Corbyn last night?"

"No," said Rosalind. "Especially since you already know it does."

Mrs. Showell frowned. "Louisa, against all my advice, decided to press Rosalind about . . ."

"Louisa was just trying to help her friend," said Rosalind. "And she had every reason to believe I might be able to do . . . something."

Devon raised his brows. Rosalind recognized that look, and the fact that he was wondering if he was going to be allowed to actively participate in this conversation.

"No one can blame Helen for having a hard time putting William's death behind her," Rosalind said.

"I suppose," admitted Mrs. Showell. "It was a hard, horrible ending to what had been a bad time for the whole family, and for poor Helen to have found him . . ." She shuddered.

Devon nodded his agreement with the words and the shudder. "That is not something she will ever forget, no matter who thinks she is supposed to. Heaven knows how long it took me to stop brooding over Hugh's death." With each word, his voice grew a little softer, until Rosalind was straining to hear. "I kept wondering what more I could have done, or should have done."

"Don't worry, Casselmaine," said Mrs. Showell. "I've talked to Louisa. She knows what she's done."

He broke a fresh roll in two and laid the halves on his plate. "William Corbyn was a good man," he said. "I knew him growing up. He was a little older, and really more a friend of Hugh's than mine, but . . ." Devon stared out the windows. "Obviously, I've had to see more of vicious men than I'd wish," he said finally. "William wasn't anything like Hugh or some others I'd known. He was more sad than anything else, I think. In pain from his wounds, certainly, and from what he had seen. Some men can't forget their wars. It . . . haunts them."

"So they seek any relief they can find," added Rosalind. "In anger or oblivion, or both."

"Just so. I think that was what William was doing. He tried to fulfill his obligations—keep his house and lands, look after his family, make plans to marry—but it was too much for him. And now Marius and Helen must deal with being left behind."

Rosalind nodded soberly. Both she and Devon understood the disruption and heartbreak of being the ones who had to carry on. They had been handed all the unlooked-for responsibility and had to endure the slow, drawn-out revelation of

facts that had previously been kept hidden, or simply ignored.

They're wrong . . . Helen's words from the night before
came back to Rosalind. *Or they're hiding something, all of
them—the coroner, Lord Casselmaine* . . .

"I have done what I can to help," Devon said. "Holding
the title brings all sorts of advantages. People listen when I
talk, and things happen if I ask. After a life of being ignored,
it's a little heady," he admitted sheepishly. "And, Rosalind,
please believe that I'm not going to ask you to break confidence, but if you do hear of something or think of something
that the family needs done, will you let me know?"

"I will," agreed Rosalind. Then, something did occur to
her. "I imagine this has all been very hard on Mrs. Graves as
well."

"Oh yes," murmured Mrs. Showell. "Poor Mrs. Graves."

"How long has she been with the Corbyns?"

"About three years now," said Mrs. Showell, more quickly
than necessary, and Rosalind wondered about that. "She is,
or was, a cousin of Mr. Corbyn's and came to help manage
the house when Mrs. Corbyn fell ill."

"Well, clearly you have a lot to talk about." Devon pushed
his chair back. "I must ask you to excuse me. We're meeting
with the Lord Lieutenant's secretary to schedule a visit to inspect the works. We have to make sure our progress is where
it should be. Miss Thorne," Devon addressed her with mock
formality. "Perhaps if the weather holds, you'd care to drive
out later and see the works for yourself?"

"Yes, thank you, I'd be most interested."

"I'll make sure the carriage is at your disposal."

Devon took his leave. Rosalind was very glad to be able to
look out at the lovely gardens and drink her tea. She did not
want her expression observed just then. There was too much
hope and fear clenched tight inside her.

One thing that last night's social sparring had made clear: Quite apart from whatever must be done for Louisa and Helen, Rosalind had to find a way to tell Devon about the family secrets she still kept, and soon. She could not let gossip reach him first. She had always known she'd have to tell him about Charlotte and her father during this visit, but she'd hoped she'd have some time to truly get to know the man Devon had become first.

Rosalind heard the door close. She turned her attention back to her breakfast, but not before she saw the sympathetic shimmer in Mrs. Showell's eyes. She knew the older woman wanted to make some consoling remark, but Rosalind found she did not have the heart to hear it properly.

"The Lord Lieutenant is coming?" she remarked. "I imagine that will be cause for some ceremony?"

"Oh, heavens yes," Mrs. Showell seized on the new topic. "There's to be a full reception and dinner, *here*, of course. Thankfully, it's unlikely to be for another month or so. Why, we haven't even finished arrangements for Louisa's wedding breakfast yet. Everything for the family is well in hand, of course. Casselmaine's staff is excellent. But the celebration for the tenants has to be planned as well, and we still must make sure of the tents and the food, and all the drink, and the music . . . oh! A thousand things. I'm sure I've filled three notebooks with the details. I'll make sure to have them when we talk later, of course." She hesitated. "Rosalind? You will keep in mind what I've said, won't you? About the ladies of the district? I know you've managed very well for yourself up until now, but . . . you are not in London anymore. In some ways the country is more difficult. It's . . . it's like one huge drawing room spread out across an entire county. All the same snubs and loyalties and schemes are brewing, but here, nothing is forgotten, and very little is forgiven. We cannot hope that some new scandal will arise to save you from being picked over."

"I will remember, Mrs. Showell," said Rosalind soberly. "I promise you."

"I'm sorry if I sound harsh. But if Mrs. Vaughn or any of the others take it into their heads that you are stirring the coals of William's death, you will lose all hope of winning them to your cause. They'll be your enemies for life."

CHAPTER 11

Several Different Species of Truth

*Such a proceeding, which naturally would acquire
publicity, would most effectually produce an
exposure . . . it would bring shame and despair . . .*

Theodore Edward Hook, *Cousin William*, or
The Fatal Attachment

After he left the morning room, Devon walked across the rotunda just as if he were heading straight down to the main entrance and the courtyard, where the groomsmen were no doubt already waiting with his horse.

But when he reached the stairs, Devon headed up to the family rooms instead.

Louisa had been given apartments midway down the family wing. Devon knocked on her door and waited impatiently until the maid opened it.

"I need to speak with your mistress, Craigey."

"I'm sorry, your grace, but Miss Winterbourne—"

"Has a headache, and she may return to it as soon as we're finished."

As Devon had told Rosalind, there were multiple advantages to being a duke. One of them was that it was very difficult to keep him out of places he was determined to get into, especially in his own house. He barged past Craigey and straight into Louisa's boudoir.

His young cousin lay, fully clothed, on her bed, staring up at the lace canopy.

"We need to talk, Louisa."

Louisa sighed audibly. She also quite visibly considered protesting, but just as clearly gave up the idea and contented herself with sitting up so she could glower more effectively at him.

"I expect you're going to tell me I'm being unreasonable and selfish." She flopped back down. "Please do let's get on with it."

"You are being unreasonable and selfish," agreed Devon. "But it seems you already know that. Louisa, this is serious. Will you please sit up and listen to me?"

His change in tone reached her. Louisa pushed herself up and swung her legs over the side of the bed. This time, she really was ready to pay attention, at least for the moment.

Now what do I say?

"Louisa, I don't know exactly what promises you made Helen about Miss Thorne, but you need to withdraw all of them, right now."

"Why?"

Devon resisted the urge to rub his forehead. Or maybe it was to tear at his hair.

"Because you'll jeopardize Rosalind's standing in the neighborhood before she's had a chance to become established. Surely you can see that." *Especially after last night.*

The gentlemen had all raised their eyebrows over the three ladies retreating from the drawing rooms in rapid succession. They'd slapped Devon's arm and tried to commiserate with him on having to deal with a household full of females planning a wedding. There were plenty of joking remarks about brides, their friends, and all high-strung girls.

But from over their shoulders, Devon watched the women

at the card games and the coffee tables. They'd gathered and whispered and smiled and nodded and kept on whispering, as they were no doubt doing this morning over their breakfast tables, and would again this afternoon around their tea tables.

A ripple of genuine consternation crossed Louisa's face, but she was not ready to give in so easily.

"Helen is convinced that she is being lied to about what happened to her brother," she said. "All she wants is to be sure of what really happened. In the meantime, the rest of you are trying to pack it all away in a neat little box and shove it into the back of the cupboard."

Yelling will not help, Devon reminded himself firmly. Louisa was not deliberately trying to be difficult, nor was she naïve, exactly. No one with a modicum of intelligence who'd lived through two London Seasons could be so. But Louisa had been lucky. She still hadn't seen the genuine ruin that the world's censure could cause.

A tapestry chair waited beside the hearth. Devon pulled it up to the bedside so he could sit down and look Louisa in the eye.

"Louisa, I know your friend is grieving, and disappointed. I know how badly she wants things to be different from what they are. I can't help that. No one can. She must come to terms with her brother's death on her own. If it helps, I can swear on my life and yours that Peter Mirabeau had nothing to do with William's death. His part in this tragedy is exactly what it appears to be. He was to take part in a duel caused by a burst of men's no doubt stupid and shallow pride."

"But how can you be so sure?" she demanded.

"Because a week before, Earnest Worthing told me what was happening, and I *thought* I'd put a stop to it."

Devon appreciated the amount of determination it took Worthing to come to him. A duel was a matter of private honor between the principals. The seconds were supposed to do their utmost to create a reconciliation, but they were also supposed to help the meeting go through and keep the secret. Not in the least because dueling had been declared a breach of the King's Peace.

When Worthing had come to sit in Devon's book room and tell the whole story, he'd done so knowing that Devon could have both Mirabeau and Corbyn arrested and hauled into court.

Worthing had come anyway.

"I can't let it go through," he'd said, his distress nearly choking him. "Corbyn is—dash it—he's not *well*. You can't duel a sick man. Mirabeau agrees, but what can he do? William has said he'll call him a coward in front of the entire neighborhood!"

"Who is Corbyn's second?"

"Bartolemew Vaughn."

Devon remembered thinking William couldn't have made a worse choice. Bartolemew was not only Cecilia Vaughn's oldest brother, he was a notorious hothead. Too many people in his life had looked down on him for being the son of a social-climbing solicitor. The taunts Bartolemew had gotten at school and elsewhere had left him with an exaggerated sense of honor that he was only too happy to indulge.

"The bloodthirsty idiot won't even *pretend* to try to make peace. I'd fight him myself, but . . ." Worthing had shrugged. "I think the little maniac would welcome it. Be proof he really is a gentleman, and all that, and . . . well, I've never been much of a shot." Worthing had laughed unsteadily. "That's why I'm here, Casselmaine. Nowhere else to go. You've got to stop this thing. Somebody's going to end up dead."

And you were right, Devon thought grimly toward his memory of Worthing.

"What did you do?" Louisa's question brought him back to the present.

"I went to Corbyn and I told him I'd found out about the

duel. I said if it went through, I'd have everybody involved arrested, including the doctor for helping a bunch of idiots breach the peace. Then I went to Mr. Vaughn and told him he'd better get Bartolemew out of the county for a month or two."

The elder Mr. Vaughn might have been ambivalent about his son's participation in a duel, but he was also openly trying to buy his way to a baronetcy. Devon's disapproval could scuttle that particular ambition, and they both knew it.

So, Bartolemew Vaughn was bundled away to Ireland, and Mirabeau had made it a point to tell friends that what was past was all past and he'd be pleased to have a drink with William Corbyn at any time.

In the end, Corbyn had decided not to return the sentiment.

"What was this idiotic duel even about?" demanded Louisa. Devon just shook his head.

"But you do know?" she pressed.

"No, as it happens, I don't. But even if I did, I would have been told in confidence."

"But if Helen could only know . . ."

"Louisa," said Devon quietly. "Please do not ask me again."

"Men and their honor!" Louisa rolled her eyes toward Heaven, looking for patience. "Thank goodness I'm not marrying a gentleman. At least I never have to worry about Rollins getting himself shot over some stupid joke somebody decided to tell after dinner! How can you . . ."

Devon could not let her get any further. "Louisa. I know you want to help your friend. That's admirable. You should help her. She cannot go on like this. She'll make herself ill. But if you draw Miss Thorne into this, you will materially jeopardize her future."

"No, I won't. It's what she *does*, Devon, and even the ladies of Almack's all keep her on their visiting lists. It doesn't get more exclusive than that!"

"It's what she does as Miss Rosalind Thorne." Devon leaned forward. "But think, will you? If all goes as I very much hope, Rosalind will be the Duchess of Casselmaine, perhaps as soon as next year. If she has already made enemies by asking questions—questions you know very well the very private and very proper ladies of this county will see as too impertinent by half—the whispering campaign will start before she and I get anywhere near the altar." *It has probably already started.* "It will be that much more difficult for her to establish a place that's already going to be a hard fight for her to claim."

Devon paused for a moment to let that much sink in. Then, he added softly, "Besides, Mrs. Vaughn and all her circle, they have friends in London they can write to at any moment. They can talk to their cronies and cousins when they come down next month for the races, and again this fall for the shooting. How many questions do we want them asking about Rosalind? Or her family?"

Devon didn't know for certain how much Louisa understood about Sir Reginald Thorne's collapse, or Charlotte Thorne's disappearance, but it was enough to realize that concerted digging into Rosalind's background would produce a lifetime's feast of gossip.

"Oh," Louisa murmured. "Oh. I hadn't thought."

"No." Devon sighed. "And to tell you the truth, neither had I. Not properly. Mrs. Showell put a flea in my ear about it last night." He winced remembering the conversation.

"There were a lot of fleas leaping about last night." Louisa tugged on her own earlobe. "I'm still feeling mine."

"But she was right."

"She usually is," said Louisa. "It's most provoking."

"Most. But here we are, and I'm asking you, Louisa, as your cousin and as a friend of Rosalind's. Please. Put a stop to this."

Louisa looked away, her mouth set in a thin line. For the

first time, Devon caught a glimpse of the woman she was about to become, and he was startled. His endearing little cousin was going to be a force to reckon with.

"Well, you will be pleased to know that the reason Helen left early last night was that Rosalind told her that she would not help find out what happened to William. So, you can rest easy on that point."

He wanted to. He wanted to thank Louisa for her news and walk away.

Devon stayed where he was.

"That may be what she said last night, but I can tell you that is going to change. I know Rosalind. Now that she's gotten hold of the problem, she will not be able to put it behind her. She was already asking questions at breakfast."

"So you admit there is a problem," said Louisa.

"In confidence, yes, I do admit it."

"But you don't want it known."

"No, I don't."

Louisa looked away. He could feel the tension in her as she clenched her jaw to try to keep silent.

"What is it you want to say?" he asked.

She shook her head, but she did not bow it. "If I say anything I'm thinking now, I will just be told I am ungrateful. Maybe I am. You've . . . you've been so kind, and you've paid for so much . . ."

"Louisa, you're family. Family is supposed to help each other."

"Yes. Yes, we are. I do know that. But." She turned and leveled her bright, gray, thoroughly Winterbourne gaze at him. "What you are asking is that I should betray the trust a friend has placed in me, and yes, thank you, I know that we are both high-strung girls on the verge of marriage, and therefore nothing we do or say can be considered more than nerves, and possibly hysteria. But Helen is sick and she is sorrowed, and you have just admitted to me there is in fact *something* going on, and that you know as well as I do the coroner's verdict was pure nonsense."

He wanted to tell her that the coroner's verdict was the sound judgment of an experienced man. But looking into her eyes now, he saw her not as the headstrong girl he wanted her to be, but as the independent adult she had become, and Devon found he could not do it.

"Louisa, I need you to make Rosalind understand it will be worse for Helen if the truth about William's death comes out."

"How can that possibly be?"

"I suspect that in your heart you already know," he said quietly. "It's possible Helen even knows, but that in her grief and anger she does not want to admit it." His mother's features swam in front of Devon's eyes. He did not want to speak his next words, but he had to. This mess could not be allowed to spread any further, and not just for Rosalind's sake. There were whole families that could be dragged down if suspicions over Corbyn's death were allowed to bloom into scandal.

"William Corbyn did not die in an accident," Devon said, and his voice was clear and steady. "There were no poachers. There was no spring gun, just as there was no hidden assassin. William Corbyn killed himself."

CHAPTER 12

A House of Mourning

She had converted her habitation into a temple of constancy and sorrow.

Althea Lewis, *Things by Their Right Names*

Shortly after Devon left the breakfast table, Rosalind also excused herself. She told Mrs. Showell she had some letters she wanted to write before waiting on Lady Casselmaine.

This was entirely true.

They both knew, however, that the retreat was really to give Rosalind a chance to collect herself before she had to meet with Devon's mother.

Devon had never said much about his parents. Rosalind knew his father's reputation was as a man who delighted in lavish parties and generous dinners. The scandal sheets printed up estimated costs of the then-Lord Casselmaine's entertainments. They also tended to speculate about the ladies in whose company Lord Casselmaine had been seen, none of whom was his wife.

Of Lady Casselmaine, the papers never had a word to say. Rosalind didn't know whether she ever came up to London at all.

She did remember one night when Devon spoke about his

mother. Rosalind had been attending Marielle Hampstead's birthday ball. Marielle was only a casual acquaintance, but Devon had managed to get Rosalind a message via a mutual friend (he was strictly forbidden to write), to say he would be there. Rosalind had worked her way up her chain of friends until she was able to beg an invitation from a sympathetic third party.

But when Rosalind arrived, Devon was not there. She had searched the crowds impatiently and danced a full two dances with even less grace than usual (which for her was no grace at all). Her mood had slid all the way from piqued to anxious before Devon finally entered the ballroom.

Rosalind remembered how her heart had leapt. She also remembered how carefully she had made her way through the crush to avoid drawing notice, and disapproval.

"I'm sorry," Devon said as soon as she maneuvered herself into place beside him. "I meant to be here earlier, but my mother . . ." he stopped. "She needed me."

"Is she unwell?" asked Rosalind.

Devon shook his head. "Not really, no, it's . . . there's been some bad news and she was not ready for it. That's all."

"Oh, I'm sorry."

"She's not a strong woman, you see. She never has been. Little things can overset her sometimes." He'd paused, and to Rosalind's surprise, a spasm of naked anger had passed over his face. "Not that this was actually little . . ." he broke off suddenly. "I'm sorry. I shouldn't be talking about any of this. Will you dance? Or walk on the terrace?"

"Let's walk," said Rosalind. Devon's dancing was no better than hers. "And you know you can tell me anything at all."

But he never had, not on that night, or any other.

Now, Rosalind and her memories stood at Lady Casselmaine's door. She'd asked Emerson to conduct her, reasoning that her chances of finding that lost parlor maid were better than those of finding her own way.

Rosalind took a deep breath. She smoothed her skirts.

You are stalling, Rosalind chided herself. She raised her hand to knock.

The door was opened by a gray-haired lady's maid. Her pale eyes raked Rosalind from top to bottom. She turned without speaking and led Rosalind into the private sitting room.

Catherine Winterbourne, *nee* Catherine Trent-Moreland, Dowager Duchess of Casselmaine, sat in front of a fire that looked pathetically small in the large hearth. Her head was bowed over her folded hands, and her lips moved silently.

What do you pray for? Whatever it was, the dowager appeared most diligent in her efforts. She did not pause or look up as Rosalind came to stand before her. Rosalind folded her own hands, bowed her head, and waited. She also, however, took the opportunity to survey the room, and its owner, from under her demurely lowered eyelids.

Lady Casselmaine was a small, sad woman. She dressed in plain black with a white cap on her hair, which was turning from ashen gray to snow white. Her wedding ring and a gold cross were her only jewelry.

Unbidden, a memory rose in Rosalind's mind, of a worn, but tidy house in a street full of tradesmen and shopkeepers. The sound of chickens, geese, and children filled the air. The house was ruled by a broad woman with a starched apron and a ladle, and the strongest tea Rosalind had ever drunk in her life.

Her son sat in a tidy parlor wreathed in the sunshine. He was Adam Harkness, principal officer of the Bow Street police station. He'd been hurt. His arm was in a sling. And as his cheerful, chattering mother brought her into the parlor, his blue eyes lit with welcome, intelligence, kindness, and something more that Rosalind did not dare let herself put a name to.

Rosalind shoved that memory aside and made herself focus on her current surroundings. The dowager's room was as Spartan as her dress. The only clutter was on the writing desk, which was piled with letters, journals, and ledgers. Clearly, the dowager carried on an active correspondence and paid at least some attention to her household. But the only decorations in evidence were two portraits, above the fireplace. It was evident to Rosalind that the one on the left depicted her late husband, and the other was her late son, Hugh.

Of Devon, there was no sign.

"Amen," said Lady Casselmaine at last.

"Amen," echoed Rosalind. She lifted her head and found herself caught in Lady Casselmaine's hard stare.

Rosalind had known plenty of looks like this, where the person regarding her believed her guilty of *being* something—too young or too old, too pretty, too poor, too clever, too pious or not pious enough, or simply present when not wanted.

Which am I to you? Does it really matter? Rosalind answered her own question with a silent negative, and then, quite deliberately, let her gaze drift to the pair of paintings above the mantel.

"I see you admiring my portraits," said the dowager. "Did you ever see the originals?"

"I did meet Hugh, once."

"Did you? Tell me about that." Lady Casselmaine gestured impatiently to the maid, who brought a slat-backed chair forward for Rosalind to sit.

"I'm afraid there isn't much to tell." Rosalind smoothed her skirts. "It was only briefly, at a supper party. I don't remember whose. I do remember I was walking into the refreshment room with my sister. She and Hugh had met before, it seems, introduced by a mutual acquaintance."

It was the fact that she had met Hugh that had made Charlotte warn Rosalind against setting her heart on Devon.

"I remember he was very handsome, and very charming," said Rosalind. "Everyone seemed to like him."

"Yes, he had many friends," said the dowager. "He liked

to bring them to see me, you know, when they were down from London. He'd pick out the choicest specimens to introduce to me, to see what they'd do, when confronted by the pious old recluse . . . But you seem surprised, Miss Thorne."

"I confess I am."

"Because you think me a fool, perhaps?" The dowager's hard gray eyes glittered. "I knew quite well what Hugh was doing. He was making mockery, of them and me. Oh, he told me he was only making sport of *them*, and wanted me to share the joke, but I knew what was in his heart. He could not lie to me, although he did try, a great deal."

Her words were as hard and sad as her gaze. Rosalind felt herself torn. She wanted to take Devon's side, here in this room where even his image was not held as equal to his wastrel father and brother. At the same time, her heart went out to this woman, who in the end believed she could do no more for her son than let herself be laughed at.

How is it you never remembered to tell Devon that you understood his brother's hypocrisy? Rosalind found her throat had gone quite dry.

"I am sorry for what you endured," she murmured at last. "Alas, what you tell me also matches with what I'd heard of Hugh's sense of humor."

It also matched with her memory of his smile and his eyes. Both were very like Devon's, but it was Devon grown cruel. When Devon looked at her, he thought she was beautiful. When Hugh looked at her, he thought she was desirable, but Rosalind also had the sense that he was tallying her flaws and squirreling them away in case they might be needed later.

He had whispered in Charlotte's ear and they both laughed, and he looked to Rosalind again and smiled.

All the cruelty she'd glimpsed a minute before was wiped away as if it had never been. Only the brilliant sunshine of him was left. Hugh had taken her hand and bowed over it, and all her breath had left her.

What haunted Rosalind later, once she'd learned more about Hugh Winterbourne, was the realization that if he'd decided to seduce her in that moment, it would have been easy.

"I knew your mother, Miss Thorne," said the dowager abruptly. "We were not friends, but we had acquaintances in common. She was much more interested in society than I was, even then."

It was a stiff and awkward olive branch, but Rosalind could not fail to acknowledge the attempt. "Mother very much enjoyed lively company."

"Yes," agreed Lady Casselmaine. "And you, Miss Thorne? Is lively company to your taste?"

"Such company might be entertaining for a time, but it can lack substance, and a steady diet may become unwholesome."

The dowager's hard jaw thrust out, and Rosalind decided she had scored another point. Whatever Lady Casselmaine had been expecting to hear, it was not a disavowal of frivolity.

"I trust, Miss Thorne, you are a churchwoman?" Lady Casselmaine said, and for one terrified instant, Rosalind wondered if the dowager had read her thoughts.

"Yes, ma'am," Rosalind croaked.

"I always attend Wednesday service, as well as Sunday. I will expect you then."

"Thank you, ma'am. I will be glad to attend."

"Devon has spoken of you a great deal." This way of leaping from subject to subject was clearly a habit with the dowager. Rosalind modestly lowered her gaze and waited. "Not when you originally met, which he should have done, of course. That he kept secret. But during the past few months, he made it very clear that you were to be invited to Louisa's wedding and that you were to assist in the preparations, and there should be no question regarding the matter."

The words were cold and bitter. But was it Devon's behavior that pained his mother, or the fact that there was so little she could do? Lady Casselmaine would not be the first person to withdraw from their household and then be annoyed to discover it left them with little power to influence it.

"I trust I have not inconvenienced you, ma'am," Rosalind murmured.

That earned her another sharp, searching stare. "I don't know what you have done, Miss Thorne, but I expect we will all soon find out. Or rather, you shall." She turned and lifted her gaze toward the portraits of her lost family.

And if Rosalind had expected to see devotion or regret in that gaze, she was mistaken. The only emotion that registered in the dowager's face was fury.

"I'm not sure I understand, ma'am," murmured Rosalind.

"No, I expect not. You believe Devon to be a good man. A righteous man."

Those words, coming from Devon's mother, sent a chill through Rosalind's heart, even as they stirred her indignation.

"Is there reason anyone should think otherwise?" she asked.

Lady Casselmaine did not answer, at least not directly.

"Do not commit yourself too hastily to my surviving son, Miss Thorne. It may be you are a good woman. I pray that you are. But a good woman would not do well in such a match."

Enough. Rosalind leaned forward and chose her words with great care. "Lady Casselmaine, of your courtesy, if there is something you feel I should know about Lord Casselmaine, I beg you would speak plainly and openly."

The dowager's mouth curled into a smile and all at once, the woman's resemblance to Hugh came into sharp relief. "You are an intelligent woman, Miss Thorne, and I suspect you have a talent for observation. I suggest you ask Devon about his elder brother, whom he carried back to this house as a lifeless corpse. Ask him to talk about all that charm and vitality, snuffed out in an instant, in a fall from a horse. There was no horseman in the county to match my son Hugh. He would never fall." She said it with the sort of certainty usually left to describe natural law. "Tell Devon I sent you with these questions. Then pay close attention to what he says about me, and about him. You may bring your observations back to me, if you will."

Rosalind had no answer.

"Please go now. I find I am very tired." Lady Casselmaine didn't look tired. There was a gleam of energy in her eyes that had not been there when Rosalind entered.

"Thank you, ma'am." Rosalind made her curtsy and left the room, passing the silent maid without speaking.

Once in the gallery, Rosalind walked slowly, without bothering to see if she was headed in the right direction. She just wanted to get away, and to think.

She had been prepared for Lady Casselmaine to be dismissive, overly pious, and to display the other regrettable qualities of the permanent invalid.

She was not prepared for Devon's mother to be so worn, cold, and cynical.

Nor to come so close to openly accusing her sole surviving son of murder.

CHAPTER 13

Complex Workings and Machinations

Sold! Who would have sold you? Arrangements
there must be in all family transactions.

Althea Lewis, *Things by Their Right Names*

After her meeting with Devon's mother, Rosalind felt a little desperate to escape the hall. Fortunately, Mrs. Showell pronounced herself quite at liberty and ready to leave on their expedition to inspect the drainage works as soon as Rosalind was ready.

"I expect we shall not be the only ones there," Mrs. Showell told her. "It's regarded as quite the local entertainment. People even bring picnic lunches, which annoys Marius Corbyn no end." She shook her head. "I will tell you the truth, Rosalind, if Helen does push through to marry Peter Mirabeau, it will be as much to get away from her remaining brother as it is for love."

Rosalind regretted she would not be present when Mrs. Kendricks arrived. This, however, was hardly the first house they had removed to, especially since Rosalind had been fitted into her position as one of society's "useful" women. What concerned her more was that she still had not seen Louisa.

As Devon promised, a carriage and driver had been left at Rosalind's disposal, and thankfully, Mrs. Showell proved quite willing to spend their drive talking about plans for Louisa's wedding. The disquiet brought on by her meeting with Lady Casselmaine was proving difficult to dispel, so it was a relief for Rosalind to fill her mind with more comfortable details.

The countryside they traveled through was a strange place to Rosalind's London-bred eyes. It was flat as a tabletop and open to the sky except for a few stands of trees surrounding the streams or farmsteads. Hedges and the occasional dry-stone wall marked farm boundaries. Gradually, the farms gave way to meadows of tall grass and brilliant flowers, which in turn gave way to beds of reeds surrounding broad ponds that sparkled in the sunshine. Here the road ran along an artificial ridge, and songbirds seemed to cling to every bobbing stem. The air grew thick with heat and the unmistakable odor of brackish water.

The countryside might be open and lonely, but the road was not. Their brougham had to keep pulling over to allow room for the wagons piled with dirt, stones, timbers, or wooden crates. Samuel, their driver, alternated between saluting the carters and cursing the ruts and holes their heavy loads tore in the damp road.

As flat as the country was, they still heard the drainage works before they saw them. As they crossed a stone bridge, Rosalind became aware of the growing cacophony ahead—men's shouts mingled with steady thumps and the high-pitched ring of metal on metal.

Soon the distant shapes at the roadside ahead resolved into a pair of parked carriages—a very fine new landau and a smaller gig, clearly for the servants of those in the landau.

"As I said," remarked Mrs. Showell, "it is quite the local attraction. Here, we may see, are some of the Vaughns. Samuel!" she called to the driver. "Bring us alongside."

Samuel complied and they drew up next to the landau.

"Mrs. Vaughn. Miss Vaughn," Mrs. Showell nodded to both ladies seated in the other carriage.

Today, Mrs. Vaughn had selected an enormous straw hat well trimmed with ribbons and feathers to keep the sun from her face. Her walking dress was likewise festooned with ribbons and lace.

Cecilia Vaughn sat across from her mother, much more sedately gowned and bonneted. Rosalind, of course, remembered Cecilia from the dinner party as one of Louisa's circle. She was slender, with a fashionably pale complexion and a pretty but solemn face. That impression of seriousness was reinforced by a broad forehead and a pair of intelligent dark green eyes. The sprinkle of freckles across her blunt nose was probably the despair of her proud and anxious mother. The bit of hair that showed beneath her bonnet was a pleasing shade of honey gold. But what truly struck Rosalind was the tired indifference of the younger woman's demeanor.

This was fleeting, however. Just as soon as she became aware that Rosalind was watching, Cecilia's expression enlivened into one of a perfectly cheerful welcome. The change was so abrupt, Rosalind wondered how many times Cecilia Vaughn had been scolded to be more friendly and smile more prettily.

"How goes the work today?" Mrs. Showell was asking Mrs. Vaughn.

"Well, I confess, Mrs. Showell," said Mrs. Vaughn. "I personally find it all a complete muddle. I brought these"—she brandished a pair of gilded opera glasses—"but even so, I cannot tell whether we make progress or not."

Rosalind found she had to agree, at least a little. Her first impression of the scene below was of a moving mass of shovels and hoists and wheelbarrows. But slowly it all began to make a kind of sense. At the bottom of the trench, men worked with picks, rakes, and shovels, digging into the earth. The loose dirt was then loaded into a massive wooden crate attached to a crane by a system of ropes and pulleys that would have been at home on a ship of the line. When the crate was full, a team of men and mules turned a great gear, like a mill wheel, to winch the crate out of the trench. Other laborers used hooked poles to catch the ropes and guide that load to a gentle landing on the high bank, where it was unlatched and the dirt allowed to spill out so men with rakes and barrows could haul it away. In the meantime, an empty box attached to another crane was lowered to the canal floor, so the laborers down below could start filling it with yet more dirt.

This was by no means the only activity. Men drove posts into the ground with huge hammers. Yet more workers slotted timbers into place to shore up the earthen banks and hold back the muck that threatened to slide down to bury the men digging and raking what would become the canal floor. Great stones were piled more than head-high in one place. Curving sections of brown tile had been stacked in another.

A ragged cluster of shacks and barns formed a makeshift village on the far side of the canal trench. Laborers came and went from these rickety structures, tools on their shoulders or mopping the sweat from their brows, all of them absolutely ignoring the carriages on the road.

It was dirty and noisy and chaotic, and in the middle of it all, there was Devon.

At the moment he was talking and gesturing to a crowd of the workers. It was impossible to tell from this distance how his direction was being received.

"Ah, now!" cried Mrs. Vaughn. "I think I spy . . . Yes, Cecilia, wave, my dear. There is Mr. Corbyn coming out just there!"

Rosalind stared in the direction Mrs. Vaughn pointed. One of the shack doors had opened again and a tall, broad man in jacket, waistcoat, and trousers came out. The sunlight glimmered on his watch chain and buttons.

Cecilia waved dutifully. But the man, Marius Corbyn, paid

no attention. He looked down at his work, and his workers, and then immediately went back inside and shut the door.

Mrs. Vaughn lowered her opera glasses and shook her head. "Well. So much activity," she said, and Rosalind thought she detected a trace of embarrassment, possibly at the way Mr. Corbyn had entirely ignored them. "It is all very much beyond me. But Mr. Corbyn tells us all it can be done, does he not, Cecilia? Even with such inferior workers as Lord Casselmaine has procured."

Cecilia blushed. *What is that for?* wondered Rosalind.

"Inferior, Mrs. Vaughn?" inquired Mrs. Showell.

"Well, I certainly do not mean to criticize his grace," said Mrs. Vaughn. "But really, his decision to bring yet more Irishmen into the district! Why, we already have to deal with positive hordes of them at the races every year—lounging about, stealing sheep, poaching off everybody's land, and drinking whatever they can find! And he's *employing* them! *Paying* them! I daresay they work cheaply enough, but everyone knows that they will only take that money and turn it into yet more drink!"

"But steady employment will surely decrease the amount of idle mischief men do," said Mrs. Showell. "And where men work, they do not starve, and are therefore less inclined to steal, or poach."

"It is certainly a great experiment, and I for one hope it comes out according to his grace's expectations. Mr. Vaughn has his doubts, may I say, as does Mr. Corbyn."

Cecilia blushed again and looked down. She might have been the picture of a modest girl hearing the name of an admirer.

She might be, but she is not.

"Mr. Corbyn has a very strong sense of what is right and proper," said Cecilia.

"There!" said Mrs. Vaughn with great satisfaction, as if Cecilia had performed a particularly clever trick. "Now, I declare a halt to this very dull subject, and we shall move onto something much more pleasant. Miss Thorne, Mrs. Showell may have not mentioned it to you, but we are planning a little card party. I wanted to be sure you know that you are included in the invitation. I do so hope we will have a chance to get to know more of each other." She beamed. "I want to be sure you are introduced to all the best society of our county, before *certain persons* can try to keep you all to themselves!"

"Certain persons?" inquired Rosalind innocently.

Mrs. Vaughn leaned conspiratorially across the gap between their carriages. "Now, Miss Thorne, you need not be afraid to tell me. I'm sure Lady Pennyworth has already been importuning you. She is quite the resident at the new hall, is she not, Mrs. Showell?"

"She is the bishop's wife and as such the dowager consults her frequently on church matters," said Mrs. Showell, obviously a little concerned, and annoyed, by this turn in the conversation.

"And she is quite pleased to let the rest of us know it," Mrs. Vaughn snapped, but in the next breath, she became entirely consoling. "You mustn't let her discourage you, Miss Thorne. There are many of us who are delighted to welcome you here!"

"I thank you for your invitation, Mrs. Vaughn," said Rosalind, ignoring the blatantly rude remarks. "I should be glad to attend your card party, as long as we have no other fixed engagements?" She turned inquiringly to Mrs. Showell.

"None at all," said Mrs. Showell, and Rosalind knew she did not imagine the trace of disappointment underneath the words.

This whole time, Cecilia sat in silence, watching the work being done below. *What are you thinking?* Rosalind wondered.

"Excellent," said Mrs. Vaughn. "Now, have you brought

your luncheon? Phillips!" Mrs. Vaughn twisted around to speak to the two maids and two footmen who were waiting with the gig. "You may unpack the luncheon. What do you say, my dear Cecilia? Shall we send Phillips down to Mr. Corbyn and invite him to join us? Cook has made that splendid pigeon pie he enjoyed so much when—"

But Cecilia cut her off. "You know very well, Mother, that Mr. Corbyn does not approve of the custom of luncheon. He says it belongs to ladies and Frenchmen."

"No, I did not know," said Mrs. Vaughn, and Rosalind thought she sounded rather impressed. "How did you unearth this little tit-bit?"

"You have frequently admonished me to pay attention, Mother," Cecilia said. "So I do try."

In another family, this might have been spoken with gentle humor, but that was not the case between these two. Mrs. Vaughn looked offended. Cecilia ignored her.

"Miss Thorne," she said. "I was thinking of taking a walk while lunch is being readied. Would you care to accompany me?"

"That sounds delightful, Miss Vaughn. That is, if . . ." She looked to Mrs. Showell.

"Oh, you girls go ahead," said Mrs. Showell. "Mrs. Vaughn and I will be quite comfortable where we are."

It seemed to Rosalind, however, that Mrs. Vaughn did not look at all happy with the suggestion and was wishing for a way to refuse.

"Not too far, Cecilia," she admonished finally. "And be careful of your hems. Should Mr. Corbyn see you, you would not wish to appear as if you were one of the laborers."

"No, Mother," said Cecilia placidly.

Cecilia and Rosalind were helped down from their respective carriages by the groomsmen and handed their parasols. Cecilia picked her way carefully down the road, more mindful of her mother's watchful gaze than her hems, Rosalind thought. She wore an ordinary lavender sprigged walking dress rather than any shade of mourning. She and William Corbyn had only been engaged, not married, so mourning dress was neither expected nor required for her. All the same, it seemed to Rosalind there was a resignation about Cecilia that spoke of some unmarked grief.

But not necessarily for William himself.

You need to stop thinking like this. Rosalind looked over the busy construction so she could keep her face turned from Miss Vaughn. *You have plenty of problems of your own. And they now include the fact that Mrs. Vaughn clearly hopes to enlist you as an ally against Lady Pennyworth.*

With all the cacophony from the work site, it did not take long before they were out of earshot from the carriages. Only then did Cecilia speak.

"Miss Thorne, I was hoping to ask after Louisa. Is she well? I sent her a note this morning but haven't received a reply yet."

"I believe she will be well. I confess, I have not seen her today, either. Perhaps Helen Corbyn would know her state of mind better."

"She might, but . . . Helen and I do not speak much anymore." Cecilia paused to glance back at the carriages, in case anyone might be coming toward them. "You see, Helen blames me for what happened to William."

"You?" said Rosalind, surprised. "How is it she blames you?"

Again, Cecilia hesitated and glanced behind them. When she did speak, her voice was so soft, Rosalind had to move close to hear her.

"Because I knew about the duel, and I said nothing to her."

Rosalind touched Cecilia's sleeve in gentle sympathy. "Can you tell me what happened?"

"My eldest brother, Bartolemew, is, was, a great friend of William's. William asked Bartolemew to be his second for the duel. And"—Cecilia swallowed—"Bartolemew told me what was happening. He all but bragged about it." Tears glistened in her eyes. "Of course, I begged him to put an end to it. I reminded him my future depended on this marriage, but he wouldn't listen."

"That must have been terrible for you."

Tears trickled down Cecilia's cheeks. She pressed her palms against them in a kind of soft panic and began rooting in her bag for a handkerchief.

Rosalind immediately pulled hers from where she'd tucked it in her sleeve and handed it to the girl so she could wipe eyes and nose before the telltale traces of red formed.

"I should have gone to Helen," Cecilia whispered. "To warn her. I didn't. I went to William instead." She pressed Rosalind's handkerchief against her eyes. "I tried to get him to call it off, Miss Thorne, I swear I did."

"I'm sure." Rosalind looked over her shoulder toward the carriages. There was as yet no sign of anyone approaching.

"But no matter how I begged, he said—he said many things, but in the end he said he would go through with it, no matter what. He said he was not going to let Bartolemew or . . . or anyone, besmirch his honor, or mine."

"Yours?"

"As his wife," she said, but she said it too quickly, and she looked at Rosalind far too steadily. "His honor is, would be, mine. Or at least, he saw it that way. And he asked me to hold my tongue about the matter and told me not to worry. He promised me he was not actually going to shoot Mr. Mirabeau. He swore that he would raise his pistol to the sky before it came to that. I accepted his reassurances and said nothing more.

"So, Helen's right, you see. It is my fault."

CHAPTER 14

A Momentary End to Secrets

*I think a renewal of your visit would be indelicate
under the circumstances, and might lead to
disagreeable results . . .*

Theodore Edward Hook, *Sayings and Doings*

Helen Corbyn had a long list of reasons for wanting to get married. First among them, however, was that it would finally allow her freedom of movement. A married woman was allowed to go where she pleased, when she pleased, with whomever she pleased. An unmarried girl, however, could not take two steps out of doors without a maid, a chaperone, and quite probably an invitation, preferably in written form to be produced on demand.

"It's ridiculous," Helen muttered as she rode—sedately proper on her sidesaddle—beside Fortuna's carriage. "All I want to do is see my fiancé."

"You cannot be causing more scandal at this stage, Helen," Fortuna reminded her. "Please try to be patient."

Helen knew she should be grateful that Fortuna was willing to help at all. Unfortunately, that willingness did not stretch as far as allowing Peter to come to the house when no one else was home. She was, however, quite ready to take a drive into town, where a little bird had told her they might happen to run into Peter at the Red Lion.

Helen had learned to place a great deal of faith in Fortuna's little birds, and this occasion gave her no cause to doubt them. When they came up the high street, Helen saw Peter's gelding, Agamemnon, being walked by a groom near the Red Lion public house.

Fortuna signaled for the carriage to stop and then asked their footman to ask Peter's groom to ask the pub's house boy to take a message to Mr. Mirabeau to say that Mrs. Graves would be glad to speak with him, if he was free.

Because, of course, an unmarried lady could not walk through the door and ask for herself. Neither could she be the one to send a note asking the unmarried man to come and speak to her in the public street.

Helen tried to keep herself calm. Atalanta, however, had already picked up on her agitation and danced uneasily. Helen patted the mare's neck. She tried not to think that Peter might refuse to come out. They hadn't spoken in days, and the last time they did talk, they'd come very close to quarreling, again. He had to have heard about Helen's embarrassment at the new hall by now. With what she had to tell him today . . . it might prove too much. He might decide it was better to just drop her altogether.

A scene won't worry Peter, she reminded herself. *We've laughed over far worse.*

Like the time Peter accidentally tore the train on Margaret Aldgate's dress and almost had to duel her pig of a brother over it. Then there was the day Helen had decided to try riding Atalanta astride and fallen. She wasn't hurt, but Peter had known she'd get into trouble. So, he snuck back to the house, stole the sidesaddle, helped her change it out, and led her home in proper style—all so her mother wouldn't lock her in the house for a week.

That was the Peter she wanted back—the one who she

understood and who understood her; the friend she could laugh with and circumvent ridiculous rules with and plan the future with and . . . and . . .

Wretched Miss Thorne, Helen thought sourly.

Wretched Miss Thorne because Helen had lain awake all night with their conversation playing over in her head.

She truly had not considered that anyone might believe *she'd* killed William. The whole idea left her sick. It meant that Lord Casselmaine, and the coroner, had not lied to protect some unknown person. They'd lied to protect her. It meant that the ladies in their smug circle, and her friends, and *Marius*, might all be going along with the lies because they thought she was the guilty one.

What made it worse was that she actually had thought about killing William.

She'd thought about it at night, muffling her sobs after she'd had things thrown at her, because William was drunk again and terrified of something he alone could see. She'd thought about it when she saw him holding his head and raging at her about all the things he believed were her fault. She'd thought about it when he disappeared for another week, or fortnight, or month in London, leaving everything in disarray and her with next to no money for the house-keeping, while Marius himself shut into his room and declared that the house was her business and she must rise to her place.

At all those times, she'd thought about taking one of the weapons from the gun room and putting an end to the whole horrible business.

Helen wiped at the tears with gloved hands.

"It will be all right," murmured Fortuna. "I believe we may trust Mr. Mirabeau."

"Do you really?" breathed Helen.

"Yes," she said firmly. "And, in fact, here he comes."

Again, Fortuna was right. The public house door opened,

and Peter walked out with Earnest Worthing. He spotted her at once and waved his hand, letting her know he would be there in a moment, then turned to say something more to Mr. Worthing.

Cares nothing for keeping me waiting, thought Helen peevishly, then wished she hadn't. She didn't want to feel this way about Peter. Between the bouts of nerves and the waves of pointless anger, it sometimes seemed she was losing her grip on herself by slow, horrible inches.

Peter left Worthing's side and crossed the street, touched his hat brim to Fortuna, who nodded from her place in the carriage. Only then did he come to Helen's side.

"Miss Corbyn. I was hoping to see you today. Worthing and I were just meeting this fellow about a brood mare he's selling. I would very much like your opinion before I make the purchase."

He said it like a peace offering. Helen didn't feel peaceful. She did not want to look into his eyes and see him saying, *I'm trying. Really, I am.*

She did not in the least want to understand this was hard for him.

But she did, and it was, and she felt herself melting and— blast him and her, and everything—she felt the tears beginning again.

"Perhaps we could walk a ways?" Peter suggested. "Fortuna can follow in the carriage."

Helen looked toward Fortuna, who was of course watching and interpreting the whole exchange. The two women nodded to each other in silent agreement.

"Yes, all right. Let's."

Peter held up his hands to help Helen down from Atalanta. They both knew she didn't need it, but it was one more gesture he could make to let the watching world know that he still regarded her with kindness.

Helen accepted his help. She also handed her reins to the footman.

"See that Atalanta is kept walking," she told the man. "She's skittish today." *As we all are.* Then, Helen took the arm Peter offered her and let him lead her away.

It was not a market day, but the town was still bustling. The air was filled with the usual mix of odors from animals and the distant scent of the fens baking under the summer sun. Men shouted from the public houses. Workers stumped up and down the streets with barrows and bundles and tools. Women strolled from shop to shop in their clusters of three and four, and everyone dodged the horses, donkeys, carts, and carriages. Helen welcomed all of it. The crowd granted them a chance to be private in public.

But much to her frustration, Helen found herself unable to speak. Her mind raced—inventing and discarding different openings. She knew her cheeks flushed and her eyes glistened, and she knew Peter saw that.

"You can tell me anything," he said quietly. "I'm not afraid."

But I am. "Peter . . . I need to tell you about dinner at the new hall last night."

"I'd heard something about it," he said. "Some kind of upset between you and Louisa Winterbourne, was it?"

"Me, and Louisa, and her friend Miss Rosalind Thorne."

"What had Miss Thorne to do with it?"

Helen steeled herself. She made certain her expression was calm, and that her hand lay lightly against Peter's arm. No one passing could be given reason to look at them twice.

"Miss Thorne is a London woman who helps solve . . . difficulties . . . ladies might find themselves in."

Helen watched the implications of this settle into Peter's thoughts.

"Helen! You took your family business to a stranger!"

"What choice did I have?" she shot back. "No one I know is willing to help!"

"That's because those who care about you also know that there's nothing to be done! It was an accident!"

Helen clenched her jaw. If she answered now, she would scream.

Unfortunately, Peter misinterpreted her silence.

"Helen." Her name was a harsh whisper. "You cannot possibly still be thinking I shot William from behind."

Thank goodness for the bonnet that hid her face from so many. Thank goodness for the crowd intent on its own business, and for Fortuna following at a discreet distance so all the world could see this was perfectly right and proper.

Because what she said next was anything but.

"Why wouldn't I think it? You were ready to shoot him from the front."

"It was a duel, not murder," said Peter wretchedly, but doggedly.

"What on earth's the difference?"

Peter stopped dead in his tracks to stare at her.

"God in Heaven, woman, how can you not see!" He dropped his voice to an urgent whisper. "I was ready to meet him face-to-face, with honor! I admit, I had my differences with him. I know how he was with you, and Mrs. Graves, and, well, God help poor Cecilia. But your brother was a gentleman and he deserved to be treated that way. Besides, if I already had an appointment to stand and shoot at him, why would I go skulk in the bushes to do it? What good would that do my name, or his? Or yours come to that?"

It made sense. Ridiculous, awful sense, but sense all the same. Helen's thoughts and breath seemed to tie themselves together into one huge knot.

"Do you think I killed my brother?" she asked.

The words came out all in a rush. There was no intention behind them. She was sure she had not meant to speak them at all.

Peter's eyes all but started from his head. "Good God, *no!* Of course not!" He looked over his shoulder, watching to see if anyone they knew had stopped to listen or watch.

Then he pressed her hand.

"Helen, I know William treated you badly. I know he was violent when he drank. If you had lost your hold . . . it would be . . . it wouldn't be all right, but it would be . . . I don't know, forgivable, understandable. Damn me, there is no way to say any of this!" He took her other hand. "I love you, Helen, and I love you because I *know* you. If you'd thought William was going to hurt somebody else—Fortuna or Cecilia perhaps, or that he was in pain he could not express—"

Helen reached up and pressed her fingertips against Peter's mouth to silence him.

Someone will see. This is not proper. But she couldn't bring herself to care. She could not bear to see the mix of pain and love in his eyes. Neither could she bear her feelings as his words rang through her. Because Peter understood so many things that were ugly and true, and he was still standing here.

He had not left her a jilt. He could have. No one would have blamed him. All the blame would have been on her. She was the one who could not sufficiently manage her appearances, and she was the one who had not been able to hide her broken family as she should.

But Helen knew Peter, too. She knew when he was speaking the truth, and that was what he gave her now—the precious, confusing, horrible, wonderful, untidy truth about him and her and William and everything else.

She kept her voice low. *But please hear me, hear every word I say and everything I mean.*

"I don't believe you killed him," she said. "But I know you still haven't told me everything. And I know the coroner lied." He tried to open his mouth, but she shook her head. "Please, Peter, don't. I do know. What kind of accident gets a man shot in the back without leaving any trace? You were there! You saw it!"

"I saw a horrid mess."

"No, Peter. Don't try to rewrite what we both know. Not now."

He sighed, turning his face toward the horizon for a moment. "Very well, and you should know . . ." He swallowed. "After I'd sent you away with Worthing and the doctor, I had a look around the area. I wanted to see if there was a gun or a mantrap or anything. If there had been, it was already gone. I didn't see any other footmarks, either, but then, it was bare ground and still frozen pretty hard," he added quickly. "If somebody else was there, they might not have left any traces."

Peter wasn't just a crack shot, he was a hunter. He knew something about the woods and the wild. His words could not be taken lightly.

"Peter, you know I'm not a coward. . . ." *At least I didn't used to be.* "But I'm afraid of what people will say about us. I don't want to risk losing you to gossips. We have to know what happened. If it comes out as a scandal, at least it's *out*, and no one can ambush us, or our family, with it later." *Because Miss Thorne was right. It's the secrets that will destroy us.*

She was shaking. She had just put herself on display. Her mother would have been appalled and would have spent a good hour lecturing Helen on the fact that no man wanted— or, indeed, needed—to see a woman's true face.

He'll leave now. I've offended him. I've shown myself to be ridiculous and hysterical and . . .

Peter took her hand again and this time held it between both of his. "I love you," he said. "I want you for my wife. I swear, I mean to care for you and your family as I would my own, and damn the whole world and whatever the world may say."

A tear escaped from Helen's eye. She didn't care.

"Peter, I am about to ask you to take a leap of faith. Another leap." She covered his hand with hers. "Will you come with me?"

His smile stopped her heart. "I trust you, Helen. I will follow you anywhere."

She believed him and she loved him. She wanted to kiss him then and there, where the whole world could see. But, of course, she could not. She could only thread her arm through his and bask in the warmth of his smile, and the surge of confidence and, yes, nerve she felt running through her.

I will follow you anywhere.

Now, if only she could be as sure of where she would be leading him.

CHAPTER 15

A Catalog of Events From the Peaceful Countryside

There is no such thing as falling in love, now-a-days: you may slip, slide, or stumble . . .

Maria Edgeworth, *Tales of Fashionable Life*

"Mrs. Vaughn," said Rosalind. "I was wondering if you could tell me what is Mr. Corbyn's role at the drainage works?"

After Rosalind and Cecilia returned to the matrons, their viewing party had all settled onto blankets. Plates of the famous pigeon pie (which was indeed excellent), cold meats, cheese, and cakes were passed around. Mrs. Vaughn had proved more than willing to provide a steady stream of conversation to accompany the luncheon. This consisted of her recounting feats of shopping, alternated with the heartbreak of raising nine children. Mrs. Showell had evidently heard most of these anecdotes before. She knew exactly when to supply a polite "Well!" or "Goodness."

While her mother talked, Cecilia nibbled and drank. If she should happen to be questioned, she smiled and made some small remark, but for the most part she maintained a quiet reserve.

As well she might. *It is my fault.* Those words played themselves over in Rosalind's head as she watched Cecilia sitting across from her—quiet and modest, and trying not to draw anyone's attention to herself. Rosalind knew what it was to have to hide heartbreak, and guilt. She wished she could say something, anything to bring a little comfort.

But there was nothing. The only way she could help was to make polite conversation and give Cecilia some room to remain quiet while she smoothed out the edges of her feelings.

Mrs. Vaughn beamed. "Oh, Mr. Corbyn has designed the whole business. The Corbyns have been in the district since the Conquest, you know. They are deeply attached to the land and very interested in making improvements."

"Mr. Corbyn made an extensive study of similar work being done in Lincolnshire," added Cecilia, unexpectedly. Rosalind caught her gaze, but Cecilia's green eyes betrayed no hint of untoward meaning. "He became convinced that the methods could be adapted here." She nibbled a bit of cheese. "It was Colonel Corbyn who recommended Mr. Corbyn to his grace."

"Oh yes. Poor, dear Colonel Corbyn." Mrs. Vaughn sighed. "It was natural enough, of course, that he should recommend his brother to Lord Casselmaine, but quite apart from that, Mr. Corbyn has such a *superior* mind. I can barely understand half of what he says sometimes."

"And, of course, William invested heavily in the project himself," added Cecilia.

Why do you mention these two facts in particular? wondered Rosalind. *The money and how it was the colonel who involved his very clever brother?*

"It was Colonel Corbyn's investment that helped convince the neighborhood that the thing could be done at all," put in Mrs. Showell. "Casselmaine had remarked more than once that raising the capital has been as hard as digging the canals."

Cecilia sipped at her glass of lemonade.

Rosalind wondered about Cecilia's relationship with William Corbyn, and how they had agreed to marry. She wondered how Cecilia felt about the fact that Mrs. Vaughn was trying to shift her attention to Marius Corbyn.

Because Cecilia clearly knows something about the family, possibly both families, that she is afraid to tell me. Then, she told herself, *I must stop thinking like this. This is none of my business.*

"Speaking of his grace!" Mrs. Vaughn smiled archly. "It appears we are to be favored with a visit. Or perhaps I should say, Miss Thorne, you are."

Rosalind had been seated with her back toward the works. She turned now and saw Devon making his way up the bank to the road and their picnic spot.

"Good afternoon, ladies." He bowed politely. "I hope you've been able to enjoy yourselves."

He was rumpled and muddy and sun-bronzed, and a sheen of sweat covered his face. But he looked happy, Rosalind realized. Thoroughly, openly happy.

The sight did very odd things to her heart.

"Oh, indeed, sir, it is always most edifying," Mrs. Vaughn burbled. "I could have wished that we had Mr. Corbyn to explain to us some of the finer details, but dear Cecilia reminded me we could not possibly interrupt the work."

Dear Cecilia had of course done no such thing, and the look on Devon's face said he knew that. At least it did to Rosalind.

"Thank you," said Devon blandly. "Mr. Corbyn has been meeting with the surveyors today about the new channel. But I'm sure he'll be at your card party and will be glad to tell you anything you could wish to know."

"There, Cecilia!" Mrs. Vaughn beamed at her daughter. "I told you Mr. Corbyn would not disappoint!"

Cecilia let her gaze fall modestly and made no answer.

"Well, sir, you must excuse us." Mrs. Vaughn patted her

daughter's hand. "If I do not get Cecilia indoors soon, she'll turn positively brown. Her complexion is so delicate."

"We cannot possibly risk Miss Vaughn's complexion." Devon bowed again. "Mrs. Showell, shall I escort you and Miss Thorne back to Cassell House?"

"That would be most welcome, thank you."

Rosalind caught Mrs. Vaughn's conspiratorial wink. She wondered how soon news of this little bit of gallantry would begin making the rounds.

She wished suddenly and intensely for London's anonymity. There, she and Devon could walk on the streets or in the park without being known. No one would care whether he smiled at her, or offered her his arm to help raise her to her feet, or try to catch the exact tone she used when she murmured her thanks.

Or, as Cecilia was doing, look on and wonder how it all might affect them.

After all the usual delays of readying the carriage, harnessing the horses, and Devon fetching his own gray gelding, they were able to set off back toward Cassell House. The late-afternoon air had grown still and heavy; Rosalind was grateful for the breeze created by the carriage's motion. Devon rode beside them, on the left hand, which was nearest Rosalind, while Mrs. Showell made herself comfortable on the farther side.

Shortly after the drive began, Mrs. Showell let her head nod and closed her eyes. She even gave a soft snore.

Devon and Rosalind arched their brows at each other. Devon grinned and nudged his horse a little closer to the carriage's side. Rosalind rearranged the light driving rug across his aunt's lap.

"Well, where do we begin?" Devon asked. "Scenery, weather?"

"Everyone's health?" suggested Rosalind.

"The condition of the roads or the drainage works?" added Devon.

Rosalind considered. "Probably the drainage works. I believe I'm expected to take an interest."

"And have you?"

"I've tried to find some reading. There seem to be a lot of different opinions on drainage and canals."

"Oh, believe me, I've heard most of them." Devon's mount stumbled over a rut, and Devon patted the creature's neck. "And I'll probably hear them all again. This is going to take . . . well, I'm only hoping I won't have to leave a lot of half-dug ditches for the next duke." He glanced down at their chaperone. "Do you think Aunt Showell is really asleep?"

"Probably not," said Rosalind. "But it's the best she can manage to give us some privacy."

"I'll thank her later. I'm sorry it's all been a rush so far," he added quickly. "I should have put the dinner off, but . . . the project needs money, and cooperation . . ."

"And that requires dinners. I know," said Rosalind. "It's all right."

Devon rode on in silence. Rosalind let him have his moment.

"I've missed you, Rosalind," he said finally. "And I'm sorry it took me this long to come back to you."

"There's nothing to be sorry about," she said at once. Devon looked away and Rosalind flinched. "I'm sorry now. I'm talking in platitudes and I don't mean to. It's just, there's so much . . ." The words fell away. *Now. You must let him know now.* "Devon . . . when we really do have some privacy, there's some things I need to tell you about, well, the past." *And the present.* "I should have done it as soon as you invited me to come down, but . . ." She stopped. "I've no good explanation, I just didn't."

"Maybe because you weren't sure you would accept my

invitation," he said quietly. "You may have thought you'd be engaged elsewhere."

It was the closest either of them had come so far to mentioning Adam Harkness.

"Perhaps," she agreed. "But I'm here now."

"I'd noticed, believe me." Devon gave her a very different sort of smile. Rosalind was aware that she should have been offended by that look, but instead she was . . . intrigued. "Would this Sunday suit you? For private conversation, that is? I was thinking we might drive out to the castle after church."

"You have a castle?"

"Oh yes," he said loftily. "My estate comes with all the frills and furbelows. We can have a picnic." He paused and looked quizzically at her. "If you're not tired of picnics after what was surely a fascinating afternoon with Mrs. Vaughn."

"I think a picnic with you would make a delightful contrast."

She smiled and he laughed, and something in her eased. Suddenly, Rosalind felt content just to sit back and enjoy the sunshine and the green scents on the breeze and to have Devon so close riding beside her.

The moment did not last.

They had left the marsh and meadowlands behind and returned to the neatly hedged fields. The droning complaints of sheep lifted themselves over the sounds of their carriage and horses. The road ahead narrowed to a lane winding between farmsteads and stands of trees. As they passed into some very welcome shade, angry shouts broke from up around the bend.

There was the sound of splintering wood, a donkey's bray, and a woman's shriek.

Mrs. Showell came awake at once. Her hand flew to grip Rosalind's arm as if she thought Rosalind would leap from the carriage.

Devon stood up in his stirrups, straining to see ahead.

"Oh, damn and blast the man!" He dug his heels into the horse's side and sent it cantering ahead. From his seat on the box, Samuel slowed their team.

"No, no," said Mrs. Showell. "It may be we can help."

The set of Samuel's shoulders said he didn't agree, but he kept the horses stepping.

The brougham rounded the bend. Three men stood in the road. Samuel pulled the team up short.

Rosalind leaned over the side of the carriage to see better, and what she did see was that that all three men carried shotguns slung across their shoulders. Another pair of men, similarly armed, emerged from the farmhouse. One held a burlap sack. The other yanked on a rope that had been knotted around the wrists of a pale man wearing a laborer's smock and breeches.

Devon had reached the gap in the wall that separated the farmyard from the road. At the same moment, the man holding the rope jerked it mercilessly, causing the laborer to drop to his knees.

"Crease!" Devon reined his horse to a halt. "What's the meaning of this? This isn't Vaughn's land!"

"What's happening?" cried Rosalind to Mrs. Showell.

"A gamekeeper's raid." Mrs. Showell craned her neck. "That one standing there watching is Nicholas Vaughn's man, Archibald Crease."

A stout woman ran from the house, screaming at the top of her lungs.

"Your grace! Your grace!" She burst through the gate and fell to her knees beside the laborer. "Help us!"

The man named Crease ignored the farmwife and touched the brim of his cap to Devon. He wore corduroy and moleskin, with stout boots on his feet. His face was tanned, lined, and unshaven.

"It may not be Mr. Vaughn's land, your grace, but that's

the trouble, you see," Crease told him. "For we've found Mr. Vaughn's property here, where it's no business being. Timmons, show his grace, why don't you?"

The man with the sack opened it up and pulled out a quartet of dead hares.

"These was under the cot in the shed where this one"— Crease nodded toward the laborer—"has been sleeping off his drink."

The farmwife glowered up at Crease. She also helped raise the laborer to his feet and leaned him against the wall.

"I never took them hares, yer honor," the laborer gasped, and his accent was distinctly Irish. "God as my witness, I've done nothing."

"Then you've naught to fear, have you, laddy me boy?" sneered Crease. "But you will have to explain how these little beasties came to be under your cot, now, won't you?"

More shouts tumbled up the road, accompanied by the sound of many feet thudding against dirt. Rosalind twisted around, but the bend made it impossible to see who was coming.

Devon heard it, too.

"Dear God," he breathed. "Samuel, take the women straight back to the hall. Tell McCleod and La Platte what's happened."

Samuel touched up the horses immediately. "Out of the way, damn you!" He slashed his whip toward the gamekeeper's men so they were forced to jump back and clear the lane.

The sound of running grew louder. Rosalind twisted around in the other direction, just in time to see a crowd of mud-spattered men brandishing shovels and picks charge around the bend.

The gamekeeper and his men saw them, too.

"Guns," snapped Crease.

"First man who touches a weapon will find himself in jail

on a charge of disorderly conduct and attempted murder!" Devon bellowed.

To Rosalind's horror, Devon also backed and turned his horse, putting himself broadside between the gamekeepers and the onrushing crowd.

"Let me out!" Rosalind fumbled for the door handle, even though the carriage was gaining speed. "I have to . . . !"

"Rosalind, no!" Mrs. Showell held her tight. "We cannot delay the message!"

Mrs. Showell was right, and Rosalind could do nothing except watch until Devon and the armed men all vanished from sight.

CHAPTER 16

The Possibility of Trouble

*How to get quietly rid of the fiend was, therefore,
the great and principal point for consideration . . .*

Theodore Edward Hook, *Cousin William*, or
The Fatal Attachment

If there was a thing Devon hated, it was poaching. Maybe it was fairer to say, what he hated was the rabid attachment his fellow landowners had to their particular beasts and birds. That desire to stock their larders and entertain their friends led them to hire and arm whole regiments of ignorant, bad-tempered men under the title of "gamekeeper." The law gave those men the perfect freedom to stop and search a woman with a basket on the road, or roust out the house of anyone they took a dislike to. Traps were set that could take a laboring man's leg off, or shoot him dead if he tripped the wire.

For rabbits. For pheasants and foxes and hares.

And yet they still seemed baffled at the fact that honest men could grow resentful of such overzealous protections.

In front of him, at least two dozen workingmen raced up the road. At his back, all six of the gamekeepers carried shotguns and a willingness to use them. The farmwife—Mrs. Soady—had abandoned her lodger and run for the house.

Devon couldn't blame her a bit.

Where the hell is Corbyn? How did he let these men leave the works? The immediate answer sent a chill through Devon's blood. His horse danced uneasily. Devon patted the beast's neck and took tighter hold of the reins.

The loose gang of men stuttered to a stop three yards ahead of him. *A good sign. Nobody willing to charge right in.*

It also gave him a chance to recognize them.

"Now then, Doyle, Jimmy, Connor," Devon called. "What's all this about? Has Mr. Corbyn called a half holiday?"

"Saving yer grace's reverence, we did that for ourselves." Doyle was the head of the biggest labor gang employed at the drainage works. He was the one who spoke to Devon when there were complaints among his men. He was also the one who made sure the men did their jobs as they promised. He could swear a blue streak in Gaelic or English, and he was willing to deal fairly when fairly dealt with. As such, he was trusted, and managed to keep decent relations with the heads of the other gangs. At least, he managed to keep it so their problems stayed between them and did not unduly affect the work. Despite what Vaughn said, there had been no more than common drunkenness and the occasional fight among the itinerant laborers. That, Devon knew, was largely due to Doyle and his lieutenants.

Now, Doyle planted his sharp-bladed spade in front of him, like a knight of old standing guard at the drawbridge.

"We heard yer man here"—Doyle spat in the dust toward Crease—"had plans to roister the house while poor Arthur Sullivan was sick abed. Said he was no sick, but off poaching, as if Sullivan was no more than a sneakin', low-life thievin' liar such as you might meet on the king's highway. Said he planned to teach us all a lesson with some of his fine master's rabbits and all."

"You're a lousy, lying son of an Irish whore!" Crease shouted. "And drunken thieving poachers, the lot of you! I've got the proof!"

"Crease!" bellowed Devon. "You'll shut your damned mouth or I'll shut it for you!"

Then, as if matters weren't bad enough, the farmhouse door flew open. Old Soady himself came charging out, an ax clutched in his gnarled hands. His eldest boy followed hard behind him, carrying a scythe.

The gamekeepers' men shifted uneasily. Two of them snapped their guns closed. Soady raised his ax but kept his eyes on Devon.

Devon didn't let himself flinch. "Go on with what you were saying, Doyle," he said.

"Well, sir," said Doyle. "When I hears this tale from my men, I says that bearing false witness is a lowdown trick that is spoken out against in your church and our own. Surely, I says, no honest Christian in the steady employ of a fine English gentleman would lay a foul charge of poaching at the feet of an innocent man. But the lads"—he jerked his chin toward the men behind him, with their pickaxes and their hammers—"they all insisted they should come see for themselves, and so now we have."

"And Mr. Corbyn was happy to let you all go, I'm sure?" Behind him, Crease snorted. Devon heartily wished he could order his horse to kick the man in the ribs.

Thankfully, Doyle ignored Crease. "Ah, well, your honor knows Mr. Corbyn. He's a strict one about working hours."

A fresh rumble of agreement sounded from the ragged ranks of laborers. Devon's horse whickered and backed several steps before Devon was able to get it under control again.

"One of the lads—can't say that I recall exactly who—thought there might be some objections on that account," Doyle went on. "Though we'd be down and back as quick as ever a man could, of course. But that worried lad might have taken the precaution of bolting the office door, not wanting the man to meet with any sad accident if some other of the lads—again, I'm not sure just who—might take exception to being told to stick to the work while a friend an' a brother was being put in danger of his life." Doyle spat again. "For the crime of being sick abed."

On the other side of him, Crease jerked his arm, bringing his gun off his shoulder and into position to fire. Devon urged his horse forward, just enough that Crease's weapon was now aimed straight at him. Devon looked down the barrels, and he looked at the man who held the gun.

"Get me the sack, Crease."

Devon had pulled his brother out of gaming hells. He had made his way across the frozen fens on a dark night to bring a midwife to farm women who would have died without some help. He had once, quite literally, stood at the head of a company of militia and read out the Riot Act to a gang of Luddites.

He had never been as worried as he was now.

Crease straightened his shoulders. His finger went to the first of the gun's double triggers. Devon heard murmurs and movement from the laborers but did not dare look back.

"You will give me the sack and your gun, because your only other option is to shoot," said Devon quietly. "And as soon as you fire, the rest of these men will be on you before you can draw breath. Ever seen a man beaten to death, Crease?" Devon dropped his voice. "I have. Now, give me that gun and that bag."

Crease hesitated, just long enough for Devon's throat to close around his breath. Then the gamekeeper uttered a whole string of blasphemies, but he also broke his gun and handed it over to Devon. Devon checked the breach and slung the gun over his own shoulder.

Crease gestured for his lieutenant, Timmons, to retrieve the sack from the ground and hand it up to Devon.

Devon snatched it from Timmons's hand. He undid the knot and pulled out the string of sad and scrawny hares. They were none too fresh, either, by the smell.

"Mr. Soady?" called Devon to the farmer.

Soady had always impressed Devon as a man with good sense and he used it now. He put the ax down on the wall before he stepped forward and touched his knuckle to his forehead.

"Yer grace?"

"Do I remember you telling me you've been having a rare trouble with rabbits in your cabbages this year?" *Come on, Soady. Pick it up.*

Soady did not fail him.

"Yes, yer grace. Very true. Like to have short commons this winter, they've et so much."

"Well. These are plainly wild hares, not preserved animals. They're too raggedy." He shoved the gruesome string back into the sack. "But mistakes get made and no real harm done. Soady, get Sullivan there loose, will you?"

Devon met and held Crease's gaze. "I'll keep these. Soady, you can come up to the house tomorrow and talk to Mr. La Platte about your losses. The two of you can square up accounts on the quarter day. I'll tell him to expect you."

Crease glowered at him, as if he wanted nothing more than to snatch his gun back, which he probably did.

"Mr. Vaughn will want to hear about all these goings-on," Crease said. "The law says—"

Devon cut him off. "I am fully aware of what the law says."

The law said gamekeepers had perfect freedom to "investigate" persons they suspected of poaching or holding poached game, on the road, in a field, in a home, or wherever else they might be. The law said that poachers must hang for their crimes, no matter how young. The law was perfectly ready to carry that sentence out, all on the word of a man like Archibald Crease.

Mr. Vaughn had frequently expressed his fondness for all such laws.

"All right, Crease," said Devon. "As I'm sure Mr. Vaughn will be hungry for news of everything that's happened here, I suggest you hurry back to the house and tell him the whole story. You can also let him know I'll be glad to meet him at his earliest convenience so we can talk the matter over. Now." He rested the sack on the saddle bow and then laid the gun on top of it, closed, with the safety catch slid back. "I don't think you or your men have any further business here, do you?"

Crease's gaze slid past Devon to the laborers behind him.

"You've got my gun, sir," he said.

"Yes, I do."

A whole host of ugly calculations flickered behind the gamekeeper's narrowed eyes, but he did the only thing he could. He turned and jerked his chin at his men and started down the road toward Vaughn's land.

Devon didn't let himself move until the keepers had vanished from sight. Only then did he sling the gun across his back and dismount.

Soady had got the man, Sullivan, free from the ropes. Sullivan, on his feet again, was chafing his wrists.

"How are you feeling, Sullivan?" Devon asked.

"A might poorly still, yer honor." In fact, the man was swaying on his feet and his face was as red as if he'd been hours in the sun.

"All right. Back to bed with you. I'll send my apothecary around to see if there's anything to be done. Now then, Doyle, a word with you." Devon jerked his chin toward the hedgerow across the way.

Doyle handed his shovel to his second and strolled off easily at Devon's side, far enough that they were out of earshot, but not out of sight.

"All right, Doyle?" Devon asked.

"Well enough, yer grace," he replied amiably, but he was not in any way relaxed.

"Glad to hear it." Devon glanced back at the men. They were starting to mill about. *Standing down*, he thought, *but still watchful*.

"Doyle, if you and the men go back to the works, *and* let Mr. Corbyn out of his office, *and* make sure there's no further unrest tonight, I give you my word that no one will be docked their day's wage for making sure of the well-being of a friend and brother."

The long pause and the sharp eye Doyle gave him clenched Devon's guts.

At last, the man nodded. "It'll do. I can take that to the men. But, again, savin' yer grace's honor, whether or not there's 'further unrest' "—he made an excellent imitation of Devon's accent—"is not entirely up to us, if you take my meaning."

"I do," said Devon. "But I will point out it was a very good thing that I was on hand to work through this . . . misunderstanding with Vaughn's keeper. I might not be able to be so quick next time, and then it'd be a sorrowful group of families burying their men and begging for their bread because there's none to earn it for them. If you take *my* meaning."

"That I do, sir." Doyle touched his knuckle to his forehead, but there was no trace of humility in the gesture. "That I do."

Doyle turned his back and raised his arms. "All right, lads! We've seen what there is to see here! Come on now, back to work. I'll tell yez all about it as we go. Come on, now!"

He stumped back to his men, retrieved his shovel, and began urging them all back down the road. English gave way to Gaelic, and there was some bitter laughter mixed in with the curses.

But they went, all of them, disappearing around the bend and leaving no one but Devon and the farm family.

"Thank you, your grace," breathed Soady. "For what it's worth, Sullivan's been a'bed wi' the fever all day. My missus 'as been seeing to him. Crease and 'is boys brought those rabbits to the purpose."

Why am I not surprised? "Make sure you give yourself a margin for the damage done in the search, Soady." Devon hoisted himself back up onto his horse. "And have one of your sons run straight up to Mr. La Platte and tell him the danger's past. I've got to get back to the works and make sure all's right there."

"Your grace." Soady touched his forehead.

Devon knotted the sack onto his saddle bow and kicked the horse into a trot. It wasn't until he was sure he was out of sight of the farm that he urged the beast into a canter. He needed to be sure none of the workers had taken advantage of the chaos, and his absence, to air a few personal grievances with Corbyn, and one another.

He thought about the anguish on Rosalind's face as Samuel drove her away to safety. He wanted to get back to the house at once, to assure her everything was well. But he couldn't.

The best he could do was hurry.

CHAPTER 17

A Brief Postponement of the Worst

*Opinions had changed; and, on opinion, almost
all power is founded.*

Maria Edgeworth, *Tales of Fashionable Life*

Later, Rosalind would find the time and breath to admire
Samuel's driving skills.

Just then, however, she was busy clinging to the brougham's side, trying not to be thrown out of her seat, and—to
her shame—trying not to scream and further panic the horses
or driver.

Mrs. Showell clung to her own seat like grim death.

Rosalind closed her eyes, but that only made things worse,
because now she could clearly see Devon caught in the middle of two gangs of angry, armed men.

Please, let him be all right, Rosalind prayed. *Please, please,
please.*

After what felt like a year, the carriage barreled through
the gates of Cassell House and into the courtyard. The
grooms and footmen ran forward to take hold of the horses
and open the carriage door. Rosalind all but toppled out onto
the cobbles, shaking with fear and the rush of the journey.
Mrs. Showell jumped down behind her.

"Mrs. . . ." began the footman.

"No time," rapped Mrs. Showell. "Where is Mr. La Platte? He must be found at once. If he is out on the estate, I need a message taken to him. At once, do you hear!"

"Yes, ma'am." The man bowed and gave orders to another younger footman, who took off running.

Mrs. Showell took Rosalind's arm. Rosalind was not sure who was supporting who as they staggered into the foyer to be exclaimed over by the maids and someone very familiar to Rosalind.

"Miss Thorne!" cried Mrs. Kendricks. "What on earth . . . ?"

Oh, thank heavens! "There's been an . . . incident. Mrs. Showell needs to sit down," said Rosalind to her housekeeper. "We'll need tea immediately."

And I need to sit, too, and catch my breath, and oh, please, let Devon be all right. . . .

"The blue salon," said Mrs. Northey, the housekeeper for Cassell House. "Mrs. Kendricks, if you could go with the ladies, I'll give orders for tea. Betsy, you go with Mrs. Kendricks."

Rosalind and Mrs. Showell were efficiently ushered into a stuffy room done in powder and delphinium blues. While Mrs. Kendricks helped them off with bonnets and cloaks, the girl hurried to open the windows and bring in the air.

Rosalind met Mrs. Kendricks's inquisitive gaze mutely. She still had not found her voice before Mrs. Northey entered the room, followed by a footman with a silver tray.

"Tea will be up directly, and I've brought sherry. You will have a glass, ma'am?" Mrs. Northey was pouring before that lady answered. She handed a delicate glass to Mrs. Showell and another to Rosalind.

Rosalind gulped the wine gratefully. The road dust had packed her throat at least as tightly as her fear.

The salon looked out onto the courtyard, and Rosalind could see Samuel already had a crowd of liveried men around him. They could hear his voice but couldn't catch more than one word in three. The coachman waved his arms and all at once, men and boys scattered, even while others were arriving from what seemed like every direction.

Help is coming. Rosalind pressed her hand against her stomach and took another swallow of sherry. *It may not be needed. It may already be over. Devon may already be on his way home.*

Someone was speaking to her. Rosalind jerked her head around to see Mrs. Kendricks standing beside her.

"I'm sorry," she said. "I didn't hear you."

"I said, you should know, Miss Thorne, that Miss Corbyn and Mrs. Graves are here," said Mrs. Kendricks. "They've brought Mr. Mirabeau with them."

Rosalind stared at her housekeeper, dumbfounded. *Oh, not now!*

"They were told you were from home, but Miss Winterbourne went in to see them and decided they should all wait until you returned. . . ."

"Where are Miss Winterbourne and her guests?" interrupted Mrs. Showell.

"Upstairs in the drawing room," said Mrs. Kendricks.

Mrs. Showell gulped her wine. "Rosalind, I have to ask you to deal with them. I must speak to Mr. La Platte immediately, and there may be other orders that need to be given, and I suppose someone ought to inform the dowager."

"Of course," said Rosalind as firmly as she could manage.

Mrs. Showell touched her shoulder. "Devon will be fine," she said. "There have been other disputes, you know—over pay or some punishment for drunkenness. He's always restored calm."

"Of course." Rosalind mustered a smile, and hoped that she looked like she meant it. "I know Devon is an excellent manager."

"He should be, after handling Hugh and his father all those years."

"Yes, exactly," agreed Rosalind, trying not to feel how

tightly her fingers gripped the stem of her sherry glass. "By comparison, a few disgruntled workingmen will be nothing at all."

A few workingmen, a few brutal gamekeepers eager to assert their power, a farm family outraged at the violation of their home . . .

Mrs. Showell was clearly running down a similar list in her own mind. Rosalind squeezed her hand. Mrs. Showell nodded, squared her shoulders, and strode out of the room.

"Will you go up to your guests, miss?" asked Mrs. Northey.

Rosalind shook her head. She didn't want to lose the view of the courtyard, and the gates. "Bring them down here, please. And make sure there's enough refreshment and . . ."

There was something else, she was sure, but she couldn't think what it should be. So, Rosalind just gestured for Mrs. Northey to go.

As soon as Mrs. Northey left, Mrs. Kendricks seized Rosalind's hand. "You're cold as ice, miss! What in heaven's name has happened!"

Rosalind blurted out what she'd witnessed in as few words as she could. She had to get over the shock and gather her wits. She could not be falling apart, not like this. Not yet.

"Miss." Mrs. Kendricks turned toward the door.

She was out of time. Rosalind shut her mouth and drew herself up straight.

The door opened, and Louisa, Helen and Fortuna hurried inside. A slim and well-dressed young man, whom Rosalind assumed must be Peter Mirabeau, trailed in their wake.

"Rosalind, what on earth?" cried Louisa. "You look like you've been caught in a raging gale!"

Rosalind put her hand up to her hair. "There has been an emergency."

"I should say!" Mr. Mirabeau went straight to the window and stared out at the crowd of male servants still gathered in the yard. "And looks like we're about to get some news."

Through the gate galloped the shaggiest pony Rosalind had ever seen. A little boy clung tightly to its rope bridle. At once, men clustered around, catching the bridle and shouting questions. The boy shouted back, and a cheer rang out among the men. Rosalind couldn't catch what was said, but the tone of relief was unmistakable. So was the way Samuel rubbed the boy's head and helped him down from the horse.

It was good news. It was over. Devon was all right.

Rosalind's knees buckled under the weight of her relief, and she sank back onto the sofa.

Louisa was right beside her, taking up both her hands. "Rosalind, for heaven's sake, what's happened? Someone . . . Helen, ring for tea. Mrs. Kendricks, find a blanket and . . ."

"No, I am well, I am," insisted Rosalind. "And tea is already on the way. There was some . . . trouble on the way back from the drainage works."

Now that she was in front of others, Rosalind could remember her deportment. She could speak clearly and calmly, because that was what she was trained to do. There would be tears later, and more shaking, and a whole host of other indignities, but those would wait until there was no one to see. She was able to relate the facts to her little audience with at least some semblance of detachment.

"Crease," Helen spat the gamekeeper's name like a curse.

"The man is a brute," said Fortuna grimly.

"Cecilia tried to get her father to fire him, but Mr. Vaughn won't budge." Louisa threw up her hands. "The poachers, I can understand. Sometimes they're hungry, or the rabbits are eating their crops, or they need a little extra to get through the winter. But *Crease* . . . !" She shook her head. "It's not fair!"

"No, I agree," said Rosalind.

"But surely it's over now?" Louisa indicated the courtyard and the rapidly dispersing crowd.

"I'll go find out, shall I?" Mr. Mirabeau didn't wait for an answer. He just pushed the window farther open and—much to Rosalind's surprise—hopped right out into the courtyard. He shouted to someone, and a footman came running over.

"I think I like your Mr. Mirabeau," murmured Rosalind to Helen. "He's very direct."

Mirabeau and the footman spoke for a moment. Then Mirabeau nodded and fished a coin out of his pocket.

"As we thought!" he declared as he returned to the window. "Whole thing's broken up. When the boy left, Crease and his men had been packed off empty-handed, and the workers had already started back for the digs. Nobody hurt. His grace should be on his way home shortly. Gave over a farthing for the boy for his troubles and all that." Mirabeau looked at the windowsill and hesitated. "I'll just go round the front door, shall I? Pardon me." He touched his forehead and hurried away.

Helen was blushing as well. "He normally doesn't . . . well."

"It's not a normal day," said Louisa stoutly.

"You must have been terrified, Miss Thorne," said Fortuna.

"I admit it," said Rosalind. "I've been in difficult circumstances, but nothing like that."

Fortuna nodded, and then after a moment's hesitation, she asked, "What of Mr. Corbyn?"

"The man, Doyle, said he'd been locked in one of the offices. I'm sure he's out by now. Lord Casselmaine will have made certain." As soon as Rosalind said it, she felt positive that was why Devon had not yet returned. Of course, he would have gone to the digs first to make certain everything was as it ought to be.

"Locked up? Oh dear," murmured Fortuna. "Mr. Corbyn will not get over that in a hurry."

"I should think not," said Helen. "Oh Lord. I wish . . . I wish everything would just stop. Just for a minute!" She sat on the edge of a tapestry chair, her posture as controlled as ever.

"I'm sure we all feel the same," said Fortuna. "And I must apologize, Miss Thorne, for having intruded at such a time. Had we known, obviously, we would not have come."

"Of course," answered Rosalind. "But we can safely assume the worst has passed. Ah, and here is the tea, and Mr. Mirabeau."

Indeed, the housekeeper and the young man entered the room together.

Thank goodness for tea, thought Rosalind. The ritual of pouring out, of passing cups, of inquiring who would have bread and butter and who cake, gave everyone time to compose and adjust themselves.

"You must know why we've come," said Helen at last. "As you can see, I've spoken with Mirabeau."

"She's told me everything," added Mirabeau. "She thought, that is, we thought, it would be best if I came here to let you know I am not afraid of whatever might be discovered."

So. Her bluff, such as it was, had been called. Rosalind set her cup down and folded her hands.

"And you, Mrs. Graves?" Rosalind asked. "What is your opinion?"

Fortuna took the time to sip her tea before she answered. "The matter of Colonel Corbyn's death has been shamefully handled," she said carefully.

Louisa, Rosalind noted, was staring at her tea cup.

"I am very sorry to say it," Fortuna went on. "But since you ask, that is what I think. I'm sure much talk has been encouraged that should not have been, and the distress to all the family has been considerable. I have tried to encourage Helen to take her concerns to Lord Casselmaine . . ."

"Fortuna, Lord Casselmaine does not want to hear me," said Helen hoarsely. "He has made that very plain."

"But, Helen . . ." began Fortuna.

Louisa put her cup down on the table. "Casselmaine thinks Colonel Corbyn killed himself."

They all turned to stare at her. Louisa responded with a defiant lift of her chin.

"He told me," she said. "It's why he made the coroner bring in a verdict of accidental death. So the family wouldn't have to bear the consequences." Louisa met their astonished expressions, and her determination seemed to wilt, at least a little. "I'm sorry to have just . . . come out with it like that, but I didn't want any of you thinking Casselmaine was doing something, well, not right." She looked right at Rosalind while she said this. "He's only trying to help."

Rosalind expected Helen to make a passionate denial of this possibility. The only sign of distress Helen permitted herself, however, was a slight trembling of her chin.

"I had thought of that," she said at last. "How could I not, given the way he was? I thought perhaps he provoked the quarrel with Peter"—the glance she gave him was filled with apology—"because everything had just become too painful. But—" She swallowed and could not go on.

"But it's the same problem with my having shot him," Peter finished flatly. "If William had already planned on dying in the duel, why kill himself ahead of it?"

"Perhaps he thought you would not come," suggested Rosalind. "Or would not shoot."

"He was dead before dawn," said Peter. "I was not late. Or at least, Helen wasn't late. I hung back to give her time to get there ahead." He met Rosalind's gaze. "You can ask Earnest Worthing if you don't believe me, Miss Thorne. He was my second, and he was there for the whole of it."

"What about Colonel Corbyn's second?" asked Rosalind. "Bartolemew Vaughn?"

Helen looked to Mirabeau, who sighed.

"Bartolemew Vaughn was probably the worst possible

choice for a second," he said. "My man, Worthing, went to
him to try and hash it all out, but instead of trying to make
peace, it was more like Vaughn wanted to start a fresh fight
with Worthing." Mirabeau shook his head. "Anyway, somebody, somewhere got wind of what was happening, because
a week before the appointed day, the Vaughns packed Bartolemew off to Ireland."

Rosalind thought about Cecilia, haunted by her own guilt.
It is my fault. And yet, she had tried her best to stop the
tragedy, and now it seemed she was not the only one.

That was when she saw Louisa was looking out the window. *She knows something else.*

"The Vaughns may have packed Bartolemew off," said
Helen. "But he didn't go."

Now everyone was looking at her, especially Mirabeau.

"You're surprised?" she answered. "Everyone knows it.
He went to London instead, maybe even to find his brother,
the one who's been cut off. But Emmaline George's brother
swears he saw him skulking about the Traveller, probably
looking for money or something."

Mirabeau was looking uncomfortably into his empty
sherry glass. *What part of this troubles you?* Rosalind wondered. *And didn't Cecilia tell me her brother was back? Is it
possible she doesn't know?*

"Suspicion," said Louisa suddenly. "That's what's happening!"

Helen, Louisa, and Mirabeau were all staring at one another. The tension between them was palpable, but it was
Fortuna who spoke.

"I believe you're right, Louisa." Fortuna turned to Rosalind. "I'm sure you know by now that Mrs. Vaughn is set on
having Cecilia marry Marius," she said. "Or at least, to get
him to offer for her. The Vaughns most certainly still want
the alliance. There are some serious property considerations,
but it would also allay suspicions."

"Because an offer, whether or not it comes to fruition, will mend appearances and confirm that Bartolemew had nothing to do with William Corbyn's death," said Rosalind, slowly.

"Yes," agreed Fortuna. "The Vaughn family is . . . diligent when it comes to protecting their own."

"Mr. Mirabeau," said Rosalind carefully. "What was the duel over?"

"No," said Mirabeau firmly. "I won't do it."

"Peter . . ." began Helen.

"No," he repeated. "This was a private matter, and it involves my honor as well as his. You may ask me anything you like, and you have my word, I will tell the truth. But the reason for my quarrel is between myself and William, and I will not tell it."

Even if it is allowing his killer to go unnamed and unknown? But before Rosalind could manage to form the words, the door opened and Mrs. Showell came in.

"Is there any news, Aunt Showell?" asked Louisa at once.

"Yes, yes, I've had word from Summers that Casselmaine is home. Everything seems to be all right. I'm sure he'll be in shortly." Her eyes narrowed. "And from the looks on your faces whatever you have all been talking about since I left has hardly been pleasant."

Louisa got to her feet. "Helen, you and Mr. Mirabeau should probably go before Casselmaine arrives."

"No," said Rosalind. "It is too late for that. You should all remain where you are. Mrs. Northey." She turned to the housekeeper. "Will you please tell his grace there are guests in the blue salon?"

"Rosalind!" cried Louisa. "You know Casselmaine will be angry if he finds us all here!"

Rosalind was too tired to argue, or to pull a veil of discretion over her words. "Yes, he will be angry. But at least he will know what's happening."

"Rosalind!"

"Louisa," she said sternly. "If Lord Casselmaine is angry, we will face that. I have told you all, I will *not* be responsible for bringing yet another secret into this house!"

They were all staring at her. Her cheeks were heating, not from the anger, but from having her anger heard. Which was ridiculous, but it was not to be helped.

Mrs. Northey looked to Mrs. Showell, who nodded.

That was when Devon, still in his dusty and disheveled work clothes, walked into the room.

"I see Parliament is in session," he remarked. "You will forgive me for being late for the sitting."

CHAPTER 18

The Perils of Private Conversation

Purblind man can judge only by the outward act.

Althea Lewis, *Things by Their Right Names*

"Casselmaine, is everything all right?" asked Mrs. Showell.

"Everything is calmed down," Devon replied. "All right will take longer. Mirabeau." He paused to nod to the young man. "Good to see you. Miss Corbyn. Mrs. Graves. Miss Thorne." They all returned polite murmurs of greeting. Devon ignored them. He was looking at Rosalind. She returned his gaze calmly.

"Your grace?" Helen stammered. "Is Marius . . . ?"

"Mr. Corbyn is fine." Devon crossed the room to the sherry decanter and poured himself a glassful. "He is angry, and I don't know how I'm going to convince him to stay on with us. Being locked in a hot shed for several hours may have pushed him too far." Devon looked deep into the sherry before he drank. "Now." Devon surveyed them all. "Is anyone going to tell me what's been going on in here?"

"Miss Corbyn is asking for my help," said Rosalind.

Devon swung round to face his young cousin. "Louisa! I asked you specifically—"

"Louisa is not to blame," Helen interrupted. "I have come

to Miss Thorne entirely on my own. I do not believe that William killed himself."

Fortuna's face went white. Helen, for her part, drew herself up. When she spoke, it was with a frozen, dignified certainty. "I also do not believe William was done in by a mantrap. He was shot, by some person, in the back. And before you try to tell me I cannot possibly know, I can. I have seen men shot before."

Very deliberately, Devon set down his sherry glass. He turned to Mr. Mirabeau.

"I confess I'm a little surprised to see you in this."

"You shouldn't be," answered Mirabeau. "Helen is to be my wife. It's my duty to make sure she's heard." He spoke calmly, but firmly. "If you'll forgive me, sir. She's not some hysterical housemaid, and"—he paused and swallowed, but found his words—"I was there, too, you'll recall, and she's right. Corbyn was shot in the back. I found no sign of spring gun or anything else, and given how cold it was . . . he can't have been dead for more than half an hour. I remember thinking if we'd been just a little sooner, we would have heard the shot."

Devon lifted his gaze to meet Rosalind's. He was exhausted, and he was angry. His voice was thick with both as he spoke to her.

"I am going to ask you all to excuse me and Miss Thorne, if you please," he said. "Mrs. Kendricks, you will stay, in case Miss Thorne wants anything."

That last, of course, was for propriety's sake, and because Devon knew as well as Rosalind that Mrs. Kendricks would take Rosalind's secrets to her grave.

Mrs. Showell got to her feet at once. "Yes, of course. Mrs. Graves, you did just say that you and Miss Corbyn wanted to be home in time to meet Mr. Corbyn when he returned from the digs? We should have Samuel bring your carriage around immediately. Louisa, come help me. . . ."

Still chattering, Mrs. Showell efficiently and politely herded the visitors from the salon. Mrs. Kendricks closed the door behind her and stood beside it, her hands folded and her eyes distant in that universal pose of a servant pretending to be invisible.

So much pretense.

Rosalind was tired to the bone and she sat back down, rather gracelessly. Devon, on the other hand, circled the room. He closed first one window, then the next. He looked out into the courtyard for a long time—watching all the business of the footmen ordering the grooms to order the boys to begin the business of bringing horses and carriage to the door.

"Rosalind?" Devon said finally. "What are you doing?"

At this moment, I am sitting here trying not to collapse into tears or exhaustion. But that, of course, was not what Devon meant. "Mostly, I seem to be listening to people plead with me to either help find out what truly happened to William Corbyn, or advise Helen Corbyn to stop asking questions."

That was plainly not the answer he had expected.

"So, it was not just Louisa," he said.

"No. What you saw after dinner yesterday night came from me telling Miss Corbyn I would not make any inquiry around her brother's death, because I would not help her keep a secret from her fiancé. I thought this would put an end to the matter. I'm afraid I underestimated her. Well, both of them, in fact." Rosalind's smile was brief and rueful. "This morning, Miss Corbyn told Mr. Mirabeau all her suspicions, and what she'd done about them, and probably a good deal else. His response, as you saw, was to agree to come here and help plead her case to me again. They were all here when Mrs. Showell and I arrived, and I am sorry it happened." She turned her face toward the windows. "Now is hardly the time I would have chosen."

Outside, Mirabeau and the footmen were helping Mrs.

Graves into a light touring carriage. Then he and Miss Corbyn mounted their horses. As soon as she was settled in the saddle, Helen turned around and gazed back toward the house. It was too far to see the expression on her face.

"I can't believe Fortuna Graves is complicit in this," muttered Devon. "The rest of them may as well still be children, but she's a grown woman of some hard experience. She should have held them back."

Yes, thought Rosalind. *She should have. Why didn't she?*

"Cecilia Vaughn spoke with me today as well."

Devon stared at her in disbelief. "What did Miss Vaughn have to say?"

It is my fault. Except if William killed himself, it couldn't be. But while Devon had relied on Louise to spread the word to Helen, he hadn't thought to make sure Cecilia heard.

Unless she had heard and had not believed. Or she feared William was likely to do himself an injury and felt she had not done enough to stop it. Or . . .

Or, or, or . . . Wearily, Rosalind dragged her thoughts back to her current conversation. "What Cecilia had to say matters less than the fact that she felt the need to speak at all. Devon, Cecilia is in a very difficult position. Now that William Corbyn is dead, Cecilia's mother is trying to maneuver her into a marriage with Marius Corbyn. She doesn't want the match, but she's being pressured into it, possibly to protect her brother Bartolemew."

Devon was staring at her. "Bartolemew was sent away. I made sure of it."

So. The someone who got wind of the duel was Devon himself. Rosalind wondered who told him.

"He did not go," said Rosalind. "He's been seen in the district. And if I, a stranger to the neighborhood, has found that out, you may believe that some or all of the Vaughns already know it. Other neighbors, such as Lady Pennyworth, may also know, and as the Vaughns are not universally popular with the older families in the district, they might be looking for a way to use it. Add in Helen's ongoing suspicions, and life may be about to become very difficult for the Vaughn family, especially poor Cecilia."

Devon let out a long breath. "You haven't even been here two whole days."

"This is how I maintain my living, Devon. I listen, I watch. I find the problems and I sort through them, and yes, I work to get people to talk to me even if they don't want to. I had thought to be doing it on my own behalf while you and I . . . well . . . came to know each other again. But I do not seem to have been granted that luxury."

Devon sighed, and the look in his eyes made her heart shrink. "I thought I'd dealt with all this."

"You clearly had, for a time."

"Next you're going to tell me that people will be talking about that as well."

"You already know they will be, if they aren't already."

"Yes," he agreed, and fell silent.

Rosalind, however, could not let him remain silent. There was a question she needed answered, and it could not be put off.

And if this is the beginning of the end of us, then that is as it must be.

Rosalind took a deep breath.

"Devon?" she said. "Why did you lie to Louisa?"

CHAPTER 19

Suspicion and Speculation

*If the mark is in the forehead, it is reasonable to
conclude that the murder has been committed.*

Althea Lewis, *Things by Their Right Names*

Devon's head jerked back as if Rosalind had dealt him a
physical blow. "Louisa said I lied?"

"No," answered Rosalind. "She said you told her William
Corbyn killed himself."

"He did." Devon spoke with regret, and with perfect seriousness. Rosalind had seen him at his best and his worst. She
knew without question that he believed what he was telling
her now.

"But how can that be?" she demanded. "Helen and Mr.
Mirabeau both saw the body. You heard them just now. They
say he had been shot in the back."

Rosalind was angry. She was tired. This was as far as possible from any conversation she wanted to be having with
Devon. She suddenly and soundly resented Helen Corbyn for
laying this matter at her feet. Equally, she resented her own
foolishness for having been glad to receive that letter in the
first place.

I am guilty as Alice of assuming any friend of Louisa's

*would be a little girl with little problems, and that this would
all prove a pleasant distraction from my own worries.*

Devon circled back to the hearth where he'd left his sherry
glass. He picked up the glass and set it where it belonged on
the silver tray with the decanters. It was an instinctual reflex
to fix the first little thing that came to hand.

She understood the impulse very well.

"I also saw the body, Rosalind," he said finally. "Miss
Corbyn and Mirabeau saw a loved one lying dead in the faint
light of a foggy morning. They were distressed, confused, and
frightened. The scene itself must have been an utter mess. I
was with the coroner as he completed his examination, in
good light, with plenty of time to review the details."

Devon sat down in the tapestry-backed chair, so he would
be closer to eye-level with her. He rubbed his hands together,
as if remembering a chill, or an unwelcome touch. "William
Corbyn was shot through the heart. The wound was inflicted
by a double-barreled pistol, not a dueling weapon. It was
held close against his chest. I asked the coroner to call the
death an accident so he could be decently buried, and so
Helen and her family could be spared at least some measure
of heartbreak."

Rosalind bowed her head. She knew how suicide cast a
pall over the entire family. Alice and George Littlefield endured not just personal impoverishment, but personal isolation when word got out that their father had killed himself.

Rosalind felt herself slowly and awkwardly adjusting to
this news. She believed Devon. What he said made sense, and
yet, Cecilia Vaughn's desperation still rang in the back of her
mind. Cecilia believed Helen was endangering herself by
keeping alive the questions and rumors around William's
death. But if Cecilia was worried that William's suicide might
be made public, why was she talking to a stranger? Why not
enlist Louisa? If Cecilia did not think Louisa would listen,
why not got to another friend? Surely there were other people close to her who could help, starting with Fortuna Graves.

Why turn to me?

"Rosalind," said Devon. "I understand that you want to help, but truly, this is not your problem to solve."

"Perhaps not, but it has been brought to me." Rosalind rallied her wits. She must find a way to make Devon understand the trouble went much deeper than a few scattered rumors. "It will not, however, stay with me. Helen's grief and suspicion will not permit her to let the matter go. In her distress, she has managed to convince both Louisa and Mr. Mirabeau to take her side, and you know as well as I do that Louisa's nature will not permit her to keep silent on a matter she feels deeply about."

Devon acknowledged the truth of this with a small, tight smile.

"Let us lay aside the very real possibility that these doubts could be preyed upon to make trouble." Against her will, Rosalind remembered Lady Pennyworth and her knife-sharp smile. She imagined that lady pretending to believe Helen's concerns about William's death, and telling some little story to plant the thought that the Vaughns had more to do with the affair than supposed. She could not permit poor, pale Cecilia to be used in that way.

"If I simply repeat a story Helen has already heard, she will continue to reject it out of hand, and she will continue to talk." Rosalind paused, struggling to put the jumble in her mind in the proper order. "However, if I do ask some questions, it may be that I will be able to find some independent proof that Colonel Corbyn did die by his own hand. But at the very least, I will be able to legitimately urge both Helen and Louisa to have patience until I have more facts in hand." Rosalind paused as a new idea came to her. "I might even be able to buy enough time to make sure the wedding is not disrupted."

Devon scrubbed at his face with both hands and then looked hard at them. Dirt stained his palms and more streaked his face. He should go wash, rest, and change. So should she.

Neither one of them moved.

"I wanted to show you my home," he said to his stained palms. "I had planned to sweep you off your feet with the beauty of this place. I wanted you to be able to see yourself as part of this setting, this life here. Instead . . . good Lord, Rosalind, you haven't even gotten to see the gardens properly yet."

She shook her head. "Nothing ever seems to go as planned for us."

"No, it doesn't," agreed Devon. Then, he paused. "What do you *want* to do, Rosalind?"

Rosalind was not asked this question very often, and she found she had no answer ready for him.

Rosalind looked out at the courtyard. It was empty of activity now. The gates were still open, showing the way out.

What do I want to do?

"I want to drive out with you, so you can show me the whole countryside," she said. "I want to read and talk with you. I want to remember old acquaintances and form new ones. I want to see these magnificent gardens properly, and the ruined castle, and hear all about the lost servant girls haunting the upper halls. I want Louisa to be splendidly married while I hand Mrs. Showell endless numbers of handkerchiefs because she keeps soaking them through with tears of joy."

The words poured out of her. Too many and too fast. It was positively unseemly, but she did not stop.

"I want to dance on the lawn in the twilight after Louisa and Mr. Rollins leave on their wedding trip. I want to dance with you, Devon, and ruin my slippers doing it, because I still cannot waltz, never mind jig step. I want to spend time with you—the way we never got to when we were so filled with feeling for each other all those summers ago." At last, she was able to draw breath. "I want all these things, but I also want to help."

Devon was staring at her. Rosalind felt an unwelcome flush of shame spread across her cheeks. But even so, she could see that Devon's whole expression was one of warmth, and not a little bit of amazement. Then, he stood and walked to her chair. He lifted her unresisting hand and he held it. His hand was warm, and the touch of it was strong. His fingertips were rough and the nails ragged and dirty. And Rosalind felt a rush of giddy warmth through the whole of her.

"Then let us make these things all happen, both of us, together." He smiled—his unfair, devastating smile that had been her weakness from the very first time she saw him.

"And the rest of it?"

Devon's smile faded. Rosalind felt its absence like an ache. He pressed her fingers warmly, a kind of promise that she was more than willing to accept.

"You will be careful?" he said. "There's a lot of high feeling in the district right now. I would hate for your . . . inquiries to be used as an excuse to inflame unrelated grievances."

"About poaching?"

"About the fear of poaching at least, yes. Then there's the resentment against the new workers, or rather, against the Irish and the Scots, who just happen to make up the majority of the people actually doing the digging on the works." Devon huffed out a sharp sigh. "And then there's all the usual tensions. You're right about the Vaughns and the Pennyworths. They're at perpetual loggerheads, and any one of them will seize on any excuse to take sides and make what trouble they can."

"Ah, the peaceable English countryside," murmured Rosalind. "I cannot think why I waited so long to visit."

"I imagine you are finding it quite a change after all the pettiness and social climbing of a London Season."

"I look forward to discovering the regenerative properties of fresh air and tedium."

"When you do, let me know."

They both pulled faces at each other, and the atmosphere between them eased.

"I will be careful," she promised him. "And I will do my best to find a way through." *For both of us.*

"I ask only that you do not shut me out, Rosalind. Let me . . . be there for you and with you."

Rosalind's mouth went dry and she was very aware of a fluttering in the base of her throat.

I've missed you, Devon. "I will try."

He smiled again and so did she, and in her heart, she felt their unsteady beginning become just a little firmer.

Rosalind wanted to keep her attention on this feeling of coming together again. She did not want to feel any nagging uncertainties bubbling in the depths of her mind.

Like the fact that just because a man was shot at close range from the front did not have to mean he shot himself. Especially when if he wanted to die, arrangements were in hand.

Especially when there was one hotheaded Bartolemew Vaughn lurking in the background. Especially when Bartolemew's parents seemed very sure he needed protection.

Or they do.

Especially when Devon did not mention when, or whether, anyone found that double-barreled gun that shot him.

CHAPTER 20

What Is Said Behind Closed Doors

It was clear she was aware of my feelings and suspicions—still more clear that the matter would not rest here . . .

Theodore Edward Hook, *Cousin William* or
The Fatal Attachment

Louisa, it turned out, had decided to wait for Rosalind in her apartments.

"I'm sorry!" Louisa leapt from the chair as soon as Rosalind entered her private sitting room and ran to embrace her. "You must believe me, if I'd known what you and Casselmaine were going through, I would *never* have invited Helen and Peter to wait!"

"I know, Louisa." Rosalind extricated herself from her friend's embrace, which threatened to become tearful. "And it's all right." *At least I hope it will be.*

She was so tired, and while her conversation with Devon had given her much hope, it had also raised fresh doubts. She needed time and space to think about both.

But Louisa did not notice Rosalind's abstraction. She was too deep in her own outrage.

"What can Casselmaine have been thinking!" she cried.

"Telling me William killed himself! As if lying to me would help Helen—"

Rosalind cut her off. "He might not have lied." She would set aside the question of the gun for later. It did not serve her now.

"But you heard Helen—" Louisa began.

"And I heard Devon." Rosalind sank into the chair by the fire and tried to find the words Louisa might actually be ready to hear. "Louisa, you have to consider the possibility that Helen made a mistake."

"Oh, not you, too!"

Rosalind forced herself to keep her voice steady. "Louisa, either we consider that Helen made a mistake, *or*"—she held up her hand to forestall the next outburst—"we consider that Devon lied, first to you, knowing full well you would repeat the lie to Helen. And that he embellished that same lie again just now, to me." She paused to make sure Louisa truly understood what she had just said. "Do you really think he's done that?"

It was not an idle or scolding question. Rosalind was very aware that she and Devon had been apart for years. They had both changed. Louisa, however, had been living in his house for two years now, when she was not in London for the Season. At this point, she might know Devon better than Rosalind did.

Rosalind found herself holding her breath.

Louisa twisted her fingers, and blushed, and smoothed her skirts. "No," she said. "I don't think he'd deliberately lie to you. I'm sorry, Rosalind. I'm probably making a horrid mess of things. I just . . . I want to *do* something."

"I understand, believe me," Rosalind told her. "But it has to be the *right* something. That means we have to be willing to consider that Helen is wrong."

"Or that Casselmaine is," added Louisa.

Rosalind nodded. "Yes, not lying, just mistaken."

"How do we find out?"

"We ask questions."

"What if no one will talk to us?"

Rosalind shook her head. "Keeping secrets is difficult. When someone is lying publically, it's generally possible to find it out, especially if one exercises multiple avenues of inquiry."

Louisa's eyes lit up again. "Such as?"

Rosalind considered. Her head was beginning to ache and she desperately wanted another cup of tea, in peace this time. She could not, however, let this opportunity pass. They actually had very little time to sort this disaster out if they wanted to be clear of it in time for Louisa's wedding.

Which gave Rosalind a new idea. "Louisa, would you be willing to enlist your Mr. Rollins to the cause?"

Louisa looked startled. "Gladly, but what can Rollins do?"

"William Corbyn was visiting his banker in town. It might be beneficial to know who his banker is and what business Colonel Corbyn was conducting there."

"Oh! Yes, of course. I will ask at once. Now." Louisa suddenly became quite serious. "He may not know, or be able to say. He has to be very careful about confidential business matters."

"Of course," said Rosalind. "But you can ask, and if he does not know the answers, he may be able to say who would know."

Louisa tilted her head. "Is this what you do? It's like trying to find out who has an extra ticket to a popular concert."

Rosalind smiled tiredly. "This is what I do, and it is exactly like that, except it's a question of information rather than tickets."

"Who else have you talked to?"

But this time, Rosalind shook her head. "I'm not ready to say just yet, Louisa. But I very much need your help for the next few days." She leaned forward. "I will be more likely to find what we need to know if I work discreetly and without arousing unnecessary suspicion." *Although it may already be too late.* "I ask you to help buy me a few days. Do your best to convince Helen that things are being done, and that she needs to keep as calm as she can and wait while . . . certain letters are answered, for instance."

It did not feel like much, but it was evidently enough for Louisa to seize upon.

"Oh, Rosalind!" she cried. "I knew you wouldn't let us down."

Oh, Louisa, sighed Rosalind in her mind. *I do hope that's true.*

But she had no time to say so, because just then a knock sounded on the door. Mrs. Kendricks moved to answer it.

"Now who . . ." began Louisa. Then she saw the look on Rosalind's face. "Oh." Louisa blushed.

Rosalind's supposition was correct, and Louisa's blush was justified, because as soon as Mrs. Kendricks opened the door, Mrs. Showell sailed into the room.

"I was afraid I would find you here," Mrs. Showell said to Louisa, who for once did not seem to muster any righteous indignation. "Honestly, Louisa! I know we must all make allowances for a young bride, but you must cease plaguing poor Rosalind. She's exhausted." She took her niece's elbow firmly. "I'm going to inform Mrs. Northey you will be taking your dinner on a tray tonight, Rosalind. Mrs. Kendricks—"

"I'm fine, truly," interrupted Rosalind. "Louisa is here because I needed to speak with her." Mrs. Showell looked entirely skeptical, but Rosalind did not give her time to object. "I am glad you're here as well. I am very much in need of your help."

"Rosalind, please, tell me that this has nothing to do with Helen's ridiculousness about her brother's death."

"She's not ridiculous." Louisa gently but firmly removed her elbow from her aunt's hold. "She only . . ."

"Louisa, I am not going to continue this argument," said Mrs. Showell wearily. "It has already been a very long day."

"I was hoping to ask what the dowager's reaction to the news about Devon was," said Rosalind.

Mrs. Showell seemed taken aback. Louisa looked tempted to add something, but Rosalind shot her a warning glance, and for once, Louisa subsided.

"Well," said Mrs. Showell. "For an agreeable change, my sister appeared genuinely concerned about her son. She even asked to be informed when Casselmaine returned."

"Mrs. Showell," began Rosalind carefully. "Devon said that when William Corbyn died, Lady Casselmaine became quite ill. . . ."

"Rosalind." Mrs. Showell rubbed her forehead. "I have no interest at all in continuing that particular subject."

"I know, but you've seen for yourself that my presence here has created a storm." Rosalind leaned forward. "Whether any of us want it this way, or whether it could have been prevented, is beside the point. I believe the situation will worsen, if only because Mrs. Vaughn thinks she can make some kind of use of me against Lady Pennyworth." *Or* vice versa.

"Oh, those two! I swear I don't know—" Mrs. Showell stopped herself and narrowed her eyes at the younger woman. "Rosalind, are you serious?"

Rosalind nodded. "I know Devon hoped that the coroner's verdict would quash any rumor or scandal around William Corbyn's death. It hasn't worked. There are too many secrets left beneath the surface, and they were brewing even before I came."

Mrs. Showell was silent for a time. Rosalind very much feared she was trying to find a polite way to tell Rosalind that she was too new to the district to be sure of any such thing.

"I was afraid of something like this." Mrs. Showell sighed and sat on the sofa in front of the hearth. "Mrs. Kendricks, will you send for tea? It appears we are going to be here awhile yet."

CHAPTER 21

The Deeds of Banished Men

*We have fallen into the discussion of a subject
which an hour ago I thought I could rather die
than touch upon.*

Theodore Edward Hook, *Sayings and Doings*

Rosalind had, of course, hoped Mrs. Showell would agree to stay and talk. There were many questions she needed to ask. She just wished that good lady did not look as tired as she herself felt.

"I suppose I knew the matter could not be put off forever." Mrs. Showell gazed with forlorn fondness at her niece. "I had hoped we could at least get Louisa married before it all came to a head."

Louisa came to sit beside her aunt and took her hand consolingly. "We will make it right, Aunt. You'll see. Rosalind can see through a brick wall, if she wants to, and have you ever known me not to get my way?" She beamed and Mrs. Showell actually laughed.

The tea arrived. Mrs. Showell performed the work of pouring out, and Rosalind drank her cup thirstily, grateful for the calming warmth and for the presence of stout slices of brown bread and new butter.

"Now," said Mrs. Showell when she'd drained her own cup. "What is it you plan to do, Rosalind?"

"I don't know, entirely," Rosalind admitted. She refilled Mrs. Showell's cup and tried to gather her own wits. But no ordered image came to her mind. Instead, what her thoughts showed her was Mrs. Vaughn, picnicking on the grass beside the drainage site, her plumes bobbing in the wind and her energies directed toward engaging Mr. Corbyn's interest for her distant, worried daughter.

"Mrs. Showell, what can you tell me about Cecilia Vaughn?" asked Rosalind. "Was there any problem with the engagement to William? Did Cecilia have any other beaus?" Rumors of Cecilia being seen with another man or engaging in other unexpected behaviors could very well trigger a duel with a short-tempered man.

It could also be feeding Cecilia's conviction that Colonel Corbyn's death is her fault.

"There was no other beau that I knew of." Mrs. Showell looked to Louisa, and Louisa shook her head. "And, of course, Mr. and Mrs. Vaughn were perfectly *thrilled* to have their Cecilia engaged to William Corbyn."

"Especially once the late Mr. Corbyn died and William inherited," muttered Louisa. Mrs. Showell gave a disapproving frown, but did not disagree.

"Was Cecilia thrilled with the engagement?" asked Rosalind.

"She always seemed content," said Mrs. Showell.

Louisa pulled a face at her teacup.

"What is it?" Rosalind raised an inquiring brow.

"She was happy with the betrothal, I'll say that," said Louisa. "But it never felt like she was happy with Colonel Corbyn himself, personally, if you see what I mean." Their expressions must have signaled they did not, because Louisa frowned. "When Rollins comes into the room, I feel . . . warm, like the whole world has just gotten that much brighter, and it shows. I know it does. But when Cecilia and Colonel Corbyn were together, I never saw that kind of warmth between them. Not even a little."

"Not everyone shows their feelings as openly as you, Louisa," said Mrs. Showell.

"Yes, I am aware of that, but this was more than Cecilia being reserved. How to explain?" She furrowed her brow. "Cecilia talked about wedding plans. She talked about all the frustrations between her and her family, and about Corbyn Park and all the improvements she was planning, and how nice it was going to be to have Helen there, even if it was just until Helen married Mirabeau. But Cecilia never talked about *William*, do you see what I mean? She never said anything about presents he sent, or drives they took, or what he said to her over dinner. None of that."

"And when he died?" asked Rosalind. "How was she then?"

"She was shocked, of course," said Mrs. Showell. "As we all were."

Rosalind looked to Louisa.

"It was the same," Louisa said. "She *was* shocked, and she was very much worried about what would happen to her next, but she wasn't grieving. Even allowing for greater reserve," she added, glancing sideways at her aunt. "I could be mistaken," she acknowledged reluctantly. "Cecilia and I are not particularly close." She paused. "Cecilia's not really close to anyone."

"She's certainly not a social creature," agreed Mrs. Showell. "She almost never comes to the public assemblies, which is perhaps just as well, as there was never any question of Cecilia having even a modest Season."

"Wasn't there enough money?" asked Rosalind.

"Oh no, there was plenty of money. It's . . ." Mrs. Showell paused, searching for words. "A woman with nine children to supervise may be excused if she is perhaps overly diligent when it comes to finding places and matches for them. But, I promise you, Rosalind, in all my years, I've never seen anyone quite like Hildegarde Vaughn. She manages her children's futures as if they were a string of horses and she was the stable master. The expectations for each one were laid out when they were small, and they have all been made to understand that if they disappoint, they will be . . ." She hesitated.

"Cut off?" suggested Rosalind.

"It's already happened to one of the boys," said Mrs. Showell.

"Bartolemew?"

"Oh no. His banishment is strictly of a temporary variety. This is the second son."

"Lucian," put in Louisa. "Of all the boys, he's closest to Cecilia."

"This is the first I've heard of him," said Rosalind. But in her mind, she saw Cecilia's worried expression. *It is my fault.*

"The Vaughns never mention him anymore," said Mrs. Showell. "I've heard Mr. Vaughn went so far as to black his name out of the family Bible. It's said Lucian left, or was thrown out of the house, in the middle of the night. No one in the district has seen him or heard of him since. At least, no one who has said anything to me."

"Is it known if he's still in the country?" asked Rosalind. *Or still living?*

"Mr. Mirabeau would know if anyone does," said Louisa. "Or Mr. Worthing. They were all friends together."

So, of the three eldest Vaughn children, one was packed off for his part in a duel, one was cut off from the family entirely, and one was being used as a pawn to increase the family holdings.

In Rosalind's experience, when children were raised by ambitious parents, they tended to develop ambitions for themselves.

"We know that when Bartolemew Vaughn was sent away, he did not go to Ireland as he was supposed to." Rosalind spoke slowly, letting the thoughts come together in her mind. "He went to London instead. Why is that? Could he have gone to find Lucian?" A person who was thrown onto their own resources would naturally gravitate to the capital, where opportunities, and the chance for anonymity, were greatest.

"It's possible," said Louisa.

"But I can't think why," said Mrs. Showell. "Bartolemew's a scalawag and a hothead, but he isn't a fool. If Mr. Vaughn found out he was talking to Lucian, Bartolemew would be risking his entire inheritance."

"Maybe he means to forge a reconciliation between his father and his brother?" suggested Rosalind.

"My dear, I doubt Bartolemew knows what the word means."

As Rosalind considered this, an unwelcome idea bloomed inside her. Mrs. Showell obviously noticed her change of expression. If she guessed its cause, she said nothing about that. She just set her cup down.

"Come, now, Louisa. This really has all become too much. I insist on your lying down before dinner, if only so I can have a nap myself, and Rosalind looks like she's ready to fall asleep in the bread and butter."

"I am rather tired," murmured Rosalind.

Louisa came and kissed her cheek. "Thank you," she said. "For everything."

Mrs. Showell took her niece out of the room. Rosalind stayed where she was with the remains of the tea, and a series of most unpleasant thoughts swirling through her mind.

Rosalind remembered that first night, in the matron's circle. She remembered Mrs. Vaughn's disavowal of London life and how much she liked the country.

She remembered how at the time, she thought lady protested too much. At the time, Rosalind had believed this praise of country society was a way for Mrs. Vaughn to flatter her neighbors. But what if it was something else?

What if the Vaughns had needed to leave London? It would hardly be the first time that London had become too difficult or dangerous for a family and they decided to settle in the country instead.

Mr. Vaughn had been a solicitor. Solicitors could become involved in so many different sorts of dealings.

This is all speculation, Rosalind tried to tell herself. *I know nothing. My mind runs this way because of what happened to my family, and to me.*

But it would explain a great deal. If Bartolemew and Mr. Vaughn had quarreled, proud, hotheaded Bartolemew might have decided he would not take his disgrace quietly. One way to fight back might be to deliberately seek out his even more disgraced brother, Lucian. For Lucian's part—a young man who was cut off from family and friends could easily find himself in desperate straits. Such a man could become bitter and might be convinced to go along with a brother's scheme to get some of his own back.

What if the brothers had decided to try their hands at blackmail?

What if William Corbyn had found out?

What if Cecilia did?

CHAPTER 22

An Unexpected Caller

*The hope of quitting the solitude of a house made
dreadful to me was tempting . . .*

Theodore Edward Hook, *Cousin William* or
The Fatal Attachment

Peter rode from Cassell House with Helen and Fortuna all
the way to the front door of Corbyn Park. Helen was
grateful. Fortuna had been unusually quiet since they left the
hall, and Helen found herself growing progressively more
nervous. She needed the sense of steady reassurance Peter's
presence provided.

Situated on a low hill above the fen country, Corbyn Park
was a wide, U-shaped, half-timbered edifice with a slate roof
and diamond-paned windows. There was a gravel yard in
front, along with a kind of courtyard-cum-kitchen garden.

Peter stayed mounted on Agamemnon while the groomsmen helped Fortuna out of the carriage and placed the step
so Helen could alight from Atalanta. As soon as she was on
the ground, she lifted her hand for Peter to bow over.

"All will be well, Helen, I'm sure of it," Peter murmured.
Then, more loudly, he added, "I won't stay. Mother and Father will want all the news about what happened out at the
digs today, and they'd better hear it from me before the gos-

sips get to work on it." Peter touched his hat brim to Helen and to Fortuna, who was now standing on the steps, and rode away down the park drive.

Helen watched him for a long moment before she turned and faced her home's open doors. She found herself hesitating. Again.

Helen hated this feeling of being afraid to walk into her own house. Outside, she might ride, or shoot, or do anything. Inside, though, she must be constantly on her guard. She must listen down corridors and around corners before she walked ahead.

She supposed she should be used to it by now. After all, it had begun when she was a child. Mother was always ready to scold any shortcoming in Helen's deportment, dress, or expression. After Mother died, her watchful eye was replaced by William's violent unpredictability. At any time, day or night, there might be a headache, or a rage, or a fit of despair. She might wake up in the morning to find out he'd tried to hurt himself again overnight.

And if she walked into the wrong room at the wrong time, he might try to hurt her again, too.

She had been as patient as she knew how to be. Following the doctors' advice, she'd ordered the household, the servants, and everything else she could think of, entirely for his care and comfort. She rallied all her girlhood training to hide her true feelings and keep up family appearances. She prayed, endlessly, for yet more patience.

Despite all her efforts, though, Helen had come to fear her brother, and to hate him. Worst of all, what came to her first when she saw him lying dead was sick, guilty relief.

That was why she had to find out what happened. She was sure the truth could ease the guilt. She could finally stop starting at shadows and listening around corners. She'd cease to imagine she still heard William's slow, faltering step, or the sound of him pouring himself yet another brandy.

Helen shook herself inwardly. This would accomplish

nothing except to make her morbid and melancholy. She lifted her chin and walked sedately into the house. Fortuna stood in the slate-floored entrance hall to let the maid remove her cloak and bonnet. If Fortuna wondered what had kept Helen lingering in the courtyard, she said nothing about it. Instead, she turned toward the head footman who was coming down the stairs carrying a canvas satchel.

"Has Mr. Corbyn returned yet, Wilcox?" Fortuna asked him.

"Not yet, ma'am."

"Is that the mail bag?"

"Yes, ma'am."

"I'll make sure Mr. Corbyn gets it." Fortuna held out her hand. The footman hesitated, but handed it across, and bowed and left them.

Fortuna faced Helen, her expression serious, and quite resigned.

"I imagine you would like to talk, Helen. Why don't we go to the book room? I can leave the mail bag there."

The book room was at the end of the western wing. By the peculiarities of the house that had been built in Tudor days and expanded on at random intervals ever since, the book room was connected to the little suite that served as Marius's private rooms. Its shelves were filled with volumes on building and architecture, where they weren't overflowing with papers and plans. There was a map cabinet in one corner and a filing cabinet in another.

Fortuna closed the door behind them. The draperies were closed, leaving them in an afternoon twilight.

"What is it you want to say?" asked Fortuna. She sounded tired, and worried. Helen's heart quailed.

"Do you think we can trust her?" Helen blurted out. "Miss Thorne, I mean."

Fortuna sighed. "You are a little late with the question, aren't you? You have already trusted her, and so we have no choice but to continue to do so."

"Fortuna—"

"Helen, please don't," said Fortuna quietly. "You have done this thing. It is happening. Choice has been removed."

"But you can't believe that William really did kill himself."

Fortuna rested the mail bag on Marius's desk, but did not let go. With her eyes adjusted to the dim light, Helen could see how tightly her cousin squeezed the canvas satchel.

"What I believe is neither here nor there. It's . . ." Whatever Fortuna had planned to say, she let it go unspoken. "Helen, you have a good heart," she said instead, her voice so tightly controlled that Helen feared something might soon break. "I want you to do well, I do, but you must learn there are reasons we are told to be discreet."

"What are you talking about?"

Fortuna shook her head. "Nothing. Never mind. Forgive me. It has all been too much. I need to rest and change for dinner. The one thing we do know is that Mr. Corbyn will be in an utterly foul mood when he gets home."

"He's already home and he already is."

The book room's inner door was pushed open and there stood Marius—disheveled, stubbled, and angry.

"Thank goodness you're all right, Marius" said Fortuna. "We'd heard the most distressing news."

"Well, I'm glad someone takes what happened today seriously." He dropped his leather satchel onto the desk and himself into the wingback chair. "To hear his grace tell it, it was all an afternoon's lark on the part of some of our more high-spirited lads."

"We were at the new hall when Miss Thorne returned, and—" But as soon as the words left her, Helen knew she'd said the wrong thing. Marius rounded on her.

"At the hall! What were you doing up there!"

Helen was so taken aback, it was Fortuna who had to answer. "Helen wanted to give Miss Winterbourne the good news," she told him. "She and Mr. Mirabeau have entirely made things up."

"Yes, that's right. Louisa's been so worried, I wanted to call and make sure she knew right away." Good Lord, she hated the tremor in her voice, and the way her stomach turned over as Marius glowered at her.

But slowly, he subsided. His expression smoothed, and if he didn't exactly manage to look pleased, at least he tried to become pleasant.

"Please believe me when I say that is excellent news, Helen," he said. "It's just that I've had a wretched day and . . . well, I've had a wretched day," he repeated, mostly to himself. "But there. Well. Should Mr. Mirabeau make any mention of wanting to come see me for a private interview, you can assure him I am at his disposal at any time."

"Thank you, Marius." *And thank you, Fortuna.*

Marius got to his feet and came back around the desk. He rested one heavy hand gently on her shoulder.

"I want you happy," he said. "I want you settled, and bringing Corbyn Park the heirs it so badly needs. I've been writing some of our cousins as well," he added. "To invite them to stay."

"You have?" Helen tried to rub the look of blank surprise off her face.

"How lovely," murmured Fortuna.

Marius actually smiled. "What you both mean is, what has gone so wrong with Marius that he is actually seeking out human company?" He sighed and turned toward the window, pulling back the drapes far enough to allow in a shaft of afternoon sunlight. "But I think it's time we faced the reality that all the acknowledged branches of the Corbyn family have an interest in the park. They *should* feel they are welcome here. We know that wasn't possible while William was alive. But that's changed." He drew his shoulders back, visibly mustering his determination. "You know I do not agree with Lord Casselmaine on much, but he's bringing his family back together, and that has been well done." Marius gazed out over their formal, old-fashioned gardens. "Very well done, indeed. It's what I want to do."

Helen felt a sprig of hope take root inside her. Something must have shown in her face, because as Marius glanced in her direction, he gave a very small, very wary smile. "Who knows?" he said. "I might even dance at your wedding."

"That should be a sight to see."

"I'm sure it will. I dance like a badger. The main thing, Helen, is I want you to understand this house needs you." He swallowed hard. "I need you. You're the one who is going to be able to make sure we continue as a family, and that the land is kept as it should be."

Marius's habitual, brooding intensity crept back into his eyes. Helen decided it was time to end this conversation while she could still keep her worries in check. She wanted to be able to just enjoy the fact that Marius was talking about taking part in the world again.

She caught Fortuna's eye, and her cousin nodded encouragingly.

"I promise I'll do my best," she said.

"I know it. You're . . ."

Before he could finish, they were interrupted by a scratching at the door. It opened and the butler, Wexford, came in and bowed.

"Excuse me, sir, but Mr. Nicholas Vaughn is here."

Helen felt her brows shoot up. Nicholas Vaughn was Cecilia's father.

"Vaughn?" Marius frowned. "What the devil could he want?"

"He will not say, sir, but he does say the matter will not wait."

"All right," said Marius, even though it plainly was not. Marius hated the Vaughns almost as much as Lady Pennyworth did. When William had announced he was marrying Cecilia, there were rows for days. Helen had spent so much time riding out, she'd all but injured Atalanta by overworking her. "Better show the man in."

"And we should go, Fortuna," said Helen. "We'll see you at dinner, Marius."

Marius waved in agreement and dismissal, but made no other answer. Helen took herself out into the corridor, one step behind Fortuna.

It was not until later that Helen realized Fortuna still had the mail bag with her.

CHAPTER 23

Purely Domestic Concerns

*He who trusts a secret to his servant makes his
own man his master.*

John Dryden

Wednesday dawned under lowering skies and Rosalind felt sure it must rain. But a brisk, contrary breeze drifted down over the fens and scattered the clouds, leaving behind a fine and sunny day that Rosalind, as it transpired, was able to enjoy much of.

Devon joined Rosalind, Louisa, and Mrs. Showell at breakfast. By silent agreement, they all spoke of small matters—the weather, letters from friends and family, and of what sort of progress Devon hoped for the drainage works that day. The one ripple of disquiet during breakfast came when the footman presented Rosalind with a silver tray containing a folded note addressed in the dowager's hand.

Rosalind picked it up, read the address, and put it back down.

"Thank you. Will you please take that up to my rooms and give it to Mrs. Kendricks?"

The footman bowed and removed the note, and himself. Rosalind returned to buttering her toast, very aware that everyone at the table was staring at her.

"I will read it when I have a private moment," she assured them all.

After breakfast, Rosalind and Mrs. Showell were able to spend the morning in Mrs. Showell's rooms, reviewing her lists and notebooks containing the details for the wedding.

As they talked, the footman again made an entrance, with his silver tray and another note. Rosalind gave him identical instructions.

"You are going to read those notes, aren't you, Rosalind?" asked Mrs. Showell.

"Possibly," said Rosalind. "If I receive any sign there's something important in them."

Mr. Firth Rollins arrived just in time for luncheon. Over a light meal of ham pie, greens, apple tart, and cheese, the conversation was confined to plans for their wedding trip to the lake district to visit some family of Mr. Rollins. After that, they would spend a month with Louisa's family, before returning to London to establish their new household before the new Season opened.

They had not yet finished the tart when the next note arrived and was sent away again.

"Lady Casselmaine's going to be furious with you, Rosalind," remarked Louisa, sounding slightly awed.

Rosalind finished her bite of tart and touched her napkin to her mouth. "There are some persons who do not ever want to be seen to make a fuss, or a decision, and yet who wish to have everything very much their own way. The first rule I have found for dealing successfully with such people is to refuse to take the hint."

After luncheon, Mr. Rollins suggested a drive to Louisa, and Mrs. Showell declared that with all that had been happening, she needed to have a lie-down to recoup her strength. This left Rosalind a quiet space of time. The post had brought several replies to her initial round of letters, and she was glad of the privacy to review them with the care they deserved.

The notes from the dowager remained on her desk, untouched.

Rosalind worked diligently at her correspondence, answering kind and gossiping letters from friends with descriptions of the countryside, the grand house, and the drainage works. She avoided as much as possible all description of Devon, reasoning that was far too personal. She put these light notes on the tray to go out with that evening's post. She also penned a more substantive letter to Alice Littlefield. Events had reached the point where she needed Alice's connections as a newspaper writer, and quite possibly George's as well.

Then, Rosalind took a refreshing walk in the beautiful gardens, which were perfect for thinking. She returned to find another of Lady Casselmaine's notes had been added to the stack. This she also ignored.

All in all, the day was almost entirely peaceful.

The distance between "almost" and "entirely," however, loomed quite large in Rosalind's mind and weighed on her spirits.

Because the "almost" involved Mrs. Kendricks.

From the moment she rose in the morning, Rosalind knew something was wrong. As was their custom when Rosalind was visiting, Mrs. Kendricks took on the duties of lady's maid. This meant she was up and dressed long before Rosalind woke. Mrs. Kendricks also ensured that there was a pot of chocolate ready, so Rosalind could be refreshed before she dressed and went down to breakfast.

But this particular morning, while Mrs. Kendricks managed everything with her usual seamless efficiency, she also managed in absolute silence, and without meeting Rosalind's eye.

Which told Rosalind that not only was something wrong, it was serious. And unlike the dowager's notes, it could not be ignored.

Rosalind allowed herself to finish the chocolate so her

mind and nerves were relatively steady before she broached any subject. Even so, her beginning was hardly promising.

"Mrs. Kendricks, what is wrong?" she asked hoarsely.

Mrs. Kendricks had brought one of Rosalind's newer morning dresses out of the wardrobe and was brushing down the green muslin.

"Nothing's wrong, miss," she said. "Are you ready for me to take your tray?"

Rosalind did not budge. "You have not said a word to me all morning, not even about what happened yesterday."

Mrs. Kendricks gave the dress hem a vigorous shake.

Rosalind sighed. She had known this must come. She had just hoped to put it off a bit longer.

"I understand you must be disappointed . . ."

"Disappointed?" Mrs. Kendricks straightened and turned in one motion, her eyes wide with shock and—Rosalind's heart shriveled to see it—outrage. "You led me to believe that we would come here so you could finally reach an understanding with his grace."

"And I still hope that is the case."

"I'm very glad to hear it, miss."

The withering, and uncharacteristic, sarcasm in her tone sparked an equally uncharacteristic pique inside Rosalind. "Have you heard something contrary to this?"

"I've heard nothing but somethings," said Mrs. Kendricks. "This is a good house. It's well managed, with everyone in their place and living up to their work, but your name, miss, is running on everyone's lips, and that's after only being here two days!"

Rosalind felt her face go pale. Gossip belowstairs could be as deadly to a reputation as anything said in the drawing room. "What are they saying?"

"Everyone is talking about this Mr. Corbyn and how he died, and how Miss Thorne is asking questions and shows fair to be stirring up old troubles if she's not careful." Mrs. Kendricks looked quickly away. She was swallowing something harsh, that much was obvious. "Miss Rosalind, will you answer me something?"

"Yes, of course." Rosalind felt an absurd desire to fold her hands, as if facing her old headmistress.

"This business of asking questions about this poor man . . . did this only begin after you arrived?"

"No, Mrs. Kendricks," she said quietly. "I had a letter from Helen Corbyn, saying Miss Winterbourne had given her my name."

"I see."

Rosalind's spine wilted. "I'm sorry."

Mrs. Kendricks lifted her chin. "I have a right to know whether your being sorry will change anything."

"Yes, you do," agreed Rosalind. "And I do not have an answer for you."

Mrs. Kendricks stood there in silence for a long moment. At last, she said, "Is there anything else, miss?"

Tears threatened. Rosalind swallowed hard. "I will need to be ready to go to church with Lady Casselmaine this evening."

"Yes, miss."

Mrs. Kendricks collected the tray and left Rosalind alone, staring out the window at the still and silent gardens.

Mrs. Kendricks had been beside her through every disaster Rosalind had faced. She had been housekeeper to Rosalind's parents. She was there when Rosalind's father and sister vanished and the world fell apart. She had stayed as Rosalind began the long process of piecing together a new means of existence. She had worked when Rosalind could pay her, and when Rosalind couldn't. She had moved with Rosalind from house to house as her assorted acquaintances offered her temporary refuge. When those offers failed, she had moved into the tiny, shabby rented rooms in Little Russell Street, which was far too close to Covent Garden and the theaters, and all they brought with them.

Not that Mrs. Kendricks remarked on it. Oh no, never. She

had not wavered once. But the silent compact remained between them—one day there would be an end. They would return to that society that was home to them both. It was understood that Rosalind wished for that return as much as Mrs. Kendricks did.

The surest way to that goal, of course, was marrying Devon.

But now here she was—a guest in Devon's home, finally treated as her rank deserved, for Rosalind was the daughter of a baronet, and quite possibly about to be elevated to a duchess. This was her chance to make a reality of what she had always allowed everyone—beginning with Mrs. Kendricks—to believe was her fondest dream.

But what had she done instead? She had reverted to the ways of a useful woman. She had asked questions. She had interfered, and caused talk.

She had jeopardized her future, and Mrs. Kendricks's along with it.

Mrs. Kendricks was an aging woman. She had spent her life in service. Rosalind remembered she once said she'd started as an upstairs maid at ten years old. She must be tired. She must ache. She never said so, of course, but that was because of pride and expectations, not because those aches and that exhaustion did not exist.

Does she have any savings? Rosalind had no idea. It was not something she had ever really considered, let alone considered asking about.

She had always meant to provide for Mrs. Kendricks in her retirement. Had she ever said so? Had she any idea when Mrs. Kendricks wanted to retire? And if that was soon, and there was no marriage to Devon, could Rosalind provide for her? Rosalind knew her own bank account down to the farthing. There was nowhere near enough to establish even a tiny annuity. She could, of course, give Mrs. Kendricks room in her house, assuming she kept her house.

But what if things got worse? What if she lost her house? How could she ask Mrs. Kendricks to stand by her then? And what if Mrs. Kendricks had no choice? How could she find a new situation at her age?

What have I done? Rosalind bit her lip. *I have been as guilty as anyone of believing that because my servant stays with me, she must love me. I have forgotten that what affects me directly affects her.*

She tried to tell herself this was not her fault. She meant to help with a small matter, only to find it was very much larger than anticipated. The current situation she found herself in did not come about because she was curious or because secretly she wanted to be the one who found out what happened when no one else could.

It certainly did not come about because now that the possibility had become so real, she found in her heart she did not want to be Duchess of Casselmaine.

CHAPTER 24

The Foundation of a Marriage

As to marriage, what a serious, terrible thing!
Maria Edgeworth, *Tales of Fashionable Life*

Louisa was pleased that Rollins suggested a drive to the lake after luncheon. It would be a chance for them to talk and perhaps allow a little breathing space and privacy. Even better, since they were to be married in two weeks, Aunt Showell had relaxed the rules and allowed Louisa to take only her maid as chaperone.

Louisa had not met her fiancé at a ball or any grand entertainment. It had been at a perfectly ordinary dinner on a perfectly ordinary night at Casselmaine's London house. Casselmaine had been inviting bankers and investors since the start of the Season, trying to put together yet more money for the drainage works, and Mr. Rollins and his father had been among those invited.

It was the Season, so normally Louisa would have been out at some party or entertainment. That particular night, however, the invitations, or perhaps the fates, had conspired, and she dined at home.

She noticed Firth Rollins at the table. Then, she thought him amiable, and unexceptional. It was a conversation she overheard later in the hallway that led her to believe this amiable young man who might be useful to her cousin's plans needed some assistance. Or rather, his family did.

Louisa tracked Rollins down in the small gallery where Devon kept a few obligatory Renaissance-style paintings and family portraits. She approached casually and pretended to stop to examine the landscape that he was also pretending to examine.

"Good evening, Mr. Rollins."

"Good evening, Miss Winterbourne," he replied.

Louisa waved her fan. "It is very close in the drawing room, is it not?"

"Very," he replied. "I find it much cooler out here."

"There is something you should know, Mr. Rollins."

He lifted one brow. "I am all attention, Miss Winterbourne."

"I suppose I should say I shouldn't be saying this, but since I am going to, I won't bother. If your father is giving out loans to Lord Howell, he should stop. Now."

She waited for him to ask how such a little girl could possibly know anything about money, loans, or anything at all. But Rollins just looked down at her with his drooping eyes and nodded.

"Thank you," he said seriously. "I'll look into the matter."

Two weeks later, Aunt Showell came to her with a note. "This is for you, enclosed to me, from a Mr. Rollins."

The handwriting was neat and unadorned and rather small, more suited to writing figures in ledgers than notes to young ladies in their second Season. It was also quite brief and to the point.

You were entirely correct. Thank you. I hope we may talk again. Your obedient, F. Rollins

As beginnings went, it was dull. As men went, Firth Rollins was quiet, methodical, and, well, dull, at least outwardly. But suddenly, it seemed, Louisa saw him everywhere. Every rout, every card party, every concert or play, there was Mr. Rollins.

It turned out he was a credible dancer. A bit stiff, but he never trod on her toes or led her into the wrong figure, and he always managed to be first to ask whether there was a space on her card.

"You, sir, have been laying siege to me," she accused him after a particularly long country dance.

"I have done no such thing," he said as he steered her toward a miraculously empty seat. "I wished to see more of you. I discovered the means to do it and drew up a plan. And, as you see, it has worked."

She considered this. He smiled, and she considered that, too. "You dance very well for a banker," she concluded.

"Thank you."

"You have more interesting conversation than most of the men in this room."

"Again, thank you. Why do you look as if that's a problem?"

Louisa decided there was no point in beating about the bush. "I'm connected to a duke, but I've got no money of my own."

Rollins shrugged. "I'm connected to a bank that is doing very well and has recently avoided a large loss because of timely advice given by a lovely young lady with sharp eyes and a brain and a detailed knowledge of the aristocratic families of London."

"Last year I made an utter fool of myself over the death of an actor."

"Two years ago, I bought a high-flyer and a team of matched bays to go with it, and promptly overturned the lot within the first ten minutes of driving out."

"This isn't terribly romantic."

"Would you like it to be?" he inquired. "I have established

accounts with several florists, and I've been in serious conversation with my mother about acceptable gifts and entertainments, as well as how to issue the invitations and to whom. I took notes," he added.

Louisa burst out laughing, and somewhat to her relief, he grinned readily in answer. "Yes, by all means," she said. "Let us turn things romantic, but never tell my aunt I said any of this."

"You have my word." And the look in his drooping eyes said she had much more than that.

It was not a foundation for grand passion. But despite the occasional serious flirtation with the dramatic, Louisa was not really a romantic.

Devon spent generously to get her through her two Seasons, but Hugh's mismanagement of the estate had meant there would be no large settlement to back that up. Being a Winterbourne might open influential doors. The matrons behind those doors, however, knew everybody's bank balances, and Louisa's balance added up to nothing more than a pittance inherited from her grandmother. That meant she was, Winterbourne or no, the poor relation. A poor relation who was also a romantic could easily wind up at Gretna Green, and after that, back in the maternal home with a child on her knee and no future left at all.

But Rollins's family found the name to be enough. For bankers, the Winterbourne name meant a chance to be invited to Winterbourne dinner parties and make connections with Winterbourne friends.

As it happened, Louisa was rather good at dinner parties. Her accomplishments at music and painting and so forth could only pass muster among her most charitable relatives, but at conversation she had a talent.

And Rollins, with his head for figures, also turned out to have a great deal of sense. And he liked her, and she liked him. They talked endlessly—about banks and parties, and all the people at the theater, about his life, about hers. He read and sent her books, as well as flowers. He asked her opinion about whom he should talk to at the suppers and clubs he attended and whom he should avoid and whose tables he should very much try to gain admittance at.

They fit together. They worked together. She liked him. It was much more than enough.

"Shall we walk a bit?"

Louisa started. She'd been so lost in her own thoughts that she'd failed to notice they'd arrived at the lakeside. She let Rollins help her out of the carriage and accepted her parasol from her maid, Tincombe. Tincombe also climbed out to follow them up the wandering path, at a very generous distance.

The lake shone a lovely silver blue in the sunlight. Willow groves lined the banks, and the wild flags bloomed in profusions of purple, blue, and gold. Rollins gave Louisa his arm and they walked on easily.

"Do you think I should learn to fish?" asked Rollins. "It seems the gentlemen around here set great store by the sport."

"The gentlemen around here also set great store by riding about the countryside at breakneck speed and shooting at underfed rabbits."

"Not at the same time."

Louisa gave his arm a shake. "You know what I mean."

Rollins smiled. It was a very good smile. It did interesting things to his eyes, and it made her feel safe somehow. Like a warm blanket or a new spring day.

"Rollins, I need to ask a favor."

"Whatever I can do, my dear. Mind the tree root."

Louisa stepped around the offending object. "That's the problem, I'm not sure you can do it."

"Now you have me worried."

"You know this business with William Corbyn?"

"Now I am even more worried."

Louisa decided he didn't really mean that. "It seems that

before he died, Colonel Corbyn had been up to London a great deal, and, well, people are saying he was visiting his banker while he was there. It would be helpful to know what he was thinking of doing. Helen has no idea, and if Marius knows, he won't say. Well, to be frank, none of us has asked him, but I'm quite certain he wouldn't say if we did, because Marius never tells anyone anything."

Rollins arched his brow thoughtfully. "Who among us is asking this question?"

"Rosalind."

Rollins sucked in a long breath and let it out slowly. He looked so suddenly serious that for a moment Louisa thought he was going to refuse.

"I could point out that a man such as Colonel Corbyn who is getting married has plenty of reasons to visit his banker, but I suspect you would swat my arm and tell me you know that."

"Well, I would, if I wanted to be completely predictable," answered Louisa tartly. "But, you know that when some-one . . . dies . . . suddenly, sometimes money is involved."

"Sometimes, yes," Rollins agreed, blandly.

"And Colonel Corbyn was very much invested in the drainage works, and you know people say such awful things, about my cousin Casselmaine and . . ."

"And us. Yes," said Rollins grimly. "I've heard those things, too. Oh look, ducks." He frowned at the ragged line of paddling birds. "Those are ducks, aren't they?"

Louisa laughed. "Yes, dear, those are ducks."

"I shall never make a country gentleman, I'm afraid."

"Oh, thank goodness. Can you imagine me as a country wife?"

"I can imagine you as anything you choose to be."

Louisa paused to enjoy the warm, fluttery sensation that was still rather new to her. "Rosalind is hoping to stop those rumors by making sure people have real answers about, well, everything."

"You're the expert in society, and you think real answers are going to stop established rumor?"

Now it was Louisa's turn to smile. "I know, I know. But it does help. It's far better than no answer at all."

She waited for him to object. But his immediate response was limited to pulling out a small notebook from his pocket and leafing quickly through it.

"I have it here that Corbyn's London bankers were Percault and West," he said. "I know some of their people. I could ask if there'd been any . . . unusual activity before he died."

"Do you have that kind of information on all the district families?"

"I'm collecting it. It's a cross between an occupational hazard and a terrible habit." He smiled. "And now you can't say I didn't warn you." He snapped the book shut and tucked it away.

"There's nothing left to warn me about," she said. "You are a perfect windowpane, Mr. Rollins. I see straight through you."

"Oh good, because most people find me a little dense." He smiled again, and she gave his arm another shake. The truth was, most people underestimated Rollins. He had one of those faces. The other truth was, Rollins knew that, and sometimes made use of it.

"I'm just worried, Louisa," he told her softly.

"You're worried that we'll learn something none of us, including Helen, wants to know."

"Not to put too fine a point on it, yes."

"I know. I'm worried, too, but what's the alternative? You and I are leaving, and probably not coming back. We'll be fine, whatever happens. But Helen, and Fortuna, and, well, others have to stay. I don't want to leave them in a mess if I can help it."

"By others you mean your Miss Thorne?" he suggested.

"Yes, she needs this business to be finished, Rollins. So she and Casselmaine can . . . get on with things, if you see what I mean." She glanced away. "And it's my fault she's in it at all, so I have to help."

He laid his hand over hers. Not a condescending pat, but just a way to let her know he understood. Then he said, "Louisa, do you trust your Miss Thorne to keep a confidence?

"Of course I do. Do you know something?"

Rollins was silent for a while. He watched the ducks dipping below the water, pointing their tails toward the sky. "Not about the Corbyns, though."

"The Vaughns?" Louisa guessed.

"No, it's about the Mirabeaus, actually."

"The Mirabeaus?" she exclaimed. "Peter's people?"

Rollins nodded. "Something that is not generally known is how much the senior Mr. Mirabeau has invested in the drainage project."

Helen's fiancé and his family were respectable, and had been in the district forever, but they were hardly rich. "I thought it was the Corbyns who were doing the lion's share of the investing from around here."

"Oh, most of the monied men in the county are in it to one extent or another. Securing a wide pool of investors was a very intelligent move on Casselmaine's part. It helps ensure continued approval for the scheme, you see. But some families, like the Mirabeaus, well . . . they've invested far more than they can afford to lose. If something were to happen to disrupt the project, it would be very bad for them." Rollins's gaze drifted across the lake. "It could, in fact, become a matter of life and death."

CHAPTER 25

The Consolations of Religion

Her decision was neither the result of sound reasoning, nor evidence of a sense of outraged delicacy, betrayed confidence, and repentant error . . .

Theodore Edward Hook, *Cousin William* or *The Fatal Attachment*

That evening's church services were entirely unremarkable. The vicar proved to be a mild young man who took the commandment to love thy neighbor as his text and expounded upon it for the requisite quarter of an hour. The dowager listened the entire time with narrowed eyes and a tightly pursed mouth. Rosalind felt certain she was enumerating perceived faults in doctrinal reasoning.

Lady Casselmaine had met Rosalind in the foyer of Cassell House with much that same look, and all of that same silence. What words the dowager had, she reserved for her maid, the servants, and the coachman. It had been a long time since Rosalind had been so thoroughly ignored, and she found the effect more disconcerting than she would have imagined.

Normally, Rosalind would have taken comfort from Mrs.

Kendricks's presence beside her. She would have looked forward to hearing her housekeeper's observations of the congregation, and especially of the dowager. Today, however, Rosalind was all too aware of Mrs. Kendricks's determined silence, which felt ten times colder and ten times harder than Lady Casselmaine's ever could.

What am I do to? What promise can I give?

But there was none. She could not change course on the matter of William Corbyn's death now. She could offer no assurance about what direction she charted for her future, or even what she would come to believe or feel in the coming weeks.

To be without even the possibility of a plan was the worst form of nightmare to Rosalind. She took a deep breath and told herself she must have patience. She must trust that somehow, all would come right.

But things coming right and things being what she wanted were quite likely to be two different things. Especially since she felt no more certain of what she wanted now than she had when she arrived in Devon's house.

The Winterbournes, of course, had a private pew at the front of the commodious, wood-paneled parish church. This provided Rosalind with an excellent view of the rest of the congregation. As this was Wednesday rather than Sunday, the pews were only half full. Among the older ladies were a few single men, mostly in tweed coats and neck cloths, and some families with ruthlessly scrubbed, collared, and gloved children. Rosalind was surprised to see a solemn Fortuna Graves sitting toward the back. No one else from the Corbyn household sat with her.

Cecilia Vaughn was there, however, dressed in a lace-lined bonnet and a blue pelisse. A quartet of younger children and pair of sharp-eyed maids filled the pew beside her. Rosalind suspected these were some of her brothers and sisters and their nannies.

What put Rosalind in danger of actually staring, however, was the sight of Mr. Crease, the Vaughns' gamekeeper, in the very back pew. He dressed as she had seen him on the road, but otherwise was shaved and scrubbed with a clean red neckcloth. The gamekeeper she had last seen threatening the life of a sick man listened to the vicar's gentle sermon with every appearance of serious attention.

When the service ended, the congregation began the slow, shuffling business of reclaiming coats and hats, or having them reclaimed by servants; finding prayer books and gloves and other stray articles; and otherwise getting ready to depart.

"Get me on my feet, Quinn," the dowager snapped. "I have several things to say to that man."

"That man" was clearly the vicar. Rosalind found a moment to pity him.

"May I help you, ma'am?" Rosalind extended a hand. *It is time I put my attention back where it belongs.*

"Quinn is quite able to manage."

Rebuffed, Rosalind stood aside and let the dowager and her maid go first. She saw a glimmer of annoyance in Mrs. Kendricks's eye. To her own shame, she seized on to that as a good sign. *I have not entirely lost her sympathy*, she thought as they followed the dowager out of the church. She looked about her for Cecilia Vaughn, but Rosalind did not see any sign of her or her charges.

The evening was cooling. Sunset painted the sky pink and gold. As Rosalind lifted her eyes to admire the glowing colors, she saw Fortuna Graves standing underneath one of the oak trees that marked the boundary between the church green and the ancient graveyard. Fortuna met her inquiring gaze and gestured to the space beside her.

It was an invitation to come speak that was too plain to be mistaken, or ignored. It seemed, however, Fortuna was not the only one with a reason to address Rosalind. Just as she was turning toward Lady Casselmaine, Mr. Crease stepped right up into her path and touched his cap.

"It is Miss Thorne, is that right?" the gamekeeper's smile was filled with easy, if oily charm. "And how are you this fine evening?"

Rosalind drew herself up and leveled her most quelling glare. Before she could speak, however, Lady Casselmaine interrupted.

"Miss Thorne," she snapped. "Who is this person?"

"Archibald Crease at your service, your grace." The gamekeeper removed his cap and bowed deeply. "I met Miss Thorne in the duke's company t'other day and thought I'd make so bold as to inquire after her health."

Lady Casselmaine looked him up and down. "You're Vaughn's gamekeeper," she said in a tone of open accusation.

"That is correct, ma'am." Crease tried his oily smile on her. It had no visible effect.

"You caused considerable damage to a blameless tenant's cottage, Mr. Crease." Lady Casselmaine made no effort to keep her voice down. "Not to mention a costly delay and disturbance at his grace's drainage works."

Heads began to turn. Conversations fell silent. The dowager took no notice. She reserved the power of her disapproval entirely for Crease.

Crease attempted a smile, and an actual tone of condescension.

"Now, ma'am, if I may be so bold—"

"You may not," Lady Casselmaine cut him off. "I know your sort very well, sirrah. You are about to try to tell me Jim Soady, a man whose family has tended this land for generations, is harboring poachers! Well, I tell you, Crease, your employer is harboring delusions on the subject of his rabbits, and it will not do. It will not do at all! And you may tell Mr. Vaughn that Lady Casselmaine has said so."

Crease's wary eyes shifted back and forth. Not one person

moved forward. No one dared to speak. He tried to look at Rosalind, as if she was perhaps the dowager's caretaker. Rosalind lifted her brows toward him.

Crease bowed, but much less smoothly than he had before. Then he slapped his cap back on his head and stalked away. Around them, people went back to their conversations, all attempting to look as if nothing at all had happened.

Against all propriety, Rosalind stared—first at the gamekeeper and then at Lady Casselmaine.

"You appear surprised, Miss Thorne," said the dowager.

"I confess that I am, ma'am." *Again.*

"Did you think I neglect to keep myself abreast of the doings on my family's land?" She paused and sniffed. "I see you did *not* bother to read my notes."

Rosalind felt herself blush. "I beg your pardon, ma'am."

"And well you may."

"I did not know you felt so strongly regarding the subject of poaching."

"Had you read my notes, you would have known differently. Greed is a sin, Miss Thorne. 'Take heed and beware of covetousness—' "

" 'For a man's life consisteth not in the abundance of the things which he possesseth,' " Rosalind finished the verse.

Now it was the dowager's turn to look surprised. "Yes, exactly."

Rosalind took one step closer to Lady Casselmaine. She met and held that lady's gaze and spoke softly, so they should not be overheard. "If I did not believe you might address me on a matter of concern to your son and your people, ma'am, I can only plead that I had some reason to think you distrusted me and disliked my presence in your home."

Lady Casselmaine's eyes narrowed, favoring Rosalind with the exact same look she'd levelled at the vicar. Then she abruptly turned away. "Quinn, we are going to see that man."

The dowager shuffled toward the vicar, who was standing

at the side of the walk, conversing with a young couple. Quinn followed dutifully behind.

Rosalind watched them for a moment, thought and feeling unsettled by all that she had just heard. Had she misjudged this woman? At the very least, she was guilty of drawing too many conclusions from one brief meeting.

She glanced up at the church tower. *Perhaps I should remember that pride is also a sin.*

Rosalind sighed, then turned toward the oak where Fortuna had been waiting. Fortuna was still there. Rosalind could not read her expression from this distance.

Rosalind saw Mrs. Kendricks with a group of other plainly dressed women, possibly servants from the hall or from other houses. The dowager stood in front of the vicar, who was frantically leafing through his Bible.

Archibald Crease was nowhere to be seen.

Rosalind lifted her hems to keep them clear of the dust, and strolled over to speak with Mrs. Graves.

CHAPTER 26

The Persistence of Rumor

*The life of a woman . . . is a life of trial—an
existence of effort—custom has required at her
hand sacrifices which are not exacted from
the other sex . . .*

Theodore Edward Hook, *Cousin William* or
The Fatal Attraction

Fortuna wore a coat of unadorned black of an older cut. It
looked like a mourning garment that was found too good
to put away.

For her husband, perhaps?

"Good evening, Miss Thorne," said Fortuna as Rosalind
reached her. "I was wondering if you'd be accompanying the
dowager this evening."

Rosalind returned a small smile. "I believe she thought it
might be beneficial."

"Has it been?"

"It has certainly been educational." Mrs. Graves waited
for her to elaborate, but Rosalind did not. "How are you
doing? How is Helen?"

"Helen is having a difficult time. I will say I am grateful to
you, Miss Thorne, for persuading Helen to talk with Mr.

Mirabeau. He is a good man. They will do well together, and . . . it will be better for Helen if she is out of the house."

"Does Helen not get along with her brother?"

"Mr. Corbyn does not get along well with many people. You must understand," Fortuna added quickly, "he does care for his sister, and the rest of his family, but in his own way."

"And his way can seem a little harsh?" Rosalind asked, thinking of the dowager.

Fortuna considered this. "Exacting, perhaps. And it can be easy to misunderstand, even for those closest to him."

"That sounds tiring."

"It can be," she admitted.

Silence fell between them. Mrs. Graves twisted the cord of her reticule, clearly trying to work out how to steer the conversation. The twilight was deepening. So was the evening chill. Around them, people were beginning to drift away. There was not a great deal of time for indecision.

"And what of you, Mrs. Graves?" Rosalind asked, hoping she sounded merely conversational. "What will you do once Helen does marry? Will you continue to keep house for Mr. Corbyn?"

"I will take what comes. I'm sure you understand what it is to have to accommodate oneself to an uncertain life."

"Yes, indeed, but Mr. Corbyn will need someone to see to the house, at least until he chooses to marry . . ."

For a moment Rosalind thought the grave, pale woman might actually laugh. "That won't happen, at least not anytime soon."

Rosalind let her brows lift. "No? Well. The Vaughns will be disappointed."

"I find it difficult to work up much sympathy for any of them." Fortuna wound her reticule cord around one gloved finger. Her gloves and her bag were as black as her coat. All her best things were those dyed for mourning. Clearly, death had come hard to Mrs. Graves and taken a great deal, including her ability to buy herself anything new.

What is it you want to say to me? How do I help you?

"The Vaughns are new to the district, I understand," Rosalind tried.

"No shame in that, we all must come from somewhere."

"But by all accounts, they are very ambitious."

"Too ambitious by half." Fortuna looked away, as if embarrassed to be caught making such a statement, which she well might be. Women like Fortuna—*and me*—understood the levels of the social ladder to a nicety. To remark on those above you was a form of snobbery that could easily come back to bite.

Rosalind let the silence sit just long enough for Fortuna to know she didn't intend to pursue that subject. "And yet Colonel Corbyn liked them well enough to be friends with their son and to marry their daughter."

Fortuna shrugged. "The colonel liked to see Bartolemew. He liked his dash and temper and fearlessness." Her eyes went distant, filled with private memories. "I think Mr. Vaughn reminded William of what he had been before he went to war. He liked to have him around to remember when he also had been fearless once."

William. It was a small, casual slip. Probably Fortuna did not even realize she'd made it. Her expression had gone sorrowful, the look of a woman for whom grief is still fresh, but there was a good measure of anger there as well.

"So Bartolemew Vaughn was frequently at Corbyn Park?"

"Yes, more than . . . well, more than Helen and Mr. Corbyn felt comfortable with certainly."

"And you?"

Fortuna paused again, this time plainly searching for some diplomatic answer. "I could have wished for more polite company."

"But what of the marriage between Miss Vaughn and the

colonel? I confess, I understand well enough why the Vaughns desired the match, but no one has been able to tell me what engaged Colonel Corbyn's interest in Cecilia Vaughn in particular."

Now is your chance, thought Rosalind. *If you have something you wish to say about the Vaughns, I've opened the door as wide as I can.*

Because despite her demurring words, it was plain to Rosalind that Fortuna did not like the Vaughns. Was it because of something she knew as a fact? Or because their marriage plans had blighted some hope she harbored?

"It would be difficult for someone who did not know William to understand," said Fortuna. "He was plagued by the fear that he had not done his duty. It ate at him. It drove him to walk the halls at night. In marrying Cecilia Vaughn, he felt that his duty could be finally fulfilled."

"His duty to whom?" asked Rosalind.

"To his family, of course," Fortuna answered. "Who else should it be?"

Rosalind shrugged. "A man may feel duty to a legacy, an oath of service, many things."

"That is true, but in this case it was family. He spoke of the need to do right by them often when I sat with him at night." She saw Rosalind's inquiring glance. "He did not sleep well. If there was someone with him at night to talk to, sometimes it meant he drank less. That duty often fell to me."

Rosalind gazed across the churchyard. Lady Casselmaine had finished talking with the vicar and was now listening to a small cluster of ladies.

Even though there was no one near them, Rosalind dropped her voice low. "If I told you that new inquiries were to be made, what would be your opinion?"

Fortuna looked at her, and her gaze was hard. "Truly?" she asked.

Rosalind nodded once.

"No matter where those inquiries might lead?"

What are you driving at? Rosalind frowned. "I have faced very hard truths before. I am aware I may have to do so again."

The corner of Fortuna's mouth twitched, but Rosalind could not tell whether she was suppressing a smile or a frown. Her demeanor had changed. Far from becoming more relaxed, she had grown harder, and more suspicious, and yet, also more direct.

"You may have faced such truths, Miss Thorne, but there are others involved here. I have not wanted to encourage Helen in . . . behaviors that would ultimately harm her. It is not as if she or I had the power to do anything about our suspicions. We hold no sway over his grace, and his grace was quite determined that the matter be laid to rest."

Rosalind looked at Fortuna again. Every time she had seen the woman before, Fortuna had demonstrated a determination to fade quietly into the background until called for. That veil had fallen now, and in its place was a woman of stone.

Rosalind felt sure that she was seeing the reality of Fortuna Graves for the first time.

"He cares for the health of the neighborhood," Rosalind remarked.

"Yes, of course," said Fortuna. "What else could it be?"

The look Fortuna turned on her then was very close to contempt. Rosalind had the distinct feeling that Fortuna was disappointed somehow, as if Rosalind was a clever pupil who had not done well in her lesson.

Lady Casselmaine had only one woman left with her, a stooped and elderly person Rosalind did not recognize. Mrs. Kendricks was nowhere to be seen. Rosalind frowned and decided to risk another direct question.

"You think you know. Will you tell me?"

Fortuna Graves was used to life in drawing rooms. That

meant that she was used to being closely observed. But even for someone who understood that their appearance was to be under close scrutiny, Mrs. Graves's stillness at that moment was remarkable. The only time Rosalind had seen anything like it was in the person of Adam Harkness, and he had learned it waiting for highwaymen abroad in the darkness.

She's making a decision. She wants to be sure before she speaks.

Slowly, certainty did come. Its arrival was signaled by Fortuna's lowered gaze and the way she wove her reticule's drawstring through her fingers.

"When you pass a certain age, or sink to a certain low, people tend to forget you are in the room."

This sounded like a non sequitur, but Rosalind held her peace. Clearly, Fortuna had a point to make.

"Gentlemen forget you're there faster than ladies, of course," Fortuna went on. "It can have advantages. I've heard some very interesting conversations about business and banking." She paused again, staring toward the church, winding her cord around her finger, rubbing the silk braid. "There has been a great deal of talk about banking since his grace started the drainage works."

Worry stirred inside Rosalind. "I understand the project to be maddeningly expensive."

"Yes. A corporation has been formed, but I expect you know that, and that shares have been issued and so forth." Fortuna paused again, and when she spoke again, she picked her way delicately along her own train of thought. "One of the things that has always struck me is the similarity between business society and drawing room society. Success in either one relies heavily on who one knows, and how one knows them. And, of course, scandal can be just as deadly in business as it is in society."

"What sort of scandal are you referring to?"

"William was one of Lord Casselmaine's major shareholders," said Fortuna. "He put in a great deal of money. He persuaded some friends to invest as well."

"It was my understanding that he hoped his investment would help secure Marius a place as head builder on the project."

Fortuna sighed. "Miss Thorne, I know your family is close to the family at the hall, but you are a clear-eyed woman. Surely you see. William invested heavily in the drainage project. His money was financing a project that was running through its funds at a breathtaking pace. His brother is in charge of the works. If Marius has discovered something wrong, and if he told William . . ."

Rosalind felt herself go very cold. "You cannot possibly suggest Lord Casselmaine was involved in Colonel Corbyn's death because the colonel was going to pull his money from the drainage project?"

There was no apology in Fortuna Graves's expression, or in what she had to say next. "I say these things to warn you, Miss Thorne. If the wealthy have trouble, it is women like us who are caught first once the wheels start grinding." She paused as some movement behind Rosalind's back caught her attention. All at once, she changed again, drawing her soft, deferential manner about her like a veil. "Oh dear, Miss Thorne. I believe we must say good-bye for the present."

Rosalind followed the direction of her gaze to see Quinn speaking with Mrs. Kendricks.

"Thank you for your candor, Mrs. Graves." She was pleased that she managed to keep her voice steady. She did not want Fortuna to think that she was not entirely shocked by this revelation. "Will we see you and Helen at the card party?"

"We've been invited, of course, and Mr. Corbyn as well. In truth, I had not planned on attending."

"I should be sorry to miss you. I am very sensible that you have given me a number of confidences. I should like to be able to return the favor if I can."

The real Fortuna, the cold, hard woman, looked at her for a long time, trying, Rosalind thought, to gauge her sincerity.

"Well, perhaps I can persuade Helen it would be to our advantage to be there."

They said their farewells, and Rosalind went to meet Mrs. Kendricks and return to the carriage. Quinn was already helping the dowager into the brougham. Rosalind settled into place and watched the sober shadow that was Mrs. Graves climb into the little gig that she apparently drove herself and touch up the pony.

Rosalind had known, of course, that there were large sums of money involved in Devon's project. She was also aware that while a man of rank would be excused a great many things, being thought to have squandered money belonging to his peers was not on that list.

She was grateful now that she had thought to ask Louisa to talk with Firth Rollins. She only hoped it was not too late. It was quite clear that the rumors running rampant across this bit of quiet English countryside had to do with far more than dynastic ambitions, or even the death of a single man.

Was Fortuna just trying to warn Rosalind about those rumors, or did she herself truly believe that Devon was guilty of misfeasance?

Or even murder?

CHAPTER 27

Persistent Inquiries

*You directly charge me with having discovered
something which you wished to conceal . . .*

Theodore Edward Hook, *Cousin William* or
The Fatal Attachment

"Well." Alice Littlefield laid the letter she'd been perusing over breakfast onto the battered table that served equally as dining table and work desk. "It appears as if I'll be helping Rosalind execute her country commission after all."

"What does she say?" George popped the last bit of his morning toast and marmalade into his mouth.

"She says the country is lovely, the wedding is going to be splendid, and she's in excellent health. She also says Lord Casselmaine sends his greetings and his congratulations on your impending marriage." George raised his coffee cup in salute. "Further, she asks if I could take time away from finishing my manuscript for Mr. Colburn to find a pair of needles in a haystack."

"You sound unusually pleased about the request."

"I am one step closer to winning the bet I placed with myself."

George regarded her for a minute and, as usual, read her like a book. "You bet that Rosalind would not be able to let herself stay in the country."

"I did." Alice considered the dregs of her coffee. "Does that make me reprehensible?"

"No more so than the rest of us."

"It's completely wrong for her," said Alice. "I do understand the impulse. If I had a chance to trade these palatial surroundings"—she waved her chipped cup at their dingy flat—"for an estate and a coronet, I'd be off like a shot."

George folded his arms and leaned back, unusually serious, especially for this hour of the morning. "Would you really?"

"Well, it would depend on the coronet. An aging dotard up to his hips in debt with his house falling down around his ears . . ."

"And a horrible family secret in the east wing . . ."

"West wing, brother dear. All horrible family secrets are kept in the west wing. Or the tower, of course, if one has one."

"So who or what does she want you to find?"

Alice consulted the letter again. "One Colonel William Corbyn, retired. He's died recently under unclear circumstances. But before he died, he'd been making mysterious visits to London, ostensibly to visit bankers, but staying for long periods, up to a month. She wants me to find out where he stayed and what he did."

"Oh, is that all?" said George dryly.

"No, she adds in the postscript she also wants information on a Mrs. Fortuna Graves. Good Lord, the poor woman, to be saddled with a name like that." Alice paused. "Fortuna Graves," she repeated. "George, does that sound familiar to you?"

George narrowed his eyes at his coffee. "Yes. Something I read? Or heard? It must have been years ago . . ." He shook his head. "No, it's gone."

Alice drummed her fingers against the side of her cup. "I'm sure I've heard that name, but I can't remember when, or why . . ."

"Well, I must get to work, or the Major will have my head." The "Major" was what all the employees of the *London Chronicle* affectionately called their editor. George got to his feet. "Did Rosalind remember to tell you what regiment this Colonel Corbyn served with, and when?"

"As a matter of fact, she did." Alice pushed the letter toward him. George pulled out his notebook and scribbled a couple of lines.

"I can call around to Pinky Shippard," he said. "He's fetched up as a pensions clerk at the War Office. He might be able to look up something about the man."

"Pinky?" Alice quirked a brow at him. "You men and your nicknames. It is beyond me."

"Well, I'm relieved to know that something is. And you're welcome, by the by. And did I tell you I'm dining with Hannah and her mother tonight? After the concert?"

"'We're going to hear that new soprano, what's her name at the halls,'" Alice mimicked her brother's inflections as perfectly as only a sibling could. "Half a dozen times now. The exact number of times I've reminded you that tonight I will be attending this private gallery lecture by Lady Maynard's latest . . . protégé."

"Protégé?" George drew the word out well past the requisite number of syllables. "Is that what it's called nowadays?"

Alice frowned at him, but quickly relented. "Yes. Well. There's probably a number of reasons this isn't happening during the regular Season, and one of them is probably that Lord Maynard happens to be away in Ireland on estate business. I'm sure the Major will want A.E. to hint up a storm about all of it."

During the season, Alice's nights were filled with glittering parties, not as a guest, but as a working newspaper woman and gossip columnist. In the summer, she had to scrounge for other work to help with the housekeeping. Translations of articles from foreign magazines were part of her work, along with essays for annuals and gift books, and now, if all went well, novels. But she did also continue to attend those few scattered events with which London's remaining society attempted to entertain itself until Parliament returned and the Season commenced.

"So, are you going to the *Chronicle* to look for Rosalind's needle with the improbable name?" George retrieved his hat from the mantelpiece. "We can walk over together."

"No," said Alice. "There's someplace else I mean to start."

George paused and gave her a stern look. "Alice, you're not . . ."

"I'm not what?" she inquired mildly. "Be practical, George. You and I both remember that this Fortuna Graves was involved in something serious, perhaps even nefarious. Where better to begin inquiries of this kind than at Bow Street?"

Generally speaking, if a Littlefield had to visit the police station, it was George. But Alice herself had made the trip on more than one occasion, and not once did she ever find the place quiet. The entry hall was always filled with harassed and angry Londoners surrounding equally harassed clerks at their high tables and ledgers trying to sort out the complaints into those that should be answered at once and those that should be dismissed, probably with a flea in the ear. The patrolmen—both foot and horse—tromped in their great boots past this crowd, while the captains and officers threaded their quieter way through to the station's mysterious inner regions.

Alice had trained in the art of navigating a crush in some of the finest ballrooms in London. She had no trouble whatsoever in slipping, barging, and elbowing her way to the head clerk to ask for Mr. Adam Harkness.

"You may give the name of Littlefield and say that I have important information regarding an ongoing matter in which Mr. Harkness has an interest."

The clerk looked down his narrow nose at her. Alice blinked innocently back up at him. And why shouldn't she? Every word of it was true.

The clerk sighed and sent a boy darting to the back rooms. A moment later, Mr. Harkness himself emerged.

The newspapers and magazine writers might refer to any man who served at the station as a "runner," but Bow Street actually had several ranks for the men who served. The most elevated was principal officer. This post was held by only eight select individuals, of which Mr. Harkness was one. These men who might be sent anywhere in England at any moment to investigate any matter the magistrates deemed worthy, or that had been appropriately paid for.

Mr. Harkness spotted Alice at once and bowed. "Miss Littlefield. I was expecting your brother."

"George is off to the War Office this morning, and I am here on a private matter."

"Well, then, please step inside." He gestured for her to precede him through the door that led to the patrol room.

Alice had first met Mr. Harkness over the matter of Almack's Assembly Rooms, a business that had earned her the praise of her paper's editor and an opportunity to write much more interesting articles than the usual rounds of dresses and gossip. It also gained her a front row seat at the most unusual spectacle of Rosalind Thorne falling slowly, shyly in love.

Alice had never been admitted as far as the patrol room, and found her writer's eye darting every which way as she attempted to memorize its details. In contrast to the front of the station, it was a quiet place, more like a reading room than anything else. There were wooden cabinets for files and an entire wall lined with racks for newspapers. Battered maps of London, Westminster, and all the surrounding towns had been pinned to the walls. Men sat at long tables, either writing diligently or perusing papers and handwritten reports. Some of them glanced up curiously to see a woman in their midst and then went straight back to their work. One man, at the far end of the table, sat with his head bowed in deep thought. At least, Alice thought it was thought, until she heard the gentle snore.

"Don't mind him." Mr. Harkness gestured for Alice to sit. "He was out all night chasing down a gang of housebreakers."

"Goodness. If you care to give me the details, I'm sure the *Chronicle* will . . ."

Mr. Harkness smiled. That smile, Alice realized, was quite probably the source of some of Rosalind's current difficulties. It did things to the man's face that were difficult to ignore. "Tell me, Miss Littlefield, what brings you here?"

"It is an errand for our mutual acquaintance."

Mr. Harkness, when surprised or upset, could go very still. He did so now. "How does Miss Thorne in the country?"

Alice found herself examining him carefully. The man was certainly handsome enough, if one cared for such things. His features were regular and included a strong jawline, a healthy complexion, startling blue eyes, and fair hair. He had a habit of looking directly at one, especially when he was asking questions. His manner, unsurprisingly, said that he knew this was unsettling, and he did not particularly care. In that, he was very like Rosalind.

"Miss Thorne is efficient, industrious, and uncommunicative. She also has accepted a request to help a young lady in circumstances."

"So, she is her usual self, then?"

"Exactly."

And we have another way in which you two are well matched, thought Alice a little irritably. *Neither one of you will give away so much as an eyeblink without due consideration.*

"If you had any message for Miss Thorne, I'd be happy to include it in my next letter," she tried. "Or is there any question I can answer?" *Such as when does she plan to return?*

Mr. Harkness drew a deep breath. "No, thank you."

This surprised her. "Why not?" *You're not actually going to pretend you don't care . . . ?*

He was not. Mr Harkness looked to his left and right, and then leaned forward. "Because, Miss Littlefield," he said softly. "I'm afraid if I do start asking, it will turn into an interrogation, and the more I hear about his grace, the duke, and his house and lands and the pastoral ideal of him, the more I will discover I am actually a mean, petty, jealous, and small-minded man, and that is not a part of myself I want closer acquaintance with."

This was not something she found she could actually argue with, although she might very much want to. So, Alice simply nodded and Mr. Harkness simply sat back, his face as still and expressionless as it had been before.

Alice raised her voice, returning them to a more public footing.

"Mr. Harkness, Miss Thorne asked me to find out what I could about a Mrs. Fortuna Graves, a widow who is currently living with a family named Corbyn. I am remembering I heard the name; I think it was in connection with an article I read, and I remember it was something serious. . . ."

"Even grave," said Mr. Harkness solemnly.

"Sir, that was beneath you."

"I suspect it was." He smiled again. Really, the man had the bluest eyes. Alice herself had what she called a natural internal distance when it came to the male sex. In terms of personal aesthetics and enjoyment, she preferred the female form. However, even she had to admit when he smiled this man was . . . positively unfair.

"Fortuna Graves, is it?" Harkness went on. "And Corbyn? I don't recognize the names, but I know someone who might."

With that, he reached out and tapped the snoring man smartly on the shoulder. "Wake up, Tauton!"

Tauton lifted his head, coming awake swiftly and silently, and without any hint of confusion. Alice had never seen anything like it.

"What's doing, Harkness?"

"Miss Alice Littlefield, may I present Mr. Samuel Tauton? Tauton, Miss Littlefield is George Littlefield's sister."

"A pleasure, Miss Littlefield." The man stood and bowed. He was gray haired with a spreading paunch, shrewd face, and sharp eyes. *Dear heavens, do all the men here look at one's face as if saving it for later?* she wondered. And then, *If ever I write a runner into a novel, I must remember this.*

"Tauton has been with Bow Street for twenty years," said Mr. Harkness. "If your widow was involved in some event that caused her to be in the papers, he'll remember her."

"We have a notorious widow?" Mr. Tauton resettled himself into his chair. "Well, that's worth coming awake for. What's the lady's name?"

"Fortuna Graves," said Alice. "She is currently staying with some relations, the Corbyns."

"Fortuna Graves and the Corbyns," Tauton repeated. "Let me think a moment."

Tauton proceeded to do so by folding his hands across his belly and staring at the wall. His eyes remained lively, though. They flicked back and forth as if he was reading from some internal ledger.

"Ah!" cried Tauton at last, but he also shook his head. "I do recall. Oh yes," he added, more softly. "A thoroughly bad business that."

"What happened?" Alice finally had reason to bring out notebook and pencil.

Tauton blew out a sigh. "Oof. How to tell it . . ."

"I am a newspaper writer, Mr. Tauton." Alice demonstrated this fact by opening her book to a fresh page and holding her pencil at the ready. "I assure you, I will not be easily shocked."

She leveled a direct stare of her own at him, just in case he was thinking of objecting.

Tauton blinked, then looked to Harkness. Harkness shrugged, and Tauton himself shrugged in answer.

"All right," said Tauton. "Straight at it, then. This would be eight or so years ago now. Mrs. Graves, born Fortuna Corbyn, was married to a man named John Graves, a son of a good family who was working for a law firm in Lincolns Inn Fields. John Graves died suddenly of what the coroner found to be arsenical poisoning. Mrs. Graves was suspected, but the inquest was unable to bring forth enough evidence to bind her over for trial. It was quite the sensation at the time."

"How awful," murmured Alice, pencil flying across the page.

"I was just a patrol captain in those days, but I assisted the principal officer who was brought in to help the coroner uncover the evidence. I never thought she'd done it. But there was a sister living with them. Miss Arietta Corbyn, and a sad, nervous creature she was."

"If I may say, that is hardly proof of anything, sir," said Alice tartly.

"No, indeed, but there was something beyond that, which I did not like. Call it intuition if you will, but I remember the feeling. I was sure that Miss Arietta knew something—well, I was sure both of them knew something that neither could be induced to say."

"And where is this sister now?" Alice asked.

"She's dead. She died a week after the inquest."

Alice's pencil hovered over the page. "Was that poison, too?"

Tauton's face twisted. Alice hoped he was not about to express shock that a young woman would be so blunt. That always put her in a temper, and she wanted to like this man.

"No, she wasn't poisoned. She was found hanged in her bedroom."

Alice looked up. Until now, professional detachment had kept her feelings quiet. But those words sent a chill through her.

"Ruled suicide, of course," said Tauton.

Alice's fingers trembled. She pressed the point of her pencil against her notebook page to help still them.

"But I had my doubts about that as well," he went on. Alice could not tell if he noticed her tremors, but Mr. Harkness most definitely did. He did not even do her the courtesy of looking away.

Rosalind is going to have her hands full with you, Alice thought, and she was glad she could, because it helped push aside the other thoughts that she did not want.

"What was there about the . . . death to doubt?" she asked Tauton.

Tauton pursed his lips. "Nothing we could show in court. But there's a certain . . . rhythm that a practiced liar gets. It's like a rehearsed actor or singer. You can hear the difference between them and an amateur. I always did wonder if it was Miss Arietta's death that should be laid at Mrs. Graves's door."

CHAPTER 28

A Slight Chill, and a Slight Thaw

She was on her knees; not in prayer, but at the
door of the boudoir, with her ear applied to the
key-hole . . .

Theodore Edward Hook, *Cousin William* or
The Fatal Attachment

"It's a disaster!" Mrs. Showell cried.

Or rather, she tried to cry. The sound that actually emerged was more on the order of a hoarse whisper.

Rosalind and Louisa stood at Louisa's aunt's beside. Mrs. Showell lay under her thick satin counterpane, a mob cap on her head and a pile of crumpled handkerchiefs at her right hand.

"It's a mild cold," said Louisa soothingly. "The apothecary says you'll be right as rain in a day or two."

Unfortunately, Mrs. Showell was one of those normally healthy people who acted as if illness was something that could be reasoned with. "I cannot have a cold! I have a dozen calls to make today!"

"I will make the calls," Rosalind told her. "I'll leave your card, or your regrets, as appropriate." She attempted a smile. "It is something I have done many times."

"But I wanted to be with you; I wanted to introduce you properly this time!"

Rosalind was not sure that would be possible at this stage, given the speed with which rumor seemed to fly through this particular stretch of countryside. But now was not the time to argue the point.

"Where is your list of calls, Mrs. Showell?" Rosalind said briskly. Louisa, however, had taken that particular matter in hand by marching over to her aunt's writing desk and pulling the list off the stack on the blotter. She handed it to Rosalind.

"Oh, well, I suppose there's no choice." Mrs. Showell sniffed and pressed a fresh handkerchief against her nose. "I'm sorry, Rosalind. I truly am. I meant to be there with you . . ."

"Rest," said Rosalind.

"Everything will be fine," added Louisa.

Before Mrs. Showell could raise any more objections, Rosalind took up an envelope of her visiting cards and left the room with Louisa in tow, leaving Mrs. Showell to the tender mercies of her maid, who had just arrived with a steaming mug of hot barley water and lemon.

"Let me see the list," said Louisa as she and Rosalind adjourned to Mrs. Showell's burgundy and cream sitting room. "I can probably take some of these, especially the wedding-related ones." She paused. "Rosalind, I talked to Rollins. It was meant to be about Colonel Corbyn, as you asked. But we got off that subject rather quickly." She paused and lowered her voice. "I think Mirabeau—Helen's Mirabeau— might be in trouble." She stopped again. "And Casselmaine might, too."

Rosalind made herself breathe evenly. To have Fortuna tell her there was a shadow of suspicion around Devon was one thing. To have a man from a banking family say it, that was quite another.

When she was certain her voice would remain steady, Rosalind asked, "What did Rollins tell you?"

Louisa swallowed. "That the Mirabeau family is heavily invested in the drainage works, far more than they can afford to lose."

"I see."

"Do you really, Rosalind? Because you look far too calm." Louisa glanced at the doors, to make sure no one was coming to overhear them. "If the shares fail to pay dividends, the family will be ruined. So, you see, if Peter Mirabeau heard a rumor that Corbyn was thinking of selling up his shares, or otherwise pulling out . . . or that he'd uncovered what might look, if you squinted, looked like misfeasance or any such thing and proclaimed it publicly in a fit of anger . . ."

Scandal can be just as deadly in business as it is in society. Fortuna's words came back to Rosalind.

Rosalind took Louisa's hand. She said nothing for a time, allowing her friend to collect herself. And it was not just Louisa who needed that time.

While Louisa was worrying about her friend, and her friend's fiancé, she was failing to see another way in which all the pieces might be put together.

William invested heavily in the drainage project. Fortuna had said, *His money was financing a project that was running through its funds at a breathtaking pace. His brother is in charge of the works. If Marius has discovered something wrong, and if he told William . . .*

And now here was Louisa's news from Rollins. Here was the corporation again, the shares again, the money. Again. First Fortuna warning that Devon might be caught committing a misfeasance. Now the news that the Mirabeaus had involved themselves in the project to the point of actual ruin.

Rosalind wondered who else in the district had invested, and how heavily. Devon would surely know. Devon would surely suffer if his neighbors lost their money in his project.

And no matter how many or how few it proved to be, at

the center of it all sat Colonel William Corbyn, who had been to London, consulting with London men, and had returned, and now was dead. That made it only a few short steps to wondering if Devon might wish to silence William Corbyn before he could reveal whatever it was he knew.

Rosalind wondered how much more widely those rumors would spread if it was known that Devon had heard about the duel before it happened.

And it was possible such rumor might spread, because none of the persons involved would say what the cause of the duel had been.

All at once, Rosalind felt her thoughts turn to Lady Casselmaine, who knew and cared about what happened around her in unexpected ways. Lady Casselmaine had lived a long time in an uncertain house. She had watched and understood her husband's failings, and her eldest son's.

I have been very wrong about the dowager. I have not been seeing her, or her place, in the correct light.

"What are you thinking, Rosalind?"

"I am thinking how rumor seldom has more than half the facts. Sometimes not even that much."

Louisa drew back just a little, as if she was surprised. "I believe I shall have to embroider that on a cushion or something."

"Do you embroider?" asked Rosalind with her own expression of mock surprise.

"Of course, I do." Louisa lifted her nose in the air. "I'll have you know, I am a perfectly accomplished young lady."

"Then you will have no trouble accomplishing these calls," said Rosalind with a smile. "And taking note of any other rumors you might hear along the way."

Louisa's eyes sparked. "You may be very sure of that. What will you do?"

"I will take my share of the calls, of course," she said. "But before that, I believe I need to go and see Lady Casselmaine."

CHAPTER 29

What Is Held in Broken Hearts

*Love grows by constant association; so I dread to
say does hate . . .*

Theodore Edward Hook, *Sayings and Doings*

Once again, Rosalind found herself glad of the long walk to Lady Casselmaine's apartments. She went slowly, lost in thought. She thought of rumors past and present. She thought of family history and personal history, and how that might shape the way someone saw the world.

She thought how it was always the case that the same set of facts meant different things to different people.

As before, it was Quinn who answered her knock. Lady Casselmaine sat in front of her fire, her drapes drawn, her hands folded in contemplation. Her great Bible was open on the table beside her, but that was the only change in the bare and silent room.

Except for one other thing. This time, Lady Casselmaine looked up as soon as Rosalind entered.

Rosalind made her curtsy. "Thank you for agreeing to see me, Lady Casselmaine."

The dowager nodded. "You may sit."

"Thank you," said Rosalind again. A chair had already been placed at the other side of the hearth.

Was I expected? Rosalind sat and folded her hands.

"You have something to say." Lady Casselmaine assumed an attitude of weary patience.

"I wanted to give you my apology," Rosalind said. "I was much mistaken regarding your intentions, and I hope you can forgive me."

The dowager shook her head slowly. "I have no need of an apology from you."

"I offer it in any case," said Rosalind. "Perhaps it will do us both some good in the future."

Lady Casselmaine leveled her searching gaze at Rosalind. This time, it was much easier to bear. This time, she hoped she possessed a better understanding of what might be behind it.

I would have known before, had I been less afraid.

"What do you want, Miss Thorne?" Lady Casselmaine asked finally.

"I want to let you know that questions are being asked about the death of William Corbyn."

"Do you expect me to be surprised?"

"No, I was quite sure you would not be. But I am also here to ask your permission."

"My permission?" Now she was surprised, fully and genuinely.

"Perhaps it would be more accurate to say, I hoped to ask for your blessing."

The dowager's steady gaze wavered. She looked to her portraits, to her maid, and to her Bible. None seemed to offer any answers. "I do not understand you."

"Lady Casselmaine, there is a great deal happening. Friends of mine, and their friends, are much caught up in these events. If I can, I would have them escape unharmed. That includes Lord Casselmaine," she said. "And you."

"You do not need to pretend to care about me, Miss Thorne," she said, and there was acid in each word. "You care only for your prospects with my son."

Rosalind met this vitriol calmly. "Even if that were true, it would behoove me to care very much about you, because you have the capability to make my life and Lord Casselmaine's very difficult."

"I have nothing."

That belief was plainly an old one, and much like her piety, it was a shield. Lady Casselmaine did not wish to be seen as being responsible. She did not wish to be seen at all, because to be seen might lead to blame. Rosalind suspected Lady Casselmaine had been blamed for much in her life, by her husband, by her family, and most of all by herself.

And much like Cecilia Vaughn, the dowager feared she deserved all that blame.

"I disagree, Lady Casselmaine. You have a great deal," said Rosalind. "Despite your appearance of isolation, you take a great interest in the affairs of her estate and her neighborhood. You go to church several times a week, and talk with many ladies there. And I can see from here you carry on an extensive list of correspondence." Rosalind gestured toward the writing desk and its great stacks of letters. "As a result, you have heard the rumors surrounding William Corbyn's death, and his last days. And you, like many others, are afraid Devon is having money trouble.

"But you are also afraid he might have decided to follow a path similar to the one his father and his brother took. You're afraid he might be actively stealing from his neighbors, or at the very least making risky bets on the success of his drainage works and an increase in rents and income for the estate that may never happen." She paused to let all of that settle. "You are also afraid that Devon killed William Corbyn to silence him."

Rosalind expected a demonstration of shock and outrage, but it did not come.

"Why would I believe that of my son?"

"Because you believe he killed his brother."

Lady Casselmaine's gaze darted to the portrait above her mantel.

"You made that very clear when you and I first spoke," Rosalind reminded her. "You shut yourself away from the world, not to escape the world, but to try to keep yourself from confessing your fear. It was the only way you could think of to protect your last living child. But you still tried to warn me, lest I tie myself to a man you believed capable of such violence."

Rosalind had sat in many drawing rooms with women trained in careful deportment. She had, as a matter of self-preservation, needed to learn how to read the meaning in the smallest of gestures and the slightest turn of phrase. The dowager straightened, just a little. Her chin lifted a fraction of an inch. Her hands tightened against each other. She was angry. Whatever prayer or fear she kept within her heart for such moments, it was failing her.

"You are beyond impertinent," snapped Lady Casselmaine. "I have no words for what you are."

That makes two of us. "Again, I ask your forgiveness. The only reason I am speaking like this is that we are very short on time. I have told others this needs to be cleared away before Louisa's wedding can be tarnished. That is a partial truth. The rest is that it needs to be cleared away before the rumors being generated can cause real harm to Lord Casselmaine."

Lady Casselmaine shook her head. She lifted her eyes toward her portraits again. Rosalind had seen that look in church, that furious face turned toward a God who willed such circumstances into being and then left poor mortalkind to deal with them all.

"What do you want of me?" said the dowager, and Rosalind was not entirely sure who she was asking. But she could only answer for herself, so she did.

"I want to know the truth of what happened to William Corbyn."

"You do not." Lady Casselmaine brought her gaze back down to earth, and there was satisfaction and even a little determined menace in it. "No one ever wants the truth."

Rosalind gave her no time for anything more. "My father robbed and deceived his own family, ma'am," she said softly. "He is a forger, Lady Casselmaine, and if his crime becomes known, he will hang. My sister keeps him under a kind of guard, but he may come back at any time to claim what little I have left. I live with that and so does she. He ruined us, and yet we protect him because he is our father, and we cannot bring ourselves to do anything else. Had we known the truth earlier, we might have found a way to help save him. At the very least, we might have been better able to save each other. So, yes, I do want the truth no matter what it is, because I may have to save myself or those I care for again."

"And if the truth only makes matters worse?" It was meant to be a hard, direct thrust, but Rosalind just shook her head impatiently.

"I am asked that question a great deal. My only answer is that all my experience, all my heart, and all my conscience tells me it is still better that I know, because it is the only sure way to know how to act."

Lady Casselmaine's pause was a long one. Rosalind could tell nothing of what was happening behind her narrowed eyes.

"So, you mean to follow your . . . questions wherever they might lead?" asked the dowager sharply.

"Yes."

"You make no exceptions?"

"None."

Lady Casselmaine fell silent again. *You have been keeping your fears to yourself for years. You have tried to avoid being*

seen as the one who makes the decisions and does the un-
pleasant work. Now I have just confessed I am willing to do
an unpleasant task for you. But in so doing, I may reveal the
worst about your son.

You have feared this revelation for years, because you
want to protect your son, and at the same time you have
hoped for it, because you want to be vindicated for your re-
sentment of him.

Which will win now?

"I believe you," said Lady Casselmaine, finally. "Perhaps I
should not." She stopped, then went on much more softly
and with a tremor in her voice. "Will you tell me what you
find before you tell the others?"

"If I can, yes."

"What do you want me to do?"

"I want you to help me find Lucian Vaughn. The Vaughns
are as close to the heart of these matters as the Corbyns are. I
believe if I can understand the recent history of the family, I
can understand what drives them, and that will bring me
closer to understanding William Corbyn's death."

Lady Casselmaine did not move for a long moment. Then
she levered herself to her feet. Quinn did not even bother to
move forward to help. The dowager hobbled to her desk.

"I have been told he has taken a position as a shipping
clerk with Waterford and Greene in London. This is the address."

She took up pen and paper, and wrote swiftly in a clear,
flowing hand. Rosalind waited for the note to be blotted and
folded. She received it with a curtsy, as if she were the maid.

"You do not ask why I have this information," said Lady
Casselmaine.

"I assumed it is because you thought some day you might
need to know." Now it was Rosalind's turn to pause. "Do
you know why he was exiled?"

Lady Casselmaine shook her head. "No, that is one secret

the Vaughns have managed to keep entirely their own. For now, at least."

They gazed at each other for a long, silent time. It was Lady Casselmaine who turned away first.

"I am very tired," she said.

"Yes, ma'am," Rosalind agreed. She curtsied again and left the room without looking back.

CHAPTER 30

When Families Are Reunited

*I know that she is indescreet . . . and indescretion
in a woman is vice.*

Maria Edgeworth, *Things by Their Right Names*

Rosalind found her own way back to her apartments after
only one wrong turning and a pause, because for a moment she really did think she heard soft footsteps pattering
behind her. When she turned down the hallway she thought
of as her own, she saw Devon standing in front of her door,
his hand raised to knock.

"Oh!" she cried, genuinely startled. "I thought you had already left for the day."

He returned a somewhat sheepish bow. "Usually, I would
have, but I had to do some work on the books, and there
were letters that needed answering, and then I went to see
Mrs. Showell, and she said you were still in the house and"—
he gestured to indicate here he stood—"I came to wish you
good luck and Godspeed with the ladies of the neighborhood."

"So, we pass like ships in the night?" suggested Rosalind.

"Again, yes," agreed Devon ruefully.

"But you are coming to the card party tonight?"

"Let me think. A chance to ride with you and dine with you and show you off to the neighborhood in general? I would not miss it for the world."

Rosalind smiled. "Well, I shall endeavor to arrange things so I can be shown off in great style." She paused. "You should probably know, I've just spoken with Lady Casselmaine."

This clearly surprised Devon, but not in a pleasant way. "Was that your idea, or hers?"

"Mine, as it happens. I owed her an apology. I was . . . I made several incorrect assumptions about her, including that she had no genuine care for her duties, or her people."

Devon glanced up the hallway to make sure no one was coming to overhear. He stepped a little closer.

"She cares a great deal." He spoke softly, but the old anger showed plainly beneath his words. "So much she cannot bear to be near any of it."

"Lest she have her heart broken again," said Rosalind gently. "Devon, she is terrified of what she has heard."

"And what I may have done?" There was pain in those words. So much so that Devon could barely stand to look at her now. He did, though, because to do otherwise would be cowardice.

Rosalind felt her heart crack. She hoped he didn't see it. She hoped that if she moved just a little closer, he would understand she was not the one who was afraid. "She fears what other people think you may have done."

"Someone spread the rumors about the finances to her."

"Yes, and I know it might not seem like much, but consider, Devon, she was married to your father. She watched his chicanery and wastage for years. Then, all was given over to your brother, and it was more of the same. It's natural . . ."

"She should know by now I am nothing like them," he snapped.

"I think she might." Rosalind remembered the dowager's

hesitation, the trapped and hunted look in her prayerful eyes. "But she cannot stand to believe it, in case she finds herself disappointed yet again."

Devon was silent for a long time. Finally, he murmured, "Yes, I suppose that could be the case."

"It's hard when someone else has used up all the good and the love in another person and left none for ourselves."

"Yes," he said again. "As we both have cause to know."

They let that sit in silence. *So much silence between us. So much that is so well known, and yet sometimes I feel I barely know you, or myself, at all.*

"I should have warned you about all this," said Devon. "About the corporation and the complications. It is a hazard of doing public business. It puts everyone on edge." He stopped. "The project is sound, Rosalind," he said. "The money is there, and the books are open."

"I hope you do not feel you had to tell me that."

"I did have to tell you. I know you're going out to learn whatever you can on these very helpful afternoon calls of yours. I wanted to be sure you knew that I've already heard all the rumors. Including the ones that say I all but sold Louisa to Firth Rollins in return for a loan from his father."

"Oh no!"

"Oh yes," said Devon. "And, well—as much as I'd like to, I can't say this sort of thing is of no consequence. Half of what I spend my time doing now is lulling people's fears, but they are without foundation. I didn't want you to have to ask," he paused. "Or to avoid asking."

"I am not happy with any of this, Devon."

"I know." He took her hand. How had they come to be this close together? She'd barely noticed it happening.

No, you noticed. You just didn't stop it.

"Good luck today," he said. He was looking at her hand in his. Her pulse was fluttering, but only in part from his touch.

"The same to you," she said, trying to return some levity,

or at least propriety to her words. "I look forward to seeing you this evening."

"I shall endeavor to do you credit." He bowed solemnly. Rosalind returned her curtsy with equal formality. Their eyes met, each daring the other not to laugh.

It was an old game. Rosalind usually won. Not this time. This time she smiled and she laughed, and then she moved past him, ducking into her rooms and trying not to feel like she was making some narrow escape.

But from what?

Rosalind had no answer.

Mrs. Kendricks sat beside the parlor hearth, working on a careful piece of darning. As soon as Rosalind entered, she returned this to her workbasket and rose.

"I have some calls to make, Mrs. Kendricks," she said briskly. Her conversations with Lady Casselmaine and Devon had left her restless. She wanted to do something, find some way to set things in order, as if bringing discipline to the world outside could help her bring it to herself inside. "Mrs. Showell is in bed with a cold, so Louisa and I will be making her rounds for her." Rosalind paused. "If you have work you wish to see to here, you need not accompany me. I can take a footman and Mrs. Showell's maid with me."

Mrs. Kendricks's closed expression said she understood exactly what Rosalind was doing. Rosalind was not going to cease her inquiries in William Corbyn's death. This meant, from Mrs. Kendricks's point of view, Rosalind was going to continue endangering her already diminishing chances of marrying Devon.

Rosalind wanted to absolve Mrs. Kendricks of the responsibility of having to stand silently by while she continued down this road.

"Thank you, miss, but there is nothing that cannot wait. I recommend your ivory walking costume and the bonnet with the green ribbons. They are warmer, and the weather does not look so promising today."

Rosalind nodded, for she understood Mrs. Kendricks's meaning as well as Mrs. Kendricks understood Rosalind's. While she served Rosalind, Mrs. Kendricks would not hold back in that role, whether she agreed with the path Rosalind took or not.

It was so strange, this dance of rank and humility. Rosalind had never truly considered how strange before. Now that it came on her so forcibly, she desperately wanted to fall back on comfortable propriety. Rosalind shook this off.

"Mrs. Kendricks?" she said.

"Yes, miss?" Her housekeeper turned to face her. Rosalind felt her throat close. She had no rules for this, no formula, and she found herself struck mute.

No. I will run away from this. That would not be fair to either of us.

"I want you to know . . . whatever happens in these next weeks, and whatever you may choose to do afterwards . . . please choose freely. You have looked after me for a very long time, but I should not—I do not—have the right to claim the rest of your years. You must look after yourself now."

Mrs. Kendricks did not answer for a long moment. Rosalind felt a terrible, shameful flush rise in her cheeks, as if she'd uttered a rude word in church.

Her housekeeper bowed her head. "When your father left, and your mother . . . failed, I swore I would make sure you were safely, properly settled. I thought your godmother would be able to keep you, but then . . . she also failed." Mrs. Kendricks's cheeks flushed as well. These were not matters they ever spoke of. *Or ever thought we should have to.* "I could not leave you alone."

"I'm not alone, Mrs. Kendricks," said Rosalind. "And I shall not be."

"Are you certain of that? If you cannot convince—" She gestured toward the door and the hall beyond it.

Rosalind did not make her finish. "Even then, I will not be alone. I have found a way to manage, and I will continue to manage."

"But it's not right!" exclaimed Mrs. Kendricks.

What she meant, of course, was it was not proper. Rosalind was bred to a gentlewoman's life. Gentlewomen did not work or earn money for themselves. They certainly did not profit from the problems of others. They were ornaments to their society and were looked after as such.

Rosalind faced Mrs. Kendricks and summoned all her determination. "What I do is an honest existence"—*if out of the ordinary*—"and it makes use of all these skills that have been bred into me, even though I do not put them to their intended purpose."

In her mind, she pictured Alice Littlefield gleefully shouting, *I told you!* She put that aside.

But Mrs. Kendricks would not be so easily reassured. "I will not leave having failed you," said Mrs. Kendricks. "I could not live with myself."

"You have never once failed me." Rosalind paused and let her mind run back over all she had heard and seen thus far. Suspicion sprang to life inside her. "Mrs. Kendricks, have you had another offer from somewhere?"

Mrs. Kendricks looked away, but not before Rosalind saw something close to anger in her expression.

"My sister," she said quietly. "She and her husband run a guest house in Bath. Their eldest has just had her third child, and it's getting to be too much. They've asked me to come help with the house and the children, and to help make sure the place will attract the right sort of guest, you understand."

Which Mrs. Kendricks, with all her experience with grand houses and grand families, would be able to do perfectly. "That sounds marvelous."

"I have not said yes."

"I understand that. But if you do, you have all my good wishes for everyone's success, and I shall insist on regular letters."

Rosalind spoke openly and lightly. She smiled. *I mean this. I mean every single word of it with all my heart.*

"Thank you, miss," said Mrs. Kendricks. "I will consider it."

"Good," said Rosalind firmly. *I mean it. I do.* "I know you will make the right decision. You always do."

Mrs. Kendricks accepted the compliment silently. She also stayed exactly as she was. Rosalind steeled herself. "Is there something more you wish to say to me, Mrs. Kendricks?"

"Yes, miss." Mrs. Kendricks paused, and Rosalind realized she probably saw how carefully Rosalind was holding herself. "I dare say it's not what you're thinking."

Rosalind let herself smile. "It is notoriously difficult to tell what I might be thinking,"

Mrs. Kendricks pursed her lips ever so slightly. "It's not for me to say, miss."

Actually, it was, but Rosalind decided not to argue the point. Instead, she sat down on the window seat and smoothed her skirts. "What is it you want to tell me?"

Mrs. Kendricks walked over to the window and twitched the draperies back a little farther, smoothing out the folds.

"It is something that happened yesterday. Perhaps I should have told you last night, but . . ."

"I was very tired last night," said Rosalind. "You doubtlessly saw that I would not be able to pay proper attention."

Mrs. Kendricks gave her a sideways glance, but she did not contradict Rosalind's suggestion.

"It was after services, while you were speaking with Mrs. Graves, I was talking to some of the servants from the hall. They were on their half day and had decided to come to services, you see. I happened to see that man, the one that accosted you, ducking back around the church."

Rosalind frowned.

"I did not like his attitude, and I feared there might be some mischief afoot. I thought, forewarned is forearmed."

"Yes, indeed," murmured Rosalind.

"So, I followed him around the church, at a distance, of course. Well, this Crease, he slips into the vestry, taking care to look about that he should not be observed. I took myself up to the window, just to see who such a one might be talking to in a church."

"And who did you see?"

"At first I thought it might be some woman, a maid or some such." Mrs. Kendricks lifted her nose in proper indignation. "There are saucy enough creatures in these country houses.

"And it was indeed a woman, but she was a gentlewoman. I'd seen her in the church, a young woman, with four little ones and their nannies."

Rosalind drew back in surprise. "Wearing a bonnet lined with white lace? And a sky blue pelisse?"

"Yes, miss. That was her."

Cecilia. What on earth . . . ?

"They were not alone," Mrs. Kendricks told her. "There was a man with them. A gentleman, he was tall, slim, fair, and pale."

"But you did not know him?"

"I had never seen him before. He wore traveling clothes, not churchgoing clothes, so perhaps he had recently arrived. I will say, his face was similar to the young lady's. So much so, I remember thinking they might be related, perhaps even brother and sister. What I could see plain as plain was that they were arguing."

"Did you hear what it was about?"

Mrs. Kendricks shook her head. "I can say it was bad. The gentleman was shouting at the lady, and his face was twisted up something awful. The lady, she had her hands up, trying to calm him down. That Crease fellow, he was standing back and watching them, his arms folded, like it was all happening on the stage and had nothing to do with him.

"Then, the lady, she runs back into the church. The gentleman and Crease head out together, across the fields, moving sharpish, I would say, as if they did not wish to be seen."

"I can only suppose they did not," murmured Rosalind. "None of them."

Cecilia Vaughn was having a secret meeting in the church. Cecilia Vaughn who believed herself implicated in the death of William Corbyn and who was supposed to be preparing to attract the interest of Marius Corbyn. She was spending her time after church arguing with a man who looked enough like her to be her brother.

The question then became, which brother?

CHAPTER 31

A Lucrative Offer

*But there is no occasion to be always thinking of
right and wrong, and making ourselves tiresome
with our scruples.*

Maria Edgeworth, *Things by Their Right Names*

The gallery lecture was scheduled to begin early by London standards, so Alice had to leave her letter to Rosalind half-finished on the table in order to have enough time to get ready. Rosalind was surely not going to appreciate learning where Alice got her information regarding Mrs. Fortuna Graves, but she could not argue with the results.

Alice currently owned only two evening gowns, and one of them required help to get into. So, she tonight wore the simpler of the two—a sky blue watered silk that her soon-to-be sister-in-law had recently altered to update the sleeves and the neckline, and add a fresh trimming of royal blue ribbons. The gown's simplicity meant she had to spend more time curling and pinning up her hair, with yet more of those ribbons, so she'd look up to scratch. She might be attending as a newspaper woman rather than a guest, but Alice could not risk appearing down-at-the-heels or otherwise out of place. That would invite unfavorable comment, and if the hostesses decided she was a detriment to their parties, they might start requesting the *Chronicle* send someone else.

To be fair, however, if it removed her from events such as Lady Maynard's little lecture, she might actually welcome the development. Alice Littlefield's natural environment was the ballroom. Oh, she no longer played any part in the games, at least not in the usual sense, but she'd made her profession observing and recording them. After so many parties, she could read a crowd as easily as she could a newspaper—picking out the points of interest in the crush and identifying the actors who would form the natural centers around which the little social eddies would swirl.

What she saw as she hovered about the edges of Lady Maynard's private gallery was that this crowd was bored to tears. The artist—a handsome, superior man with rich golden hair and a horseman's build—led them all around the broad chamber, expounding on each canvas and broken bit of statuary. Some of what he said was blatantly false, and some of it, Alice suspected, was being made up on the spot. She saw several girls she knew from the social rounds looking at one another and rolling their eyes.

One of them caught Alice's attention and raised an inquiring brow. Alice nodded. Yes, she would indeed be giving this event the attention it deserved. She could get a full column inch's worth of innuendo out of the way Lady Maynard stared at the man as if she wasn't sure whether to crown him with laurels or drag him off for a private . . . interview.

Alice sighed. *Please let Mr. Colburn accept my novel,* she prayed to all the muses, and whatever other god might oversee the lives of writers. *I'd really rather give up the gossip columns before I become a complete cynic.*

But if she must be a cynic, she would be a dutiful one and earn her pay. It was not considered good form for her to pull out her notebook in the middle of the "party," so Alice set about noting the faces she knew among the gathering and making sure she had committed the most important names to memory. She also paid careful attention to how they were dressed, and who seemed to be standing just a bit too close to whom. She'd make notes when she got home tonight, and tomorrow, she could start the business of finding out whose spouses were where, who had stayed in town due to financial difficulties, and who simply had nowhere else to go.

She was so intent on this activity, she failed to see the little nervous woman come sidling up on her left side.

"Miss Littlefield?" she said. Alice turned. The lady was a tiny, pink-faced person, even shorter than Alice, which was saying something. Her gown was dark gray trimmed with antique lace and was of new cut and good quality.

She wasn't alone. Behind her, at a discreet distance, waited a throughgoing dandy of a man.

"Forgive me," said the tiny woman. "Miss Emma Vanderstaad, we met . . ."

"Oh yes!" said Alice. "Two summers ago, wasn't it? At Easter."

"Yes, yes," she smiled. "I have a gentleman here who was most anxious for an introduction." She gestured and the dandified gentleman stepped neatly forward. "Miss Alice Littlefield, may I present Mr. Russell Fullerton?"

Alice had been in the act of extending her hand when she froze. Miss Vanderstaad started.

"Erm. Perhaps you already know each other?"

"By reputation only," replied Alice. "I'm sorry, you must excuse me."

She swiftly turned her back and walked away. In drawing room parlance, it was "the cut direct," and it had been years since she used it. Short of cursing in public, it was the most offensive thing one could do. It told the other individual *I do not even acknowledge your existence.*

She hoped this particular individual would take the hint. But given what she knew of him, this hope was probably in vain.

I have to get out of here. Alice glowered at the crowd. *I can go. I have enough. I'll make up the rest.* But she had to at least say a few reassuring words to Lady Maynard, or that worthy hostess might complain to the Major and . . .

"Miss Littlefield?" said a man's smooth and cultured voice behind her.

She knew instantly who it must be. Alice turned. She fixed a smile on her face. Like it or not, she was in public, and there was a strict limit to how rude she could be.

She had no doubt this man knew that. "I'm sorry, Mr. Fullerton. I was just leaving."

Fullerton sighed with all semblance of deep regret. He was, of course, in the black and white uniform of male evening dress, but gold and garnet buckles shone on his shoes and on his white satin breeches. A ruby stickpin glittered in his cravat. Another ruby graced the ring on his right hand. "I'm afraid I must beg you to stay. We have much to say to one another, you and I."

"Without a doubt," replied Alice. "But I'm not sure I'd care to be caught using that sort of language in public."

She stepped up to him and leaned in, making sure her lace fan was held over her face, as if she was about to share an amusing confidence.

"Mr. Fullerton," Alice whispered. "I know you are a moneylender and a blackmailer, with a particular fondness for silly young wives who don't think they can tell their husbands their troubles." *And you may believe me, as soon as I have the proof, I will make sure your name is published in every paper in the city.* She drew back, beamed at him, and snapped her fan shut sharply. "Was there anything else?"

Alice had endured many contemptuous glances in her career, but nothing had come close to the bright hatred in this man's eyes. And yet, his voice remained perfectly smooth and entirely polite. The combination was terrifying. "Shall we sit, Miss Littlefield?" He gestured toward a marble bench that had been situated for the better contemplation of the paintings.

Damn, damn, and damn again. She couldn't leave now. Something was going on. It might involve a friend.

It might involve Rosalind.

Rosalind had crossed paths with Mr. Fullerton a summer ago. One of the women she'd helped had been one of his chosen victims. Somehow, he'd gotten word of it, and since then he'd set out to do what he could to ruin her.

Alice, who knew every last one of Rosalind's secrets, knew exactly how much danger this man presented.

She walked past him. She sat at the extreme end of the bench. Mr. Fullerton settled himself at the other end and gave her a sardonic smile. *See? You are a nervous little girl, but I shall indulge you.*

Alice could have cheerfully filleted him with a dull knife.

"What I have to say is very simple, Miss Littlefield. You are a writer of society notes and gossip, and a very talented one. I want to pay you to put those skills to work for me."

"For you?" A chill crept up Alice's spine.

"You are well-placed to receive the sort of gossip the papers cannot print. About Mrs. Prescott-Wells there, for example." He nodded toward a tall, green-gowned woman in the knot of persons still following the artist. "Or the newly engaged Miss Fetherstonehaw. She's an old school chum of yours, I believe? Or she was until she struck you off her lists." He tsked at the unfairness of that. "You would find me much more generous in my terms than either the Major or Mr. Colburn, and infinitely more reliable in my payments."

"I see now why you wanted to hold this conversation in public. Far less risk that I should slap your face." Alice got to her feet. "Do not attempt to speak with me again, Mr. Fullerton."

"I would pay triple for any information regarding Rosalind Thorne."

Alice froze again.

"I understand she is a particular friend of yours."

"Mr. Fullerton . . ."

She was not permitted to get any further. "Miss Little-field," he said softly, but clearly. "You are a practical woman. You are also in straits. You are about to enter into a new phase of your life. Your brother will be marrying soon. Your household is best described as meager. You do not have the means to keep yourself, and sisters-in-law begin to chafe at having to share rooms with relations, especially once the babies start to arrive and the money gets even tighter.

"Miss Thorne has made herself a nuisance to me and I am tired of her. I will pay handsomely and regularly for reports which give me the means to quiet her. The name her sister lives under, for example, or the whereabouts of her father."

Alice felt her face flush with anger. She would *destroy* this creature. She'd blacken his name so thoroughly across the Sunday pages he'd never be able to show his face again. She'd . . .

Fullerton smiled. "Now, before you are tempted to raise your hand, or your pen, against me, you will very kindly consider that I do not approach people without something of my own to offer. Young ladies from disgraced families also have their secrets, and some of them are too . . . impolite to be tolerated. Even in the publishing trades."

Alice walked away. She'd write a note of apology to her hostess later. A sick headache. Because she was sick, and she knew she could not stay here for another minute.

Alice also knew she would carry the memory of Mr. Fullerton's smile with her for a very long time.

By the time Alice got home, George was already there, drinking a mug of tea by the fire.

"Hello, sister dear." He raised the mug to her as she walked in. "How was the lecture? And did you have any luck finding out about your mysterious Mrs. Coffin?"

"Graves," Alice corrected him listlessly. She collapsed onto the sofa, dropping her reticule and fan carelessly beside her.

"Good Lord, Alice." George was on his feet instantly, coming to her side. "What happened?"

"I've just been offered a bribe." *And a threat.* "By Russell Fullerton."

The color drained from George's face. "What does that blaggard want from you?"

"Dirt on Rosalind. Oh, anyone, really, but mostly Rosalind."

"What did you do?"

"I left. And now I'm very tired." She tried to strip her gloves off, only the buttons got stuck and she tore at them with her inadequate fingernails. Tears stung her eyes.

"Here, here." George took her hand and undid the tiny, ridiculous buttons. "Can't afford to replace these yet. There." He let go of her so she could tug the gloves loose. He also produced a handkerchief and handed it over. "Will you tell Rosalind?"

"I'll have to." Alice sniffed and blotted her eyes. "But how? I can't write this in a letter. Fullerton . . . even Sanderson Faulks is scared of him, George. He's perfectly capable of having my correspondence with her watched."

To her infinite surprise, George was grinning. "Well, then you'll have to bring her back to London. And I happen to know the perfect excuse." George got to his feet and went to where his coat hung on the peg by the door. With a flourish, he pulled a folded paper out of his pocket.

"What's that?" demanded Alice. "What have you found?"

"Some very interesting items regarding one Colonel William Corbyn, thought to be retired." George bowed and handed her the paper.

"What do you mean, thought to be?"

"I mean he never did actually retire. He was on half pay."

"Really?"

"Really. What's more, Pinky was stunned to learn that the colonel was dead. Apparently nobody thought to notify the War Office of his demise."

Alice's brow furrowed. "But surely they knew something was wrong when he stopped collecting his pay."

"No, they didn't, because you see, that pay was still being collected." George paused to make sure he had Alice's full attention. "By one Mrs. William Corbyn."

CHAPTER 32

Polite Parlor Games

*We cannot judge either of the feelings or of the
characters of men with perfect accuracy, from
their actions or their appearance in public; it is
from their careless conversations, their half-
finished sentences, that we may hope with the
greatest probability of success to discover
their real characters.*

Maria Edgeworth, *Castle Rackrent*

According to the invitation, the Vaughns' card party was
set to follow the established formula—there was to be a
"light" supper first, followed by an evening of cards. This required that all the guests gather for a socially mandated half
hour before the dining room could be opened.

Rosalind was prepared to be watched when she walked
into the Vaughns' receiving rooms on Devon's arm. She was
not prepared for the mix of feelings inside her. As the ladies
turned their eyes in her direction, a heady blend of pride, de-
fiance, and pure bashfulness washed through her, making her
feel even taller than she was, while at the same time making
her to wish to run and hide.

The receiving room was filled with silver and gold. There

was nothing that was not frescoed and filigreed and painted with pastoral scenes. Dozens of beeswax candles burned in elaborate branching candelabras—silver gilt on tables and wrought iron in the corner. Cassel House had attempted to establish its primacy with excessive grandiosity. The Vaughns, on the other hand, had attempted a similar feat by purchasing enough antiques to attempt to fill the place with a sense of history. What the two houses had in common was a similar absence of taste.

"Your grace!" Mrs. Vaughn bustled up to them, glittering and gleaming and causing Rosalind to blink. She wore dark brocade and velvet the better to set off her vivid display of diamonds. "We are so delighted you could join us this evening."

She dropped a long, deep curtsy, from which she struggled to rise. Devon watched with a completely straight face that did him a world of credit. Louisa managed to confine herself to several rapid blinks.

"And, Miss Winterbourne, so kind of you to come to our little party. And, Miss Thorne! How do you do this evening? Are we not to have Mrs. Showell with us?"

"My aunt has a slight cold and sends her regrets."

"Oh, I am so sorry to hear it. Miss Thorne, I don't believe you've met my daughters. Cecilia, of course you know, but this is Margery and this is Julianna."

The girls approached to help welcome the new arrivals, and both curtsied warily. Rosalind saw how their gazes turned ever so subtly calculating as they took in Rosalind's remade gown, and added this to the fact that Lord Casselmaine was so clearly escorting her.

Cecilia's sisters were true beauties. They all shared that swan's neck and sloping shoulders, as well as her lovely honey-gold hair. Their choice of gowns went well with their complexions. Margery wore pastel yellow and Julianna was in delicate rose. Rosalind easily recognized them as Cecilia's sisters, and like her, they were graceful and studied in their movements. But whereas Cecilia mostly seemed distant and fatigued, Margery and Julianna possessed a latent energy. It was the sort of feeling that could crackle across a ballroom and attract a certain kind of gentleman.

These two would do well in London.

If Mrs. Vaughn is careful. If she isn't . . .

Rosalind did not permit herself to finish that thought. She was helped by the arrival of Mr. Vaughn.

"We are so delighted you could join us tonight, your grace," he bowed smoothly.

"Vaughn," replied Devon. "Good of you to invite us, and to include Miss Thorne."

Mr. Vaughn was a tall, thin man, and now Rosalind saw where the sisters had gotten their long necks. It seemed to Rosalind that Mr. Vaughn wore his dinner clothes more comfortably than he wore his own skin. He smiled at his newly arrived guests with what could be satisfaction, but there was an edge to it, a restlessness, as if he were waiting for bad news.

"I know you've only just arrived, sir," he said to Devon. "But I was hoping I might steal you away for a quiet word . . . ?"

Rosalind glanced at Louisa, who just rolled her eyes. "Oh, there's Helen. Let's go say hello." Louisa took Rosalind's arm out of Devon's. "You will excuse us, won't you, Mrs. Vaughn?"

"Yes, of course," Mrs. Vaughn smiled. "You may see we are all free and easy here! But I shall claim you later, Miss Thorne, for a hand of whist."

Rosalind smiled and promised nothing, and let Louisa lead her away. But even as they departed, she saw how Julianna and Margery stood so close to Cecilia, and how very tired she looked.

What is going on here?

Helen was on the edge of the gathering, talking to a dark girl in white and cream whom Rosalind did not know. As soon as she saw Louisa and Rosalind working their way across the room, Helen excused herself from the other girl and came forward.

"Hello, Helen, how are you?"

"Wishing to be elsewhere, and you?"

"Worried," said Louisa. "What on earth is the matter with Cecilia?"

Helen hesitated a little, as if, Rosalind thought, she did not want to admit she was concerned. "I don't know. But she does not look terribly well, does she?"

"She looks under guard," murmured Rosalind. "Has there been any . . . news of her around the neighborhood? Or her brothers?" she added. She'd done her best to make discreet inquiries on her round of calls that afternoon, but if anyone had seen either of the disgraced Vaughn brothers in the neighborhood, no one was willing to tell her.

Louisa raised her brows. "Do you think there's been bad news, Rosalind? I didn't hear anything when I was paying calls."

"Well, something's been happening," said Helen. "Old Mr. Vaughn has been to the house no less than three times in the past two days, and Marius has been growing more sour and snappish by the minute. I'm surprised he agreed to come tonight at all." She nodded toward a man standing at the fireplace.

Rosalind had seen Marius Corbyn only from a distance at the drainage works. Up close, she saw he had the same curling, sandy-gold hair as his sister and the same golden complexion, but his had been burned to a deeper brown by his days in the sun. He was lean and angled, but work had not smoothed him at all, or given him any ease in his own body. Instead, he hunched his sharp shoulders as if he was waiting for another blow.

If the Vaughn sisters had looked like guards, Marius Corbyn looked cornered.

Rosalind let her gaze flicker to where Devon stood in close conversation with Mr. Vaughn. Devon was keeping an entirely neutral face, but Marius Corbyn watched the two men as if fascinated.

In the meantime, across the room Margery was saying something to Cecilia, and Cecilia's reply left the other sister, Julianna, openly shocked.

All the while, Mrs. Vaughn was flitting, or attempting to flit, between her guests, stopping only briefly with each one, and returning over and over again to Cecilia.

"Is it just me or is something . . . off?" said Louisa.

Something was decidedly off. The question was, what was it? There were so many possibilities.

"Is Fortuna staying away tonight?" Louisa asked Helen.

"Yes, she had a headache." Helen mouthed the words, but it was plain she did not believe them. "She's been as bad as Marius recently. I can't get a civil word out of either of them." She paused and frowned.

"I see Mr. Mirabeau is not here, either?"

"Peter?" Helen seemed surprised. "Oh, I forget what a stranger you are yet, Miss Thorne. No, Peter wants nothing to do with the Vaughns, especially since the duel. He blames Bartolemew for the whole thing. They did not even bother to invite him."

Which was natural enough. And yet . . . Rosalind looked at Cecilia again, and at Devon. And she knew what was wrong. She knew at once and absolutely.

It was then that the dinner gong rang.

"Oh yes, yes, hello, everyone!" called Mrs. Vaughn. "We shall be going in now. Your grace, can I impose upon you to escort Cecilia? Thank you. And, Mr. Corbyn, perhaps you'd be good enough to escort Miss Thorne?" She beamed at Rosalind. Rosalind mustered her deportment so she was able to nod in acknowledgment and take Mr. Corbyn's stiff arm to be led to the dining room.

To her surprise, Mr. Corbyn took them directly to the middle of the table, the point absolutely farthest from either Mr. or Mrs. Corbyn.

"I'm pleased to finally get to meet you, Miss Thorne," he said as he helped Rosalind to her seat.

"And I you, Mr. Corbyn. Lord Casselmaine has said it is your design that will make the drainage project a success."

Marius Corbyn sat down exactly as he stood—stiffly and uncomfortably. "You must thank his grace for me," he said mechanically. Then, an idea seemed to occur to him. "I understand you've gotten to know Helen and Cecilia rather well during your stay."

"A little. I've been here such a short while and I'm afraid I've been so busy with Louisa's wedding, I haven't had a chance to get to know anyone as well as I'd like."

His eyes narrowed intently. At the same time, her noncommittal answer seemed to relax him.

"Well, I'm sure there will be time for that. May I ask who your people are, Miss Thorne? And where you come from?" It was an abrupt change of subject, and much to Rosalind's surprise, Corbyn smiled at his own awkwardness. "Genealogy is a hobby of mine," he said, by way of apology. "My mother was devoted to it. She believed that to understand a person, one had to understand their family."

"Is that what you believe, Mr. Corbyn?"

"I do, as it happens. After all, we know that what makes a horse is its bloodline. Why should we ignore that as a vital facet of the human being?"

"Because humans are not horses," said Rosalind.

"Indeed, they are not. Some of them are rather worse." His gaze drifted down the table, but he seemed to catch himself and focus on her again.

"You have a low opinion of humanity, Mr. Corbyn."

"I do," he admitted. "I am not sorry for it. I have seen enough to believe I come by it honestly."

"Oh, Miss Thorne, do not, please, draw Mr. Corbyn out on the subject of human nature." Julianna Vaughn, Cecilia's pink-gowned sister, was being settled across the table by an older man with a thatch of gray hair and a pair of carefully trimmed sideburns. "It will make for a dinner dreary beyond imagining.

"Answer his question instead, if you would." The whiskered man sat down beside Julianna. "Tell us of your family."

"And give us all a chance to change the subject!" added Julianna, which raised a ripple of laughter up and down the table.

Marius's jaw hardened. Before he could give voice to his very evident anger, Rosalind obliged the request. She detailed her mother's family origins in the Cotswolds, and made sure to tell the story of the dairymaid, who was said to have given a cup of milk to a thirsty Queen Elizabeth and received cows and gold as a reward. As she spoke, she watched the calculations in Marius Corbyn's eyes. He looked at her as if he could see through her skin to her blood, and was evaluating what he found there. It was as open and insolent a look as any she had ever received from a cad on the dance floor.

Thankfully, however, what her country-bred dinner companions seized upon was the subject of cattle, and there ensued a lively round of storytelling about surprisingly intelligent and mischievous cows, which at some point changed into stories of dogs and then of horses.

Marius and his discontent faded into the background. Rosalind found herself almost forgetting him, but not quite. Because at the foot of the table, Devon kept looking toward him. Cecilia, sitting beside Devon, kept her eyes on her plate but ate next to nothing. Her face was bright pink. Rosalind wondered what Cecilia's mother was saying.

Louisa was practically at the other end of the table, near enough to Helen that they were able to talk, or would have been if they hadn't been so often interrupted by Margery

Vaughn, who seemed very keen to talk about something Rosalind couldn't hear over the general babble of the table.

The dinner worked its slow, winding way from the soup down to the cheeses. As soon as each of the guests had been served their choice morsel, Mr. Vaughn pushed back his chair and stood.

"You will forgive me for interrupting your meal, but I have some happy news." He smiled and raised his glass. "Tonight, it is my very great pleasure to announce the betrothal of my oldest daughter, Cecilia, to our good friend, our neighbor, Mr. Marius Corbyn."

CHAPTER 33

A Double-Edged Betrothal

*But most of them said marriage would tame him,
and cure him, and set all to rights . . .*

Theodore Edward Hook, *Cousin William* or
The Fatal Attachment

The very moment the women removed to the drawing
rooms, the matrons all clustered around Mrs. Vaughn.
That lady beamed expansively and accepted their congratulations with open delight.

The girls, of course, crowded around Cecilia. They all congratulated her and demanded details. Cecilia's sisters kept
their stations beside her. Rosalind suspected they'd been instructed to stay at their posts for the whole of the evening, no
matter what.

Cecilia herself was blushing furiously. If any of her friends
saw the panic in her eyes, they were ignoring it.

Except Louisa. Louisa stood apart from the group, watching Cecilia. Her expression was intent, anxious, and more
than a little angry.

Rosalind stole up to her side.

"Did you know this was going to happen?"

Louisa shook her head. "There was absolutely no hint of
it, and I was *here*, in this house this afternoon, paying a call.

I don't understand it. I don't understand why she'd *agree* to it."

"It seems her mother wanted the match very badly," said Rosalind.

"But *why*? There are a dozen other men in the county just as rich and eligible. Some of them have even more land than the Corbyns, and all of them are less . . . I don't even know how to describe it . . . less of an unpleasant a possibility than the brother of one's dead fiancé."

Rosalind scanned the room, looking for something that might help settle her disordered thoughts. What she saw was Helen Corbyn. Helen had not joined the general crowd around Cecilia, either. She was seated on a small sofa toward the back of the room. She looked pale, Rosalind thought, and rather stunned.

She touched Louisa's arm and flicked a finger in Helen's direction. Louisa nodded and the two of them crossed the room to join her in the dim corner.

Louisa sat down beside Helen. "Are you all right?"

Helen just shook her head. There was a tea set on the table. Rosalind poured out a cup, added milk and sugar, and gave it to Helen. She stared at it for a minute and then drank an enormous gulp.

"Did you know the engagement was going to be announced tonight?" asked Rosalind gently.

"I knew something was happening but . . . no. Marius didn't see fit to tell me about this. Neither did *she*." Helen glowered toward Cecilia. "He hates the whole notion of marriage for himself, and he hates . . ." She broke the sentence off. "How could Cecilia agree to this! It's monstrous! She barely had any feeling for William and now . . ."

Rosalind touched Helen's hand to remind her to lower her voice. Helen started, and then realized she'd been on the verge of making a scene. Fresh panic filled her expression.

"It's all right, Helen," said Louisa.

"No, it isn't," Helen croaked. "He didn't even tell me

there was a betrothal, never mind an engagement." She glared at the wall, as if she could see through the layers of wood paneling all the way to the dining room, where Marius would still be sitting with the other men over port and brandy. "How could he not tell me . . . oh Lord." She stopped. "I think Fortuna knew. Oh my . . ." Memories were rising like a tide. Rosalind could see them shifting behind the girl's eyes. "She did know."

"That's why she's not here," said Rosalind.

"Yes. How could I have been so stupid? I caught her coming out of Marius's book room today, white as a ghost. I asked her what was wrong, but she wouldn't tell me. And then there was that business with the mail bag . . ."

"The mail bag?" Louisa repeated.

"It was that day we had the unrest at the works. We'd just got home and our footman was taking the mail bag to the book room, but Fortuna stopped him and said she'd take it. She should have left it in the book room, or given it straight to Marius. But she didn't give it to him. She kept it."

Rosalind cast a casual glance toward the larger gathering. No one was paying them any attention, not even Mrs. Vaughn. She was too busy with her friends, extolling her triumph. Cecilia was fenced in by her sisters and friends.

"Why did Fortuna keep the mail? What was she . . ." Louisa's words trailed away. "Oh."

"She was looking for a letter," said Rosalind. "One she didn't want anyone else to see." *Especially Marius.*

Helen bowed her head. Rosalind made a decision. She touched Helen's sleeve.

"Can you hold yourself together for just a few minutes longer? It will look odd if you're the only one who does not congratulate Cecilia, and you don't want there to be any additional talk."

Anger flashed in Helen's eyes, but it was quickly replaced by a much deeper weariness. "No, you're right."

"I'll come with you," said Louisa.

"As will I," said Rosalind.

The three of them stood. Louisa took Helen's arm and fixed a reasonably convincing smile on her face as they crossed to the knot of girls around Cecilia. By the time they got there, Helen was able to manage a smile of her own.

"Congratulations, Cecilia." Helen took both Cecilia's hands in her own. "I'm so glad you're going to be my sister."

"Thank you, Helen. May I call tomorrow? We have so much to discuss."

"Yes, of course, anytime you like!"

They kissed each other on both cheeks. They smiled at each other. Rosalind did not miss the fact that both of them had tears shining in their eyes. She hoped that the watching crowd took them for tears of joy.

Doubtlessly Helen and Cecilia do, too.

Cecilia pressed Helen's hands one more time and turned to accept yet more congratulations from a plump matron in a truly unfortunate cloth-of-silver turban. This gave Helen and Louisa and Rosalind an excuse to let themselves fade backward through the little crowd that kept Cecilia Vaughn at its center.

When they were finally clear, Rosalind murmured, "Louisa, I think Helen needs some air. Can you take her out?"

"Yes, of course," agreed Louisa. "Come along, Helen. We'll find a quiet spot and pretend you're quizzing me about dressmakers. What about you, Rosalind?"

"I've a tear in my sleeve. I'm sure there's a retiring room. I'll have someone send for Mrs. Kendricks."

She said all this looking straight at Louisa, who nodded briskly.

As the girls took themselves farther into the interconnected drawing rooms, Rosalind moved to the door. She very deliberately caught Cecilia Vaughn's eye. Cecilia saw, and understood. She said something to the girls and came over to meet Rosalind at the door.

"Congratulations again, Cecilia," said Rosalind. "I wish you very happy."

"Thank you. It's all a bit overwhelming." She spoke the words by rote. She'd probably said them several dozen times already this evening.

"I imagine. If I may be horribly trivial, I was in need of the retiring room . . . ?"

"Oh yes. I'll show you." Cecilia looked back at her sisters. The tallest of them shrugged wearily. Evidently, the duty of guarding their sister was beginning to pall.

Outside the drawing room, the corridor was cool, still, and dim. Cecilia inhaled the fresh air deeply. Some little bit of color began to return to her cheeks.

"Your mother looks quite pleased," said Rosalind as they walked toward the foyer.

"Yes," Cecilia said it like a guilty admission. "Father, too."

Despite the fact that they were quite alone, Rosalind lowered her voice. "And you?"

"I'm delighted, of course." There was not a trace of sincerity in Cecilia's words. "Is—I hope Helen is not getting a headache. She looked a little startled when Father made the announcement."

"Perhaps she did not realize it would be made public tonight. I'm sure she thought that your mother would like to have a separate engagement party."

"Yes, well." Cecilia made a weak, dismissive gesture. "They wanted the thing signed and sealed."

Rosalind lifted her brows in polite inquiry. Cecilia declined to answer.

"And how did your brother receive the news?" Rosalind asked. "Was that why you quarreled the other day?"

Cecilia froze at once in her tracks. "How did you know about that?"

"My maid saw you in the church. I don't believe anyone else did."

"Oh." Cecilia had been looking pale, now color flooded her cheeks, and for a moment, Rosalind was afraid she might start to cry. "Bartolemew is pleased. He's been in London, you know, and he's back now, and he . . . well, he's pleased. He's not really supposed to be home yet and didn't like me reminding him of it. But I promised I'd speak with father and make sure he's able to return for the wedding. It will be soon, it . . ."

They had reached the doors of the dining room. The sound of masculine laughter reverberated through the carved wood.

"Why are you lying to me, Cecilia?" breathed Rosalind.

"Because I have to."

Rosalind opened her mouth, but Cecilia held up her hand. "*Please*, Miss Thorne. I understand you want to help Helen. I do. But you must ask her to have patience. I will explain everything as soon as I can."

Rosalind wished she did not have to be so cold. She wished she had time to convince Cecilia she truly was her friend. But she did not have the time. "Is it Lucian you're protecting?"

The look of mingled fear and determination Cecilia turned on her then was heartbreaking.

"Miss Thorne, I'm going to ask you one last time, please do not go any further with this. Help Helen, but leave me out of it. I have no wish to become your enemy, but there are promises I have made that I am determined to keep, and I will not be interfered with."

She turned and strode away then, heading back to the brightly lit rooms to endure the guardianship of her family and the congratulations of her friends.

Anger burned through Rosalind. *What is being done to this girl?*

To all these girls?

CHAPTER 34

The Complexities of Domestic Arrangements

*In this marriage . . . I secure a place in the world,
which I flatter myself I shall be able to fill with
effect at all events.*

Theodore Edward Hook, *Cousin William* or
The Fatal Attachment

Rosalind was still trying to collect herself when she heard footsteps coming down the gallery. She had just time enough to smooth out her features before Earnest Worthing strolled around the corner.

He drew up sharply when he saw her. "Oh, sorry! I . . . erm . . . They still at it in there?" He nodded toward the closed dining room.

"I'm afraid so, yes."

"Then I'm glad you're here. Surely between the two of us we could find an excuse to keep me from having to go back in, eh?" He grinned, an amiable, slightly foolish grin. Then, a thought struck him and he bowed. "Damme if I don't forget my manners. We've not been formally introduced. Earnest Worthing at your service."

"How do you do, Mr. Worthing?" Rosalind made her curtsy. "Miss Rosalind Thorne."

"Ah! Thought so. Heard your name at dinner and so on. Well, Miss Thorne, can I escort you someplace? Or fetch a wrap? Really, anything will do to avoid another of Vaughn's damned—'scuse me—arguments about poaching."

Rosalind smiled. "Well, I believe I have become rather confused as to my way back to the card rooms. If you could oblige me by being my escort, Mr. Worthing?"

"Gladly, Miss Thorne." He bowed again. "This way, if you please."

At another time, Rosalind reentering the drawing room at the side of an unmarried man might have raised eyebrows, but in this case it did not. It was clear from the way the younger women greeted him that Mr. Worthing was regarded as something of a harmless pet. The fact probably annoyed him privately, but he bore it with good grace. He walked Rosalind to a chair and saw her seated comfortably.

"Anything else?" He made a positive pair of puppy-dog eyes at her, which did nothing to reverse her impression of pet status.

"Will you sit for a moment, Mr. Worthing? I'm sure the gentlemen will be arriving shortly."

"Be glad to." He dropped himself into the wing-backed chair with the loose-limbed casualness of someone who was at home in the whole world. "How are you finding your stay here, Miss Thorne?"

They made small talk for a bit. Rosalind was very careful to keep her body language reserved. The younger Vaughn misses, clearly having imbibed their lessons from their mother, shot a series of curious glances in her direction. When she did not give them anything to see, they eventually lost interest.

"I was surprised not to see Mr. Mirabeau at dinner," she said eventually. She spoke casually, depending on the general noise of the conversation to cover her individual words. "But I understand he and the Vaughns don't get along."

"Putting it mildly," said Mr. Worthing.

Rosalind clicked her tongue. "That's so sad. I wish I could be of some help. . . ." She paused as if an idea struck her. "Do you know what his dislike stems from?"

"Well, now, that's a longer story, and not all mine to tell, you see. But Mirabeau, he was friends with Lucian." Mr. Worthing eyed the shifting gathering again, to make sure no one had heard him utter the forbidden name. "You've probably heard of him by now."

"He broke with Mr. Vaughn."

"That's it. We all liked him, but he and Mirabeau were chums since we were boys together. Backed each other up at school, all that. When he was sent packing, Mirabeau lost his temper, said some things he shouldn't."

"It seems Mr. Mirabeau has a habit of intemperance."

"No, actually, he's a good sort. Levelheaded. I mean, he'll go along with the lads on a lark, but it's never any more than that." Mr. Worthing stopped and added, softly but seriously, "That damned duel . . . never should have happened, never should have even come close. Not Peter's fault, no matter what anyone says."

Rosalind had met so many young men like Mr. Worthing. They were born to a certain degree of wealth, and the expectations for them were always high, but always vague. They were sent to schools, less to study and more to get to know one another. Some of them broke away from the established path and found a living in business or politics. Most of them, however, spun a comfortable cocoon of family, house, and land from which they never emerged. They had servants and wife and amusements, and got on with things day to day, but always seeming mildly bewildered that nothing ever seemed to quite matter. They stayed that way unless and until something happened—misfortune or war or some other event to jolt them out of the benign course of their lives. That was when their character might be revealed to themselves, as well as to the world.

William Corbyn's death had clearly been such a jolt to Mr.

Worthing. It seemed to Rosalind that he was still struggling to understand what his actions meant, to himself most of all. Rosalind liked him better for that struggle.

"It's very sad when friends fall out," said Rosalind. "Sadder still with families."

"Yes, you've hit it there. Still, where there's life, there's hope, eh? Always a chance to make it right, if only a chap can see it."

"Do you think there's a chance that L—that Peter's friend will reconcile with his father?"

Mr. Worthing considered this. "Maybe not with his father. That's a tricky business. Don't have all the details, don't want 'em. But tricky, tricky. Still, he might yet make things right with his mother, and his siblings, and after that"—Worthing shrugged—"who knows?"

"Do you think he's in touch with any of the family?"

For the first time Rosalind felt she had the full focus of Mr. Worthing's attention. "Now, Miss Thorne, I suspect you of trying to wriggle a confidence out of me, eh?"

Rosalind dropped her gaze. She could not force a blush, but she did manage a credible show of mild discomfort by smoothing her skirts and resettling her hands.

"I'm sure Lady Casselmaine would warn me against the dangers of idle curiosity."

"And much more than that, I'll wager." Mr. Worthing laughed. "Natural thing, curiosity, and a man'd be surprised if you hadn't heard a few things, what with getting to know his sister and so on. . . ." Mr. Worthing grew serious again. "Let me say that I shouldn't be at all surprised if some of the family know where he is. As I said, where there's life, there's hope. Maybe even reconciliation."

His gaze was lingering on Helen as he spoke, and an idea sparked inside Rosalind.

"Indeed, such a reconciliation happened with the Corbyns, I believe?"

It was a shot in the dark, but it hit home nonetheless.

"Well, after a fashion," drawled Worthing. "Things changed a lot after William got back from the wars, but he was trying to make it up." He shook his head sadly.

"Were the brothers close as boys?"

"Practically lived in each other's pockets," said Mr. Worthing. "Depended on each other, you know. Had to. Their father was . . . well, let's say the man kept both eyes and both hands on the future, if you take my meaning. Didn't have much time for anybody hanging about in the present, if you take my meaning."

"I do, Mr. Worthing."

"Old Mr. Corbyn and Vaughn made a pretty pair, I can tell you." Mr. Worthing's voice dropped to a near whisper, but Rosalind still heard the anger in it.

"They were friends?"

"Wouldn't use that word, exactly. More like they'd agreed to stay out of each other's way. I remember when William and Cecilia's engagement was announced; it was like the pair of them thought getting Cecilia to marry William would unite the clans, if you see what I mean. Give the two old duffers an excuse to never get into a fight in the first place."

"A sort of preemptive truce?"

"Just so, Miss Thorne. Just so. Now, old Mrs. Corbyn, she was nowhere near as happy with the arrangement."

"Mrs. Corbyn?" Rosalind felt her brow furrow.

"Nearly came to blows with Mrs. Vaughn. Right over the soup at one of the Ablehavens' dinner parties. Was a sight to behold, let me tell you. Not a woman to make a scene, Mrs. Corbyn, but there it was."

"What was Mrs. Corbyn's objection to Cecilia?"

"Didn't like the family," he said promptly. "Didn't like their looks or their background. Very big on background was old Mrs. Corbyn. Hobby was drawing up family trees. Would drag them out and show them to you on a moment's notice. Had the Corbyns' line traced practically back to when the Romans first landed."

She believed that to understand a person, one had to under-stand their family, Marius Corbyn had said of his mother. He'd also said, *We know that what makes a horse is its blood-line. Why should we ignore that as a vital facet of the human being?*

"But old Mr. Corbyn overruled his wife," said Rosalind.

"No idea how," said Mr. Worthing. "But he did it, stiff-necked old bastard—I beg your pardon, Miss Thorne." Rosalind waved this away. "Of course, William and Cecilia helped that along."

"William *and* Cecilia?"

"Oh yes." Worthing nodded, a little surprised at Rosalind's surprise. "Cecilia was very keen on the match, in her quiet way."

That did not sort at all with what Louisa had said.

"Mind you," Mr. Worthing went on, "I suspect any chance to get out from under her mother's thumb would be welcome, but she went to Mr. Corbyn with William saying they wanted to get married and they'd elope if they had to, but they'd really rather not, and that settled the matter."

Why hadn't Louisa told her about this? Was it possible she hadn't known? That beggared belief. A romantic attachment so powerful that both parties were willing to elope rather than be separated, that would very quickly become the talk of the neighborhood.

What on earth could have driven such a declaration? An oppressed girl might consider a scandalous elopement prefer-able to remaining in her parents' house. But what reason, short of passionate attachment, would William Corbyn have to agree to such an action, and such a marriage?

There are promises I have made that I am determined to keep, Cecilia had said.

Whatever those promises were, they were powerful enough that Cecilia was willing to enter into a marriage with a man she knew hated her family in order to see them through.

CHAPTER 35

Unfortunate Encounters

*The ancient, true, & Principal Uses of Inns,
Alehouses & Victuallying-Houses is for the
receipt, Relieving & Lodging of Travellers &
for the Supply of the Wants of the People . . . but
was never meant for the Entertainment &
harbouring of Lewd & Idel People to spend &
consume their Money & their time in a lewd
and drunken Manner.*

Charge to the Grand Jury of Surrey, 1736

It's a damnable business, thought Peter Mirabeau as he stared glumly at the low, seedy inn that was known simply as the Traveller.

The place squatted right on the edge of the fens. Men's voices bellowed out some raucous song he didn't understand. More men clustered around the stone horse trough, passing a jug back and forth between them.

Mirabeau's grip tightened involuntarily on the stout walking stick he'd brought with him and he stepped into the doorway.

The great room was filled with smoke, and the odors of alcohol and unwashed men. As shadowed as it was, Bartolemew Vaughn stood out clearly among the laborers and farm hands. He spotted Mirabeau in the doorway and raised a glass of . . . whatever they served in this place. Idly, Mirabeau thought it might possibly be a good bottle. Everyone knew half the smuggled (or poached) goods that passed through the county wound up in the Traveller's cellar. Vaughn motioned for Mirabeau to come in. In answer, Mirabeau turned and walked back out into the yard to where he'd secured his horse.

He wasn't about to let any of the inn's men touch Agamemnon, so he'd left the gelding tied to the post in the yard. Mirabeau patted his horse's neck and let him nuzzle his gloved hand. *Wish I'd thought to bring some sugar. Going to be a long night for us both.*

Fortunately, Vaughn did not choose to keep him waiting. Bartolemew ducked under the Traveller's low doorframe and emerged into the moonlight. He was a tall, rangy man with a long face and large, liquid eyes and that dark golden hair that all the Vaughns possessed. The combination gave him a poetical air that he was quick to use against any woman who caught his fancy.

He carried a brown bottle in one fist and a crockery mug in the other.

"Drink?" Vaughn waved the bottle at Mirabeau. Mirabeau shook his head. Vaughn shrugged, poured a measure of—whatever it was—into the mug and tossed it back. He smacked his lips and stared up at the stars.

"I've brought what you asked—" Mirabeau began, but Vaughn waved the bottle and cut him off.

"No good, I'm afraid," he said. "I've changed my mind."

"What do you mean?" Mirabeau had been doling out funds to keep the man away from the Corbyns, especially Helen. The blaggard was not above using what he knew about William to make her life a misery, and he might just try to extort money straight from her, if he couldn't get it from anywhere else.

Helen was going to be furious if she found out about this

meeting, but Mirabeau was willing to risk it. He was willing to risk anything to keep this man away from her.

"I mean I don't need your charity anymore." Vaughn lowered his gaze and grinned. "I've made it all right with the pater, you see. I'll be reinstalled in the family domicile before the fortnight's out."

"Does Lord Casselmaine know you're coming back?" asked Vaughn. Casselmaine would be none too pleased, especially with all these new questions being raised about William Corbyn's death.

"What's he got to do with it? This is between me and my father, and if his very nobby grace is smart, it'll stay that way. If not"—Vaughn shrugged—"well, on his head be it." This time he took his drink straight from the bottle. "So." He leaned in close enough for Peter to smell the fumes on his breath. "If I was you, Mr. Mirabeau, I'd take yourself and that most excellent horse out of here, before any of these fine fellows"—he waved toward the cluster of men who were passing the jug about—"decide to do something about the both of you. Oh." He held up the bottle, pointing a finger at Mirabeau with the same hand. "And if you are a very good boy, when I return I won't let word of our little meetings slip to his grace, or that tasty fiancée of yours."

Fury surged inside Mirabeau. "You mention her again and I will stop your filthy mouth."

For a moment, he thought Vaughn was going to make him put actions to his words, and for that same moment, he knew he'd relish the chance. But Vaughn shrugged and pressed his finger to his lips. Then he grinned again—that damnable, insolent grin—and strode back to the inn.

As soon as Vaughn was out of sight, Mirabeau untied Agamemnon, threw himself onto the horse's back, and rode straight out of there.

What the devil just happened? He's clearly up to something. Never knew the man to turn down money. . . .

The truth of the matter was, Mirabeau had been paying Vaughn to stay away since that horrible morning when he was supposed to be dueling William Corbyn. Vaughn was supposed to be in Ireland, of course, but everyone knew the bloodthirsty idiot had never actually gone. He wasn't going to miss his chance to participate in a duel and finally prove himself a gentleman.

So, on the morning of the duel, Mirabeau went out early and intercepted Vaughn on his way to Corbyn Park. Vaughn might overflow with temper and pride, especially when he also overflowed with drink, but he was also perpetually in need of funds. It hadn't taken long to agree to a price to turn him back.

Since then, Mirabeau wondered if he'd done the right thing. He knew Worthing saw him on his way to find Bartolemew that morning. He knew that by keeping this secret, he was helping keep Helen's worry alive.

He'd wondered more than once if he was now paying bribes to a murderer.

No, Mirabeau told himself, as he always did. *That's impossible*. Vaughn had already been half-drunk that morning when Mirabeau had met him. It was possible Vaughn had taken his money and still gone on to the meeting place with Corbyn. It was *not* possible that a drunken Bartolemew Vaughn could have shot a soldier like Colonel Corbyn.

Unless it was an accident.

Mirabeau shoved that thought away.

He thought he'd given Bartolemew enough to put an end to the matter. The problem was, in Bartolemew's eyes, Mirabeau had revealed himself to be a soft touch. That meant another payment out of Mirabeau's pocket every time Vaughn came sneaking back and looking to make fresh trouble.

But he'd kept on paying. He'd done it for Helen's sake and, yes, his own. Helen was desperate for answers and when Helen got desperate, she also got forgetful of consequences. She didn't need to be tempted to seek those answers from the likes of Bartolemew Vaughn.

Hope Miss Thorne can clear this up for her. Hope things get better soon. Hope . . .

I just hope. It's all I have left.

Almost, he amended. Because along with his hopes, he still had Helen, and if didn't get a move on, she'd be angry.

He nudged Agamemnon into a cantor and then a full gallop. A gentleman never kept a lady waiting.

It was well past midnight when Mirabeau finally rode up the drive to the Vaughns' house. He'd timed it well. The yard was busy with groomsmen, footmen, and outriders, rushing to and fro with their torches and lanterns, getting the carriages ready for the party guests who were making their exits.

One of the features of the Vaughns' yard was a dramatic, spreading oak tree. As he'd agreed with Helen, Mirabeau stationed himself there, making sure to stay deep in the shadows. He dismounted and wrapped Agamemnon's reins loosely around a lower branch. He hoped she would not be long. The night had grown chill, and Mirabeau's worries about what the hell Vaughn was up to were being replaced by worries about keeping his best horse standing for too long.

He shouldn't have doubted. Helen, as always, was true to her word. Even from here, and even though she wore a dark cloak with the hood up, he could tell it was her. He knew exactly how she moved, and how she held herself.

She slipped smoothly between the shifting pools of light and into the shadows, arriving breathless and beautifully flushed.

Behave, Mirabeau.

"Peter! Oh, thank heavens!"

He took both her hands and squeezed them tight. Let the world see this, he didn't care. He wanted to do a great deal more, but this was already a risk for her, and he wasn't going to add to it. "I'm sorry to make such heavy weather of this, Helen. But I can't . . . I just couldn't face—them." He glowered at the Vaughns' house. Then he stopped and looked at her more closely. "Did something happen?" Vaughn's odious, drunken face reared up in his memory. If anybody had said anything, if anybody had *dared*—

"Marius is going to marry Cecilia Vaughn."

Mirabeau's thoughts pulled up to a sudden halt. *"What?"*

"Mr. Vaughn announced it, right at the supper table. I had no idea. They'd never said a word, either one of them. She doesn't even *like* him, and he hates all of them. He thinks they're . . . bad blood. Inferior stock. I swear, Peter, I don't know what's happened!" Helen's hands trembled between his. "Louisa thinks Mr. Vaughn has found a way to pressure Marius. It's the only explanation."

"My God. Do you have any idea what it might be?"

She shook her head. "None. Marius . . . he's capable of being rude and unpleasant, but he's the one of us who has no secrets. Unless he got up to something at school, I suppose . . . but what could that have been?"

"What does your Miss Thorne think?"

Helen shook her head. "She doesn't know. She thinks money might be at the root of it. I suppose it could be. If they won't tell me about a wedding, why on earth would they tell me about money?" Her words were drenched in bitterness, but Mirabeau only half heard her. He was thinking of Bartolemew, drinking and celebrating—yes, that was the word, *celebrating*—in that foul inn. "Are you all right?"

"I don't know," she admitted. "I'm just, I'm so confused, and angry. I don't know what to do," she whispered. "I swear I'd run away, if there was anyplace to go."

Mirabeau pressed her hands. "There is. Tomorrow I'll visit your brother. Declare myself. Get his consent. We'll get married, just as soon as can be."

"Thank you, Peter." Tears were shining in her eyes. Love

and anger welled up in him. "I didn't want it to be like this. I just . . . Everything's out of control."

"It's all right. Whatever is happening . . . none of this is your fault. We'll get you out of it. Marius said he's in favor, didn't he?"

"He did. I only hope he hasn't changed his mind. Everything's gone so mad, I'm afraid. . . ."

Mirabeau didn't let her finish. "If he refuses, we elope. That's all there is to it. Not a driver in the county could catch either one of us if we decided to make a run for the border, eh?"

That actually got a smile out of her. Helen reached up and laid her gloved hand against his cheek. "I'd like to see them even try."

His heart swelled. Damn it, he could do anything in that moment. He could fly if she asked it. He took her hand and pressed a kiss into the palm, and then closed her fingers around the spot.

"Now, I best be off home before we're spotted and some Vaughn or the other takes offense. But I will be on your brother's doorstep first thing."

"You'd better be, or I'll come throw you across my saddle and run off with you all by myself."

What a girl she is! No turn of fortune could keep her down. She'd always find a way to fight.

Mirabeau kissed her then, right on the mouth, and she put her hands on his shoulders and kissed him back, and it was worth any trouble, any scandal, anything at all, to have that kiss to take home with him.

CHAPTER 36

Unforeseen Consequences

*I had been entrapped into the very snare which I
had hoped to escape . . .*

Theodore Edward Hook, *Cousin William* or
The Fatal Attachment

The rest of the evening was strained, to say the least.
The gentlemen had arrived in the drawing room while
Rosalind was still talking with Mr. Worthing. Devon had come
straight to her side. Frustratingly, the wedding announcement
threw their hope of showing themselves off to the neighbors
as a potential pairing into disarray. Devon, as the Duke of
Casselmaine and Marius Corbyn's employer, had to circulate
about the room, listening to all the cheerful speculation about
what a good thing this wedding would be for the families involved and for the neighborhood in general.

Rosalind, on the other hand, attached herself to Helen.
She and Louisa together sat with her, bearing as much of the
brunt of the gossip and speculation as they could. By unspoken agreement, Louisa diverted the girls, while Rosalind kept
the matrons occupied by detailing plans for Louisa's own
wedding and speculating what Cecilia and Mrs. Vaughn might
do for their own ceremony.

"Oh, everything will be of the finest," remarked Mrs. Ablehaven with a sniff. "Mrs. Vaughn will see to that."

But such expressions of pique were, to Rosalind's mind, remarkably rare. What struck her was how many persons seemed relieved that Marius Corbyn was getting married at all. Apparently, his dislike for the idea was no secret, and even with Helen all but engaged to Peter Mirabeau, there had been a great deal of worry about the future of Corbyn Park as a stable estate. Now that it looked likely to remain intact and in familiar hands, most people were ready to declare that Mr. Corbyn had made a sound decision.

"Not perhaps the finest pedigreed family," murmured more than one matron into Rosalind's ear. "But Cecilia herself has always been perfectly steady, and she's remarkably well-bred. Considering." This was always accompanied by a discreet glance in Mrs. Vaughn's direction. "Still. After so much tragedy, it will be good to have the house settled."

Rosalind would murmur her agreement, and change the subject.

Mr. Corbyn installed himself in a corner and let the gentlemen and matrons come to him. What he did not do was go to his intended's side. Not once. Cecilia was taken into the card room with her mother and sisters and sat down to play at whist while Marius remained in the sitting room.

As the evening wore on, Rosalind found her anger had not cooled one whit. Neither did her sense of helplessness. She longed to be able to talk more with Cecilia. But even if she went in to join the card game, there would be little chance of private conversation. She would need to find another way, and another time.

A few minutes after midnight, Marius Corbyn decided he'd stayed long enough, and rather peremptorily came up to inquire whether Helen was ready to leave.

"Of course. Just let me get my things." Helen signaled to one of the parlor maids.

"I don't believe I've had a chance to add my congratulations yet, Mr. Corbyn," said Louisa. She had been sparkling all evening, and it was only just now beginning to sound a little forced. "I wish you and Cecilia very happy."

"Thank you." Mr. Corbyn bowed. "I trust we may be."

"Let me add my congratulations as well," said Rosalind. "This will make a fine new addition to your family tree."

The look Marius turned on her then was so filled with hate, Rosalind's breath caught in her throat.

Marius did not speak. He did not even attempt to smile. He just bowed and held out his hand for his sister to take.

"Well!" breathed Louisa as the Corbyns walked away.

Rosalind found the only answer she could make was a silent nod.

The chill from Marius Corbyn's silent glance was still with her when she, Louisa, and Devon all climbed into Devon's closed carriage at the end of their evening.

"Well, that was an interesting party," said Louisa, huddling underneath the rug.

"It certainly did not lack for diversion," remarked Rosalind.

"Nor yet entirely engaging conversation," added Devon.

That, fortunately, was the extent of the conversation they all three seemed to be in the mood for. Rosalind was tired, but at the same time, her thoughts were racing. She was angry at herself for failing to do more. She should have found a way to ask more questions. She should have gone into the card room and engaged with the matrons there. She had wasted an opportunity to learn so much. What did she know now that she did not before? A little of Marius Corbyn's background, of his attachment to his mother and her attachment to the family line. She had the fact that he had been devoted to his older brother once upon a time. She also knew a little more of the ruthlessness of Mr. and Mrs. Vaughn when it came to the disposition of their daughter. She had seen the depth of Cecilia Vaughn's determination, but she still had no idea what was at the root of it.

What has she promised? And to whom? Rosalind thought of Mrs. Kendricks's description of the argument in the church. Was that about those promises? Or something else altogether?

She had to work out what was going on. Setting aside all other interest she had in the matter, Rosalind could not in conscience leave Cecilia Vaughn to the mercy of a man like Marius Corbyn, who could muster so much poison in a single glance.

Rosalind thought of the address Lady Casselmaine had given her. She would need to write to Alice and George at once, so they could speak to Lucian Vaughn. Or, perhaps, she needed to go back to London herself. Or should she stay at the hall and wait to hear what news Firth Rollins might discover about the Corbyns' financial situation and arrangements? Because this must all come back to the money and the land. It must.

Mustn't it? Rosalind rubbed her temple. *Why can't I think? What is wrong with me?*

It was cool enough that the carriage windows had all been raised. The lights from the outriders' torches created a delicate play of light and shadow against the draperies as the carriage rocked along the road. Rosalind felt Devon looking toward her, and she knew she should turn and muster some reassuring smile, but she found she could not.

Not just yet. In a moment I will. There is no need for me to be making such heavy weather of this. There is . . .

Her thoughts were interrupted then by Samuel calling to the horses. Their carriage slowed and stopped.

Devon frowned and let down the window.

"Samuel, what's the matter?"

"Riderless horse here, sir. Might be someone's had an accident."

"Right." Devon unlatched the door and climbed out. Rosalind caught a glimpse of trees standing black in the uncertain light of the moon and the torches. They'd entered one of the stands of forest that waited between the farms and the fens.

"Where is it?" called Devon. "Ah, Daniel, let's . . ." Devon's words stopped short, and he swore.

"What is it?" Rosalind craned her neck to try to see whatever it was that raised such a reaction from him.

"Casselmaine?" added in Louisa.

"It's Agamemnon," Devon called back. "Mirabeau's horse."

Rosalind scrambled out of the carriage. One of the outriders was holding the reins of a tall, dark gelding—a chestnut or a bay, it was impossible to tell in the darkness—but Devon apparently knew his markings well enough that he was already issuing orders.

"Samuel, Daniel, bring the lanterns! Have we any more torches? Spread out, everyone!"

"Oh Lord." Louisa threw aside the rug and climbed out next to Rosalind. "Let's go, Rosalind. Oh Lord! Oh, poor Helen!"

"Surely we don't need to panic yet," said Rosalind, even as she felt the fear riding inside her. "The horse may have just bolted . . ."

"Believe me, if Agamemnon just startled, Mirabeau would still be on him." Louisa was already gathering up her hems and plunged into the underbrush. "The only person I've ever seen who could ride like him is Helen. Peter!" Louisa raised her voice, shouting into the woods. "Peter Mirabeau!"

The men took up her cry. They spread out into the woods, taking the lights with them, each of them calling and hallooing. Rosalind gathered up her own hems as tight as she could and grit her teeth to wade into the darkness with the others.

"Peter Mirabeau!" she called. "Peter Mirabeau!"

There was no answer, just the shouts of the other searchers. Rosalind stumbled over something unseen and pitched forward. Her failing hand slammed against a tree, barely saving her from tumbling into the dirt.

She stood there, trying to catch her breath and staring hard into the darkness. The night's damp chill crawled over her, and the men's shouts rang in her ears. At the same time, another man's voice rose from the back of Rosalind's thoughts.

It's nothing like chasing a man through the streets.

The voice belonged to Adam Harkness. Rosalind and Alice had been sitting with him in his mother's parlor, drinking tea. Alice had finally teased him into sharing a few stories from his time when he was part of the horse patrol and hunting highwaymen.

You have to hold still. You have to give yourself time to feel the woods around you. If your man's there, the woods'll give him up.

Rosalind made herself stand where she was, her hand resting against the prickling tree bark. She stared into the darkness, willing her eyes to adjust, willing her mind to settle.

The torches moved behind her and the shadows shifted in front of her. A patch of white flashed among the fallen leaves.

"Here!" she cried. "Bring the lights!"

One of the outriders hurried up with the lantern and raised it high. Rosalind's knees buckled. What she had taken for a fallen tree limb was a man. It was Peter Mirabeau.

He lay on his back, his head at a dreadful angle. Blood soaked his collar and the front of his white shirt.

He wasn't moving at all.

CHAPTER 37

What Is Done in Darkness

The trick itself spoke volumes.

Theodore Edward Hook, *Cousin William* or
The Fatal Attachment

In the end, it transpired that Peter Mirabeau had been enormously lucky.

The moment Rosalind shouted, Devon and the other men came running. Devon knelt at once at the fallen man's side and, to Rosalind's shock, called out, "He breathes! He's living yet!"

For hours afterward, time felt distorted. All the things that needed to happen slowly happened far too quickly, and all that needed to happen quickly stretched out forever. They sent one of the outriders ahead on Agamemnon to alert Mirror House. Another was sent to rouse the physician, Dr. Stackpole.

A rug from the carriage was used to make a sling to carry Mirabeau. As soon as they had the fallen man as secure as they could make him in the carriage, Samuel drove on at a walk. Rosalind felt suspended in a net of fears—fear that any jolt might be the end of Mr. Mirabeau, fear they would not reach his home in time, fear of the dirt and the blood that they could not clean from his injuries, fear of the terrible, croaking noises that emerged from his torn throat.

Peter Mirabeau's parents were mild people who received their fallen son with determination and bewilderment. The household threw itself into motion immediately. Peter's bed was stripped of all its blankets, clean sheets were brought, along with water and bandages. A roaring fire was built in the hearth. His mother staunched the blood, and washed his face, and cried silently the whole time as he croaked and tried to struggle. His father, the butler, and Devon helped hold him down.

When Dr. Stackpole arrived, he slammed the door shut behind them all.

It fell to Louisa and Rosalind to be in the receiving room when Helen and Fortuna arrived with the dawn. Helen took one look at their pale faces, turned, and raced up the stairs. She did not return.

Fortuna heard all their news in staunch silence.

"I think . . ." Fortuna stood. "I think there will need to be a breakfast. And tea. Someone will have to give the orders." She left the room. She did not return, either.

Rosalind and Louisa sat together, clutching each other's hands, feeling the long minutes crawl past.

At long last, Devon came into the receiving room. Rosalind had never seen him so grim, or so pale.

"He's alive," he told them both. "He might stay that way if . . ." He cleared his throat. "The fever is at work already."

Rosalind left Louisa and crossed to him. She laid her hand on his shoulder. He covered it and they simply stood like that for a long moment.

"Dr. Stackpole's a good man," Devon told them at last. "He will do everything possible. We should leave. They"—he nodded toward the door to indicate the whole of the household and its additions—"have enough to worry about. I've told Stackpole and Mrs. Graves they should send to Cassell House at once if there is anything I can do."

And so the carriage was brought, and Samuel drove them home through the brightening morning. There, they had to tell the story to Mrs. Showell in the front hall, and then Rosalind had to tell it again to Mrs. Kendricks.

It was too much. When Rosalind was finally able to let her maid undress her, she fell into the bed like she was the one who had been struck down.

It was past noon when Rosalind woke. All the events of the night came flooding back to her at once.

"Mrs. Kendricks!" she called, struggling out from under the covers.

Her housekeeper was there at once. "No, miss!" she cried. "You should stay in bed. You've had a shock. . . ."

"So has everyone else," snapped Rosalind. "I need to see Lord Casselmaine. He . . . he was in a very bad way last night."

That stopped whatever protest Mrs. Kendricks might have thought to make. Between them, they got Rosalind into her simplest muslin dress and pinned her hair into a loose chignon. Barely fit to be seen, Rosalind bolted from her rooms.

Devon, as it transpired, was in his book room. When Rosalind burst in, he was standing at the window, staring out across the gardens. There was a tray with coffee and rolls on the desk, very much untouched.

Devon turned.

"There's news from Mirror House," he said. "Mirabeau has taken a turn for the worse."

Rosalind closed her eyes briefly. "But he's still alive?"

"He was when this was written." Devon held up a note. "We can only hope he still is."

"Poor Helen," breathed Rosalind.

"Poor Helen," Devon echoed her. Then he turned and looked at her properly. He moved to the desk and poured out a cup of coffee and handed it to her. Rosalind wrapped her cold hands around the cup and swallowed gratefully.

"Do they say . . ." Rosalind stopped and swallowed and tried again. "Do they say what happened . . ."

"They do not," Devon said grimly. He poured another cup for himself. "They do not need to. I saw the wound." He drank. His gaze fixed on the bookcase in front of him, but Rosalind knew that was not what he saw. "He'd been clothes-lined."

"I don't understand."

"It's a foul trick, popular with highwaymen and that kind. You string a taut line across the road, and when a man comes along on horseback, it catches him, and he's swept to the ground, and you can rob him at your convenience while he's dazed or dead." Devon stopped abruptly. "If you want to kill your man, you make it a fine wire, and you string it throat-high. It works as well as a garrote."

There was a chair at her back. Rosalind sat down, hard and gracelessly. The coffee in her cup sloshed hard. But if she did not sit, she might have fallen, for all her breath was gone.

"It was deliberate, then," she said. "Not some riding accident. Someone did this to him. They planned this, and they knew that Mr. Mirabeau would be on that road."

"Yes," Devon agreed reluctantly. "The villain must have been lying in wait, and he must have watched it happen. First, because he had to take the line down, so as not to leave evidence of his crime, and second . . ." Devon took a deep breath. "Second, because Mirabeau was not just thrown clear. He was dragged from the road and left for dead."

Rosalind's heart thudded hard against her ribs. She had no words. She stared at the steam rising from her coffee, while the horror of what had been done sank slowly through her thoughts down to her bones.

"What will you do?" she asked finally.

"I've already begun," he said. "I've sent for the magistrate and the justice of the peace. We will need to turn out the militia to search the woods for signs of . . . for whatever signs we can find. I'll need to get the gentry together. Vaughn is going to have a field day," he added grimly. "He's going to insist it's poachers, demand that the labor camps be cleared out . . ."

"But it's not poachers," said Rosalind. "It's the duel. Again. Peter Mirabeau is one of the few left living who knows the true nature of the quarrel that took William Corbyn to the dueling ground."

Devon nodded. "I've sent for Worthing as well. It's time for the man to stop standing on his honor. And . . . he needs to take care. Someone will remember him soon enough." Devon stopped. "Good Lord," he breathed. "Good Lord, I'm a fool. A fool!"

"What is it?" cried Rosalind.

"There is someone else who knew about the duel. The man who was supposed to be there, but who no one saw."

"I don't understand."

"Corbyn's second!" he cried. "If William wanted to carry on with the duel once Bartolemew was sent packing, he'd need a new second. That new second would also know the cause of the quarrel and support it, or at least pretend to."

"That person might have been the one who shot William Corbyn," said Rosalind slowly. "And might also have done this."

"I don't know who it was, and fool that I am, I have not wondered." He clenched his fist. "I've been too busy trying to calm things down to wonder."

Rosalind felt her mouth go dry. "Devon . . . is it possible that the second . . . that it was still Bartolemew Vaughn?"

He did not answer immediately. "I want to say that is impossible, and that Vaughn was in Ireland. Except, of course, there are all these rumors circulating about the district that he did not go."

"And there is something more." Rosalind steeled herself,

and she told Devon about the quarrel in the church that Mrs. Kendricks had seen. "I do not know for certain, but the man with Cecilia could have been Bartolemew."

"From that description it could have been. God in Heaven." Devon's words came out through gritted teeth. "What is happening here?"

The Vaughns and the Corbyns are to be united in marriage. The drainage works are to continue. The money from the stock dividends may yet appear. This seems vital to someone.

Unless we are wrong. Unless we are seeing it this way because we don't know what else to look for.

And there was something else.

"Devon?" breathed Rosalind.

"Yes?"

"You've seen a man . . . clotheslined before?"

"Yes," he said. "Yes, I have."

"Hugh?"

Devon nodded again. "He played cards with the wrong group of men at the tavern. He cheated, they realized it, and they took their revenge." He paused. "I could not let it be discovered that my brother was a card cheat, so the incident had to become a simple fall."

Rosalind nodded. She could not press him anymore just now. It would be unkind, and unjust. She cast about for something she could say, and what she came up with was so innocuous as to be absurd. "You haven't eaten anything."

The corner of Devon's mouth twitched. "Neither have you."

"I will have a bit of roll," said Rosalind. "But only if you will."

He sighed. "Well, then, I suppose I must, for your sake."

He took a roll from the basket, tore it in two, and laid it on a plate.

The door opened. Both of them turned. Rosalind rose to her feet.

Quinn held the door open, and Lady Casselmaine, leaning heavily on a gold-headed stick, hobbled in.

Devon froze. "Mother."

Rosalind stepped quickly aside so the dowager could take her chair if she chose. She did not choose. In fact, she ignored Rosalind altogether and walked to stand before her son.

"I have heard what happened," she said. "You are unhurt?"

"Yes," said Devon. "This outrage was not . . . against me."

"We must thank God for His mercy," said the dowager.

"Yes," Devon agreed. "Will you sit, Mother?"

Every bit of Rosalind wanted to offer to help, but she knew better by now. The dowager lowered herself carefully into the chair Rosalind had abandoned. "Tell me the whole of it, Devon. I would hear it from you."

"Yes, ma'am." Devon drew up his own chair. He glanced at Rosalind. She nodded and backed silently out of the room. Quinn closed the door behind her.

Rosalind stood in the gallery, her hand pressed against her stomach.

Please, let this be some small good that comes of all this.

With that fervent prayer, Rosalind returned to her rooms. As soon as she opened the door, she was greeted by Mrs. Kendricks holding out a silver tray that contained a pile of letters.

"The morning post, miss," she said. "I would not bother you with it at such a time, only there is a letter from Miss Littlefield that I thought might be important."

"Yes, thank you." Rosalind took the letter from the top of the pile and then remembered something else. "Mrs. Kendricks, have you slept at all? Or eaten anything?"

"I slept when you did," she replied stoutly. "And Cook sent up a tray of bread and cheese with a pot of tea."

"Good, good." She tried to mean it. She did mean it, but her mind was so very full. "Can you find out where Mrs.

Showell and Louisa are? We will need to talk as soon as possible."

"Of course, miss." Mrs. Kendricks curtsied and went to
give orders to the chambermaid.

Rosalind sat down at the writing desk, broke the seal, and
read.

Dear Rosalind, Alice wrote.

*We've had success here. The name Fortuna Graves
sounded familiar to me, and I know you will not like this,
but I went to Bow Street to ask the runners . . .*

"You mean to ask Mr. Harkness. Oh, Alice." Rosalind
sighed.

I was told a dreadful story . . .

Rosalind read Alice's clean, factual description of the cold
fate of Fortuna's husband and sister, and she shuddered.

Fortuna. Pale, restrained, *useful* Fortuna Graves. The poor
relation come to a quiet country house to help care for the
sick and for a drunken, violent man. To find herself on the
edge of families scheming over marriages and inheritance,
and heaven knew what else, and working to hide her own secrets, and such a secret . . .

"Oh, Fortuna," Rosalind whispered. "What have you
done?

*But there's more, and it concerns William Corbyn and
what he may have been doing while in town. George spoke
to a friend of his at the War Office. We have an address that
it will be* VERY—Alice had underlined the word twice—
*worthwhile to visit. I don't like to be dramatic, but you need
to return to town at once.* This last was underlined three
times.

Rosalind's jaw clenched. Her thoughts were racing, but
blessedly, they were now in perfect order. She knew what she
must do.

It would begin with finding Louisa and Mrs. Showell.

* * *

The ladies, as it transpired, were in Louisa's rooms, both huddled together at her writing desk.

"Oh, Rosalind!" croaked Mrs. Showell when she entered. "I'm glad you're here. We must have fifty requests for news, or to call, or to know if there's anything to be done."

"Some people already want to know when the funeral is to be!" Louisa brandished one letter. "Vultures!"

"Has there been any news from Mirror House?" asked Rosalind.

"Nothing," said Louisa. "Rosalind, do you think I should go round? I don't want to be a bother, but I'm sure Helen will still be there, and I know that brother of hers will be no use to anyone. . . ."

"Yes, I think you should go. Do you agree, Mrs. Showell?"

"I do." Mrs. Showell blotted her nose with a handkerchief. "Helen is sure to need her friends with her, and I cannot go anywhere with this wretched cold. I will stay and deal with these." She laid her hand on the stack of letters. "What will you do, Rosalind?"

"I have other news," said Rosalind. "I've heard from Alice Littlefield. She writes I must return to London at once."

"Why? What's happened?" cried Louisa.

"Alice and George have found us some answers," replied Rosalind. "And I sincerely hope they will help put an end to this horror. To that end, I have a favor to ask you both."

"What do you need?" asked Mrs. Showell at once.

"I need you to make sure that Mrs. Vaughn first of all, and the neighborhood in general, know that I left because I was so upset by what happened to Mr. Mirabeau I could no longer stay. I need you to say I positively fled."

"You've never fled from anything in your life, Rosalind," said Louisa.

"Nevertheless."

"May I ask why?" inquired Mrs. Showell.

"Because it may calm matters, for a time at least."

"And allay suspicions?" Louisa suggested. "Because whoever did this may still be in the district," said Louisa.

"And because the Vaughns are heavily involved. I do not
know exactly how, but they are. Cecilia's father has been visiting Mr. Corbyn. That surely was about the wedding settle-
ments, but what else? What was it that made a man widely
known to be opposed to marriage in general, and to marriage
into that family in particular, have such a change of heart?
And then there is Bartolemew Vaughn coming and going in
all the shadows, and Lucian Vaughn who has vanished, and
Cecilia who is trying to keep her secret promises."

"And Mrs. Vaughn who will by fair means or foul secure a
future for her family," added Mrs. Showell.

"A family that has already been displaced once," added
Rosalind.

Louisa nodded. "I do not care what she says, she resents
having to move from London. She's very bad at hiding it."
Determination sparked in Louisa's eyes. "You can count on
us, Rosalind. I'll make sure all the girls hear you were weep-
ing into your tea as your maid packed."

"Thank you." Rosalind pressed her hand. "And don't
worry. I'll still be back in plenty of time for the wedding."

"But should you?" Louisa's brow furrowed. "I never
thought I'd say such a thing, but, Rosalind, I'm worried for
you. I don't wish to sound like I'm returning to the dramatic
old days, but if somebody's trying to silence people—"

Rosalind cut her off. "If that is so, our true safety lies in
exposing this person as quickly as may be. And that is exactly what I intend to do."

CHAPTER 38

Upon Returning Home

Such marriages may be *happy, but I fear seldom* are.

Theodore Edward Hook, *Cousin William* or
The Fatal Attachment

"Rosalind!" cried Alice Littlefield as she threw open the door to her tiny flat. "Good heavens! Did you come straight here?"

"I had little choice, I'm afraid." Rosalind stepped inside and hugged her friend. "Russell Street is entirely shut up. I've sent Mrs. Kendricks ahead to begin opening things up, but I didn't want there to be any more delay."

It seemed to Rosalind that preparations for the drive back to London took almost as long as the journey itself. As she was absolutely unable to tell Mrs. Kendricks how many days they would be gone, she insisted on packing up all of Rosalind's belongings.

Rosalind longed to speak with Devon before she left. She had so many questions, and she wanted to offer him what reassurances she could, but the justice of the peace, and the magistrates, and a representative from the Lord Lieutenant had all arrived, and he was closeted with them. Rather than delay her departure any more, she wrote him a letter, and felt her heart crumble a little further.

It is not a good-bye, she thought as she sealed it. *It is nothing like a good-bye. Why would I even think that now?*

Traveling by private carriage had many advantages. Changing horses at the roadside inns was accomplished seamlessly. Any request for food or drink from the landlord was paid for by their driver out of the money Devon had ordered be given him. Even so, the drive itself took a full ten hours, and given their late start, they were required to stop at a staging inn for the night. Rosalind desperately wanted to carry on straight through, but that would have involved arriving in London in the dead of night, with no house ready to take them in.

As it was, it was still quite early, but Alice and George kept business hours, not society hours, and Rosalind had no fear of turning up on their doorstep before nine o'clock.

"Well, take off your bonnet and sit down." Alice gestured toward her table, piled, as usual, with papers and writing implements. "George is already gone to work. I'll put the kettle on. There's so much to tell!"

"Your letter was uncharacteristically short on details." Rosalind settled herself in the offered chair. After the ease and grandeur of Cassell House, she expected to find the Littlefield's cramped and dingy flat a shock. As indeed it was, but only because of how much it felt like a return home.

"I'm sorry about the brevity." Alice hung the copper kettle on the hearth's hob and added a bit more coal to the fire. "I can only say I had good reason."

"What's happened?"

Alice sighed and came to sit at the table. "I'm going about this the wrong way round, I'm afraid, but . . ." She moved some papers aside so she had space to fold her hands. "I was attending a private gallery lecture, and I . . . met . . . Mr. Russel Fullerton."

Rosalind felt herself blanch. "Oh, Alice."

"He offered me an unspecified sum for becoming one of his spies, and for giving him information about you." She paused. "He specifically asked for your sister's address and your father's whereabouts."

"I see," murmured Rosalind.

"I feel like I should reassure you I told him nothing."

"As if you would ever be capable of working for such a man. Well." Rosalind endeavored to put a brisk note into her voice. "Do not worry, Alice. I have understood for some time that Mr. Fullerton might become a problem, and I am already taking steps."

Nothing short of the end of the world could dampen Alice's curiosity. She leaned forward, scenting a good story. "What steps?"

Rosalind smiled. "Mr. Fullerton is very fond of collecting letters. Well and good. I have taken to collecting certain letters of my own, a number of them from ladies who bear old titles and prestigious names. I've made copies and given the originals over to Sanderson Faulks for safekeeping. Should it become necessary, I will instruct him to bring them out."

Alice beamed wickedly. "Will you let me see them?"

"I promise you, Alice, should Mr. Fullerton prove to be unpersuadable, you will see them all."

Alice drew herself up, all her natural spirits quite visibly restored. "Then we may dismiss Mr. Fullerton for the time being. Now." She picked up the nearest pencil and rapped it sharply on the table in imitation of a teacher bringing a classroom to order. "What on *earth* have you been up to in the country?"

While Alice made up a pot of harsh, scalding tea and produced some apples and boiled eggs as refreshments, Rosalind told her the entire story of what had occurred since she first arrived at Cassell House, ending with the awful events that had so very nearly killed Mr. Mirabeau.

"A note reached us at the inn this morning," Rosalind concluded. "Mr. Mirabeau is still fighting his fever, but it has not broken yet."

Alice listened to all this with wide eyes and twitching fingers. Rosalind could see how she longed for her notebook and pencil, and silently thanked her for her self-restraint. Probably the matter would end up in the papers, but it should not be until they knew what story could best be told.

And definitely not before we know who else might be endangered.

"Well!" exclaimed Alice when she finished. "Even by your standards, Rosalind, that is . . . it's incredible."

"And now it's your turn, Alice," she said. "Tell me what you've learned. You said George had been to the War Office?"

"Yes, and it seems that no one actually bothered to tell them your Colonel Corbyn was dead."

Fortuna had been intercepting the mail bag. . . .

"Come to that, no one told them he was retired, either."

"What?" said Rosalind, startled.

Alice nodded. "Somebody was still collecting his half pay and advertising themselves as Mrs. William Corbyn." Alice fished a letter out of her piles of paper. "And she has an address." She handed the paper to Rosalind.

Rosalind read it. She was not at all familiar with the street or the district. "We must . . ."

Alice was already on her feet. "There's a hackney stand at the end of the road. Bank the fire, would you? I need to find my reticule."

They had to inquire of three separate cabmen before they found a driver who knew the address George had given Alice. All during the ride, Rosalind felt herself becoming increasingly restless, and not even Alice's lively gossip could calm her down. At last, her friend, rightly perceiving that Rosalind was not attending, fell silent.

Rosalind had no doubt Louisa would do her best to paint a picture of Rosalind fleeing to lock herself into her own house, but she did not expect that to lull the suspicions of whomever had attacked Colonel Corbyn and Peter Mirabeau for long. She was certain that if they were not already on their way to London, they would be soon.

But *who*? Old Mr. Vaughn, or his son, or both of them together? It could even be Mrs. Vaughn. Rosalind did not believe that lady could wield gun or line herself, but Archibald Crease was her servant as well, and he was plainly deeper in the family confidence than was usual for a gamekeeper. He could have been acting on her orders, to save her family's reputation and preserve the futures she had planned.

And what of Marius Corbyn? What did he know and how, and what future did he truly hope to carve for himself out of this rubble pile of events? What had Cecilia told him about his brother and their relationship?

What had Cecilia told anyone? Rosalind clenched her jaw. What had she told Bartolemew in the church? What did she know about why Lucian was cut off from his family, and did that mystery feed off of this other?

She shook her head. *This is no good, Rosalind Thorne. You will worry yourself into irrationality, and then how will you be able to do any good at all?*

The cabman drew the hackney over to the side of the road and brought them to a halt.

"Are we there?" Alice called.

"Just about," answered the driver. "But there's some 'at 'appenin' up ahead. You ladies might want to wait 'ere."

Lost deep in her own thoughts, Rosalind had not paid much attention to their surroundings. Now she saw they were in a cobbled street that was older, but still of good appearance. Blocks of houses stood between tidy shops and brick-walled yards with iron gates.

Ahead of them, as the driver said, the way was blocked. A crowd had gathered, including several carts that had pulled up crosswise in the street. Youths of assorted ages had climbed up on them and were now straining to catch a glimpse of whatever might be happening beyond.

"Uh-oh," murmured Alice. "I don't like the look of this."

"Neither do I." Rosalind climbed out of the cab and paid the driver. "Will you wait?" she asked him.

He eyed the crowd, and then Rosalind, and shrugged. "Not forever, mind."

Alice came to stand beside her on the cobbles. "I suppose it's too much to hope that whatever is attracting so much attention might have nothing to do with us?"

"I'm afraid so, yes," said Rosalind. "Have you your notebook, Alice? We may need to call on A.E. Littlefield."

Alice pulled her book and pencil from her bag. She held these in one hand while she gathered up her hems in the other. "Once more into the breach, dear friend."

Together, they marched forward. Rosalind let Alice take the lead. Her life as a newspaperwoman and attender at social crushes had given her a pair of sharp elbows that she used with alacrity and extreme accuracy. Rosalind herself trod on a few toes and may have upended one idling porter's sack to move him out of their path.

With these impolite but effective efforts, Rosalind and Alice soon found themselves through the wall of bodies, just in time to see a house door fly open and a small boy run shouting into the street.

"*Monstruo!*" he screamed. "*Demonio!*"

A burly man burst out of the dark doorway behind him. The man grabbed the boy by the collar and jerked the child off his feet. The boy screamed again. The crowd gasped and then roared its disapproval as the man scooped the boy into his arms.

"Back off!" bawled another man to the crowd. "This ain't none of yez business, no how!"

Rosalind opened her mouth to say something to Alice, but she never got the words out. Another scream cut through the air—a woman's this time and from inside the house.

Two more men emerged from the doorway. Between them they dragged a struggling, black-clad lady. She tried to kick out but was hampered by her heavy skirts.

"Mama!" cried the boy. "*Monstruos!* Let her go!"

"Hold still, blast you!" The man tried to clap his broad hand over the boy's mouth. The boy responded by sinking his sharp teeth into the tough's thumb. The man hollered and dropped him.

"You stop!" the boy cried, on his feet instantly and charging up the house steps. "You let my mama go!"

He dove for the nearest assailant and managed to get his slim arms around the tough's knees. The woman, his mother, tore briefly free. The tough kicked out, and the boy toppled backward. The crowd roared again. The toughs shouted threats. One of them grabbed the woman's arm and twisted.

Rosalind and Alice moved. Rosalind swept straight up to the house steps. She called on the spirit of every governess she'd ever displeased and every boarding school teacher who found her where she was not supposed to be and thundered.

"What is the meaning of this!"

CHAPTER 39

How Far a Mother Will Go

The restraint which the customs of the world have put upon the conduct of females renders the best among them more or less hypocrites.

Theodore Edward Hook, *Cousin William* or
The Fatal Attachment

All the toughs froze like statues and stared at Rosalind as she planted herself at the foot of the steps.

"Good afternoon." Alice's clear voice rose up from the edge of the crowd. "I'm A.E. Littlefield from the *London Chronicle*. Can you tell me what's happening?"

The distraction was just enough. The boy wriggled free and kicked the big man in the ankle for good measure. Rosalind swept down, scooped him up, and climbed the stairs, elbowing the startled toughs aside as she went.

"A woman, from the newspaper?" Some man laughed.

"One of many," replied Alice calmly. "You'd be surprised. How did the business begin? Why is this child being torn from his terrified and heartbroken mother?"

Rosalind handed the boy to his mother, who had retreated to the doorway. Rosalind then stood herself squarely between the tiny family and the ruffians.

"'Ere now!" shouted the man who had been attempting to

tell the crowd this was none of their business. He was carrying a hefty wooden club and he brandished it toward Alice.
"You clear off!"

Alice ignored him. She was standing in front of a wagon
piled with men and boys. Her pencil was already flying
across the page.

"Bugger if I know what it's about," the wagoner was telling her. "But that one's making a pig's breakfast of the job."
He spat toward the burly man who'd tried to hold the boy
and was now wrapping a dirty handkerchief around his
wounded thumb.

"G'wan, covey!" the wagoner shouted. "Answer the girl!
What 'cher think you're about? Takin' babes from wim-
mins!"

"Exactly." Alice turned to face the burly man. "What do
you think you're about? And who told you to come here and
create such a disturbance?"

"And if you do not leave immediately, I shall summon the
watch, and you may explain yourself to them," announced
Rosalind.

The nearest ruffian attempted to draw himself up. He was
a pale little man with a flattened nose and one distorted ear.
"Now, madam, you don't want to do that. This is the law,
see?" He puffed out his chest.

Rosalind gave him her best withering glance. "I've never
seen the law look so unshaven."

That got a laugh from the assembled crowd.

"But if you are the law," she went on, "I suggest we pro-
ceed at once to Bow Street. You can explain yourself to the
magistrates, and I will do the same."

"Yeah! 'Ow'd you like that? Bow Street!" shouted somebody from the back of the crowd.

"Bow Street wi' the lot a' yez!" cried somebody else

"Bow Street! Bow Street!" The rest of the crowd took up
the chant. Fists began pumping in the air. "Bow Street!"

Someone raised a shovel. Someone else raised a wooden stave.

"Bow Street!"

The flat-nosed man glowered at Rosalind, grinding his teeth hard. Rosalind kept chin up and gaze direct. The flat-nosed man leaned forward. He smelled of sardines, beer, and tobacco, and for a moment, she thought he was going to grab at her and try to throw her down the steps.

"Bow Street!" shouted the crowd. "Bow! Street!"

"You're messing with things you know nothin' about," the ruffian shouted at Rosalind. Then he jabbed his finger over her shoulder toward the mother and child. "You! We'll be back for that boy. He ain't yours to keep no how!"

The woman responded in outraged Spanish laced with a few perfectly intelligible English words, none of which Alice was going to be able to put in the paper.

The four ruffians drew together in a bunch. Two produced smaller clubs from their pockets, and all of them dove together into the crowd. The crowd roared, but it parted and let them run away down the street to a crescendo of shouts and very rude jeers.

And for a moment no one was paying any attention to the women on the doorstep.

"I think, señora, we should get inside," said Rosalind.

"*Sí, sí, sí,*" the woman agreed, hugging her boy tight against her. "Come in. All, please come in."

Alice and Rosalind followed the stranger inside and shut the stout door against the noise of the celebrating crowd.

They found themselves in a neat but dim little foyer. The woman set her boy down. She gave him a series of instructions in rapid Spanish and sent him pelting down the central hallway.

"Please." She gestured for Alice and Rosalind to enter her front parlor.

Like the foyer, the room was tidy and well appointed. The

furniture was comfortable, and everything was clean. In this, the interior of the house matched the exterior and the general flavor of the neighborhood. Rosalind, however, saw the plain signs of a household under stress. There were gaps in the arrangement of ornaments and an outline on the wall that showed a painting had recently been removed, probably to be sold. The dust had begun to settle on the mantel and table-tops, and the fire had not been laid, nor the grate swept. Probably because the servants had also recently been dismissed.

The woman took a wing-backed chair beside the fire. She was almost as tall as Rosalind, with sandy brown skin, thick black brows, and a long, Roman nose. Her black hair had been swept back into a braided chignon and pinned with black lace in place of a matron's cap. Two gold hoops hung from her ears. Her dress was black crepe, and at her throat she wore a small gold crucifix. A gold wedding band flashed on one brown hand.

She gestured toward the slick velveteen sofa, inviting Rosalind and Alice to sit.

"I must . . . I . . . thank you," she said, speaking more to her hands folded in her lap than to her guests. "I apologize. My English is . . . not as good as it should be, especially when I am upset."

"It's better than my Spanish, certainly," Alice told her. "Can you tell us why those men were trying to take your boy?"

"*Mentirosos!*" The woman spat. "Those men are liars! They say they take my boy to his father's family! But I have had no letter! I have had no . . ." She stopped, apparently remembering that there were secrets she should keep to herself. "My husband is dead these six months," she said, clearly trying to formulate some story that would make sense on the spot. "His family . . . his family have made it clear they do not want me, or the boy. I do not know why those men came for him now."

"Was your husband Colonel William Corbyn?" asked Rosalind.

The woman regarded Rosalind with her dark, suspicious eyes. "Who are you to know this?"

"My name is Rosalind Thorne. This is my friend Alice Littlefield." Rosalind decided to take a risk. "We're friends of Cecilia Vaughn."

"Cecilia!" cried the woman. "Is she all right? Her last letter was not good. I have been so worried. . . ." She stopped abruptly and her cheeks colored as she realized she might have said too much.

"She was fine when I left her," said Rosalind, recognizing this might not be deeply reassuring. "Were you aware of her engagement to Marius Corbyn?"

Mrs. Corbyn nodded. "I knew it was coming. I told her not to do it, but she said there was no other way to buy time. She said she hoped it would not come to her having to go to the altar with the man."

There are promises I have made that I am determined to keep, and I will not be interfered with.

"You were the one she was trying to protect," said Rosalind. "She said she had made promises, and she would keep them, and that there were others involved. She meant you and your son."

Mrs. Corbyn glanced reflexively toward the door. "I have met her only once, but she is a good woman. She is also in a very difficult place. When William . . ." Mrs. Corbyn faltered. "When William died, I expected us to be cast to the winds, but Cecilia wrote to me. She said she wanted to make sure my son had his birthright, but she asked that we be patient and remain quiet. She said there might be trouble."

"And she was right," said Rosalind.

Alice was also looking toward the door, her expression tight, as if she smelled something unpleasant. "Will you two excuse me for a minute, please?" She got up and walked out before they could answer.

Her departure seemed to rally Mrs. Corbyn's nerve. "Miss Thorne, you come here with all these names and kind offers of help. You will forgive me if I think the timing is . . . the word . . . convenient for you, as you come when my trouble is worst." She drew herself up, shoulders and back as straight as any headmistress could ask for. "You should not make the mistake of believing me friendless. As soon as those . . . men knocked on my door, I sent for help. He will be here shortly."

"I understand," said Rosalind, and she did. Mrs. Corbyn had every reason to be cautious, and to make sure the strange woman sitting in her parlor knew that there was somebody expecting her to be home, whole and well.

Rosalind thought then of Cecilia, so determinedly keeping her many secrets—secrets from her family, and about her family, and about her coming marriage. She looked up at Mrs. Corbyn. She decided to make another leap.

"Your friend, whom you sent for, is he Lucian Vaughn?"

Mrs. Corbyn did not answer directly, and neither did her suspicion lighten one bit. "You will tell me how my life becomes any of your concern."

It was not a request Rosalind could reasonably refuse. She drew in a deep breath and began to talk. Mrs. Corbyn listened in silence, her gaze fixed on Rosalind's face, alert for any hesitation or prevarication. Around them, the room was quiet, except for the ticking clock and the dull patter of rain against the windows.

When Rosalind finished her story, Mrs. Corbyn bowed her head, but only briefly. "Miss Thorne, you say it was Helen Corbyn who brought you into this?"

"Yes."

"But she did not tell you about me?"

"I don't believe she knows about you."

Mrs. Corbyn shook her head. "I cannot say. I certainly do not know her." She paused. "I had thought William died in an accident. It was what Cecilia and my friend told me."

"It was what she surely believed at the time," said Rosalind. "But the facts have proven it to be otherwise. I am sorry."

"So am I," said Mrs. Corbyn, and for the first time there was a tremor in her voice. "But you do not tell me who sent those men to take me away."

"Because I don't know, not for certain," said Rosalind. "It could have been Bartolemew Vaughn, or perhaps either Mr. or Mrs. Vaughn."

Rosalind thought of Cecilia meeting her brother in the church, of how Vaughn was there to listen. She thought of how everyone's first belief was that William Corbyn had been killed by a spring gun set to catch poachers. She thought of Devon, white and shaking, telling her about the foul trick of clotheslining, something known to highwaymen. Perhaps to other outlaws as well.

The gamekeeper, Crease, would be well versed in such tricks.

As Rosalind was considering all these unpleasant possibilities, Alice came back into the room, looking grim.

"You have a lovely back garden, Mrs. Corbyn," she said. "The view from your kitchen window is quite excellent. It let me see quite clearly the man with a battered face watching from the alleyway behind it."

Mrs. Corbyn surged to her feet. So did Rosalind.

"Let us get you to safety," said Rosalind to her. "We can go now."

"*You* want to take me away now?" Mrs. Corbyn laughed. "Forgive me, Miss Thorne, but I do not choose to risk myself and my child with another set of strangers."

Rosalind found that she could not blame her at all. "Then let me send for help. I know one of the principal officers at Bow Street and . . ."

"A runner!" cried Mrs. Corbyn. "No! Those men work for whoever will pay!"

"We may trust this man. I know him well, and he already

knows something of this situation. With him, you will have the force of law behind any . . ."

Mrs. Corbyn smiled, and it was as sharp and cynical a smile as Rosalind had ever seen. "Your English law, Miss Thorne, is not very kind to women, or foreigners, or to those who do not belong to your church." She touched her crucifix.

"Please," said Rosalind urgently. "You and your boy are not safe here. Your husband is already dead, and an attempt has been made on another man who knew his circumstances. Those men have not left you and may make another attempt to snatch you and your child. They may come at night next time."

Mrs. Corbyn's expression filled with fear, but also with anger.

"There are some things I must get," she said. "Where are we going?"

"Yes, Rosalind, where?" asked Alice.

Rosalind looked at the clock. It was just going on noon now. The ragged chorus of London church bells began its slow tolling outside. There was only one place she could be traced, and yet would be certain of welcome at this time of day. "We'll go to my sister's."

Alice looked startled but said nothing. "Very well, but what do we do about our friend? He's sure to follow us."

Rosalind considered this and then turned to Mrs. Corbyn. "Señora, do you have a spare cloak and bonnet I could borrow?"

CHAPTER 40

The Importance of Family

*If I had but kept my feelings snug until the thing
was settled, all might have been well.*

Theodore Edward Hook, *Cousin William* or
The Fatal Attachment

Anyone taking an interest in that (usually) anonymous house in that respectable street around the hour of half past twelve would have seen two ladies leaving by the front door. Both of them were well cloaked and bonneted against the thick fall of rain. They walked to a coaching inn in the next street to hire a conveyance that might be thought to be rather large for just two.

Shortly afterward, another woman, also well cloaked and bonneted, and carrying a small grip and pressing a small child against her shoulder ran out the back door and down the alleyway, disappearing around the corner of the brewer's yard. She was very swift of foot and evidently knew where she was going. So much so that by the time the man with the flattened nose rounded that same corner, he found the grip, the cloak and bonnet, and the pillow dressed in a boy's jacket and cap dropped on the ash heap. The woman herself was nowhere in sight.

What he said and did after that would be rejected for inclusion in any news story Alice might choose to write about the incident.

At that moment, however, Alice, Mrs. Corbyn, and her son were more interested in making sure the driver of their hired, closed carriage stopped in time to meet Rosalind, who, hatless and coatless against the pouring rain, was running to try to catch up with them. Alice pushed the door open, grabbed Rosalind's hands, and helped pull her into the carriage.

"Go!" shouted Rosalind as she tumbled into the seat.

The driver was a man who relished a challenge. He cracked his whip and the carriage lurched and bounced into the London traffic with such speed and force, none of the women inside had any breath left for talking.

The pretty square where the carriage eventually stopped was much more sedate than the street they had left. Everything about them was brand-new. The peaceful central green was enclosed by a freshly painted iron rail. Gleaming white houses stood behind stoops that gleamed in the watery sunlight.

Rosalind paid the driver and ushered her charges up to one particular door. She rang and was answered by a slender maid with a placid but intelligent face. The girl did not bat an eye at this strange collection of individuals, but invited them all to step in while she took Rosalind's card up to her mistress.

It turned out there was no need. Her mistress was already coming down the stairs.

"Rosalind!"

Rosalind smiled ruefully at her sister. "I apologize for invading your home, Charlotte. It's an emergency. May we come in?"

Charlotte Thorne was two years older than Rosalind. She

was just as tall and possessed a rich fall of hair the same dark shade of gold. But where Rosalind's form had always been generous and well-curved, Charlotte cultivated a fashionably slender frame that looked supremely graceful in her exquisitely simple ivory tea gown.

Charlotte looked at Mrs. Corbyn in her widow's black and disheveled, excited, little Philip beside her. Her brows raised.

"This is Señora William Corbyn and her son, Philip. Señora, this is my sister, Charlotte Thorne."

"So very good to make your acquaintance, señora," replied Charlotte. "Hello, young man." Then, "Hello, Alice."

"Hello, Charlotte," said Alice. "You are looking well."

"Thank you." Charlotte turned to her maid. "Elizabeth, please tell Cook we require tea and extra cakes. Well," she said. "Won't you all step up?"

Charlotte led them up a gently curved staircase into a sunlit sitting room. Everything was new and laid out in perfect taste. The lines of all the furnishings were full and simple, with only a very few feminine frills.

It was a room, Rosalind thought, perfectly calculated to make a gentleman feel at home. Which should not have surprised her. Charlotte was a courtesan, and had been for some time. It was part of the reason each of them kept the other at a distance.

It was painful to acknowledge that among the other reasons was Rosalind's relationship with the man who was the Duke of Casselmaine.

At first, Charlotte tried to send little Philip down to the kitchens, promising there would be treats, but it soon became evident that neither mother nor son was willing to be separated, so instead, Charlotte produced a pile of illustrated magazines and, much to Rosalind's surprise, a box of lead soldiers. She glanced at Charlotte, Charlotte shrugged. Little Philip was delighted, and proceeded to dump them all out on the floor and then line them up in ragged formations.

Seeing her guests settled on sofas and chairs, Charlotte sat in an overstuffed chair in the little alcove of the bow window. The pale afternoon sunlight caught her golden hair. She looked like a painting, an effect that was surely both calculated and practiced.

"So, tell me, Rosalind," said Charlotte. "How does his grace?"

"Very well, thank you."

"I won't send my regards. That would be very awkward for us both." She paused. "I'm sorry, Rosalind, that was beneath me."

Rosalind shook her head. Mrs. Corbyn was looking at her uneasily. So was Alice. Rosalind couldn't blame them. "Charlotte, I am going to have to ask a whole set of favors from you. I have no right but . . ."

"But you have nowhere else to go," said Charlotte.

"Yes," agreed Rosalind. "I'm sorry, I . . ."

Charlotte waved her hand. "We'll talk about it later, when we can be private. What is it you need?"

"Two gentlemen will be arriving shortly. We sent the messages from Señora Corbyn's house before we left. One is a Mr. Lucian Corbyn and the other . . ." She hesitated.

"Rosalind," said Charlotte firmly. "I've already agreed to help. You can spare me your blushing delicacy."

"Yes, I'm sorry. The other is Adam Harkness from Bow Street."

Her sister's eyes narrowed into a look surprisingly similar to the one Mrs. Corbyn had given her earlier.

"You and he and . . . the rest of your entourage must be gone before eight o'clock, Rosalind. I have an appointment I cannot break."

"It is my hope we will be gone well before that. We cannot risk being traced here."

Again, Charlotte's brows rose in delicate surprise. "My dear sister, what have you gotten yourself into?" She stopped.

"Perhaps we should wait for your gentlemen to arrive. That way you will only have to explain once. Alice, tell me how you have been? I am an *avid* reader of Society Notes."

Charlotte's performance as hostess was flawless, Rosalind noticed with mild amazement. She drew Alice into an animated discussion of the latest novels and sought Rosalind's opinion on several developments among the board of the Almack's Assembly Rooms.

Charlotte's cook had produced a full luncheon; in addition to the requested cakes and tea, there were sandwiches of bread and butter, or paté and chutney, as well as slices of cold game pie.

This was when they discovered Charlotte spoke fluent Spanish. As food was served by her efficient and unobtrusive maid, Charlotte chatted with Mrs. Corbyn. Rosalind was able to follow along well enough to understand that Mrs. Corbyn's family was originally from the countryside near Toledo, that she had aged parents still living in their village, that she had lived in London with her son since his birth, five years previously. Mrs. Corbyn grew more relaxed and animated under the spell of her native tongue, assisted by tea and good food and the calm, ordered surroundings of Charlotte's parlor.

They were still enjoying the lunch when the downstairs maid came in with a pair of cards on a silver tray. Charlotte read them both.

"Your gentlemen have arrived, Rosalind. Elizabeth . . ."

"I'll be hanged if I'll wait another minute!" called a man's voice from down below. Feet thundered up the stairs.

A slim man with a shock of honey-gold hair burst into the room. "Maria!" he cried. "What the devil is going on!"

"Lucian!" Little Philip bounded to his feet and ran to the man. "Lucian! I saved Mama!" He wrapped his arms around the new arrival. Lucian Vaughn rubbed the boy's head absently, but he stared at Mrs. Corbyn.

"It's all right." Mrs. Corbyn was also on her feet and crossing the room. "We are safe here."

"So we all hope." A second man entered the room. "But I second the question. What on earth is going on?"

The last time Rosalind had seen Adam Harkness, he had been laid up in his mother's parlor with a badly wounded arm. He looked considerably better now. He had clearly been summoned from the station, for beneath his plain blue coat, he wore the scarlet vest that marked him as a "Robin redbreast," an officer of Bow Street.

Rosalind found herself staring at him, as if starved for his details. His eyes were as blue as they had always been, the line of his jaw as strong and clean. She knew if she inhaled deeply, she might just catch the scent of him, leather and paper and fresh air and . . .

And what kind of fool am I making of myself?

She might not have an answer to that, but she could not help notice that she was not the only one staring. Adam Harkness had the bluest eyes she had ever seen, and those eyes were fixed on her as if he wished never to have to look away again.

Rosalind felt her shameful, fickle, entirely too-excitable heart bang insistently against her ribs.

Charlotte cleared her throat. "Rosalind, I think you had better introduce us, don't you?"

Rosalind blinked. So did Mr. Harkness.

Alice snorted.

Rosalind's ability to move returned with a rush. She could have also wished it was not accompanied by a sharp burning sensation in her cheeks, but there was little she could do about that.

"Please forgive my manners," she said. "Mr. Adam Harkness, Mr. Lucian Vaughn, if you will permit me . . ." Rosalind introduced all the room's occupants.

"Gentlemen." Charlotte did not rise. "Do sit down. We

have been expecting you. There is luncheon available, if either of you are hungry, and I have some excellent wine, or there is brandy if you prefer." She smiled mockingly at Mr. Harkness. "The duty on which has been fully paid, I hasten to add."

"I am certain everything in this house is of excellent quality and perfect legality," replied Adam dryly. He sat himself on the sofa beside Alice. "I must say, Miss Littlefield, you do know the most interesting persons."

"I cultivate a wide-ranging acquaintance," she said loftily. "It keeps the conversation from growing stale."

"Look, you." Vaughn marched to Mrs. Corbyn's chair and took up a position beside her as if appointing himself her personal guard. Perhaps he was. Philip plopped himself happily down at the man's feet with a set of the soldiers. "The lot of you may want a pleasant afternoon's chat, but I want to know what's going on. Maria? What are you doing here?" He gestured at the exquisitely appointed room, clearly at a loss for words.

"Well, Miss Thorne?" said Mr. Harkness. "I'm afraid it's a very good question."

"Yes, you are correct." Rosalind sat in the overstuffed chair she'd been occupying before the gentlemen's abrupt entrance. "For me, this story began with a letter from Helen Corbyn, but I think the real beginning was some time ago." She looked at Mrs. Corbyn.

"You don't have to say anything you don't want to, Maria," said Mr. Vaughn, his eyes were fixed on Mr. Harkness.

"No," said Mrs. Corbyn. "I will speak. Miss Thorne, and . . . these others, they have already saved us twice today." She took a deep breath.

"As you already know, I am from *España*, near Toledo. My family is of no importance. My father was a farmer of some small prosperity. We grew oranges and almonds and olives. When the fighting came to our part of the country, it was very bad. One morning, I woke early to find a wounded English solider hiding in our barn.

"My father hated Napoleon, so was positively delighted to hide an Englishman from the invaders."

"This was William Corbyn."

"Yes." Mrs. Corbyn reached down and touched her son's head. "William was wounded in his side. Very bad. Fever came, as it does with such a wound, and in the heat of summer, we all thought he must die. But by the grace of God, he lived, and over many months he grew strong again. We told people he was my mother's cousin. No one believed that but . . ." She shrugged. "Even considering our family name, none of our neighbors was quite ready to betray my father to looters and conquerors."

Rosalind knew what it was to have to be discreet and speak in coded language. She understood that some significant phrases could be used to cover a wealth of meaning, and be repeated so often they slid easily off the tongue. She heard that quality in the way Mrs. Corbyn said "considering our family name," and "none of our neighbors were quite ready to betray." She looked again at Mrs. Corbyn, and especially at her crucifix.

"My brother was the one who was supposed to look after William," Mrs. Corbyn went on. "But mostly, those tasks fell to me. This was not an accident. I made it happen. William was handsome. I was a romantic peasant girl." She shrugged. "I taught him a little Spanish. He taught me a little English. I kept him amused. I was a pretty girl, and love happened, as it does. Perhaps I trapped him a little. Perhaps he took advantage of me a little."

"These things are never as simple as they are in novels," murmured Rosalind.

Mrs. Corbyn smiled briefly. "You English and your novels . . . *Madre de Dios*, I do not know whether to laugh or cry."

Alice kept her expression studiously blank. "And after a while you realized there would be a child?"

"A farm girl knows much more about these things than a city girl. I was terrified. I assumed that I would be shamed, and left alone. But William, in his awful Spanish, got the truth out of me. And much to my surprise, he asked me to marry him. The priest brought the church register to the house. He was not happy, especially because William was not Catholic, but he did it, anyway.

"About that time, things finally became too much for the neighbors. Their dislike of our family combined with their fear of the very blond English bringing trouble down on the village. William and my father talked and decided it would be best if I was sent to England. He sent a letter to a friend"— she nodded to Mr. Vaughn—"to come meet me and help me."

"You? Not Marius?"

"Even William knew he shouldn't spring a Spanish wife and baby on Marius," said Lucian blandly. "It was me and Peter Mirabeau who did most of the errand running and letter carrying. Earnest Worthing a little, too, as he could."

Rosalind remembered sitting with Mr. Worthing in the Vaughns' parlor, the sound of general conversation covering over their much more private words.

We all liked him, he said, speaking of Lucian. *But he and Mirabeau were chums since we were boys together. Backed each other up at school, all that.*

"Through his good friends, William saw me placed in a decent house," said Mrs. Corbyn. "He made sure I had a tutor to teach me English and reading and writing. When the war was over, he came home and I thought our married life would begin."

"Have you any proof the marriage did take place?" asked Adam quietly.

In response, Mrs. Corbyn opened her bulky bag and pulled

out a thick bundle of papers. "I thought it would be best if I brought these, in case." She passed the papers to Adam.

Most of the papers were in Spanish. The one Rosalind could read was an English birth certificate for Philip Alphonse Corbyn, signed by the attending midwife and Colonel William Corbyn.

Adam passed Rosalind the papers written in Spanish. Rosalind passed them to Charlotte. She leafed through the documents, asking a few questions of Mrs. Corbyn as she did.

"The register of the marriage," said Mrs. Corbyn. "And a letter from the priest who married us. The deed to the house signed over to me for use during my lifetime. The formal acknowledgment of Philip as his son. William insisted we should have our own copies of these things. If his plans did not go as he hoped and it became necessary to reveal the marriage, he did not want his family to be able to contest his word and say his son was illegitimate."

"It is exactly as she says." Charlotte handed the papers back to Mr. Harkness. "It would take a very clever and very expensive solicitor to make this amount of documentation go away."

"You said 'if your plans did not go as you hoped'?" said Mr. Harkness. "What were your plans?"

Mrs. Corbyn sighed. "When William came back to England, I thought he would reconcile with his family, and bring myself and Philip to his home. And at first all seemed well, but then . . ." Her voice trembled, and Mrs. Corbyn swallowed. "The letters began."

"His mother was ill, and his father. He could not upset them. His brother, too. He told me . . . he told me many things, but it came down to this eventually. His family would never accept his marriage to one such as myself. They would never accept the child. He cried. He did not have the courage to give up his inheritance, not even for his son.

"By then I knew of the troubles he brought back from war

with him. Of the drinking and the fits of temper. And by then, I was . . . I was tired, as was he. I did not have the strength to stay married to such a man who needed so much and if he came to me against his family's wishes, he would bring nothing but his broken self. So, we conceived a plan. . . ." She swallowed again.

"He'd marry Cecilia and arrange to adopt your child," said Alice.

Mrs. Corbyn stared at her. So did Rosalind and Charlotte. Alice smiled.

"I *am* a novelist. If this was my story, that is how I would write it."

Mrs. Corbyn laughed, once. "I see I must apologize, señorita. Yes, that was it."

"Cecilia's promises," said Rosalind. "They were to you and your son."

"I said I would only go along with this plan if the woman he was to marry knew and agreed," Mrs. Corbyn told them. "I will lie for myself, for my family, but I would not engage in a conspiracy that might ruin the life of an innocent girl who might otherwise have a good life of her own."

"And you knew about all this?" Mr. Harkness said to Lucian.

"I didn't like it, believe me," Vaughn said. "And I wouldn't have gone along if Cecilia hadn't come and begged me."

"She wanted to get away from her mother," said Rosalind. "Into a home of her own."

"That was part of it." Lucian nodded. "To tell you the truth, I'm not sure I understand all of it, but it was a way for her to escape, at least a little, from the path that had been dictated for her. And as William's wife, well, if certain things came to light, she'd be protected."

"Certain things?" inquired Mr. Harkness.

Lucian turned away. "You said there was brandy, Miss Thorne?"

"On the sideboard," Charlotte gestured. "Do help yourself."

Lucian Vaughn poured out a large measure of spirits and sipped. He looked surprised, and sipped again.

"This is very good."

"I prefer to be surrounded by fine things," said Charlotte. "There is so much unpleasantness in the world. But do go on, Mr. Vaughn. We are all of us enraptured."

Rosalind ducked her head so no one could see her entirely inappropriate smile. But when Lucian resumed his speech, all urge to smile fell away.

"As you know, my father was a solicitor before he turned country squire. His particular area of expertise was estate law, and special pleadings in cases where affairs could be especially tangled." Lucian paused. "He also had an interesting specialty that was less talked about. My father, you see, is a forger."

CHAPTER 41

Professional Specialties

A man who sells his conscience for his interest
will sell it for his pleasure.

Maria Edgeworth, *Tales of Fashionable Life*

*F*orger. The word hung heavily in the air. Rosalind could not help but look to Charlotte. Charlotte looked out the window.

"He practiced this specialty as part of his larger legal practice," Lucian went on. "Suppose, for example, a man died and left behind a young wife, or perhaps a first wife, or a poor cousin who was insufficiently provided for. My father would go to visit them on pretense of estate business. He would talk about the complexity of the affairs, and how it was unfair that this person should be so neglected in the will. He would hint that if he had sufficient inducement, things might be found to turn considerably in that person's favor."

"And if that person agreed . . . ?" prompted Alice.

"It was amazing how many of the wills my father worked on had codicils expressing regret at having so neglected some member or another of the household and settling large sums of money on them." Lucian took another long swallow of brandy. "There now, Mr. Harkness. I have just confessed that my father is a low criminal."

"So you have." Mr. Harkness folded his hands. "And if the matter ever comes to court I shall testify exactly to what I have heard."

Lucian glared at him, trying to sort out what sort of promise he'd just heard. Mr. Harkness returned the look calmly, and silently.

"Was that why you broke with your father?" asked Rosalind.

"Yes," said Mr. Vaughn. "I had been set to start reading law, a fact which annoyed my older brother no end, since we were all supposed to be playing at genteel pastimes these days." He shrugged. "Anyway, I was looking through some casebooks of my fathers, and I found some letters." He stopped. "We quarreled. I left. I felt terrible about leaving Cecilia on her own, but I could not stay."

So there it was. Rosalind folded her hands. Very simple in the end, as so many things proved to be. Lucian Vaughn found out his father was a forger, and left. He said nothing, because he would not destroy the prospects for his brothers and sisters who must remain behind.

Rosalind found herself regarding Charlotte again. This time, Charlotte looked back. She also looked very tired.

A new thought came into Rosalind's mind. "Did Colonel Corbyn leave a will?"

"Cecilia writes that he did," said Mrs. Corbyn. "At first, they thought he did not, but one was found among his private papers."

"By whom?" asked Mr. Harkness sharply.

"That I do not know," Mrs. Corbyn told him.

"But," said Mr. Vaughn. "Given Cecilia's new engagement and my father's former profession, you can see how this complicates matters."

"Because it's possible that your father offered to forge the will, in return for Mr. Corbyn agreeing to marry Cecilia," said Rosalind.

"Which certainly puts this Marius Corbyn in the thick of this," said Alice.

"Oh, he was already there," said Rosalind. "The question is, in what capacity? He was most certainly trying to prevent little Philip from inheriting." *And I should have guessed something like that was behind this matter. It was all as plain as day. It began with his desire to see Helen married and with children as soon as possible. He wanted her to have heirs of her own to fight for, just in case Mrs. Corbyn should try to put her son forward.* "He would never willingly acknowledge the marriage or the child."

"How can you be sure?" Mr. Harkness asked.

"Mr. Corbyn is a great believer in the importance of heritage and bloodline. He . . . he has a hierarchy of human worth he adheres to. Such men do not tend to rate persons they believe to be of Jewish descent very highly."

"How diplomatic you are, Miss Thorne," said Mrs. Corbyn acidly. She also did not deny this remark on her family's background. The way she talked of her family's relationship with their neighbors had led Rosalind to wonder if her people were *conversos*, Jews who had converted, willingly or not, genuinely or not, to Catholicism to save themselves from the horrors of the inquisition. Now she had her answer.

"There is only one problem," said Mrs. Corbyn. "Marius Corbyn didn't know about myself and Philip."

"I'm sorry to contradict you," said Rosalind. "But he most certainly must have. If he did not know at the time his brother died, somebody told him afterwards." She looked to Lucian.

Lucian nodded and polished off his brandy. "Yes, my father could have told him, and yes, that's my fault.

"My brother Bartolemew came up to London six months or so ago. He found me, I'm not sure how, but he did. He said he'd had enough and wanted to break with the family. I agreed to help, and that if he'd move to town, I'd teach him the shipping business and help him to a place.

"At first, all seemed to be going well, and I was glad to have him with me. But Bartolemew kept asking about my quarrel with Father—how it had come about, how much I knew for certain, how much I could prove in court if it came to it, how I had found any of it out. And I talked." He added to his empty brandy glass. "It can be lonely, when you're apart from your family, and I thought he might be the means of putting me back in touch with my brothers and sisters. Gradually, however, it began to dawn on me that Bartolemew had a plan of his own, and it did not involve becoming a shipping clerk."

"Blackmail?" asked Alice.

"Oh no," said Lucian. "Much simpler than that. He'd simply have our father arrested and tried, and then he'd inherit. Forgery, you may well know, is a hanging offense."

"Yes," said Rosalind. "I am quite aware of that."

Mr. Harkness said nothing at all.

"But." Alice frowned. "If your brother Bartolemew turned your father in, wouldn't your father just make a new will and write him out entirely?"

"Ah!" Lucian held up one finger. "That was the especially clever part, you see. He planned to tell our father that I was the one who turned him in. All very neat, you see?"

"Neat is one word for it," said Alice. "Charlotte, may I have some of that brandy? I'm afraid another cup of tea just now is not going to be enough."

"Help yourself, Alice," replied Charlotte placidly.

For a time, the only sound in the room was Alice pouring herself a perfectly ladylike measure of brandy and then drinking it off in a fashion she never learned in boarding school. It was Mr. Harkness who broke the silence.

"Here, then, is what we know," he said. "And you will please correct me if I am wrong on any point. We know Colonel William Corbyn married Mrs. Corbyn while still abroad. He then arranged that she and her child, whom he fully acknowledged, should come to England. He stated he did intend to reveal the marriage to his family."

Mrs. Corbyn nodded. Philip, sensing his mother's distress, climbed into her lap. She wrapped her arms around the boy and held him close.

"But the family's disapproval was considerable. Colonel Corbyn felt himself compelled to conceal the marriage, to shield all the parties. The plan then became that Mr. Corbyn should enter into a marriage of convenience with one Cecilia Vaughn. They would adopt the child and raise him, while you, Mrs. Corbyn . . . ?"

"I hoped I would be able to take some little money and go home to my parents and family." Mrs. Corbyn kissed her son. He reached out one finger and poked at one of the gold hoops she wore in her ears. "I was content enough with the possibility. If my love for William did not last as it should, I can only plead that it is difficult to always be the hidden one."

"Yes, it is," agreed Charlotte.

"And you were happy to leave your son?" asked Mr. Harkness.

"Happy, sir?" Mrs. Corbyn's cheeks colored. She laid a hand on the back of her son's head. The child squirmed and slithered back down to the floor and his soldiers. "No, of course I was not. But what could I give him? A life of shame and poverty? With his father, he would have everything. And despite his troubles, William was a good man. He loved our son and would do his best by him."

Mr. Harkness nodded and turned to Lucian Vaughn. "From what you say, Mr. Vaughn, quite a number of people knew about Colonel Corbyn's secret marriage. A Mr. Mirabeau, a Mr. Worthing, and of course, your brother, *and* your sister, and perhaps later, your father."

"Yes," said Lucian. "And if Father didn't tell Mother, she still probably found out on her own."

"And Marius Corbyn," added Rosalind.

"And Marius Corbyn," added Mr. Harkness blandly. "So, all these persons were in on the secret. Then William Corbyn is found shot dead by person or persons unknown, after having agreed to participate in a duel. The person he was supposed to meet and shoot with . . ."

"Peter Mirabeau," said Rosalind.

"Denies having gotten to the meeting place in time to do it. With him were the sister, Helen Corbyn, and Mr. Worthing."

"And Helen Corbyn is engaged to Mr. Mirabeau," said Rosalind.

"Did Helen know the colonel was planning to become a bigamist?" asked Mr. Harkness.

"I do not know. But it may be . . . it very well may be that her cousin Mrs. Graves did."

"Ah, yes. Mrs. Graves," said Mr. Harkness solemnly. "Of whom we have a serious report."

A woman with nowhere to go if she should be turned out of Corbyn Park, and who may have already committed at least one murder.

Mrs. Graves who surely knew about the duel, because she tries to know everything. Her position could have been endangered by Helen's marriage, but even more so by William's. No wife likes spare relations hanging about their new home, especially spare relations with secrets and pasts. Mrs. Graves drives her own trap and could have driven out that morning.

Rosalind bit her lip.

"At the time Colonel Corbyn dies, no will is found. Which is unusual for a man ready to go out and die," Mr. Harkness went on. "But a will is found later. I presume it leaves everything to Marius Corbyn?"

"This is what Cecilia tells me," said Mrs. Corbyn.

"But it could well be a forgery, and Marius could have bought and paid for it by agreeing to marry Miss Vaughn," said Rosalind. *And Fortuna could have facilitated this, with the understanding she would be paid, or allowed to stay at Corbyn Park.* "Does Miss Vaughn know about her father's . . . specialty?"

Mrs. Corbyn nodded. "She wrote me many letters, both before and after William died."

Mr. Harkness sighed. "And of course, you did not go to a lawyer with any of your troubles, because there is no money to pay."

"Yes," she nodded. "And because such a man might well cheat a woman alone."

"And because we would have had to find a man who could be counted on not to alert my father," added Lucian. "He was disgraced, but he still has friends, and spies."

Rosalind thought of Helen's story of Fortuna and the mail bag. "Did you ever hear from a Mrs. Graves?"

Mrs. Corbyn shook her head. "No, I do not know that name."

"But Cecilia Vaughn and you, Mr. Vaughn, did ally with Mrs. Corbyn and her cause, and were presumably trying to work out some solution for her child to gain his birthright that did not involve the destruction of the Vaughn family. Which may well prove impossible."

"Yes," agreed Lucian.

"And that is where matters stood as of today, when these men turned up on Mrs. Corbyn's doorstep to attempt to forcibly remove her and her child."

He looked around the room. No one answered or contradicted him.

Mr. Harkness stood smoothly. He walked up to Mrs. Corbyn, and he bowed.

"Mrs. Corbyn, I need to make certain you understand some things. I am a king's officer. What I have heard here is a story of murder, and attempted murder, and as such; it is a breach of the King's Peace. I wish to make this plain, because you and your son will be directly affected by what is found."

"Yes," she said. "I understand."

"What you do or do not do about this, that is up to you."

"Yes," she said again.

"Very well," he said. "I think it's time I leave you. That is . . ." He stopped. "Unless you might need somewhere to stay?"

Mrs. Corbyn looked to Mr. Vaughn. "We should not go back to the house. It is not safe."

"You can stay with me for the time being," Lucian told her. "It's only bachelor rooms . . ."

"I may have something better," said Mr. Harkness.

"You?" Mrs. Corbyn was openly surprised. "Where?"

Mr. Harkness gave them both his best smile. "My mother's," he told them. "There are still a crowd of us at home but always room for more, and I can make sure the patrols take special care to mind the street while you are there."

He was watching Mr. Vaughn as he spoke, waiting for his reaction.

"All right," agreed Lucian. "Better for us all, anyway, Maria, and probably a deal more comfortable for you and the boy." He pulled out a notebook and pencil, and wrote something down. "My address." He tore the page out and handed it to Mr. Harkness. "Should anything be needed."

"Thank you." Adam tucked the page into his pocket. "And thank you for your hospitality, Miss Thorne." He bowed. "Miss Rosalind, Miss Littlefield, can I escort you anywhere?"

"You may indeed, Mr. Harkness," said Alice. "Charlotte, it was good to see you again."

"It was good to see you as well, Alice. I very much look forward to reading your novel."

Charlotte rose gracefully to her feet. "Rosalind. You will let me know if there's anything I can do to help?"

This might have been a polite nothing, but Rosalind looked into her sister's eyes and saw, against all expectation, she meant what she said.

"Alice," said Rosalind. "I'll join you and Mr. Harkness downstairs in one moment."

"Of course, come along, everyone. It's high time we returned Miss Thorne's parlor to her." Alice took little Philip's hand. "Do you know, when I was your age, I was champion at sliding down bannisters?"

Mrs. Corbyn screeched in shock, just a little, and scolded, also just a little, and the door closed behind them all.

"Why are you doing this, Charlotte?" said Rosalind. "I do not deserve any help from you."

Charlotte smiled. "You need not think I am a martyr, Rosalind. I am well past that." She sighed lightly. "But I think you can see for yourself that for the moment, I am very well set up. The life of a woman such as I am, however, is inherently precarious. It may be that a day will come when having a sister who has connections to the good and the great is of help to me." She spread her well-kept hands. "Therefore, it is in my own best interest that I should keep myself in good stead with such a sister."

"And that is all? Your self-interest?"

"Will you allow me to believe that it is?" Old regret flickered in her sister's merry eyes, and Rosalind felt her heart twist. "It is much easier for me."

Rosalind bowed her head. "Of course, Charlotte. If you like."

"Thank you."

They said farewell. They did not embrace, and when she heard the sitting room door close behind her, Rosalind did not look back.

CHAPTER 42

Reunions

*I stand here . . . perfectly ready, whenever I
am suitably called upon, to afford to the world
generally every explanation of the affair it may
consider requisite . . .*

Theodore Edward Hook, *Cousin William* or
The Fatal Attachment

Out on the rain-washed street, the odd little party of Mr.
Vaughn, Mrs. Corbyn and her son, Adam, Alice, and
Rosalind gathered in consultation.

"I need to get back to my office," said Vaughn. "I'll have
to tell my employer . . . something, and ask for time away, I
expect."

"That would probably be wise," agreed Mr. Harkness.

"Alice," said Rosalind. "Would you agree to go with Mrs.
Corbyn to Mrs. Harkness's house?"

"Of course," Alice said promptly. "Don't worry, señora,
you will like Mrs. Harkness, and, Philip, you will have a raft
of boys to play with. Should you like that?"

"Hurray!" The boy bounced up and down, tugging at his
mother's sleeve. "When do we go, Mama?"

"We go now, I imagine," answered Mrs. Corbyn, putting a
hand on her boy's head, to calm him, at least a little.

"Yes, now," agreed Rosalind. "You take the carriage and tell the driver to come to Little Russell Street once Mrs. Corbyn is settled and you've gotten home."

Alice looked at Rosalind and at Mr. Harkness. "I hope George doesn't have plans tonight. I can't believe how much I'll have to tell him." She beamed at Rosalind, and the smile said: *You will be telling me the rest of this story, whether you want to or not.*

The carriage came around the corner. Rosalind had no doubt her sister had space in a livery stable or a private mews for the conveyances belonging to her callers. Their driver received his instructions without comment and helped Mrs. Corbyn and Alice into the carriage. There was some small delay while Philip tried to insist he was big enough to ride on the box, but eventually the door was closed and the carriage drove away, and Rosalind was left standing on the cobbles with Adam Harkness.

He bowed deeply, sweeping his hand out in a gesture that indicated she should walk on. Rosalind returned an equally deep curtsy and did so.

"Do you suppose you and I will ever have a dull and ordinary meeting?" he asked.

"It does not seem so. How have you been?"

"Quite well, as it happens. Busy. Most of our principal officers are scattered about the country looking into matters in the provinces. I'm practically on my own at the station." He paused. "How does his grace, the duke?"

Rosalind walked on for a time without answering. They reached the high street. The busy, noisy world of London, with its carts and vans and porters, maids and footmen, and housewives with their baskets flowed around them.

"He is wrestling with a host of troubles," she said. "Many of them inherited with the family title."

Mr. Harkness folded his hands behind his back. Rosalind was grateful for the broad edge of her bonnet that made a shield between them. He was too close as it was. She did not want to feel the twist inside of her. She should not want to talk over all Devon's troubles with this man, and hear his opinions and his ideas, but she did. The urge was a strong one, and it was far more dangerous and telling than any tug on her heart from his blue eyes or handsome face.

"I suppose you sent Mrs. Corbyn to your mother's because you did not entirely trust Mr. Vaughn."

She was blatantly changing the subject. Mr. Harkness ducked his head, so she could see him around her bonnet's edge. He knew what she was doing and why. He also simply smiled softly, and he let her.

"He's a member of this Vaughn family. He spins a good story, but there may be lies tucked inside it that we haven't seen yet. I thought it wasn't wise to leave a woman and her child in his hands just yet." He fell silent. Rosalind stepped around a stray heap of slop.

"And then there's Mrs. Corbyn herself," Adam said, so softly Rosalind barely heard him.

"Mrs. Corbyn?" echoed Rosalind. "What do you suspect her of?"

"I suspect her being a mother of a child," he said. "As such, she might not be so resigned to this plan of giving up her child as she would have us believe. Perhaps she took her papers down to the country to force Colonel Corbyn to declare the existence of a marriage, and a legitimate child. Perhaps the colonel refused her, perhaps he even threatened to take the child, anyway. . . ."

"As would be his legal right as the acknowledged father," Rosalind finished. Adam nodded.

"Perhaps she decided she would risk anything but that. She's a farm girl and grew up in war. It's quite likely she understands how to handle a gun. Perhaps she went to Corbyn Park in secret to confront William. Perhaps she did not like the answers he gave her."

"And then what? Conspired with Cecilia?"

"Or your Mrs. Graves," said Adam.

"To what end?"

He touched her arm. Rosalind drew up short. A youth on horseback barreled madly up the street, a bare foot in front of them. She caught her breath and let it out slowly. "Thank you."

He bowed, just a little, and they walked on. The streets were growing busier, and Rosalind began to recognize some of the houses and yards. They would be home soon.

"Now that the colonel is dead, Philip Corbyn inherits, as long as his mother can prove he's legitimate, and with all those papers, it seems she can. In that case, she becomes his trustee until he is of age," said Adam.

"You're forgetting Marius Corbyn," Rosalind said. "I doubt he would accede to such a development quietly."

"Oh no, I'm not forgetting him," said Mr. Harkness. "I'm just pointing out that the pieces of the picture we have fit together in more ways than one."

Yes. A whole host of memories swirled in Rosalind's mind— conversations, letters, glances, silences. The all piled on top of one another. She felt she should know the truth. She felt she did know, but the answer was still buried beneath all the confusion and reluctance that had built itself up so high inside her.

"But if Mrs. Corbyn killed Colonel Corbyn, who hired those men to take the boy?" asked Rosalind slowly. "She did not do that to herself."

"It would have to be someone who was afraid Mrs. Corbyn would renew her claims, but who could not be sure of proving she was the one who killed her husband."

That could describe Marius. Or Cecilia, or Helen. Any of the Vaughns. And, of course, Mrs. Graves.

They had reached Rosalind's neighborhood. It was in some ways Mr. Harkness's as well, for they were not so far from Bow Street here. Rosalind stopped and turned to face him.

"Mr. Harkness, will you come back with us?" She spoke briskly, not in the least because she had to get the words out before she changed her mind. "We need your help in this and . . ." She stopped. "I am certain Lord Casselmaine will pay your fees."

Adam considered this. "Very well," he said. "I will inform Mr. Townsend that this is an urgent matter for the Duke of Casselmaine. I'll also send Sampson Goutier around to Mrs. Corbyn's street to make himself comfortable in one of the local taverns. It may be that these bully boys were known in the neighborhood." He lifted his nose then, as if he caught an unfamiliar scent on the wind. "You say that the district in general around Cassell House knows you left?"

"Yes, I could not conceal it. I asked Louisa to say I fled in tears, but that may or may not have fooled anyone."

"And by now our bully boys will surely have told their employer what happened at Mrs. Corbyn's house today." He looked over his shoulder as if he thought to see them coming up the street. Perhaps he did.

"I think, Miss Thorne, that whoever is in pursuit of Mrs. Corbyn and her child may be upset if they do not find her, and they may suspect that you know where she is. I also think that if you stay in London tonight, you should not stay alone, and that you should leave for the country again as soon as possible."

He was of course right. She wanted to object, but she could not.

"Oh dear," she muttered.

"What is it?"

"Mrs. Kendricks. We only just returned." Rosalind smiled ruefully. "She's not going to forgive me."

CHAPTER 43

The Road From Town

The two great essentials for the formation of a villain,—a good head, and corrupt heart.

Catherine Cuthbertson, *Rosabella: Or, A Mother's Marriage*

As it transpired, Mrs. Kendricks had not actually unpacked. "I thought it best to wait and see what news you came back with, miss," she said. "There have been a great many changes of late."

Rosalind's first instinct was to say "I'm sorry," but she swallowed the words. "Under other circumstances I would suggest you remain here and follow after later," she said. "But Mr. Harkness believes that may be ill-advised."

"Yes, miss," agreed Mrs. Kendricks, and the words were cold.

Rosalind could not blame her. "Have you any new letters from your sister?"

"As it happens, I have, miss. After you are settled, I thought I might take a holiday, if you can spare me."

"I think that's an excellent idea, Mrs. Kendricks. Perhaps I will take a little holiday as well."

"Perhaps that would be for the best."

Perhaps it would. Rosalind certainly felt the need for a

holiday. But before that, she felt the need to get back to Cassell House as soon as possible.

Again the convenience of a private carriage was very much felt. Samuel advised against traveling through the night, but he could have them ready to go at any time after daybreak. And with Samuel, Mrs. Kendricks, and—at her very firm insistence—Alice, and once he'd heard the entire story, George in the house, Rosalind could hardly be said to be spending the night alone. In fact, she and Alice shared a bed, and George stretched out on the parlor sofa. In the morning, Mrs. Kendricks had to send to the baker's for extra muffins and a fresh jar of tea.

Just as Samuel was loading Rosalind's trunks onto the carriage, Mr. Harkness rode up the street, mounted on a bay gelding.

"I see you took my advice, Miss Thorne. Good morning." He nodded to the Littlefields.

He wore a plain jacket, his red vest, and his old-fashioned tricorn hat. But there was something else about his appearance.

"A sword, Mr. Harkness?" said Rosalind. "How romantic."

"We are dealing with dangerous men," he replied calmly. "And since Parliament decided to cease funding the highway patrol, things have been getting rougher on the roads again. I should rather have such a precaution and not need it than need it and not have it."

Rosalind found this was not something she cared to think about at present, and instead faced Alice. Alice stood up on tiptoe and hugged her.

"I wish I could go with you," she said as they parted. "You're sure to have all the fun."

"Don't worry, Rosalind," added George. "We'll keep an eye on everything here for you."

"But not a word to the Major until we know how it all works out," said Rosalind sternly.

"Our solemn promise." Alice raised her right hand. "Besides, the Major will want the whole story so he can know how best to chop it up and dole it out." She caught Mr. Harkness's quizzical expression. "You have your work, we have ours. Take good care of Rosalind, sir, or you'll also have the rough side of my tongue."

"I shall guard her with my life," he replied.

Their farewells finished, Rosalind and Mrs. Kendricks were enclosed in the comfortable confines of Devon's carriage. As both women were experienced travelers, they soon settled themselves down for the journey. Both of them had their workbaskets, their books, and their letters to keep them busy.

And, of course, Rosalind had her thoughts—endless rivers of thought—about William Corbyn's death and about the attempt on Peter Mirabeau. About all the persons who might have been driven to take such rash and desperate action, and about how she felt sure the answer was in what she already knew.

About herself and Mrs. Kendricks.

About herself and Devon Winterbourne.

About herself and Adam Harkness.

The London and Westminster streets were rough and loud but soon gave way to the quieter length of the turnpike. At each gate, Adam would fall behind, because he would stop to talk with the keeper, but he soon caught up with them again.

They made their first stop at an inn some four hours out from the edge of Westminster. While Samuel saw to the change of horses, Mrs. Kendricks went inside to negotiate a basket of provisions from the landlord. Adam disappeared entirely.

Rosalind stood in the yard, feeling a little bereft. Being caught between worlds was an uncomfortable feeling. It gave her an awareness of her precarious balance. No matter which way she let herself fall, she would have no one to praise or to blame but herself.

"You look much distracted, Miss Thorne."

Rosalind jumped. Mr. Harkness positioned himself so she could see him around her bonnet's sheltering rim. "I'm sorry."

He probably was not, but Rosalind let that go. "I was just thinking of all the events surrounding William Corbyn," she lied.

Adam nodded, and she thought she sensed a rather undefined air of disappointment in him.

"I can't fathom how you even begin with this one," he said. "When I am thrown into a murder, it generally begins with a body to view. Or at least the written report of the body."

"And in this case the body has been buried for some time," said Rosalind. "And the reports are all . . . contradictory, to say the least."

Adam nodded. "That's hard, because when there are far too many reasons *why* something might have happened, it's good to be able to concentrate on *what* happened."

"Yes," murmured Rosalind. "Yes, it would be at that."

"I came to tell you Samuel has the horses ready. We should go. It is still broad daylight, I know, but I am convinced lingering on this road is not our best plan."

Rosalind looked at him sharply. Rosalind remembered that Mr. Harkness had made his original reputation as a member of the highway patrol. It was a body of men who had been astonishingly effective in its eradication of bandits along the roads leading to and from London, to the point where highwaymen themselves had almost retreated into romantic legend.

Almost.

Their journey resumed. The inn fell behind, and the woods enclosed them. Adam rode on the left-hand side of the carriage. He kept an easy seat on his sturdy gelding, but there was an air of extra attention about him.

There was no other traffic. They were alone on this road. Mrs. Kendricks was reading a letter, perhaps from her sister. Rosalind ignored all her work and books, as well as the enticing scents rising from the hamper that now shared their traveling compartment. Instead she stared out the window.

When I am thrown into a murder, it generally begins with a body to view. Or at least the written report of the body. Adam's words repeated themselves in her thoughts. There was something there, and it was important.

The reports are all . . . contradictory, to say the least, she'd told him, and this was true.

When there are far too many reasons why *something might have happened, it's good to be able to concentrate on* what *happened.*

What did happen? They did not know. Helen and Peter said William Corbyn had been shot from behind. Devon, however, swore that he'd been shot from the front, and at close range. And with a weapon that was not a dueling pistol.

But Helen and Peter had found no weapon. So the weapon must have been removed.

Rosalind sat up straighter.

If William was shot at close range, someone would have had to walk up to him. He would have to allow that.

It would have to be someone he knew, and trusted.

Devon said there should have been a man there to stand as William Corbyn's second.

Someone whom he could have confided in and trusted to hold his tongue around outsiders.

Who was a liar, who wanted William Corbyn dead. Rosalind's breath caught in her throat.

Someone close. Like a brother.

Someone who could not stand the idea of a person of inferior stock inheriting the family land and distorting the family tree.

Like *his* brother.

His brother who could have goaded him into the duel, who would have known how to play on his injured honor, who could have spun tales of fresh insults.

Fully awake and alert now, Rosalind struggled to let down the window. As she did, she saw Mr. Harkness urge his horse forward. She heard him say something to the driver but could not distinguish the words. A moment later, she heard their driver call out and crack his whip. The carriage picked up its pace.

That was when the horses screamed.

CHAPTER 44

Stand and Deliver

*Not one instant would elapse before I would be
face to face with them in the field, were there a
legion of them...*

Theodore Edward Hook, *Cousin William* or
The Fatal Attachment

Later, Harkness would reflect on the difference between reality and fiction.

In a novel, there would have been a heat-stirring chase. There would have been descriptions of desperation, of daring, and of the carriage being surrounded and the horse's reins seized. Perhaps a fellow with a bunch of lace at his throat would leap from a running horse onto the team's lead fore.

In reality, there was the high, horrible sound of beasts in sudden agony. The lead horses reared back. The carriage driver screamed, too, and the carriage bucked and teetered sideways. Somehow, Harkness jerked back on this horse's reins hard enough that the beast veered from the road and into the trees. It too bucked and shook, but Harkness managed to keep his seat. As soon as he had the horse under control, he backed and turned the animal so they both faced the road.

Just in time to see the carriage crash onto its side.

All four carriage horses, still screaming, fell with it. Tangled in the harness, they fought to stand again, kicking at one another. They cried in heart-wrenching agony for help, mercy, freedom as they fought one another. His own horse shuddered and kicked and tried to run.

The driver was sprawled on the ground, hurt, unconscious, perhaps even dead.

Now the attackers poured out from between the trees.

Ambush.

Four of them—one on horse, three on foot, ready and waiting. Caltrops on the road too could have taken the carriage down, and Harkness had no time to think of how Miss Thorne could be hurt or dead inside the fallen conveyance because the attackers were already swarming the carriage.

Harkness drew his saber and drove his heels into his horse's ribs. A cry of rage and revenge tore from his throat as he charged.

All four of the men stopped what they were doing, stunned stupid. Harkness had to steer the gelding in a circle wide enough to keep away from the maddened carriage horses.

The first shot rang out.

Harkness's hat flew from his head. Hot claws raked his cheek, but Harkness felt nothing after that. He wheeled his mount again and bore down on the man with the gun, saber held out straight ahead like a bayonet. Harkness's first blow caught the man in the head. The man screamed and toppled backward. Harkness wheeled again, charging back toward the carriage.

"STOP AND STAND IN THE KING'S NAME!" he roared.

No one listened.

One of the outriders grappled with one of the outlaws. The other three lay on the ground—two were still, one, like the tangled, tiring carriage horses, was struggling to rise. The smallest boy had somehow escaped harm and was among the plunging horses, knife out, fighting to cut the reins before they killed themselves.

The last outlaw finally tore the carriage door open. He plunged his head and arms inside.

"GET YOUR . . ."

The outlaw reeled backward, screaming and clutching at his eye. Harkness's horse reared again, and this time, he barely kept his seat.

Rosalind Thorne rose from the carriage like an avenging fury, a pair of scissors in her grip.

". . . HANDS OFF ME!"

The man screamed again and tried to scramble away. The outrider had laid his attacker low and jumped onto the man, so they fell, tussling. Hating every second of delay, Harkness reined in his horse, jumped down, knotted the reins hastily around a fallen branch, and ran forward to help the boy with the carriage horses.

The next moments were fully occupied with trying to get the beasts free without anyone—horse or human—getting killed. When at last Samuel, swearing profusely, hatless, coat torn, joined the boy, Harkness ducked away and ran behind the carriage.

Miss Thorne was bent down beside the carriage. Mrs. Kendricks had been propped up against the roof. She was cradling her arm, but she was alert. Although it hurt to do so, Harkness judged them both well enough and turned his attention to the outlaws.

The one who'd shot at him was dead, or good as. Harkness, left cold by the need, and praying Rosalind did not see, made sure of it. The man Rosalind stabbed had collapsed on the ground and very clearly was not going any farther.

The one Samuel had fought was awake, but groggy from his beating. Harkness kicked him once to roll him over, then knelt on his back, yanked off his cravat, and bound his hands behind him.

Slowly, the world behind him quieted down.

When he stepped away from his man and looked up again, it was to see Rosalind coming toward him, brisk and efficient, with a ridiculously small handkerchief clutched in her fist.

"You're hurt," she said.

That, of all times, was when Harkness's strength gave out, the world spun, and to his shame, he fell to his knees.

For Rosalind, the attack was a haze of noise and riot punctuated by moments of perfect clarity.

The first came when the carriage stilled and she lifted her head, knowing she was not dead. Rather, she was tangled in Mrs. Kendricks, who was crying in pain, and she knew any moment the door, now above her head, was going to be opened, and possibly not by a friend.

The next came when she saw the workbasket spilled out across the same windows she was lying against.

The next came when the door was indeed torn open, and Rosalind Thorne looked into Marius Corbyn's hate-filled face.

She remembered the sensation of her arm stabbing upward, but not much beyond that.

In fact, she remembered nothing at all until she was helping one of the outriders gently extricate Mrs. Kendricks from the carriage. Her housekeeper hoarsely insisted that she was fine, miss, fine, she was not so old as she looked, but her arm . . .

Her arm was very clearly broken and needed to be set by someone competent immediately, and they had no one, and Rosalind wanted to scream.

She did not. She settled Mrs. Kendricks as comfortably as possible and went to see to Mr. Harkness, who fainted shortly afterward.

Rosalind, her mind numb and filling rapidly with a strength-sapping fog, wished she was in London.

In London, she would have been able to send at once for a physician. She would have been able to call out through the window for her neighbor Annie Kettle, who was a nurse and midwife. She would have had plenty of linen and better scissors and fresh water and tea and spirits.

In London, she would have been able to *do* something.

In the woods as they were, all Rosalind could do was stand around stupidly while the men—those who could still speak—discussed where to go, and who should go and who should stay with the women and the ruined carriage.

She'd used her bloody scissors to cut strips of petticoat to bind up Mrs. Kendrick's arm as best she could, and tried to ignore the fact that her housekeeper had to bite hard on a glove to keep the pain from making her scream out loud. All the while, she listened to the men talking about setting the carriage upright, but one of the axels had been broken in the crash, and now the whole conveyance was just so much kindling. Besides, despite everyone's efforts, the carriage horses were dead. One died in the struggle, and the others had broken their legs and had to be put down. That left only Mr. Harkness's saddle horse. The last inn was two or three hours back, but there was another only one hour ahead, so someone who could ride would have to go on.

Which meant the boy or the one uninjured footman, a man named Griggs. Samuel's injuries had caught up with him and he had fallen down insensible. As for Adam Harkness, he had lost more blood than he realized and, in fact, had come closer to dying than he should have.

Rosalind knew that because in the last of the useful daylight, she'd stitched the side of his neck closed where a piece of shot had grazed it. Others had caught his ear (he'd lost the lobe and it bled even more profusely than his neck), and his jaw, and his cheek, and his scalp.

"This is the second time you've been wounded in my service," she murmured as she tried to daub the blood away, at least a little.

"Anything for milady," he answered.

"You're lucky to have both eyes."

"I'm lucky not to have met you with a pair of scissors."

"That man . . ."

"He won't hurt you, Rosalind. I promise."

"He's Marius Corbyn."

Mr. Harkness stared at her. She nodded. "He killed his brother. He went with William to the dueling ground as his second, and shot him, and left him there. I suspect he did it because he could not bear to have a sister-in-law such as Mrs. Corbyn." She paused. "Since his hirelings would have reported that we met, he may have assumed that she and her son were to be traveling with us."

Adam stared up at Rosalind. She saw his injuries afresh and yes, he was profoundly lucky to still have both eyes. What he would also have before too much longer was a fever. Sweat already beaded his forehead. And she had nothing to give him to help, and Mrs. Kendricks was hurt and trying to remain stoic, and she didn't know for certain where they were, and neither did anybody else, and she was cold and she was frightened, and there were dead horses and dead men, and she wanted very much to cry and she couldn't do that, either.

"Get me on my feet," said Adam.

"You should be rest . . ." she began, but even in the deepening twilight she could read the expression on his pained and pale face, and gave it up as a lost cause. Instead she did as he asked and helped him to stand.

Adam limped a few steps, but then straightened and strode to the place where Marius Corbyn had been propped against an oak tree.

Someone, not Rosalind, had bandaged his head. A dark, distorted spot stained the torn linen. But he was alert, and he watched the two of them approach. Pain and shadow turned his angled face into a series of sharp lines and dark hollows.

He was still dressed as a gentleman. He still wore his

watch chain and his cravat and his long coat. Gloves protected his hands. He'd lost his hat somewhere.

"Marius Corbyn?" said Adam. Marius let his head loll sideways so his remaining eye could look up at Mr. Harkness. Rosalind found she wanted very desperately to be ill. She had never injured anyone before, not like this. That she did it to save herself made it no better. She somehow wanted to explain, to smooth it all away.

She bit her tongue, hard.

"Marius Corbyn," repeated Adam. "In the king's name, I charge you with the willful murder of one Colonel William Corbyn, to which you will answer in . . ."

Marius closed his eye. For a minute, Rosalind thought he'd fainted. But then he turned his head, and he cried out in pain. He also hawked and spat onto the leaves.

"Give me some water," he croaked.

"There is none," said Adam. "You'll have to wait with the rest of us."

Marius grunted.

"Why, Mr. Corbyn?" Rosalind asked him.

"Why?" The word rasped painfully in his throat. "Because I will be damned and in hell before I see my family home and land turned over to some conniving, foreign, hook-nosed *whore* and her mewling, half-breed bastard!" He stopped, licking his cracked, dirty lips. "Bad enough that his *grace* is so in love with his own benevolence he doesn't see how those creatures he's bringing in to grub in the mud and swill their whiskey are going to keep breeding until they drown the entire kingdom! We're going to be torn down, by *them* and the men like him who help them breed! Give them useful work, he says. Improve their lives he, says. They're animals! You can't improve them! You can only lock them up, along with their brats and whores!"

"Which is why it was so important for Helen to get married and begin having children," said Rosalind. "So she would feel the need to defend the land against Mrs. Corbyn and her son."

"Don't call her that!" he screeched. "She is not his wife! That brat is not his son!"

"No, sir," said Adam quietly. "I'm afraid you will have to do so much better than that."

Marius tried to rise, but it was too much. He cried out in pain from the effort, but fell back against the tree. Rosalind's own confusion made her head spin. But even as she struggled to keep sense and strength together, she became aware of a new sound.

Hoofbeats, from up ahead on the road. The rattle and jingle of harnesses as well. Someone—a lot of someones—was coming down the road in a tearing hurry. Rosalind turned to face this new calamity, and she teetered. Adam caught her arm, but he staggered as well and they both only barely managed to stay upright.

It was horses. A half dozen at least, and a carriage, and a wagon.

"Rosalind!"

It was Devon. He pulled his horse up harder than he should and threw himself from the saddle. Rosalind held up her hands, meaning to say she was unhurt, and then she realized she was still covered in blood.

Devon caught her by both wrists. "You're hurt."

"Not me." It was only a small lie. "Mr. Harkness and Mrs. Kendricks, and Samuel . . ." *Everyone. Everyone is hurt.*

"I've brought the doctor," Devon was telling her. "There's a carriage and a wagon coming as quickly as they can. Are you sure you're not hurt? There's blood . . ." He turned her palms over.

"It's not mine." *I don't think.* "It belongs to Marius Corbyn." *And some others.*

The world swayed around her. Devon's hands pressed

against her shoulders. "Fortuna came to us. She was the one who told us he had left, gone to London. We met your footman on the road."

She blinked up at him. She was not entirely sure she was understanding what he said. She felt Adam Harkness move yet closer beside her, in case she should fall. Which she might. She rather wanted to fall.

"You've done enough, Rosalind," Devon whispered. "You can rest now, if you want."

As if they had been waiting for permission, Rosalind's knees buckled and she sank gently to the ground. Devon held her hands, but it was Adam Harkness who guided her carefully the whole, slow way down.

CHAPTER 45

Differing Conclusions

*The human heart, at whatever age, opens only to
the heart that opens in return.*

Maria Edgeworth, *Castle Rackrent*

"You were not exaggerating," said Rosalind. "Your estate does come with all the frills and furbelows."

Devon smiled and held out his arm. Rosalind looped hers through it.

The day was gloriously sunny. Mrs. Showell and Mrs. Kendricks sat on piles of quilts and pillows under the grand old oak. Mrs. Kendricks's arm still had a ways to go before it was healed. However, the bonesetter—a clear-eyed, gray-haired woman with strong, deft hands—pronounced the break a clean one, and thus far, they'd managed to keep both fever and infection away.

Neither chaperone made even a small pretense at following as Devon led Rosalind around the corner of the tumbling pile of Norman stonework. Moss and ivy laced and spotted the tumbled stone with green. A trio of crows pecked at the pebbled ground.

"Three for a marriage," said Rosalind.

"We shall have to tell Louisa," said Devon. "This delay's been rather hard on her."

"I think it's been harder on poor Mr. Rollins," remarked Rosalind.

"Miss Thorne, that remark is positively bordering."

"Is it, sir? I hadn't noticed."

It had been decided that Louisa's wedding should be put off until after Marius Corbyn's trial, and until Peter Mirabeau was pronounced fully and finally out of danger.

"I'll not have one of my bridesmaids required to act happy while their own fiancé needs them," Louisa declared stoutly. "I'm sure all the civilized world will understand."

Whether the civilized world would, the neighborhood did. Even Louisa's fretful mother wrote consolingly when she got the news the wedding trip would have to be put off for a month. That, Rosalind suspected, had more to do with the fact that Louisa would be living at someone else's expense for a while longer before her family must host her even for a little while. Mrs. Winterbourne had always preferred to keep her shillings where she could see them.

What no one said out loud was that this time was also needed for the district families to adjust to the new reality. Marius Corbyn had killed his brother and had tried to kill Peter Mirabeau. Of this, there could be no doubt. He had stood up in court and declared as much, as if in the ruin of his mind he expected the magistrates to understand the importance of keeping a woman of such parentage from taking residence in Corbyn Park.

Perhaps he did. In this, however, he was mistaken. The mistake was his last.

After the trial, Devon referred Helen and Mrs. Corbyn to his London lawyers to draw up some agreements. Corbyn Park would be given over to Helen and Peter upon their marriage. A share of the estate income would be paid into a trust for Philip, with Mrs. Corbyn acting as his trustee.

"I do not think it wise we should reside in the district," Mrs. Corbyn said. "There will be much bad feeling."

"I wish I could say you were wrong," said Helen.

"But I am not," she had replied with that hard, cynical smile Rosalind had become so familiar with. "It is all right. We will be fine, my son and I."

"I hope that you will write, and that we may visit."

Mrs. Corbyn had drawn herself up. "I would like that very much."

Rosalind and Devon had reached the sunny side of the ruins. The ground sloped gently away to a field of wildflowers. The sound of sheep and cows drifted up from the farms below. Birdsong was everywhere.

Rosalind, forgetful of bonnet and parasol and even her complexion, turned her face toward the sun.

"This is how I wanted to see you," murmured Devon.

"It is how I wanted to be seen," Rosalind admitted. "Devon . . ."

He shook his head. "No, Rosalind. You don't have to."

"Well, one of us must." She paused. The mischievous breeze blew her bonnet ribbons across her cheek. She pushed them down. "I remember when we drove out to the drainage works, when I saw you coming up from the digs, mud-stained and disheveled and tired, and I remember then thinking how happy you looked then. And I remember thinking, I wonder if I could ever make you so happy."

"My happiness . . ." He shook his head. "I don't even know what my happiness is. And that's part of the problem, isn't it?"

"I'm afraid it is. But I think you've made a beginning."

"I hope so." His eyes narrowed. Rosalind recognized that particular look now. He was thinking of his drainage works, his house and his lands; of the men who must be calmed and placated, of how he must interview and hire a new builder, possibly a team of them, capable of taking over from Marius Corbyn.

Poor Marius Corbyn, driven by his own hatred off the edge of the world.

The trial had been a huge sensation. Alice and George had

come down from London to represent the *Chronicle.* On their heels had come a flood of the morbid and the curious, turning the entire county into one great carnival, or so it seemed. Devon had had to get the Lord Lieutenant to call out the militias to help keep order.

Adam Harkness had stayed at Cassell House, first to heal and then to be on hand to take testimony from the witnesses along with the local magistrates. Devon had written to Mr. Townsend specifically to praise the excellent work of his principal officer.

Lucian Vaughn had come down to be examined, and then to testify, and when he left, he took Cecilia with him.

That had been a matter of patient negotiation, with Rosalind standing as witness.

"You cannot go," Mrs. Vaughn had said. "We are your family, Cecilia, you owe it to us. We are destroyed! You will stay and you will help rebuild. For your sisters' sakes, your father's sake, for *my* sake."

"Mrs. Vaughn," said Rosalind. "I understand you are upset, your losses are particularly grievous just now, with Bartolemew departing so suddenly for America." Bartolemew had evidently decided that it would be prudent to put some room between himself and this particular set of legal proceedings, and had left before the trial. "I do not, however, think you quite understand the particulars of the situation. At the moment, William Corbyn's will, which was so conveniently discovered several months after William Corbyn's death, is not being examined. This could change. Information can be given to the magistrates that they will find difficult to ignore."

Mrs. Vaughn stared at Cecilia, as if she was the one who had spoken. "You would participate in the slander of your father who loves you, who . . ."

"I am going to London," said Cecilia. "I will write, if you choose to receive the letters. I will be staying with Lucian."

"Not one of us will have anything further to do with you!" cried her mother.

"Perhaps that is just as well." Cecilia stood, and Rosalind stood with her.

"Your father will order you to stay!" cried Mrs. Vaughn. "You are underage, you cannot . . . !"

But Cecilia walked out of that room filled to bursting with its gaudy antiques and did not once look back.

"Have you heard from Cecilia?" Devon asked, seeming to read her thoughts.

"I have," answered Rosalind. "She is settled in London and asks me to call when I return."

"I'm glad of that. She's had a very bad time."

"She's not the only one." Rosalind pressed her hand against his arm.

"Do you mean me?" He smiled softly. Oh, it was still such a beautiful smile. "My worst was over and done with years ago."

"No, I don't believe that's true. But I think it will be one day."

Devon had not told her exactly what had passed between him and his mother the day she left for London to discover Mrs. Corbyn and Philip, but to Rosalind's surprise, the dowager had.

"I wished you to the devil when you first came, Miss Thorne," she'd said. They'd sat upstairs in her private parlor. Quinn had made tea. Rosalind had taken a polite sip and had decided perhaps she would not have any more. It really was that close to undrinkable.

"And now?" Rosalind asked.

"Now I do not know." Lady Casselmaine looked up at her portraits. "Now I wonder if I should not wish for you to stay a little longer."

Rosalind bowed her head.

"Devon tells me he found Hugh had been thrown from his horse," the dowager went on. "He says it was done by means of a line strung across the road. He says it was done . . . because Hugh angered the wrong people in a gambling game, and they robbed him of the money on the way home."

"I thought it might be something of the kind."

"I feared it would be," breathed Lady Casselmaine. "I have sat here and nursed that fear for many and many a day."

"And now?" asked Rosalind again.

"I don't know," said the dowager. "But I know that these rooms seem rather smaller than they used to. Perhaps it is time to open the doors a little."

Rosalind and Devon reached a part of the crumbling wall where a bramble rose had knotted itself into the ivy. One faded blossom remained defiant in the late-summer sun. Rosalind touched it, and a small shower of petals rained onto the weedy ground.

"I will miss you, Rosalind," Devon said.

She turned to face him. "Do not think that I regret one moment of our time together. You have always been one of my truest friends."

"I hope that I shall remain so."

"It is my hope that you will find a lady who understands this place as you do." *And your heart as I do.* Rosalind, however, found she could not say so much at this time.

"But what will you do?"

She smiled. It was that worry that had kept them from having this conversation until now. *What will I do?*

"I will return to Little Russell Street," she said, and she hoped her jocular tone did not sound too forced. "I will continue to make myself useful, I expect. Although some or the other of the details will have to change." Mrs. Kendricks had written to her sister to say she would be coming to stay at her guest house in Bath.

"You're frightened, Rosalind, I can tell. Don't—"

She held up her hand. "Yes, I am frightened, and that is my responsibility to deal with, not yours. Since my father left us . . . since my father left us I have been taught very firmly to understand that my only security lies in strict adherence to the rules of appearance and propriety. Now it may be that I have to step beyond those." All at once Rosalind pictured the dowager in her tiny, Spartan room. *Perhaps it is time to open the doors a little.*

"And I do not know what really lies across that particular threshold," she went on. "The stories we are told are very grave."

"You don't . . ."

"Devon, I have said this is my responsibility."

"I know that it is, Rosalind. But grant me the courtesy of understanding that I will worry about you, especially living alone in London. It is not safe."

Rosalind smiled indulgently. "Actually, I was thinking of asking Alice to come stay. Now that George is getting married, their current arrangement will begin to feel . . . crowded. I believe she and I shall do very well together."

"I believe you shall, but if I can ever help in any way, you will tell me, won't you?" He smiled, although slowly. "Because if I have to find out for myself, I'm going to be severely angry and I may be driven to descend upon your house in all my ducal might and majesty."

"From which my humble neighborhood might never recover. So, I promise. I do, Devon. In fact, I swear it."

"You do not have to swear to me, Rosalind."

He leaned forward slowly, giving Rosalind plenty of time to pull away if she chose. She did not choose. She tilted her face up to his, and he kissed her.

It was a gentle kiss, hopeful and sweet. Rosalind let herself relax into it, savor it, want it. It was not like being pulled back into memory. That was what Rosalind had dreaded. But this kiss was not any sad longing for the children they had been. This was the grown man and woman, sharing this place and this time.

And learning how to say farewell.

Devon drew back from her, and he smiled.

"Whatever is waiting for you, Rosalind, it is something far different, and I suspect far greater, than a coronet and a country estate. And I want you to have it, all of it."

"No fear, Devon. My time of denying myself entry into my own life is done. I do not know what I am or what I should be, but this time, I am going to find out."

"Well, I think we should find out if Mrs. Showell and Mrs. Kendricks have left us any lunch."

"And I think if Mrs. Showell has eaten all the shortbread, I shall be most put out."

Laughing together, Rosalind and Devon turned and strolled back to their chaperones and their luncheon, to toast their future with lemonade and to enjoy together one more perfect day in the summer sun.

EPILOGUE

Do not in a moment of phrensy like this, make a confidence which you may hereafter repent.

Theodore Edward Hook, *Cousin William* or
The Fatal Attachment

The woman was rather too easy to spot. She stood out amid the high summer of Hyde Park like a poppy in a wheat field. She wore an orange silk turban of astonishing size, decorated with dyed plumes, and a jeweled necklace that cost at least as much as the entire rest of her brocade and lace gown, gloves, kid half boots, and beaded reticule included.

"Mrs. Vaughn?" Russell Fullerton approached her bench and bowed. "Mr. Russell Fullerton, at your service."

"You have brought my letter, as I requested?" she asked sharply.

So. There were to be no pleasantries, nor any delays. Good. Fullerton was used to dealing with women who stammered and danced about their subjects. That did not mean he enjoyed it.

He brought his wallet out of his coat pocket and extracted the letter. Mrs. Vaughn examined it thoroughly. When satisfied this was the original, she folded it tightly.

"I will keep this, if you don't mind," she said.

"Very prudent of you." He favored her with his best smile.

It had no visible effect. Oh, she was going to be a challenge. That was all right. He hadn't faced a good challenge in a long time.

"You may sit." She glanced toward the opposite end of the bench.

He bowed and obeyed, lifting his coattails out of the way as he did and folding his hands on the top of his walking stick.

"Now, ma'am. Exactly what is it you have to tell me about Miss Rosalind Thorne?"